Ford's voice rose a

m

She was, after a

"Doing what I ask and satisfying me sexually must be your first priorities." Ford paused for a long time, and when he spoke again, his voice sounded as if he now had his emotions under tighter control. "I'm afraid this is my fault. You trusted me to guide you in how to perform your role and I've been lax in addressing your mistakes with the punishment they merited. I will to make up for that today. Do you understand my intentions?"

"Yes," she answered cautiously, her anger being edged out by fear.

"Evangeline," he snapped, and his voice had the tone of correction. "This is your punishment position. When you're in it, you will address me as Mr. Hawthorne or sir." Ford sat down at his desk chair in front of her so she could see his face. His jaw was clenched tightly and his mouth pressed into a thin line, but his eyes sparked with something wild.

Leaning back in his chair, he folded his arms across his chest. It gave the impression that he was in no hurry, as if he had all day to stare at her, prone and bound naked before him. The idea chilled her. How long would it be before being held in this position became very uncomfortable?

Ford's eyes wandered over her for a few moments before continuing in his coldest, business voice. "When you agreed to this arrangement, our deal was that we did things my way or you leave this house. It's always your choice to continue, but if you refuse my wishes, you must leave immediately and forfeit the rest of your money. So I ask you now, with the understanding that you have no idea what I intend to do to you…do you trust me?" He lowered his voice to a wicked tone that sent shivers through her body. "Will you stay and take your punishment?"

He leaned forward so his face was close to hers. She could feel his breath on her cheek. She could smell his vanilla-and-leather cologne, which always made the scent-memory of sucking his cock for the first time in the library flash through her head. She studied the way his long eyelashes framed his dark green eyes, the curl of his strong lips, arching into those sexy dimples, his mouth so close to hers. Breathing heavily, he was so keyed up that the energy seemed to be jumping from his skin.

She knew why. According to Charley, though Ford desperately craved the kink she was providing him, he'd never let himself explore it before. Had he ever even done this? Tied someone up since that fateful time when he was sixteen and caught in the early days of his kink? Charley had clued her in. Ford needed her — not just to be at his sexual beck and call — but to be tied to his desk, braving his dark punishment, submitting to his strong will, and enduring whatever pain he wanted to make her feel for him. This was the fire he was missing.

Evie was sure she could do it. Even though she was frightened, she trusted him, and she could endure almost anything. But what Ford didn't understand is that nothing physical he could do to her would hold a candle to the pain he was capable of causing her heart. Her and Charley's. Ford might enjoy bondage and corporal punishment, but in matters of the heart, he was being a true sadist and he wasn't even aware of it.

She was mindful of her own breathing, heavy now, and the blood rushing in her veins, heating between her legs. With a deep breath she had one of those thoughts that whispers through a person's mind, but no one never says out loud.

I'm not sure there's anything I wouldn't let this man do to me.

Would she stay and endure her punishment?
"Yes I will, Mr. Hawthorne," she whispered.
"Punish me."

Come When Called

~THE COMPLETE SERIES~

Piper Trace

Copyright © 2015 Piper Trace

www.pipertrace.com

ISBN 978-1514125908

Cover design by Mark Henry

ACKNOWLEDGMENTS

A special thank you to Meghan Miller for believing in this book way back when and urging me to write male/male. You gave me confidence when I needed it, held my hand, and played Draw Something with me until the wee hours—an integral part of the writing process.

Thanks also to Karen Booth and Jessica Lemmon for all of your help with this book, and for reading random parts of it countless times...even some of the dirty, redacted parts (Lemmondrop...), and for all of your editing help and advice!

Thanks to the Cabal girls for asking about it a million times and urging me to release it upon the world: Shana Gray, Cara Carnes, Anya Richards, Sasha Devlin, Cassandra Carr, Amy Ruttan, A.M. Griffin, Danica Avet, Lea Barrymire.

Thanks to Julie Naughton for all of your support and cheerleading, and for being the first person to read Come When Called in its evolved state from start to finish and loving it. I still remember the moment you told me. Dreamy sigh.

Thanks to my own romance hero, my husband, who doesn't know what's in this book (shh, let's not tell him).

And finally, of course, to you, Dear Readers. I hope you enjoy the world of COME WHEN CALLED.

Sign up for Piper's newsletter to hear about new releases and giveaways at www.pipertrace.com!

Contents

~THE INCIDENT~ 1

~THE OFFER~...55

~CHARLEY~ 109

~DEEPER~ 177

~DARKER~...233

~THE PUNISHMENT~ 291

~THE SUNRISE~ 345

~THE INCIDENT~

CHAPTER ONE

*F*ORD HAWTHORNE'S SINFUL looks were already enough to give Evie butterflies, but hell, even his fidgeting sent her into naughty daydreams. Dreams about his bed, a place she imagined as a candy-shop of sexual titillation, the likes of which she'd never seen before in her pedestrian life. If only she could be Ford's sexual focus for a moment. Just one lick. That might tide her over.

Except of course it wouldn't. Not for as long as she'd been craving the man.

Evie swallowed against her lust and blinked until she was solidly back in the law firm library's tweedy seat instead of writhing naked in her client's Egyptian cotton sheets. It wasn't an easy feat. She'd been saving her pennies a long time for a shopping spree in this man's candy-shop. And she'd worked up quite a sweet-tooth.

Stop looking at his fingers.

Stop looking…

The thought trailed off as Evie watched Ford's long fingers stroke the mahogany of the table. His index finger caught the corner of the contract and curled it up with a flick again and again. The skin of his large hands was smooth perfection. No scars. No calluses.

They were the hands of a rich man, engaged most often in activities no more arduous than holding a cell phone, a martini, or the elbow of a long-legged beauty. Having been pampered all his life, Ford might've grown up pretentious and unapproachable, especially to service-providers like Evie, yet he was anything but.

Though she was only a paralegal working under John Martin, the senior partner who proudly claimed Ford, the firm's biggest client, as his own, Ford treated Evie as if she ran the place.

Flick…flick.

She'd been thinking about him flicking her nipples like he was flicking the paper, and her nipples hardened under her pinstriped shirt, which was work-appropriate only when closed three buttons higher than Evie currently had it fastened. She bit the inside of her cheek.

"Evie?" Ford's voice boomed in the silence of the otherwise empty library and she stifled a yelp. Heart hammering, she met his eyes before looking away, whispering, "Sorry." She collected a stray lock behind her ear with one sapphire-tipped fingernail, trying to look casual, and then clasped her hands firmly in her lap.

Oh god. Distracted by her fantasy starring Ford—as her sexual fantasies normally did—had she trailed off mid-sentence?

It was mortifying.

But worse, it was stupid. She'd spent the last six months trying to get away from a man with money and power who had no need for her, not to mention the fact that carnal thoughts about Ford could cost Evie her job.

She pressed her lips in a firm line, ignoring the heat smoldering between her legs, the same way it always did when he was around. She had to be masochistic to even be attracted to a man like Ford. He was the heartbreak equivalent of a ticking time-bomb.

But, damn, he came in a really sexy package.

Cocking his head, Ford studied her with his dazzling green eyes. But then, everything about Ford was dazzling, really. It was almost disheartening to be around him, since she couldn't have him.

He had this intoxicating abundance of elegance and sex appeal, tarnished with just the right amount of cocky bad-boy, and it was all off-limits to her. So, naturally, she couldn't remember any man she'd wanted more.

Meeting with Ford to do his legal work often bordered on torture, especially the longer Evie went celibate. When he teased her about something, which he often did, he pursed his lips up into this

2

mix of playful pout and sexy smile that made her want to fuck him on the table.

"Evie, love—" He slid his chair toward her, his wonderful, deep voice as plush as velvet. "I'm bored with this contract. Distract me." He narrowed his eyes. "You seemed distracted. Tell me what you were you thinking about."

They were at the point when all the subtle flirting for months had grown into barely-concealed innuendo. Ford might think they were at the point where it was inevitable something would happen, the question being only when and where. But Evie knew something he didn't—that nothing *could* happen between them. Ever. Not only was Ford a client, and getting involved with him would be a serious conflict of interest, resulting in her immediate dismissal from the firm—zero tolerance—there was also a more menacing reason that went by the name of John Martin, her boss and crazy-ass ex-boyfriend.

"Tell me," he repeated, his tone edging on command now.

"No," she said, a little too loudly. "I mean, nothing. I wasn't thinking about anything." Her face grew hot and she shifted sideways in the orange-woolen chair. It occurred to her the industrial fabric would be scratchy on her bare ass.

What was wrong with her? She needed to pull herself together.

Sucking in a fortifying breath, she tugged down on her short length of pencil skirt, which fell a good four inches shy of her knees. Why had she worn it to a meeting with Ford? If she'd had a best friend, that friend would demand to know what in the hell Evie thought she was doing. Evie was asking herself the same thing.

The green, glass-shaded library lamps threw shadows on the high walls of leather-bound books around them, providing a false feeling of seclusion that wasn't helping. The blackness outside the windows, dotted with the lights of Atlanta, reflected Evie and Ford's cozy vignette, their figures intimately close, their bodies nearly touching.

It was too dark, too private, and they were too alone.

She knew better than to meet him late at night in the deserted law firm. Infamous for wanting to control every aspect of his legal work, but busy running an empire, Ford often requested meetings with his legal team, which consisted of John and Evie, at odd hours. John used to join them, but for the past year, John had more and more let Evie shoulder the load of his work, micromanaging her with calls for status updates to create the ruse that he was fully involved. So lately, more often than not, it was just Ford and Evie working together. Alone.

For John, what had started as "therapeutic" drug use to allegedly give him the energy he needed to handle the workload and stress of making senior partner at the firm, had been spiraling out of control for the last year. Evie's excellent legal work, being passed off by John as his own, was the only thing keeping him from being fired, but if Ford noticed the situation, he never mentioned it.

She didn't mind the extra work, especially since every day led her closer to the day she could leave the firm and would never have to see John again. It was such a cliché that the daughter of a drug addict would somehow, even in the posh world of top law firms, find a druggie to hook up with. And her carefully cultivated quiet life had disintegrated because of it. The lesson was not lost on her. When she was free, she'd start over and fix it all again, finally find a way to feel safe.

But in the meantime she was apparently dead-set on creating more problems for herself. When Ford had called earlier that day asking for this after-hours meeting, Evie had actually gone out at lunch and bought a shorter skirt.

She may as well have bought an incendiary device, for all the sense it made.

Looking in the mirror in the dressing room, she had told herself that making a man like Ford, John's most important client, want her—even if John didn't know about it—was just her way of rebelling against her ex for the terrible situation he'd put her in. But now, as she sat in the library feeling helplessly aroused, looking at Ford's impossibly handsome face, her heart pounding nearly out of her chest, she knew her choice in wardrobe had little to do with John. A sinking, sick feeling clutched her stomach as she considered whether "rebelliousness" was just a glamorous, rationalized synonym for "self-destructiveness".

She smiled apologetically—he *was* the client after all. "We've been at this for a while. Would you like to take a break?"

4

"Thought you'd never ask." He mirrored her smile, his dimples transforming his face from merely very handsome into *Oh. My. God.*

Evie could lose herself in those dimples. Ford's dimples were one of the many reasons he was infamous around the law firm. When he flashed those babies, the polite feminine constraints of every woman in the room fell away like the clothing in their imaginations.

He stretched and ran one of his large hands through his thick, always-tousled hair, and it fell back into place as perfectly mussed as before he'd touched it. Ten years her senior at thirty-six, Ford was starting to go salt-and-pepper at his temples but the rest of his hair was a shiny dark-brown, which set off his green eyes in stunning and stark contrast.

Her coloring was much lighter than his, her eyes a clear blue and her hair a dark-blonde. John had once said her long, wavy hair made him think of the ocean in front of his family's beach house in Cape Cod. The day after she'd ended their relationship, she'd chopped her hair off to her chin so the only thing it would remind him of was her hatred for him. It had since grown out to brush her shoulders.

Evie tucked a loose wave behind her ear again and pulled out her phone to check emails. Her eyes focused on the screen but her brain didn't register any of the bolded, unread messages. Instead, she just kept thinking about Ford. She had it bad tonight.

She'd seen pictures of him in the society pages of the local newspaper and he seemed to be perpetually emerging from shiny, black cars with gorgeous, long-limbed women — models, heiresses, CEO's, even the occasional movie star. How might Evie look taking his hand and stepping out of a limo? Would everyone recognize she was faking it? That she didn't belong?

Ford pinched the bridge of his nose between his thumb and forefinger, and Evie glanced up at the movement. She could see his arm and chest muscles outlined under the fitted material of his tailored shirt. Obviously the man had time to do more than make money. He probably kept firm by doing things like swimming or playing football, or somehow otherwise getting sweaty with some male-model-looking friends, all shirtless. *Then, back to the locker room, where they all get naked...*

Realizing she was staring at Ford instead of her phone, she snapped her eyes back down to the small screen and made a show of scrolling and mumbling about the mountain of unread emails there. He touched her arm and she nearly jumped.

"It's good of you to meet me this late," he said quietly. He swept his eyes over her hair and face. "You shouldn't be stuck with a client in a law library on a Thursday night." He nodded toward her phone. "Am I keeping you from somebody?"

"Oh, no." She waggled the phone. "Work emails." She smiled, hoping it didn't look as rueful as she felt. "There's nowhere else for me to be."

That's right. I have no life.

"Oh come on. Surely you have a boyfriend. Or two?" He raised his eyebrows, his bright eyes glinting mischief.

"No!" She laughed. Nothing could be further from the truth. In fact, since the day she'd lost her virginity she couldn't remember a more celibate time in her life than the last six months. So it was killing her to be around Ford. "I spend all my time working. I guess I'm between boyfriends." Or maybe just "after boyfriend" if she couldn't get away from John long enough to ever safely date again.

"All your time working? What about family?"

Evie's derisive laugh escaped before she could quell it.

Cocking his head, Ford narrowed his eyes. "Mommy issues?"

"Uh, no," she said firmly. "I haven't spoken to my mother in years." Why was she telling him this?

"Daddy issues?"

"Stop that!" But she couldn't help but grin at him, no matter how rude he was being. He was just so charmingly infuriating. "I've actually never met my father," she added quietly.

"Ah." His voice was low and serious, and he nodded sagely. "Definitely daddy issues."

Her mouth dropped open. "I can't believe you said that!"

His grin widened. He enjoyed flustering her. "If I had a dollar for every time someone couldn't believe—"

"You'd be what? Richer?" she interrupted. "You're already filthy rich."

"That's right. I am." His smile faded and he tilted his head, studying her. "You're alone in this world. Just like me."

Staring at him in silence, she was at a loss for a response. Ford Hawthorne...alone? No. People must flock to this man. She thought back to the ladies in the limos.

"So that means you're all mine?" he asked softly. "Tonight, I mean?"

"I don't have anywhere else I need to be, so I guess I'm available for anything you need." Clamping her lips shut, she turned away to hide the blush she felt heating her cheeks. She'd only meant available professionally, of course.

I think.

She was trying to play it cool, but she suspected she was about as subtle as a blinking, neon sign, Vegas-style, pointing at her head and proclaiming, "This gal wants to screw your brains out!" His grin said as much.

"Anything I need?" Ford tipped his head and his glittering eyes caught hers. "I must warn you, Evie Radmin. There is a lot I need from you." Slowly and deliberately, he brushed the bare length of her leg between the hem of her skirt and her knee.

She sucked in her breath and panicked. Without thinking, she swiped his hand away and laughed as if he'd been joking, hoping he didn't notice the slight maniacal edge to her giggles.

Geez, god. This man was going to be the death of her. Maybe literally, if John found out.

"Mr. Hawthorne, we're never going to get this done." Turning her attention back to the contract, she tugged down on her skirt again. "You're going to have to behave if we have any hope of finishing this tonight."

Would he notice the rise and fall of her chest as her breathing picked up? The probable pink of her cheeks, hinting at her arousal? Being alone in a room with him was like being in a cage with a hungry lion.

Ford leaned closer. "I don't think you don't want me to behave." His graceful voice stroked over her skin and she wanted to stretch and purr. "And no one has succeeded in making me behave since my father died when I was eighteen." He dropped his gaze to her legs. "Don't try and make me start now. I assure you, it won't work." He trailed the backs of his fingernails over her skin. "Besides, I've decided I don't intend to behave around you anymore," he murmured.

His last comment tore through her, realigning every one of her thoughts to his intentions. And she hoped his intentions were bad. Really bad.

Still, her survival instincts screamed a reminder about her situation with John, and she opened her mouth to shut Ford down, but the look on his face made the words flee her head. She saw the desire that mirrored her own, but there was also a hint of vulnerability she'd never seen before. Had it come from his mention of his father's death? Or was he...lonely?

How could this charismatic man, capable of literally charming the pants off most any woman, possibly be lonely?

She mentally flipped through the pictures of the steady stream of society-page women, one more long-legged than the next. Though she *had* noticed it was never the same woman twice, and she'd only ever heard him mention one friend—someone named Charley. She knew from his legal history that he had no living relatives.

The thought was so incongruous with what she knew about Ford. Could it be true? Instead of a playboy with an enviably perfect life, could Ford be an attractive, lonely man taking advantage of his golden façade to keep everybody at arm's length?

And then she saw it there in his eyes, and she wondered how she'd never seen it before. Loneliness. His gorgeous, jewel-colored eyes hid it well, but there was definitely a dusky sadness there under the surface.

Her resolve softened and she ached to let him touch her. Maybe they did have something in common. She was lonely too. Always had been. Never knowing what she was going to walk into at home had made it impossible to have close friends growing up. It'd just been easier to keep everyone away to avoid embarrassing explanations.

But with Ford she didn't feel her normal self-protectionism. She felt a reckless and unfamiliar urge to give him anything he wanted to take from her. It was scary as hell, and thrilling.

Though, knowing her, she was just being self-destructive. What could be a better distraction from her trouble than more trouble? Without brushing his fingers off her knee again, she went with it, and ventured a challenge. "No one ever asks you to behave? And that's never struck you as a problem?" She raised her eyebrows, her pulse quickening with the suddenly-personal exchange.

His eyes flashed and the timbre of his voice dropped low and dangerous as he took hold of her chair and yanked it easily around to face him, making her gasp. "Problem or not, I'm tired of behaving around you. And I think you're tired of me behaving." His gorgeous eyes were dark with an intensity that told her he wasn't playing anymore.

Excitement laced with panic tremored low in her body. She wasn't going to make it out of the room without carnal knowledge of Ford. She couldn't decide whether to be thrilled or terrified about that.

"Ford, don't make me hurt you." Evie's voice shook. "The firm would kill me." There was no conviction behind her words. She bit her lower lip and reached a trembling hand up to her hair, but he grabbed her wrist and pulled it toward him instead. Evie let out a quick "oh" of surprise.

"I saw this before and I wanted to ask you about it," he said, studying her hand, his voice holding a hint of wonder. Following his eyes she realized with relief that he was referring to her cobalt-varnished fingernails, not her shaking hands. "I've never seen a lawyer with a blue manicure."

"It's not a manicure. I did it myself. And you know I'm a paralegal, not a lawyer." She was so aware of her hand in his, her cool skin against his warm. She wanted to straddle him and feel the rest of his skin against hers. Bite the buttons off his shirt.

Ford had all sorts of bulges and ridges she'd only seen in her imagination. She'd love to explore them in person. Instead, she tugged her fingers out of his grip and tucked her hands safely under her thighs.

"Why blue fingernails?"

"I just like them," Evie mumbled, looking away. The color of her nails was against the firm's dress code and she'd get in trouble if Ford mentioned it to any of the partners. They'd never notice her nails on their own. The mostly middle-aged men who populated the firm were either too busy to pay attention to her, or too busy paying attention to her ass or tits to notice the finish of her nails.

"*You* are a non-conformist." Ford's voice was accusatory, but his smile was good-natured.

"I am not! I'm just...individualistic."

She moved to scoot her chair away from him, but her eyes met his and the sudden intensity in them held her still. Tilting his head, he examined her with sharp eyes. "You are a fascinating creature, Evangeline. Different than most women I'm around."

She pulled her head back, frowning. Maybe she wasn't as refined and educated as the women he normally socialized with, but she wasn't sure she liked being called different from them. She touched the skirt she'd bought for their meeting. She didn't want to be different from those women. For once, she wanted to be the same. She wanted to show him she could be just as comfortable in his world as in hers. Even if she was faking it. Ignoring the worried voice in her head, she leaned toward Ford and set in motion a runaway train she didn't have the power to stop.

Her sexual self—not work-Evie, but private-Evie—reared up and took over, pushing all her job and ex-boyfriend concerns out of her head. Without any thought to the consequences, Evie licked her lips, leaned forward and said, "Different? It seems to me that you've always found me to be...interesting." She parted her legs a fraction and his eyes flicked to her knees where his hand still lay lightly against her skin.

How many business negotiations had she witnessed him dominate? How many times had she sat in awe as he effortlessly turned the tables on powerful, brilliant people and got exactly what he wanted?

What had she been thinking?

Because without skipping a beat, Ford leaned forward too, his mouth only inches from hers. Then he didn't just call her bet, but

raised it. "Evie, love, you're right." He squeezed her knee. "So let's make things *really* interesting. Put my cock in your mouth."
Just like that.

CHAPTER TWO

UT MY COCK in your mouth.

Ford said it as casually and as comfortably as if he'd merely suggested they go for coffee. Eyes widening, Evie sat back and her mouth popped open. Ford gazed unapologetically back at her. Her lungs felt flattened, like the moments in kung fu class when she had the wind knocked out of her and she lay on her back, praying the air would come.

Goddamn, this man had balls.

She shut her mouth, trying to process. Opening it again, she managed a strangled, "Excuse me?"

She and Ford had flirted before—a lot—but if this was flirting, it was some type of guerilla-warfare flirting.

He shrugged, his posture managing to look like a rugby player's in spite of his crisp, custom-made shirt and silk tie. "I'm a bit obsessed with your lips and, if we're being honest, I want to come in your mouth." He pursed his lips, seeming to gauge her reaction.

She choked on a breath. "We're not being honest. I'm being flabbergasted and you're just being rude."

He raised one eyebrow. God, he could even do that.

"If I'm being rude, you should be offended. Evie, do you find it offensive that I want your lips around my cock?" He leaned forward, and she swore she could feel his heat.

13

She touched her bottom lip. She'd long ago chewed the gloss off it. Ford wasn't ruffled. In fact, his eyes danced, his dimples tugging at her heart and other places.

He wants to come in my mouth.

His words should offend her, shouldn't they? Yet they didn't. Instead her pussy was throbbing with a warmth that demanded action. From the look on his face, he had all the confidence in the world he could make her do what he asked. Even in the library. Even in the middle of a business meeting.

His voice turned soft, like cashmere. "You want me as much as I want you. I'm certain of that." He dropped his head and spoke in a tone that was almost self-conscious, something she had never heard from him before. "Besides, I've been staring down your shirt at your extraordinary breasts all evening." He moved his eyes slowly back up to hers, his mouth quirking into a smile. "You were aware of that, I'm sure?"

Evie's heart skipped in its staccato rhythm. She moved her fingers to the lowest button on her shirt, which she'd undone just before Ford had arrived for their appointment. He caught her hand but didn't pull it away from her blouse. "Evie, don't. Please. Your curves are fantastic. You must know what you do to me."

She couldn't drag her eyes from his. He twisted his hand over hers so the backs of his fingers brushed against the bare flesh on the swell of her breast. She sucked in a lungful of air. Electricity danced over her skin at the graze of his fingers, instantly tightening her nipples even more.

Her quickening breath caused her breasts to lift against his knuckles and his eyes flicked down to her chest, lingering there. She couldn't let this happen, not in the law firm library. Reluctantly, she lowered her hand, still enclosed by his, and his hand dropped away. She barely had time to register her pang of disappointment before Ford reached out and abruptly pulled her chair even closer to his. Wrapping his large hands around her knees, he squeezed his fingers into her bare flesh.

Tensing, she made a noise like a whimper. A spark lit in his eyes at the sound, and heat flooded through her body, pooling between her legs. She could feel her slickness as she grew wet for him.

"Evie, I've been hard for half this evening. I'm aching for you."

A groan escaped her lips before she could bite it back. Ford was hard for her right now. She was drawn to him as if she was magnetized and he was hardened steel. "I can't." She whispered so weakly she wasn't sure he'd heard it.

"You can," he said firmly, brushing his fingers across her skin, bringing up goose bumps. Alarm rustled in the back of her mind. If he kept being so goddamned insistent, she was going to do anything he wanted.

"Mr. Hawthorne, maybe we can go somewhere? Away from the office?" Her voice held a clear edge of panic now. If they were going to go through with this terrible and thrilling idea, at least away from her office would only be half as dangerous. Right?

"No. Here. We've worked together for a while now. I'm sure you've noticed my need for control?" His voice dropped an octave. "It doesn't end with my legal work. I want you the way I choose." A rush of heat slammed through her, concentrating between her legs. She'd never felt anything like it. "I choose here, and I choose now."

Evie's respiration and heartbeat accelerated even higher. In his verdant eyes she saw an unwavering aim to have what he wanted from her, and rather than push him away, she nearly pulled his hands against her crotch and begged him to take it.

Her pussy throbbed now, excitement making it difficult to keep her thoughts straight, and he continued unmercifully. "I think you love this. I think you are wet through your panties for me right now."

"Don't," she breathed. She looked down to see his long fingers caress her inner thighs, her fantasies come to life. He'd rucked up the hem of her short skirt, his fingertips less than four inches from the crotch of her panties. Biting back a groan, she tried in vain to suppress the vibrant thrill that crackled through her at the sight of him touching her so insistently.

Summoning all her remaining strength, she closed her hands over his, but when she looked up to finally put a stop to the out-of-control situation, she watched him wet his lips deliberately, his piercing eyes burning into hers. The sight of his slick tongue made her go weak. She needed that tongue in her mouth, on her nipples, on her clit. She let go of his hands and let hers drop in surrender.

He could have had her in that moment—taken anything he wanted—had he pressed forward. Never had she been so thoroughly seduced. But instead he furrowed his brow and blinked. A pained look reflected briefly in the set of his features before he looked away and took a deep breath. "Not like this," he murmured as if to himself, running his fingers through his hair in a reflection of her own nervous habit.

His lips curved up, but the emotion didn't reach his eyes. He looked somehow sad under his weak smile, which confused her. She shifted uncomfortably.

"I want you to know something about me." His voice was quiet. "You are beautiful, of course, but that's not why I want you. I can count on one hand the number of people in this world I enjoy being around and you're one of them." His eyes held hers steadily. "That might mean nothing to you, but it means a great deal to me. It makes me want you in a way I've never experienced." He pressed his fingertips into the flesh of her legs and smiled when she jumped, the muscles of her core constricting in a twang of pleasure. "Perhaps it's the way you treat me."

"I don't treat you in any special way."

His eyes lit. "That's exactly it. People fawn over me. But not you."

She winced, knowing her bosses wouldn't think much of that revelation, given he was the firm's most valuable client and, thus, certainly deserving of fawning. "I'm not really a 'fawner'."

He looked down and compressed his lips into a thin line. "You'd think I'd like being treated so special all the time, but I don't. I despise it."

Under Ford's cultivated verve was a controlled and guarded man, so when he lifted his head and Evie caught the honesty on his face, it looked strangely raw on him. His voice matched his expression. "Except when it comes to you." He paused and inhaled deeply, as if he was choosing his words carefully, or collecting the courage to plow ahead. "With you, I find myself wishing you

16

wanted to please me in every way. I can't stop thinking about how I might make you want to please me." He swept his eyes down to her nipples again, which she knew were blatantly beckoning to him against the front of her shirt, betraying her attempts to de-escalate the situation. "I come here more than I need to. I purposely pick times that are inconvenient to John so he'll let you take the meeting. I pay an exorbitant amount by the hour just to be around you."

Evie's mouth dropped open. "Wait...you *like* me?" Her mind flashed again to the leggy women and refused to believe the possibility.

Ford frowned. "Yes, but I don't want to mislead you." He looked her square in the eye as if he needed to get the message across. "I don't engage in relationships. I've tried and they don't work for me, so I just don't anymore. I don't miss them." His eyes softened. "I don't want there to be any misconceptions between us. I want you. I want you more than I've wanted a woman in a very long time."

At his admission, desire rocketed back full-tilt in Evie, and he seemed aware of it, feeding off her subtle body-language. He moved his hands again along her skin, up and down, squeezing his thumbs against her inner thighs, causing her to shudder with every stroke upwards toward the heat between her legs. "And I know how to make a woman feel very good. I could make you feel very good."

Now it all made sense—the ladies in the limos. *Never the same woman twice.* Now she knew why. Ford didn't have girlfriends. Ford only had sex.

She'd never had a man come right out and tell her he only wanted to have sex with her, but she wasn't surprised. She'd known through all of her growing lust that he wasn't a happily-ever-after kind of guy. And hadn't she learned her lesson anyway, trying to find that elusive ending?

With a ringing clarity she realized Ford's prohibition against relationships was perhaps the only way she could be with him. She couldn't date anyway, not with the situation with John.

God, could she really do this? She hadn't had an orgasm brought on by the touch of a man in so long.

Ford's offer to make her feel very good in her sexually-neglected condition was like dangling a fresh-baked chocolate chip cookie in front of her after a long week of strict dieting, telling her to "go ahead, put it in your mouth."

Could they meet just for sex now and then, without John or the firm finding out? She imagined them having sex in Ford's limo, in a luxury hotel room, lounging next to his pool. Her stomach flip-flopped as her rationalizations began to work, breaking down her walls. As long as they both went into it with clear expectations, she couldn't get hurt. In fact, it was very honest. Everything was completely clear. And that felt safe to her.

Her aching desire was becoming critical. She swallowed hard. She was going to require some attention soon—either from him, or if she wasn't going to do this, she was going to need some time alone. Glancing at the lofty shelf of legal volumes behind him, she wished desperately they were anywhere but the firm's library. She swallowed again, trying to moisten her dry throat. In her fantasies this had gone a lot smoother.

"Now that I've laid it out, you can make a decision." And with that disclaimer, Ford was back. The unusual vulnerability vanishing back into his familiar mischievous confidence. His eyes glinted, lively with power.

Sliding his hands down, he closed his fingers around the backs of her knees and jerked her closer to him so she was now wedged between the muscular spread of his parted legs. She grabbed the sides of her seat, her heart beating a wild drumbeat under her hard-nippled breasts.

He moved his hands up her thighs, pressing her legs apart, causing her skirt to ride further up. Leaning in until his face was close to hers—his mouth close to hers—he whispered, "I am successful because I make good choices. *You* are a good choice." He caught his fingers just under the already indecently high hem of her skirt and forced it the rest of the way up her legs. "Let me," he growled.

"I'll lose my job."

"Evie…" He breathed out her name as if it were something decadent, his lips close enough to warm hers. Her body quivered as

18

the weight of her need swamped her. It took everything she had not to press her lips to his. "When you picked out this short skirt to wear for our meeting, tell me you didn't hope I'd do exactly what I'm doing now." He squeezed his fingertips into her thighs again. "Now move your hands so I can do it." She hadn't realized she'd placed her hands over his again, trying to stop his progress.

He was so close to her wet pussy, his fingertips digging into her skin, his mouth nearly on hers, and she suddenly couldn't remember why she was fighting him. "Okay," she whispered, her voice hoarse.

The moment froze. She was acutely aware of the sound of their breathing, both ragged, both heavy. Then the corners of his mouth rose and his eyes flashed triumph. She knew that smile. She'd seen it before at the negotiation table, always at the point when Ford knew he'd won.

Damn him and his dimples.

"Yes, love," he breathed and slipped his hands under her skirt, sliding his fingers the rest of the short distance to the crotch of her panties. Every nerve in her body sizzled and she fought the urge to thrust herself against his hand.

Though his lips were so close, he didn't kiss her, but leaned his face against hers. "Now listen to me Evie." He nuzzled his nose against her cheek, his breath tickling her earlobe, making her nipples diamond-hard. His voice, the low growl of a stalking lion, coaxed her. "It's past eight o'clock at night. Everyone's gone home." He pulled his head back, his leaf-green eyes meeting her blue ones. "We're completely alone."

He shifted, moving one hand to the back of her head to cup her skull in his palm. Tightening his grip, he secured a fistful of her hair and tilted her head back to look up at him. She gasped. It didn't hurt, but his handling was oddly forceful and she was stunned when a powerful spasm of lust reverberated from her core at the rough treatment.

He inclined his face, his hand still gripped in her hair. She could almost feel the brush of his lips on hers as he spoke. "In fact," he purred, "I could bend you over this table right now and fuck you until you screamed and no one would even hear." He put emphasis on the "fuck", hitting the K hard, and the raw sound of the word affected her physically, as if he'd run his tongue down her body.

Her body was shouting at her, "*Bend over the table! Bend over the table!*" betraying her determination not to get caught screwing a client in the library. She managed a barely audible, "You could?"

He pushed his other hand the remaining fraction of distance up her inner thigh and found the spot she knew he'd intended. He stroked one strong finger down the wet satin between her legs and this time she didn't even try to stop her moan as his fingertip pressed hard over her swollen clit. "Yes," he said simply, "I could."

"Oh god," she closed her eyes and whispered, forgetting everything except how much she wanted this man. How long she'd wanted him. Human beings aren't meant to be solitary creatures and Evie had gone too long without touch because of John.

Her need to be close to a man—to touch him intimately and be touched by his strong hands in return—clawed to the surface and took over. That neglected, essential instinct in her would not be denied this chance. It was as if she'd been in hibernation and was now finally awaking to a warm and glorious sun. And she wanted to bask naked in it.

She licked her lips. "Please."

Kneading three fingers against the fabric that clung to her engorged labia, Ford kissed Evie on the cheek and then moved to her ear, dropping kisses in the indentation under her earlobe before nuzzling his way down her neck. Her head dropped back and her lips parted as wildfire seemed to surge through her veins.

"My pretty Evie," he whispered against her skin. "I think you need to come." He adjusted the movement of his fingers to a circular motion that made her head swim. From somewhere deep in the recesses of her thoughts came a small, worried voice—*you should make him stop.* But her visceral need for touch, intimacy, release, told that voice in no uncertain terms to *fuck off.* Moving his lips against her ear he asked, "Do you want me to make you come?"

Daring to touch him, she lifted a hand to the bicep of the arm and she could feel the cords of his muscles roll under her fingertips as he worked his fingers against her pussy. His solidly built arm felt like a buttress under her palm, and she closed her eyes and gave herself over to him. He felt strong. Safe.

How was it this man felt safe to her when there was nothing safe about him?

A glowing euphoria was expanding from the center of her core under his skilled fingers. She was amazed—it wouldn't be long before her pleasure exploded into an orgasm that promised to be spectacular. And badly needed. Before she had time to second guess, she nodded her head vigorously, whispering, "Yes, yes," against his hot cheek.

"Yes what? I want to hear you say it."

Frustration and unease twisted in her, but not wanting to give him a reason to stop touching her, she followed his instructions. "I want you to make me come." Her voice sounded meek, reflecting her embarrassment. She wasn't shy, but she'd never flat-out asked a man to give her an orgasm before.

Pulling his head back, he met her eyes, his green ones hooded and smoldering. He stilled his fingers and she nearly groaned at the loss. "Then here are my terms, Evangeline. First, you must do exactly as I say." He raised his eyebrows as if challenging her to protest. When she didn't, but only stared back at him, open mouthed and—she was sure—wide-eyed, he continued in a purr. "After I make you come—and I will make you come—it will be my turn. You are going to kneel between my legs, do what I tell you to do, and then you're going to let me come in your mouth, and you're going to swallow it." He raised a hand to her chin and pressed his thumb across her bottom lip. "Agreed?"

Holy hell, he was negotiating their sexual encounter.

Yet, though she'd been close to climax moments before, somehow his taking charge had shifted the potential of her orgasm to another level. A level she didn't even know existed. And she wanted that orgasm.

Ford's voice was low and intimate. "Evie, after I'm done taking care of you, you will want to please me. I'm willing to guarantee your satisfaction." Amusement played around his lips, quirking them into that bad-boy, pursed smile of his that made her crazy. She had to close her eyes to block it out so she could think as he continued. "If you don't have the best orgasm of your life, you are free to forfeit your end of the bargain. Do we have a deal?" He lowered his lips back to her neck and nuzzled her skin as he waited for her answer.

The best orgasm of her life?

God yes, we have a deal.

Actually, she'd agree to anything if he'd keep talking to her like that and touch her again. Her frequent fantasies of Ford involved him spending a lot of time with his head between her legs, his face wet with her juices. And she could use that "guaranteed" climax.

Only Ford would negotiate a sexual transaction the same as he would any other business deal. How many times had they sat at that table and planned negotiations together for Ford's development deals? The only difference here was that Ford was sucking her earlobe and bartering to exchange orgasms. Could she approach it with the same kind of business mindset?

She'd have to, given that she and Ford couldn't have a relationship, each for their own good reasons.

Taking a deep breath, she got down to business, concentrating on the terms and attempting to analyze whether she was getting a good deal. It was hard to put thoughts together with Ford nibbling under her ear, but she didn't become a top paralegal without learning how to think fast under less than ideal circumstances.

It felt like a win-win. Maybe even better than a win-win. Evie truly enjoyed giving blowjobs—relished it, even. But what kind of negotiator would she be if she took his first offer? "I will agree to your deal," she spoke the words next to his ear, her head thrown back as she fought to keep her voice steady. "But only if you use your mouth to make me come, not just your fingers. I want the full treatment."

He pulled back, beaming a smile at her, his dimples triggering a sensuous twinge between her legs. He looked proud. "I knew you wouldn't let me down, love. And I will happily agree to that concession." His deep voice vibrated through her, his lips so close to Evie's she could feel his breath on her. "That had been my plan all along. I can't wait to taste you." His eyes practically blazed. She'd never seen him so vitalized. It was almost as if…

Yes. This was really doing it for him—bargaining over their sexual encounter.

It was certainly a first for her, and, she had to admit, it held a unique appeal in its candidness. Everything clear up front. Everyone gets what they want.

Licking her lips, Evie tried to let out a slow, controlled breath in an effort not to look rattled. "Then, Mr. Hawthorne," she said in her best, professional voice, "I believe we have a deal."

She'd just negotiated an oral contract for oral sex with the hottest man she'd ever laid eyes on. She could have laughed out loud. It made her feel powerful and risqué, and the combination was quite an aphrodisiac, so said her hard-as-pebbles nipples and her throbbing pussy.

"Excellent." He sat back, eyes dancing with delight. "Let's establish a safe word."

"A safe word?" Her stomach twisted as she tried not to sound as stunned as she felt. Certainly she knew what a safe word was, but something like that was for people into extreme sex. It wouldn't be needed for anything like what she'd just agreed to. Would it?

"Love, we've made an agreement in which you've promised to do everything I ask. It's important for both of us that you know you can stop at any time if you're not comfortable or if I'm hurting you. Do you understand?"

"That sounds reasonable." And it did. A safe word. Something she could blurt out that would make any discomfort or pain cease immediately. A swell of warmth sparked to life in her chest. Something about Ford establishing this kinky-sounding safe word made her feel protected. He was concerned for her, putting her choices first. She liked the concept of a safe word.

If only life had a safe word. She'd scream it in John's face.

"Good. Do you have a safe word you normally use?"

"No!" she practically shrieked. His green eyes appeared momentarily wounded at her sharp exclamation. "I'm sorry, I've just... No, I don't have one." She shifted uncomfortably.

"You've never used one?" She shook her head and an unreadable look passed over his face. "Okay," he said gently. "Then let's come up with one for you. Most importantly it should be something memorable, but something you would never normally say or think about during sex."

"Like jellybeans?" As soon as the word came out of her mouth, she felt her face flush hot. She'd said the first inane word that came to mind and was mortified at how cutesy it sounded. She should have picked something urbane or edgy, like "sommelier" or "mosh pit", not a word associated with the Easter Bunny.

But Ford grinned, dimples beaming. "Yes, exactly like 'jellybeans'. I love it." In spite of his assurances, her face grew even hotter. Had he just mentally compared her ridiculous safe word to all the others he'd "worked with" in the past?

Leaning in, he brushed a kiss on her cheek and whispered next to her ear, "You're even prettier when you blush, Evangeline." And suddenly her blush felt like that of a schoolgirl's with a crush.

This is a transaction, she reminded herself, *not a date. Keep it together.*

In an effort to focus, she took a deep breath, forcing down her misplaced affection for the completely unavailable man in front of her. The man whose cologne, mixed with his natural, male scent, made her heady as he pulled his face back from her cheek.

His flirtatious smile disappeared and his face grew serious. Her stomach flip-flopped. They had begun.

Hammering to life again, her heart was in her throat. She'd just put herself in Ford's hands with no idea what he'd ask her to do. Could she do it?

"Stand and pull up your skirt, love."

24

CHAPTER THREE

*F*ORD GAZED LEVELLY at Evie as if he had every confidence she would not defy him. She bit her bottom lip, a gesture she'd always thought she hated in women but realized maybe she'd just never truly been put in a situation that warranted it.

And this was definitely a bottom-lip-gnawing situation.

Standing up, her face still feeling flushed pink, she raised her skirt slowly until the hem inched up to reveal her panties, displaying for Ford her bare legs and the vee between her thighs, covered with red satin. She felt exposed, but she watched in fascination as his eyes traced lazily down her form. Pursing his lips in that sexy way of his, he cocked his head, taking his time in examining her. He wasn't going to make this easy.

Over his shoulder she could see her reflection in the huge windows against the blackness of the night as she stood in front of him in the library flashing her panties. The shock of that sight alone would have made her call the whole thing off if she hadn't needed the release he promised so goddamned badly.

With Ford still seated and Evie in her tall heels, he was nearly at eye-level to her crotch. He wrapped his long fingers around the outside of her bare legs. Though his fingertips felt hot against her, she shivered at the contact. The nerves of her skin felt raw, sensitized to the slightest touch.

His eyes fixed to the small triangle of red fabric that comprised the only barrier between her tingling core and Ford's face. He curled his hands around to her butt, her cheeks naked due to the thong she was wearing. Squeezing her ass, he pulled her toward him and ducked to bury his mouth and nose against the damp, scarlet satin, breathing deeply before mouthing her folds from over the fabric.

She moaned, hardly even aware she'd made the sound. What Ford had done in smelling her—tasting her—through her clothes without any prelude seemed somehow animal, instinctual. It was as if he meant to claim her. The thought made her sigh, but it wasn't a noise brought on by the actions of his lips against her. It was a sigh of pleasure, knowing what was coming.

Ford wouldn't hold back the way many people did during their first encounter with a new partner, feeling them out before they felt comfortable enough to really let loose, if they ever did. No, as he'd said, Ford was an overachiever, and she was about to reap the benefits of his drive for excellence, if she could just play along and keep up.

Between her legs, he nuzzled his lips against her. It was decadent. She couldn't remember the last time she'd been treated to oral sex. Though John appreciated the blowjobs Evie loved to perform, he wasn't generous with reciprocation. The few times she'd talked him into it, he'd performed the act with such apathy she'd stopped him out of boredom.

In contrast, Ford's lips clutched at her and drew her in as if he couldn't wait to devour her. A delightful throb steadily gained momentum in her core as he coaxed her closer toward ecstasy.

Hooking his fingers under each side of her thong, he peeled it off, dragging it down the length of her legs until she stepped out of it, her bare sex now flaunting what she was sure were engorged, rosy lips for his attention. Picking up the discarded lingerie, he stuffed it in his pocket.

"Hey, I'm gonna need those back." Evie plucked at the hem of her skirt, inching it down slightly. She felt awkward standing in front of him stripped of her panties while he raked his eyes over her.

"We'll see," he murmured. Cupping his hands on the sides of her legs, he slid his fingers up under her skirt to her hips, and looked up at her. Eyes sparking and voice alive with the same controlled excitement, he said levelly, "Miss Evangeline, I don't recall telling you to pull down your skirt. Now lift it back up or I'll have to remove it entirely."

Evie's mouth dropped open at his nerve, yet her hands obeyed him instantly, lifting her skirt as she was told, to expose herself again.

What was this man doing to her?

Normally so independent, she stood in front of him on knees weak with desire, displaying herself to him and hungry to obey his sexual demands. Clenching her vaginal muscles, she shivered at the potential there, the taut focusing of the nerve ending toward their instinctual, ultimate goal of blissful oblivion.

She longed for that oblivion. If she just gave herself over to him and let Ford take control — take his pleasure with her — then maybe she wouldn't have to think for those glorious moments when he was in charge. And maybe for the first time in six months, or perhaps ever, she could stop feeling so exhaustively alone. Let someone else take care of her, think for her. Right or wrong, it sounded so refreshing and free.

Being on her own, by default, meant she was always in charge — always the one responsible — whether she wanted it or not. And she was so tired of it. She couldn't remember a time when she was taken care of, though she knew she must have been, at least when she was a baby. When she was five years old, she'd make herself cereal in the morning, sometimes with milk if they had any, and then would dig through her mom's purse while the woman slept, passed out, hoping to find enough change so she wouldn't have to beg for a free school lunch again.

Growing up that way had created strength inside Evie, but also a powerful weakness. And it was just the leverage John had needed to use her. As a trial lawyer he knew how to read people, spot their wounds and exploit them. And that's just what he'd done to her. He'd dangled the promise of the safety and security in front of her until she'd let her guard down.

How ironic that ending up hurt and alone had only fueled her desire to let someone else be in charge. That need burned stronger than ever in her gut, and Ford was pushing all the right buttons. She'd never connected sex with a longing to relinquish control before, and the combination was like a powerful drug to that deeply unsatisfied part of her psyche.

She wasn't just ready to do whatever Ford asked her, she was excited to do it, hot to do it, wet to do it. This was a temporary solution with no strings. Perhaps giving Ford control and abandoning herself to the pleasure he promised could allow her to forget. Forget her responsibility, forget to be afraid, maybe even let her feel safe and protected in someone's strong hands for at least the time it lasted.

Still seated in the library chair with his hands on her hips, he pulled her to him, his gaze pinned to her naked mound.

Can he see how wet I am?

Moving his palms around to cup her buttocks, he squeezed her ass cheeks and pulled her against his face again, burying his nose and mouth into the neat strip of hair that disappeared between her legs. She gasped when his warm lips brushed her sensitive labia. Nothing except her own fingers and her vibrator had been this close to her clit in half a year. She had to fight the urge to clamp her fingers in his dark hair and crush his face between her legs until he brought her to climax again and again. She suspected he could do it.

He snaked his strong tongue out to explore her, and she groaned and gave in to the urge to place her hands on his head. His hair was so soft. Looking down, she forgot to breathe. Ford Hawthorne's face was between her legs, his tongue licking her, just like she'd fantasized about so many times. But this was so much better than her fantasies. She didn't have a vivid enough imagination to have come up with the way this felt. Closing her eyes, she shook her head. She didn't even know how to process the pleasure and joy that was bubbling in her, but she could lose herself in it.

He drew away from her and she groaned at the loss of his hot mouth against her flesh. "On the table," he demanded. Standing, he lifted her easily and dropped her bare bottom onto the development contract they'd been word-smithing not twenty minutes prior. He pulled the chair in front of her and helped her brace her heels on the armrests on either side of him. Reaching under her leg and around her ass, he scooped her toward the edge of the table, forcing her legs wide, until she was spread open in front of him, laid completely bare.

"Mr. Hawthorne…," she said, self-consciousness swelling again and allowing her nerves to find purchase.

"Shh. None of that, Evangeline." His tone was firm and the message clear. He wouldn't hear protests or allow her to entertain embarrassment. Laying his hands on the sensitive skin of her inner thighs, he pressed her legs wider, his eyes traveling slowly all the way down from face to her naked pussy. "Your body is so beautiful," he said softly. Leaning in, he laid a kiss above his hand on her thigh, inches from where she really ached for him to be. "But this part is especially pretty," he murmured, sliding his hand all the way up her leg and stroking a finger into her folds. She sucked in a breath as his touch sent shock-waves through her. "God, Evie," he nearly moaned her name. "You're so wet. You're ready for more than just my tongue."

She tensed, not sure whether she wanted to wrap her legs around him or remind him to stay on task. Without more delay, he pushed a finger inside, studying her as if he intended to memorize her reactions, adjust to her cues. "So tight." He looked up at her, grinning mischievously. "When is the last time you've been thoroughly fucked, Miss Radmin?"

She blinked at him and couldn't make her mouth work. The only response her brain could produce was that she wasn't sure she'd ever been thoroughly fucked. That sounded like something she'd remember.

Thankfully, Ford didn't wait for her answer. He slid his finger in and out of her slowly. "No worries, love. I'm going to make up for some of the fun you've missed."

With his other hand, he tucked his first two fingers in a vee around the sides of her pussy, trapping her labia tightly against the finger he still had inside her. Her firm clit was caught snugly between her folds so that every movement of his finger dragged her own engorged lips against her clit.

Damn. He is good.

Letting her head drop back again, she closed her eyes and whispered, "Oh god," as she rocked her hips, not able to remain still with so much pleasure building inside her. Exhaling, she realized she was holding her breath as she anticipated whatever fabulous thing he'd do next.

Lowering his mouth to her heated core, he removed his finger. He was taking his time, making her wait in agony for every new treat. He replaced his finger with his strong tongue, snaking it between her folds to dip in and taste her.

Evie moaned and let her head loll, her brain struggling to keep up with the intensity of the feelings he brought to life in her. Maybe it was her sexual dry spell or because she was so hot for him, or perhaps it was Ford's skill, but she'd never experienced anything like the mind-bending rush of desire coursing through her from his touches.

Abandoning all thought, she leaned back and shifted her weight to her arms, pressing herself more firmly into his face. He'd guaranteed her satisfaction and it had taken him less than five minutes to convince her he'd have no trouble over-delivering on that promise.

Ford moved his tongue up and down rhythmically on her, finding her clit and flicking it. She was almost embarrassed at how much she was enjoying him. Fighting the urge to squirm against his mouth, Evie arched her back, eager for his tongue to bring her over the edge and ease her need.

She should drag it out, relish it, but she was too desperate. She just needed the satisfaction of an orgasm brought on by a man who worked only to please her. It had been too long. That hunger combined with her lust for this man, and she was in over her head. Her only choice was to enjoy the ride.

He released her folds from the clench of his fingers and wrapped his arms under her legs and around until he had an ass cheek in each hand.

"Damn," he whispered against her, "I'm so hard for you I'm tempted to throw out this whole agreement and just fuck you until I'm satisfied." Evie whimpered and flexed her fingers against the solid wood of the library table, wondering if her nails could dig nicks into the oak. She looked down at him, intending to burn the sight of him between her legs into her memory for future uses on lonely nights. He met her eyes, his lips curling into a sexy smile, wet from her juices. "But a deal's a deal, Miss Radmin."

Closing her eyes, she nodded, breathlessly agreeing. "A deal's a deal, Mr. Hawthorne."

He lapped his tongue up the full length of her pussy, once, twice, before adding his finger again to fuck her while his mouth produced magic. The tingling pleasure multiplied and then multiplied again. Feeling as if she was too small in her own skin, she fought the urge to cry out to release the pent up, glorious feelings he was tonguing to life in her.

Damn, she was almost there already.

She tried to back off from the precipice, determined to make her side of the deal last as long as she could hold out. She'd never actually tried not to come before, and it seemed to have the opposite effect on her, her pleasure careening headlong toward the euphoric escape of orgasm.

Staring down at him, her eyes greedily drank in his broad muscular shoulders, his strong back. She wished he would take off his shirt so she could touch his tanned skin and watch his muscles roll and contract as he worked to pleasure her. Pausing, he looked up again, his gorgeous eyes meeting hers.

"Evangeline, do you have any idea how often I've sat across from you at this law firm and thought of fucking you with my fingers while I sucked on your clit?"

Goddamn, the things this man said.

His voice was low and sultry. "When I make you come, say my name."

Evie nodded as if in a trance, thinking she'd agree to anything as long as he didn't stop what he was doing to her. "F-ford?" she stammered, realizing she wasn't clear on his instructions. She'd never called him by his first name before, not to his face.

"No," he growled, and pushed a second finger into her without warning, making her gasp. Sucking her clit between his lips, he nuzzled his tongue against the nub while he had it trapped. She gave up holding back on her expressions of pleasure. She was sighing and moaning so much that she almost missed his instructions. "You will call me 'Mr. Hawthorne'. Now lie back."

There was something so wrong about his insisting she call him by his formal name, given he had his fingers buried in her pussy, but it magnified the idea that he was in control, and the thought did things to her. She'd think about it later, dwell on why surrendering her control fueled a raging fire in her. She'd never wanted such things before. Of course she'd never negotiated a deal with a hot billionaire for oral sex before, either.

The forgotten contracts crinkled noisily under her back as she lowered herself to the table, making the only other sounds in the deserted library besides Ford's wet kisses and her soft moans. Before closing her eyes again, she noticed the ceiling had upgraded acoustical tiles, making it fancier than a standard office ceiling.

She'd never even looked up at the library ceiling before. Of course she'd never been on her back on a library table with her legs spread before, whimpering in inevitable ecstasy. Ford was introducing her to all kinds of firsts.

Without slowing his pumping fingers, he tilted his head, sucking one side of her folds into his mouth entirely, suckling them for a moment before shifting his head to give the other side the same treatment.

Oh.

No one had ever done that before. "Please," she whispered again and she didn't know if she was begging for mercy from the onslaught of arousal so strong it felt like torment, or begging him to bring on more.

He stood but didn't move his face from between her legs, his efforts reaching a feverish rhythm. His long fingers continued to fill her and her pleasure spiked again. Her legs tensed on the arms of the office chair, scooting her slightly away from him. With a growl of displeasure, he wrapped his arms up around her thighs, jerking her back to the edge of the table again to bury his face in her aggressively. This time he settled into an unyielding cadence against her. Short, quick sucks of her clit before allowing a moment of relief as he lapped his strong tongue along her pussy, all the while penetrating her with his fingers.

She writhed, moaned, and grabbed for the edge of the table to stay pressed against his face.

Oh fuck. Oh fuck!

This wasn't going to be an orgasm, this was going to be an awakening, an act of god.

He pressed his fingers into her thighs a little too hard and the pain cut through the pleasure, but it didn't bother her. It was better. "My name," he commanded. "Say my name when I make you come." His deep voice vibrated against her and her body responded instantly.

The orgasm slammed through her like a tidal wave. "Oh god, Mr. Hawthorne. I'm coming. Mr. Hawthorne, it's so good. Oh…oh…" Her cries trailed off as she surrendered her mind to the oblivion until there was nothing but the rapture. Wave after wave of it. Nothing to think about. Nothing but what he'd made her do, made her feel.

He held her legs until she stilled. As she slowly returned to reality, she clamped her lips closed, realizing she was continuing to whisper his name over and over again like an incantation.

He untangled his arms to sit back as she righted herself unsteadily. His face glistened with the wetness from her excitement and without blinking he used the sleeve of his custom shirt to clean his beautiful face.

Even that pricey, custom shirt was disposable to him. Deep in her mind, a small voice warned her she was no different. But she was not thinking about that. Not thinking at all.

Rather than awkwardness descending as it easily could have at that moment, she met his eyes and something passed between them in the charged air. There was an intensity in his stare and neither of them spoke. The echoes of her cries in orgasm seemed to reverberate like living memories in the shadows of the somber legal books around them.

Was it like this for him all the time? Was this what went on behind the blacked-out windows of the limos? Or was this different for him too? Better?

From the look in his eyes, one thing Evie was sure of was that he'd enjoyed doing what he'd done to her. And so had she.

Maybe she should just quit her job and fuck Ford all day. She didn't need to eat, right?

"Wow," she finally managed, making him smile. He wasn't kidding. Best orgasm of her life.

"If your response is any indication, I'm guessing I delivered the satisfaction I promised, love. Now stand up. My turn." He pursed his lips into that cocky smile that showcased his dimples and always made her panties a bit wet. If she'd been wearing any. In that gravelly, bedroom voice of his, he added, "I know exactly what I'm going to do to your mouth."

A wide and wicked grin stole across her face and she looked down quickly, trying to hide it. She had no idea what he had in store for her, but the truth was she was ready to perform any lewd act this man could come up with in his sinful imagination.

She was usually more hesitant than that. Maybe she was losing her mind. Maybe the stress of the last six months, coupled with no sexual relief, had finally caused her to go crazy. But whatever it was, she was ready at that moment, with no commitment from either of them, to be Ford's whore. And that didn't sound the least bit bad or degrading to her.

Actually, it felt empowered. She was doing what felt good to her and fuck everyone else. It felt filthy and wild and all the things a smart, responsible girl should never be.

And Ford's slut was exactly what she wanted to be at that moment as she sat with her naked ass on the wet and ruined contract documents that John had reviewed earlier that day, adding only grammar-picking comments and no compliments on Evie's hard work.

No. In this moment she wasn't worrying, for once, about her long-term plan, the consequences, or the investment versus the reward. In fact she could think of nothing else but doing whatever Ford wanted as long as it would get him to do that to her again.

But, despite her enthusiasm, something nagged at her. She was playing with fire.

I. Don't. Care.

She wanted to burn and burn and burn, until all of her stress and worries were reduced to ashes, and everything left simply felt good.

He helped her off the table and she stood on shaking legs, smoothing her skirt back down as she studied his handsome face. He'd been confident enough to guarantee her satisfaction and now she knew why. Cupping her jaw in his hand, he smoothed his thumb over her bottom lip.

"In all my years in business I've made deals that have netted me billions, but I think this may be the best deal I've ever struck." He smiled and gripped her close, letting his hand trail down to her lower back and pulling her against him. For a moment, she thought he was going to kiss her—thought she might die if he didn't—but instead he spoke softly, his eyes locked to hers. "Kneel down and take me in your mouth."

Her lips parted and her still-sensitive core twanged with pleasure at his bald demand. She'd expected something like this but it still shocked her when it came. He didn't mince words. And where her first thought perhaps could have been shock, to her surprise, it wasn't. Her first thought instead was how much she wanted to do exactly what he demanded. She clenched the muscles in her well-serviced pussy realizing she still wasn't done enjoying him.

"Okay, Mr. Hawthorne," she whispered, and she knelt.

CHAPTER FOUR

WITH THE SHOCK of an early-morning alarm clock, Evie's cell phone shrilled to life in the charged, quiet air of the library, startling them both.

She jumped to her feet and jerked her attention to the table where her cell sat forgotten. She watched John's name flash on the phone's display, and reality slammed sickeningly back into her. Her stomach flip-flopped queasily, as if John had actually walked in and spied them in the compromising position.

"Fuck," Ford snarled under his breath as Evie reached for the phone with a shaking hand.

"I'm sorry. It's my boss. I've got to take this," she said, not taking her eyes from the name on the screen.

"Of course." Ford's clipped words were polite but his tone was clearly displeased at the interruption. She walked away to get some privacy. There was no telling which John she'd get on the phone, and she didn't want Ford to overhear her dealing with him. Closing her eyes she pressed the answer button. The phone had rung four times already, and John was likely to be incensed that she hadn't answered more quickly.

"H-hello." She winced, hoping John hadn't noticed the slight tremor in her voice. While he surely had no idea what he'd interrupted, she couldn't help but be freaked out that not less than five minutes ago her legs had been spread eagle with the firm's biggest client's face between them. It would be dangerous for her and Ford if John found out.

"Well gee, Eves, I'm glad you could find some time to answer my apparently unimportant phone call." Unchecked contempt oozed from John's voice. Wrapping her free arm protectively around herself, she hunched her shoulders toward the phone pressed to her ear.

"I'm meeting with Mr. Hawthorne. I didn't want—"

"Shut up. You're a fucking paralegal. You shouldn't even get to talk to a client as important as Ford Hawthorne."

Evie narrowed her eyes and inhaled silently.

He's a snake, she reminded herself. *You're better than him. He might live in a fancy house and wear expensive clothes, but he's gutter-scum. There will come a day when you'll be free.*

As soon as she finished paying him the money she owed him, she'd be long gone. But until then, she was being forced to play his bitch. And she wasn't very good at it.

Unfortunately, Evie had two qualities that always made things worse with John. Rebelliousness bordering on recklessness, and not much deference for authority. Especially an authority who so clearly didn't deserve respect.

Her voice was icy. "We don't want to keep Mr. Hawthorne waiting. What can I do for you?" She wouldn't hang up or curse at him—she'd learned fighting him only made her life more miserable than it already was, especially given that half the time John was high and unpredictable. But she wasn't about to play his cowed handmaiden either.

John coughed out a harsh laugh that hurt her ear and she flinched, angry at him and angrier at herself for cringing, though she knew he couldn't see her reaction. "Sometimes I cannot understand how you even got this job." He laughed again. "And everyone's always going on about how smart you are. You called *me.*"

If he were seven years old his tone couldn't have been more childish.

She groaned inwardly. John was high as a kite. Again. Checking her watch she saw it was almost nine o'clock. Of course he was high.

Every Thursday night he hit the city's upscale martini club after work with his litigation buddies so they could regale each other with exaggerated, or completely made-up, tales of their legal triumphs and snort lines of coke at their outrageously expensive, private, VIP table. He was probably fifteen minutes from ordering a hooker. Hugging her arm tighter around herself, Evie closed her eyes.

She tried not to beat herself up at her naiveté, but now that the blinders were off, she couldn't help but feel like an idiot. A now-jaded idiot. But then, John had put on quite a show when they'd been together, his courtroom acting skills on full-bore. He'd shown her exactly what she'd wanted to see, and she'd lapped it up.

But this time, resentment overwhelmed her better sense. "Jesus Christ, John," she hissed, gripping the phone with both hands in her frustration. "You're so smashed you don't even remember calling me. I'm hanging up so I can finish your work. Don't call me back."

"Listen, you little bitch. You —"

"Put John on speaker."

Evie gasped and whirled around at the sound of Ford's voice. He stood less than five feet away, his posture stiff, fists clenched at his sides. "I-I'm sorry, Mr. Hawthorne. This will only take another moment and I'll be back with you." Trying to muster a perfectly normal smile for him, her heart pounded in her ears, her blood cold. She mentally raced back over her words, trying to gauge what Ford might have heard.

"We are putting him on speaker-phone. Tell him." He nodded toward the phone she'd let drop from her ear, and she saw in the set of his jaw that he was not going to be talked out of it. Slowly, she raised her cell back to her head, trying to assess the damage this was going to cause.

Dammit. Why hadn't she just mollified John and gotten off the phone without incident? Was she that self-destructive or did she just keep forgetting that John had the means to have her hurt? And he'd made it clear he was capable of it.

John's weedy, irate voice was yelling through the earpiece, but she didn't allow her brain to process his rant. Instead, she locked her eyes to Ford's, concentrating on the deep, green intensity in his stare and finding comfort in the fury she saw in them. Something in his stance or the blaze behind his eyes spoke through the connection they shared, and she knew his anger wasn't directed at her.

Calmly, she opened her mouth. "John, Mr. Hawthorne would like to speak to you." John didn't stop his tirade, and she repeated the sentence again, louder, adding, "He's asked me to put you on speaker-phone. I'm going to do that now."

Ford reached for the phone and she handed it to him, not dropping her eyes from his. For a moment, Ford let the phone fall to his side, ignored, and reached out to take Evie's hand. He closed his large hand around hers and squeezed, giving her a slight smile before turning and pulling her along behind him, back to the table where they'd been working and playing.

Studying her phone, he clicked on the speaker button and set the cell on the table, all the while keeping a solid grip on Evie. Now there was only silence on the other end of the phone. "Good evening, John," Ford said, his voice sounding calculatedly unemotional.

"Mr. Hawthorne." John's voice boomed a little too cheerfully and Ford closed his eyes and shook his head once, a small, neat gesture that Evie caught only because her attention was tuned to him as if her life depended on it. Maybe it did. "Let me call you on a conference phone. No need to conduct this business on Evie's cell. What conference room has Evie set you up in?" Familiar muffled snuffling noises came over the phone, which Evie recognized as John wiping his nose with tissues she was sure were dotted with blood.

"We're in the library, John. There is no conference phone in here. Miss Radmin's cell phone will do just fine."

"Evie!" John's voice had the same exaggerated tone one might use to scold a dog. "Seven conference rooms stocked with luxury furnishings and state-of-the-art equipment, and you take Mr. Hawthorne to a table in the library? Mr. Hawthorne, I truly apologize. If —"

Ford interrupted before John could continue, his beautiful voice holding the hint of a razor's edge. "*I* asked Evie if we could work in the library. Those luxury conference room chairs your firm boasts are so large that two people cannot sit close enough together to review the same document. Nice for putting on a show, but worthless when it comes to getting actual work done. And I'm quite fond of your library tables. I find them to be just the right size for Evie and me." Ford squeezed Evie's hand and glanced a crooked smile her way. She felt her face blush, and she covered her mouth with her free hand as a pleasant thrill crackled to life low in her belly, catching her off guard in the midst of the scary mood she'd been dumped in.

"Oh." John's clipped response belied nothing about what he was thinking and he used the pause to sniff a few times again.

Ford plowed ahead. "Thank you for the phone call to check in on Evie's progress, but I assure you we're nearly done and don't require your help. Evie is taking excellent care of my needs, as always." Ford used his grip on her hand to pull her against his side, tucking their clasped hands between them. Standing together like that, they faced the phone, and John, side by side.

Evie couldn't help it—she felt a huge wave of affection for Ford. He always flirted with her and teased her, but now he was also taking up for her and protecting her. And with Ford's well-muscled arm pressed against hers, she realized it was the first time in a long time that she actually felt safe.

"I'm glad to hear it, Mr. Hawthorne. This firm takes great pride in handling your legal affairs. We only want to ensure you have the best possible service."

"I do." Ford turned his body, shifting his attention to Evie. Reaching up, he brushed her hair behind her ear in an echo of her own habit and tipped her chin up to meet his eyes. "Whatever you pay her, it's not enough. I've worked with a lot of attorneys," — Ford inclined his head toward the phone and raised his eyebrows, pausing for effect, and brought a smile to Evie at the private joke— "and Evangeline has one of the best legal and business minds I've ever encountered."

Her stomach quivered, full of butterflies, and she wasn't sure which was stronger—her pleasure over what Ford had just said about her, or her fear of how John would react to it. Ford was pushing him, and pushing an unstable guy like John could have bad consequences.

"Well," John's voice came across tight over the line. He wouldn't like the idea of Ford admiring her work, possibly over his own. "Evie is certainly a valued paralegal. Without the benefit of all of the experience and education that we attorneys have, she still comes up with some clever thinking now and again. With the benefit of my guidance and refining, sometimes her ideas are quite useful."

Snapping his head back toward the phone, Ford bristled, mirroring Evie's body language. His clenched jaw sharpened his profile, and he took a deep breath, drawing himself up to his full, impressive height.

Oh no.

"Okay John, because there is no question that you are an arrogant asshole, I'm going to be completely honest with you." Ford's voice was scary in its calm quietness. "Your value to this firm has a direct correlation with your ability to retain me as a client. Do not think for a moment I'm ignorant of that fact." John made some blustering sounds on his end of the phone, but Ford plowed on. "The truth is, the only reason I use you as my attorney is because Evie works for you. There is nothing especially interesting or skilled about you any more so than a thousand other overpriced lawyers."

Noises sounding like John shifting the phone to his other ear came across like static. "Mr. Hawthorne," he started, his tone toeing the line between placating and offended.

"No." Ford cut him off cold. "You are unprofessional. You interrupted our meeting—that you skipped—to abuse your paralegal. And I'm not an idiot. It's clear you have a problem. Every time I see you, which is rarer and rarer—thank god—you are high." Evie's mouth dropped open as she looked back and forth from the phone to Ford, horrified.

"Mr. Hawthorne!" John was not giving up easily.

"Don't insult me by acting surprised. I'm wealthy and I move in wealthy social circles with a lot of bored and aimless people. You don't think I know a cocaine problem when I see one? Now unless you want me to complain to the senior partners, you will leave Evie and me to finish your work without any further disturbances. At all."

There was silence on the other end of the line. In the still moments Evie wondered if Ford could hear her heart beating.

"I'm coming down there." John's voice was cold when it came slinking back into the hush of the room.

Jellybeans, Evie thought and pressed closer to Ford, angry at herself even as she did it. After all the time she'd spent in self-defense classes, progressing eventually to advanced kung fu, John could still make her cower. These days, after all of her training and skill, she could probably kick John's ass around the library, yet here she was pressed against Ford, praying John would stay away.

This could not continue. She had to find a way to get out of the firm and away from that man. She was so tired of living in fear.

Ford dropped her hand and wrapped his arm around her shoulder, squeezing her against him. Something in Evie melted for him at the calmness the gesture brought her.

"Don't even think about coming here tonight." Ford's voice boomed through the room. "Do I need to call my private security? He's waiting with my driver in the car."

Silence again. Sniffing. Then a restrained, "Evangeline, we'll talk tomorrow", before the line went dead.

Neither she nor Ford moved, letting the silence wrap around them. Then Evie turned and looked at Ford, not sure what to do. He raised his eyebrows, his mouth curling into a pleasant smile that was totally unsuited to the circumstances. "Wow," he said in perfect deadpan, "you must really enjoy working for that guy."

Though a moment before she'd felt a million miles from the emotion, Evie burst out laughing. When she'd caught her breath, she asked, "Do you really have a bodyguard waiting in the car?"

"No. I drove myself here, alone." Ford's grin showcased his dimples and without thinking Evie touched his waist, her desire for him stronger than ever. Adrenaline from the exchange with John still surged in her veins, and she felt as though she must be radiating desire like heat waves over blacktop in July.

"Good." Her wide smile mirrored his. "Because I thought 'waiting in the car' was a dumb place for your bodyguard to be."

Ford's brows pulled together momentarily before he laughed, and the deep, reassuring sound of it carried her even further from the distress she'd felt moments earlier. "That's what you were thinking during that exchange? That I was mismanaging my security?" He wrapped his arms around her and she beamed up at him, relishing the feeling of being held against his firm, well-built frame. It had been a long time since she'd been in the arms of a man.

"Okay," she admitted, "I was also thinking that my underwear is in your pocket and the documents are going to need to be reprinted."

Ford's grin took on a mischievous tinge that reached his glittering eyes. "I was also thinking about your red panties in my pocket."

Looking up at him from the band of his arms, Evie's stomach tightened. Her weakness for Ford was too powerful to resist, consequences be damned. But sexual weakness and emotional attachment are two different things, she firmly reminded herself, and with what she'd been through recently, Evie could compartmentalize with the best of them. In fact, she was banking on that.

Ford's captivating voice became all business again. "Before we were interrupted, you had work left to do." He touched her cheek. "And I intend to see that you finish it." Ford flicked his eyes to hers and now his voice was husky. "You don't know how many times I've imagined pushing my cock between your lips." He wet his own lips with a slow, deliberate swipe of his tongue, the tongue that had just made her lose her mind on the library table. "Kneel down so I can do that to you."

The space between their bodies was suddenly too much for Evie. A noise escaped her that sounded like a whimper as she fully surrendered herself to the moment. She wanted him to shove his cock into her mouth, to take anything he wanted from her.

Their agreement allowed her to enjoy their tryst without wondering if it was going to work out, where it was heading, would John hurt them both, would Ford hurt her? Her solitary life for the past six months had been a living nightmare of worry and constant stress about her problem with John and the money she owed him.

How would she get out of her situation? Where would she go? Could she be safe again?

But if she let Ford take control, she'd be free, at least for those moments.

She knelt in front of Ford on legs quivering with adrenaline and lust, and he sat back in his chair. Placing her hands on his thighs, she looked up at him for direction.

She'd never touched him sexually before, in spite of all the times she'd fantasized about it. But if she was going to do it, she wasn't going to ignore the dynamic between them driving the pulse of excited blood through her pussy—the dynamic they'd created of him being charge. The idea of it was making her crazy with lust. She'd analyze it later. Maybe.

Meeting his smoldering gaze, she offered him the cue for what it was that she really wanted—for him to command her. "It sounds like I don't have much of a choice in the matter, Mr. Hawthorne." Not moving her eyes from his, she silently telegraphed her permission for him to control her—no, she begged him to do it.

His eyes softened and his lips parted in what looked like surprise, and for just a moment, Evie could swear she saw a look of honest affection sweeten his beautiful features. Then it was gone, replaced by a mask of dominance that made her tremble with a nearly manic level of arousal.

She fought the urge to look away, afraid for him to see the truth in her eyes of what she would allow this man to do to her, what she wanted him to do to her. She was frightened of that truth herself.

But he seemed to understand what she wanted, maybe even more than she did. His deep voice thrummed through her like a current and heat sizzled in every nerve ending as Ford looked down at her with the face of an angel and said the wicked words she would look back on later as those that ruined her sexually for any other man.

"I'm tired of asking politely. Suck my cock now, Evangeline. I've been patient long enough."

A feral groan bubbled from her throat. He grabbed her hands and pulled them into his lap where his erection had swelled noticeably against the front of his trousers, pressing her hands against his hardness. He felt substantial and strong, and without meaning to she made an appreciative "mmm" sound and moved her fingers over the soft fabric, exploring the contours of his erection.

God, he felt good.

Ford's smile spread and he closed his eyes, crooking his lips in an expression that evinced delight in what she was doing to him. "Yes...make me come," he whispered.

He pushed against her hands, grinding her palms on his stiff penis. She trembled as a shudder of pleasure swept through her. Until then the kinkiest thing she'd ever done was deep-throat a cock, something she had a surprisingly unique talent for, so it unnerved her to discover that she was enjoying being...

What was it called? Being given orders? Being forced? Was she into some kind of kink she'd never realized before?

She was nearly as curious as she was aroused. She didn't want to just play—she wanted to dive in and find out what was making her so out of her mind with lust. She wanted to test the limits. Stilling her hands, she stopped touching him and met his eyes, her body quivering with anticipation of Ford escalating the encounter. Praying he would take her cue and understand what she wanted from him.

He did.

A shadow flashed across his face. His beautiful voice was now kissed with an ominous promise, and he said what she wanted to hear. "Are you going to force me to persuade you, love? Because I will if I must. I have no intention of stopping. You are going to make me come."

At his brutish words, desire exploded in her—a wild yearning she'd never felt. And then understanding clicked into place like a firecracker going off in her head. She realized what it was he was doing that turned her on so thoroughly.

She was enjoying being dominated. Mastered.

She'd never felt such all-consuming excitement. It was as if she'd been set on fire, set free. She wanted him to make her do it, to use her body for his pleasure, to take what he wanted from her.

Refocusing her attention back to his still fully clothed erection, she stroked him through the fabric, loving the way he felt under her fingers. He took her chin in his hand and tilted her head up to meet his eyes, pressing his thumb across her bottom lip again. She parted her full lips for him obediently and he smiled, pushing his thumb into her mouth. "That's my girl," he breathed.

Evie closed her lips around Ford's thumb instinctively and sucked it, not moving her eyes from his. He shut his eyes and groaned, sending a thrill through her at the masculine vibration of it. Sucking harder, she caressed him with her tongue, wanting to give him a taste of what she could do to him.

He must have liked it, because at that, he brought his other hand to his waist and fumbled with his belt buckle, one-handed. He seemed to be in a hurry to get his cock out of his pants.

She moaned at the thought of him so anxious to free his erection and the noise drew a hiss of breath from him. Pulling his thumb out of her mouth, he lifted out of his seat enough to yank his pants down in one swift movement.

His cock, now free, bobbed heavily in front of her face and she reveled at the sight of it. Swollen and standing temptingly erect, it looked purple in its need for release. She wanted it in her mouth. Ford didn't take the time to remove his shirt. Instead he hastily unbuttoned the lower buttons and settled back, spreading his shirt apart to keep the fabric out of the way and throwing his tie over his shoulder.

He wrapped one of his large hands around his cock and there was still a substantial portion of it left visible.

His cock was glorious. No wonder the women coming out of the limos with him are always smiling.

Below his fist, the skin of his scrotum was drawn tight, darkened and, she was interested to see, shaved clean. She'd never felt particularly drawn to that part of a man's anatomy before, but Ford's smooth balls looked so enticing pillowed at the base of his dick that she found herself wanting to snake her tongue around their smoothness, draw them one at a time into her mouth to suck them too. She began to press her thighs together rhythmically as she knelt, encouraging the good feelings growing there again.

Looking as he was and sitting like that, still half-dressed in a monogrammed shirt with his silk tie thrown over his shoulder, he looked like a complete gentleman visiting a whorehouse to get his cock sucked by someone who knew what they were doing—absolutely naughty. Very sexy.

Stroking his erection, he stared at her, his eyes dark and fiery. "Now Evie," he commanded. "Put my cock in your mouth."

The way he looked at that moment—so refined, yet so dirty—and with his silky voice commanding her to service him, it made her out of her head with hunger for him. Evie squeezed her legs together hard against the throbbing in her pussy and nearly came on the spot.

CHAPTER FIVE

ORD HAD UNCOVERED a primal need she hadn't realized she'd been missing—the need to be sexually dominated, to be someone's plaything. And Ford seemed as thrilled as she was to find a partner with whom to explore his apparent complementary need to control. Their gazes still locked together, Evie whispered, "Yes, Mr. Hawthorne," and saw a flicker of what looked close to joy pass over his features. The affection they'd shared for months seemed to solidify in that moment into something sturdy and believable, unlocked by their mutual kink.

Evie felt his thighs go rigid under her fingers and his jaw flexed. He reached for her, his eyes glinting like a predator's. "I can't wait. I need to fuck your mouth *now*." He wrapped his free hand around the back of her head and pulled her face toward his lap, using his other hand to tilt his cock to her lips. Although it seemed wrong to enjoy such treatment, the idea of what is right and proper made no difference to her swollen clit. She loved what he was doing to her. It felt deliciously wrong of him to push her head down to his erection, demanding she suck him.

His normally refined speech became ragged. "I'm going to fuck your mouth. I've waited so long to do this, and you're going to swallow my cum." She moaned low in her throat as his crude words sent her further toward unfamiliar levels of arousal. Without thinking any more about possible consequences, she opened her mouth to swallow him like he insisted. He tangled his hands in her hair and pushed her mouth down onto his cock with a long, low groan.

Tasting his tangy pre-cum, Evie swirled her tongue against the hot skin of his erection. His cock filled her mouth completely, connecting Ford and her in a way she'd only fantasized about until then. She wanted to reach up and caress his balls, feel the weight of them in her hand, but she kept her hands where they were— gripping his strong thighs. Ford was in control. That's how they both wanted it, and so she pleasured him with her mouth and waited for him to tell her what he wanted from her.

"Oh yes…god, like that." His silky voice had turned rough and husky. She felt his leg muscles contract under her fingers. With his hands in her hair controlling her, she let him move her head up and down on his cock slowly, taking him in her mouth however he wanted it. Tilting her head back, she looked at him, drinking in his reactions. His eyes slid shut and he let his head drop back in ecstasy. "Your mouth feels amazing. Just like I knew it would."

She'd wanted for so long to devour him, and so she did. Even though Ford was the one receiving the pleasure, Evie greedily relished every detail of the act—the clean smell of his skin, the salty taste of his pre-cum, the stiff tension of the muscles in his thighs. She hadn't been prepared for how hot it made her and she showed him—sucking and licking him as though his cum down her throat was the thing she wanted most in the world.

He grew even harder in her mouth and stood up on shaky legs, pulling her up to kneeling and tightening his grip in her hair. "I'm going to fuck your mouth now." His voice was tight with strained control, but his words were clear and brazen. He held her head still with both hands and slowly rocked his hips, pushing his thick shaft between her lips, in and out, fucking her mouth like he said he would, gently at first. She was easily able to accept his thrusts—he wasn't aware of her unique talent.

With practiced control, he pressed his sizable cock against the back of her mouth as he thrust, a little deeper each time. Evie knew he was working up to see what she could handle, and she was ready to show him just what she could do. Ford had everything he could want in the world, except maybe someone who could do what she could. And what she could do made her feel powerful—to have a man in awe of her abilities, make him putty in her hands. As Ford pulled back in preparation for another gentle thrust, she pulled her mouth off his cock and looked up at him, whispering simply, "More. All of it."

He looked down at her, hesitating, his eyes narrowing in consideration, and then a wicked smile teased the corners of his mouth. "Okay, prepare yourself."

She took a deep breath and dropped her eyes to the task at hand, concentrating on relaxing her throat. When she closed her lips around him again, he thrust forward with his hands still firmly in her hair, burying his entire hard length down her throat. She adjusted her position, swallowing against the urge to gag and flattening the back of her tongue until the discomfort passed.

He pulled her head hard against his erection until he had no more length to force into her throat, and at that point his knees buckled. Releasing a hand from her hair, he grabbed at the Property Law bookshelf to steady himself as she pulled her mouth off his cock to gasp in a deep breath before swallowing him again, this time on her own. He groaned so deeply she thought he was going to come instantly, but he didn't. Instead he found his balance again and made a low, animal sound as he began thrusting into her mouth in earnest, finally gasping "Oh god" like a liturgy every time he plunged his shaft to the hilt into her wet mouth. With each thrust that took him deep into her throat she could feel his hands tremble in her hair. It didn't take long after that.

He grunted as he pumped his hard cock in and out, and she worked her breathing around it and her tongue against it, keeping her lips wrapped tightly. He moaned loudly one last time, stilling completely for a moment, and then she felt his hot cum explode down her throat. She made an appreciative noise around his pulsing erection as she eagerly drank every drop of the liquid she'd spurred from him. He pressed her face against him with one hand to hold himself deep in her mouth as he came, keeping himself upright with his other hand on the bookshelf as he rode out every last wave of his orgasm in her mouth, whispering, "Goddamn, Evie. Goddamn."

Finally spent, he pulled out of her mouth, collapsing down onto the institutional upholstery of the dark wooden chair, the exact copy of several that populated the dim library. She worked to catch her breath as his legs shook under her hands. When he looked down at her, his face was dazed, causing a thrill of pride she felt to her toes.

She had rocked Ford Hawthorne's world.

He probably hadn't expected that. Still aroused for him, she slowly licked him clean as he grew soft under her tongue.

She'd discovered her talent for deep-throating when an old boyfriend had challenged her to see how far she could take him into her mouth. Much to his surprise and delight, with a little practice she was able to take his considerable cock all the way down her throat. She apparently had an excellent and natural control over her gag reflex, or not much of a gag reflex at all. When she was done and he'd come so far down into her throat that she hadn't even needed to swallow, he'd stared at her in disbelief. "What?" she'd asked. "Was that good?" Reading his continued shock, she'd realized what she'd done was special.

After that, just like some men inspire a much-whispered-about reputation for having a particularly amazing technique in bed, Evie had her own secret weapon. And "unleashing" it for the benefit of her current lover always turned her on like nothing else.

Ford had that same kind of look on his face as Evie's old boyfriend when she'd performed that first deep-throat blowjob—half amazement, half elation. She was still kneeling between his legs, the soft hair on his thighs tickling her fingertips. He stared at her for a moment, then in a visible effort to collect himself, cleared his throat and straightened his posture. Wetting his lips, he blinked a few times.

Evie pulled herself back up on her chair to give him room as he stood to re-dress. She'd thought she might feel awkward at that moment, when their heat had been sated and the ugly light of the library fluorescents put the work setting back into sharp focus, but there seemed to be no way to dampen her mood. Desire still drove a pounding and distracting pulse between her legs. She kept thinking about his cock, anxious for him to touch her again.

When his clothes were tucked neatly back into place he pulled her onto his lap, his strong arms handling her as easily as if she were a child. Wrapping her up, he kissed her cheek. "Evie, love, that was... My god. That was everything I imagined it would be." He paused, then, "No—it was so much better." He didn't have a definable accent that she could identify, but his confident voice was layered with such an educated and proper manner of speaking that it somehow sounded as if he did.

He buried his face in her hair and breathed deeply. "So smart, so professional. I never would have guessed you could suck me off like that," he whispered against the nape of her neck, making her smile. Strange sometimes, the things that make you proud.

The surrealism of it all kept twanging against her thoughts. A man who she was not dating—a client!—just complimented her on the way she'd "sucked him off", and she was flattered. Grinning as if he'd given her the greatest praise she'd heard from a suitor. Yet she wasn't frightened by the interaction, or disturbed by it. She was excited. She wanted more. This was different. Fun. Maybe a little wrong, and she was loving every minute of it.

"You are a rare find, and I love to possess rare things." His voice was silky, and he nuzzled his lips against the delicate skin under her ear, sending chills everywhere.

She had only a moment to wonder what he'd meant about "possessing rare things" before he stood abruptly, setting her neatly onto her feet. His voice was formal again. "Thank you for a wonderful time." He kissed her on the forehead, lingering, his lips soft. "I'll see you tomorrow at the deal closing then," he whispered. "It was a great pleasure doing business with you."

Smiling at her teasingly, his eyes sparkling anew with his usual playboy charm, he turned and strode out of the library before she could think to call him back. Or throw a book at him. Or tackle him and screw him on the floor. Instead she just stood, astonished, and watched his tight rear end, cupped beautifully in expensive trousers, disappear from view.

She blew out a lungful of air indignantly. Their work wasn't even complete, and she was still horny. Ready to go again, in fact—deal be damned. And he took her underwear!

That jackass. How could he just leave her in this state?

Collapsing into her chair, she dropped her head onto the table. She was still wound tight with lust. She picked her head up and tucked her hair behind her ear, sighing miserably. She was going to have to take care of her lingering excitement herself, alone as usual.

This situation with John, the one that had caused her celibate state, had to stop. Maybe if she hadn't been so deprived she'd have made a better choice in the library with Ford, a choice that wouldn't have potentially put them both in danger. Only now she had another problem. One that only further complicated her already screwed-up life.

She wanted more of whatever it was Ford had done to her.

That dominion. That control. She needed it, and she only wanted it from him. Ford Hawthorne. The worst possible choice…for both of them.

*****

As Evie headed for her office, the ruined contracts in her hands, she didn't notice the sleek camera mounted in the corner of the library, winking its tiny red light as if in warning.

~THE OFFER~

CHAPTER SIX

ACK IN HER office, the scorching encounter Evie and Ford had shared in the law firm library replayed in her head as she reprinted the ruined contract documents. She was still aroused, but energized. She'd needed that encounter—needed something to reinvigorate her nonexistent sex life—and her deal with Ford had been just the thing. His controlling behavior had awakened something animal and alive in her. She'd intended to rush directly home to her vibrator to relieve more of her sexual tension, but she made it only as far as her car.

Ford's hands on the back of her head, pushing her mouth further down onto his hard cock. Insistent. Almost as if he was *making* her do it.

She couldn't even wait for the drive home.

Sitting behind the wheel of her car in the dark parking garage with her hand up her skirt, Evie rubbed her fingers desperately against her still-slick clit. She replayed it all—Ford's cock filling her mouth as he grunted and pumped into her, telling her to make him come—and she easily orgasmed.

Later at home she tossed and turned in bed, still frustrated. Using her vibrator, she called out Ford's name as she came again, this time thrusting the toy in and out of her pussy at the point of release as she imagined him bending her over the library table and fucking her hard as he'd described in her ear. Three orgasms in one day. She couldn't remember the last time that'd happened, if ever. And what both thrilled her and scared her was that she still wasn't

55

satisfied. She was hungry for more of Ford Hawthorne. But finally, exhausted, she was able to sleep.

In the morning, she opened her lingerie drawer and rifled around in the back for the good stuff she hadn't worn in some time. She settled on a sheer black bra with a black satin ribbon outlining the edges, a matching thong, and high, shiny black heels. It was a skimpy bra, just a slip of a thing, and she turned in front of the mirror inspecting her image.

Though she seemed to always be struggling to lose some amount of weight, the target amount was currently a smaller number than it'd been in a while. She had a curvy figure, too thick to be seen in the pages of a fashion magazine—a little too much ass and a lot too much up top—but men like curves, even if fashion magazines don't.

As always, she reminded herself to concentrate on what she liked most about her body rather than what she didn't. Her breasts were full, but still high enough that she could get away with going braless now and then, and her backside had a pleasantly rounded shape. Sexy, she determined.

She'd almost forgotten how to feel sexy after John.

The black mesh of the thong disappeared between the twin curves of her ass cheeks. She'd see Ford today at the deal closing. Maybe afterward he'd get up-close enough to find out where that fabric disappeared to… Her nipples came to hard points at the idea, and she considered using her vibrator again quickly before she finished dressing—she couldn't remember the last time she'd been this sexually charged—but noting the time she sighed and slipped on her fitted, black dress.

Stuffing some clean workout gear into her duffel bag, her hand brushed the suede carrying case of her throwing knives. Reassured they were safely tucked in her bag, she tossed her gym shoes on top and made her way out the door. The scary trouble she'd had with John had prompted her to take up some strange hobbies—first kung fu, then knife-throwing. The deadlier the hobby, the safer it made her feel. Clearly, knitting was out.

She hummed as she left the house, wondering how she could find time alone with Ford to celebrate the deal closing. He owed her a thorough fucking—something about "until she screamed"?—and she intended to collect. It had been way too long since she'd had sex. She practically skipped into the office.

But when the elevator doors opened into the lobby of the law firm, her bright day came to a gut-twisting halt with the suddenness of a needle raking across a happy record.

Stepping out of the elevator, she was hit with the sensation everyone was staring at her. More than one woman whipped her head in Evie's direction and then quickly looked away, as if hiding a smile. The men stared, and their stares seemed a little too much like leering. Something was up. Her heart began to pound.

They know.

She walked the excruciatingly long walkway to her office, her footfalls heavy on the institutional carpet, repeating a desperate mental mantra.

You're just being paranoid. You're just being paranoid.

She wasn't. Mr. Northland called her into his office as soon as she reached her desk. It turns out law books are expensive and when some volumes had gone missing a few years back, the firm had installed cameras to monitor after-hours activity in the library.

Mr. Northland had a beautiful black and white, high-def video of Ford and Evie's oral-sex-fest, and the clip he chose to play her was an animated little tidbit of Ford fucking her mouth, his chair pushed back against the books on Wills & Trusts, her heels splayed out behind her as she knelt in front of him.

Son of a bitch.

Mr. Northland showed her enough of the recording to ensure she wouldn't put up a fight, then fired her. John was nowhere around. Probably sleeping his night off. But even John couldn't save her job now. The violation she'd committed was a zero-tolerance one, and lawyers have a funny thing about rules.

Lawyers also have a funny thing about gossip, and everyone at the firm knew the latest. When she left Mr. Northland's office, their snickering pricked her like freezing rain on bare skin. She hurried to her own office before she made it worse for herself by throwing up on the hallway carpet. She had to get out of there. Emptying a file box onto the floor, she quickly filled it with her personal items, but her humiliation was complete when a paunchy man from security came in to confiscate her cell phone, which belonged to the firm, ensure she hadn't taken any firm property or files and escort her out the door.

Evie closed her eyes while the guard conducted his inspection of her packed box, trying to focus on her kung fu discipline and the empowerment it gave her. She was bigger than this single situation. Clinging to that thought, she centered herself and forced her head high. Hoisting the "Hey, look, I just got fired!" box, she pasted on what she hoped resembled a smile and allowed herself to be escorted out of the firm.

It seemed everyone came out of their offices to watch her go, and through some trick of the universe, the walk from her desk to the front door had grown from ten yards to a hundred. But she made it, and she was deeply relieved when the elevator doors finally closed in front of her before she started crying.

She cried all the way to her car, big snuffling heaves of sobs. Reaching into her gym bag for a towel to dry her tear-streaked face, her fingers encountered the solid heaviness of her throwing knives. Something about feeling the hardness of the steel blades pulled her back together.

She took a moment to settle her core, the same preparation she'd done a thousand times before releasing a knife sailing true toward its target. Her muscles were suddenly steady and her mind organized, as was necessary to throw a knife accurately. Her heartbeat slowed and her breathing evened. She was strong and she was capable of taking care of herself. She always had, and she'd come through worse than this. Now she just had to find a way.

She cleaned up her tears, her mind working overtime. What did she have to be humiliated about? Every woman at that law firm wished they'd been her. Everyone lusted for Ford — all of the women and some of the men. They were not going to make her feel like a failure or a whore. For what? Because she'd gotten carried away? Because she'd allowed herself to have some fun? To do something crazy? To be seduced? It wasn't like she was the first person to screw around in the office.

It wasn't even the first time *she'd* screwed around in the office. During the good times of their relationship, she and John had gone at it many times in his office when the rest of the firm thought they were working on some big project. Evie shook her head — she wasn't going to think about John and what he might do to her when he found out she'd lost her job...and why.

She shuddered, shoving those thoughts into a mental box to think about later. The fear they would inspire would only distract her, making things worse. Right now, she needed a plan. Taking a deep breath, she took inventory. She had three major problems to manage — protection from John, a job and money — in that order.

Banging the steering wheel with her fists, she let out a frustrated scream. There was no one she could turn to. There never had been. Dating John had been the first and last time she'd let herself believe in the fairy-tale, let herself believe it could happen for a girl like her. She'd been wrong. And she should have known — she wasn't the right kind of girl for those kinds of happy endings. She didn't have the right hair or the right friends. She didn't come from the right family or have the right size on her jeans' tag. She was going to have to find her own way.

The cold reality of that was no different than what she'd known all along — the same thing she'd learned growing up in her mother's home — no one was going to take care of her. If she wanted a happily ever after, she was going to have to forge it herself with her two bare hands. She could do that. She *would* do that. Counting on other people would only get her screwed, in more ways than one, she'd discovered.

She couldn't just sit there and wait for John to come looking for her. Snapping down her vanity mirror, she fixed her makeup. When everything went to shit, she could at least make sure she looked good as she was watching it go. Tucking her hair behind her ear she flipped the mirror back up. She set her jaw, her chin raised. She had no regrets. Ford had taught her something about herself and uncovered desires she'd never known she had. Desires she wanted to fulfill again. Pushing that thought aside too, she concentrated on the larger issue. She needed a job.

If she wasn't working at the firm under John's thumb, he would want the money she owed him right away. She didn't have it. She still owed him thirteen thousand dollars, and he was making her stay at the law firm until she paid him back...or else. And after what she'd seen John was capable of, she wasn't willing to risk the "or else", especially once John found out why she'd gotten fired.

She couldn't even go home because John would go there looking for her. Heart pounding, her throat swelled as tears threatened again. This job and her apartment were all she had. She beat back her fear and distress out of sheer survival instinct. She could fall apart later. What she needed now was to take care of herself.

Somehow she had to find safety until she could figure out how to get John his money. Then she could disappear. One thing she was thankfully certain of was that John wasn't fixated on her. No, he'd made that painfully clear back when she cared.

He'd conned her good about the relationship, but she was at least smart enough to learn the lesson. Men with money and power like John couldn't be trusted. They had the world for their taking, so they took.

John would leave her alone once she repaid him. Her certainty of that was solidified by the blackmail he had on her. It was his genius little insurance policy that ensured Evie'd never rat him out.

Not knowing where she was going, she attempted to put the keys in the ignition but dropped them to the floor in a tinkle of cheerful, metallic jingling. Looking down at her hands, her eyes widened. Her fingers shook as if she were in the first stages of hypothermia.

Clasping her hands together so tightly they hurt, she pulled them against her stomach, curving her body around them and rocking in her seat.

I'm going to be okay. I'm going to be okay.

She muttered it fiercely over and over until she'd succeeded in pushing out the helpless feelings of fear invading her body.

A fresh wave of hatred for John iced through her veins. She'd worked so hard to learn to control her fear of him. Safety and security were the aspirations that drove her since she was a child, yet somehow no matter how she arranged things, she could never seem to find them. When would she be able to achieve the feeling of peace that came from knowing *everything was going to be okay*? She pounded her hands on the steering wheel again, gritting her teeth, a frustrated groan escaping her raw throat.

Was safety and security a fairy tale too?

Comfort. Peace. Just for once in her life she wanted to stop being afraid. Was that too much to ask?

Suddenly she was eleven years old again, pretending to sleep on the broken down couch that was her bed. Curled into a small ball under the thin blanket, she jumped when the front door slammed open. Grateful for the cover of darkness, she lay very still, as she'd learned to do whenever her mom finally came home.

"Shh, don't wake her up or we won't have no privacy." Her mom sounded like she had a mouth full of marbles. Drunk? High? Evie never knew from day to day.

"You got a kid?" The man's voice was coarse and his words sounded wet, as if there was too much spit on his tongue. Evie stilled in her ball on the couch, willing her body to be as motionless as a statue, as unremarkable and unworthy of attention as any piece of shabby furniture in the room. Her heartbeat sounded like a freight-train in her head as she heard his clumsy footfalls coming closer.

"Stop screwin' around, Jimmy." She heard her mom stumble and giggle. "Wait for me in my room. I have to get my stuff." Evie allowed herself to breathe again when their lurching footsteps moved down the hallway and away from the couch. For the next two hours she didn't sleep until she'd finally heard them fall into silence. Passed out.

At that point she couldn't stand it. She'd finally gotten old enough to have her eyes opened to the stress and danger she was living with. Slipping off the couch, she found the keys to her mom's broken down car, pulled on layers of clothes from the black trash bag that served as her dresser — easy to pack when they got kicked out of whatever shit-hole they were currently in — and slipped out of the house. She slept in the car for the rest of the night, shivering in the chilly fall temperature, but grateful to be behind locked doors to which only *she* had the key. A place where she could lock out the world.

It was the first time she'd ever remembered feeling safe, and the feeling had been so powerful that at twenty-six she could still reach out touch that memory like it had just happened. After that, she had slept in the car every chance she'd gotten. Her mother had never even noticed.

It was moments like these when the fear crawled back up Evie's back, needling into the darkest parts of her brain to try and suck that scared little girl back to the surface. But Evie had spent years becoming the *woman* she was now, and she wasn't having it.

Bursting from the car, she fumbled her keys again. She dipped and snatched them up from the concrete with still-shaking fingers. She couldn't stay there a moment longer—not with her mind working overtime to reminisce about all the times she'd felt most helpless.

I need to pull myself together.

Panicking would not help her situation. Neither would crying and neither would sitting around and feeling sorry for herself. What she needed was a drink—a lot of drinks. Once she felt calmer she'd come up with some way to save herself. She always did.

Grabbing her purse, she locked the car and slammed open the nearest stairwell door, desperate for fresh air. When she hit the sunlight-bathed city sidewalk, she paused, bracing a hand on the grimy brick facade of the parking garage. The open air soothed her burning throat, hot from pent-up emotion. While she waited for her eyes to adjust, her heartbeat slowed to normal.

Frustration welled in her chest. Couldn't her life just be simple? Boring? She clenched her teeth against the weight of her concerns and straightened her back. Pivoting on her black patent-leather, Ford-bait pumps, she headed toward the center of the city and the nearest bar.

This was not going to beat her.

Evie's nerves steadied more and more with every solid click of her five-inch heels against the sidewalk.

CHAPTER SEVEN

*T*HERE IS AN interesting group of folks at a bar at ten o'clock in the morning.

Four men in drab and rumpled shirts were already bellied-up and drinking with their heads down. She was one of them now. Nowhere better to be.

Not wanting to talk to anyone, Evie took a seat at the far end of the bar, ordered a beer and sat down to think.

An obvious solution was to ask Ford to loan her the money, but she wasn't a complete idiot. She'd be borrowing from one man to pay another, and she didn't know Ford that well. It could be jumping from the proverbial frying pan straight into the fire. Besides, she'd learned her lesson the hard way about borrowing money from men.

By noon, she was three and a half beers in and had come up with a list of exactly zero places to look for a job. The legal community was a small one and gossip this juicy would travel like wildfire. She'd be lucky if any legitimate law firm in the state would even talk to her.

All this trouble and she hadn't even gotten to have sex with Ford. Screwing herself with her vibrator while she thought about Ford obviously didn't count. She did that all the time. Groaning, she dropped her head into her hands.

The stool beside her scraped across the floor and she smelled the mouth-watering vanilla and leather of Ford's cologne.

Oh god.

It was the last thing she needed. John was going to come for her and she had to have a plan before he found her. Ford was a distraction she couldn't afford right now. Lifting her head, she peeked at him through the fine strands of her light hair, now a bit disheveled.

Ford tucked his stool in beside hers, all smiles, all dimples. His skin was lightly tanned and he wore pale linen trousers with a breezy, untucked shirt that looked expensive, of course. He looked just as he always did—fresh, handsome, as if he just stepped out of a men's nautical cologne ad. He was breathtakingly gorgeous and the last person she wanted to see.

The bartender had noticed him—everyone notices Ford—and came over to get his drink order.

"Ah yes, bourbon, please. Give me the finest you've got." Ford smiled expectantly.

"I got Jim or Jack." the bartender growled, polishing a glass with a dingy towel and glaring at Ford. "Which one you want?"

"Black Label?" Ford asked, hope in his voice. The bartender glowered.

"Right, of course. Jack please, and a cola, and one more of whatever the lady's having." Ford turned and smiled at her, tilting his head in a charming greeting. "Hello, Evie," he drawled.

She burst out laughing. Seeing Ford in the shabby bar, watching him try to order some fancy liquor, and the bartender's reaction to him...Evie lost it. She laughed so hard tears streamed down her face. Ford watched her, a pleasant smile on his face, until her giggles began to abate.

"Are you quite done?" he asked amiably.

"Yes, yes, I believe I am...*quite.*" She wiped at the tears on her cheeks then dissolved into laughter again.

"I believe I've caught you after a few drinks, love." Ford smiled and his dimples made her breath catch. Her giggles died quickly and she had a sudden and powerful urge to kiss him, to have him wrap his strong arms around her and make her forget her trouble. She turned toward him, drawn by that urge, when he asked, "What are we celebrating?", as if he'd walked into a party.

She glared at him. Easy for him to be glib, he didn't have any of the worries she did. "You're right. I've had a few drinks. In fact, I think it's safe to say I'm drunk in the middle of the day because I got fired. Apparently there are cameras in the library and they recorded every single minute of what we did last night. Mr. Northland called me into his office this morning and played me a charming video of me sucking your dick."

Crossing her arms over her chest, she waited for his reaction to the news, but Ford kept his pleasant smile steady, and without moving his head, flicked his eyes up behind her at the row of men five seats away at the bar. Wincing, she whispered, "I said that too loud, didn't I?"

Ford pursed his lips, obviously trying to suppress a smile. Giving the men a friendly nod of his head, he met her eyes again. "No worries. I am now officially the most envied man in the place, a position I quite like to be in." He tipped his glass toward her and gamely took a sip of his bourbon, grimacing.

She groaned again and dropped her head back into her hands.

"I have a sex tape?" He sounded amused and proud. "Scandalous." She raised her head to glare at him and he beamed back at her.

She huffed. "What are you doing here, Ford?" She'd never called him by his first name before, but he wasn't her client anymore. Plus she'd had his dick in her mouth, so some liberties with formalities were probably justified.

Tilting his head, he studied her for a minute and then finally answered. "Looking for you."

She narrowed her eyes. "How did you know where to find me?"

"I haven't stopped thinking about you since last night, so I called the firm, but instead of putting me through to your office, I was transferred to Mr. Northland. He apologized to me and told me you'd been dismissed. I felt terribly about it and came looking for you. I followed my instincts to the nearest bar." He slapped the back of her barstool, an easy smile lighting his face. "And here you are! It wasn't hard,"—he leaned forward, glancing back down the bar again and adding conspiratorially—"you do stand out here, love."

"No more than you, Mr. Country Club." Evie finished her drink and moved on to the one Ford had bought her. She should stop, but even through the fuzz in her head, something Ford had said caught her attention. "Wait, you talked to Mr. Northland?"

"Yes." Ford gave up on the straight bourbon and poured it into the cola entirely.

"And he apologized to you?"

"Yes, he did. He was quite apologetic, actually." Ford set his drink down and looked at her good-naturedly.

"What for?" Her voice rose in pitch. "Was my blowjob not up to his standards? That I didn't do it twice? What in god's name did he apologize to you for?"

Ford turned toward her and pulled her stool closer to his, swiveling it so that her knees were between his spread legs, just like the night before. Leaning in, he spoke softly. "He apologized to me for your seriously unprofessional behavior...behavior that I very much enjoyed."

Leaning closer, he put his hands on her thighs, wrapping his fingers around her legs, bare due to her short dress. His voice was low and seductive and she found she couldn't look away from the snare of his darkening eyes. "Behavior that I replayed in my head when I woke up this morning and enjoyed myself again." His lips curled in a sexy snarl of a smile. "Can you picture it, Evie?"

Squeezing his fingertips into her thighs, he made shocks of pleasure ripple up her legs. Her pussy began an enjoyable throb as she was distracted by the thought, picturing his hand wrapped around his thick cock, stroking it while reliving the memory of fucking her willing mouth. Masturbating just as she'd done to the same memory, in her own bed last night.

Very nice.

She tried to focus on the immediate matter. "My unprofessional behavior? Did you defend me? Did you tell him you insisted? Hell, did you tell him you struck a deal with me for it? You're the firm's biggest client! If you demanded I not be fired they might take me back."

Her mind flashed on the idea and she leaned toward him. "Wait, is that why you're here? To tell me you got them to give me my job back?" She searched his eyes, hopeful that, for once, things had taken a turn for the better.

Taking advantage of her closeness, Ford leaned in and put his face against hers. She held her breath as he nuzzled his nose against her cheek and moved in to kiss her neck. When she felt his lips on her skin, she forgot what she'd asked him, alcohol and lust fogging her brain. Letting her head fall back, she closed her eyes, and her pulse quickened under his lips.

She trembled as his mouth moved up her neck to her ear, his tongue sending desire crashing through her. His silky voice came right against her ear, "Mmm, now that I've tasted you, I can't seem to be in the same room with you and behave." Evie's breathing was becoming erratic. "Sorry love, I didn't ask your law firm take you back. I didn't want them to." Ford sucked her earlobe into his mouth and she bit down on a moan, trying to remain cognizant that they were in a public place.

Then she processed his words. Shoving his hands off her legs, she pulled away from him and shot to her feet, knocking her stool backwards. It crashed to the floor, the ear-splitting sound reverberating through the otherwise quiet bar. Everybody who wasn't already watching them turned to stare.

"You arrogant son of a bitch," she hissed. "You didn't defend me?" Feelings of betrayal reminiscent of the ones she'd felt with John flooded her like cold lake water, threatening to drown her. She lowered her voice, speaking deliberately, slowly, her words brittle with frostiness. "If you had the nerve to come here looking for more of what you got last night, knowing I just got fired for it, you can go to hell. I needed that job, and you had the power to save it for me."

"Evie, let me explain."

But she waved him off. Her motions jerky, she picked her stool up off the floor and yanked her purse onto her shoulder. She was used to being alone, even preferred it sometimes, but right at that moment her aloneness swamped her like an anchor dragging her into darkness.

She needed to get away from all of these people. John, the

firm, Ford Hawthorne. She'd been twice-screwed over, and now she was unemployed to boot. Without looking at him again, she moved to squeeze between their stools to leave.

"Wait." Ford grabbed her around the waist, wrapping his arms around her in a vice-like grip and pulling her against his broad chest. "You're not leaving until you hear me out."

She pushed at his chest, not daring to meet his eyes lest her welling tears would spill, showing the bastard how much he'd upset her. But his voice softened. "Please, Evie." She hadn't expected the distress she heard in his tone, and it nearly wrecked what meager control she had left. Her chest hitched against a sob born of anger and frustration and she let her hair fall in her face, curtaining her eyes from him as fought to keep her emotions under control.

Even as angry as she was with him, she gave in to the comfort of his embrace, and tucked her head into his shoulder, wanting to hide, wanting to disappear, even if it was in his traitorous arms for a moment until she composed herself. She was in trouble, and God help her, she felt protected wrapped against him like that. The feeling was intoxicating as it filled those holes in her—her desperate need for safety—even though he was one of the things she needed protected from. And yet, she couldn't bring herself to pull away.

Just a minute in his arms, and then she'd leave and never look back.

He caressed her shoulder blades, down to her lower back, his fingers kneading her tense muscles. "Shh, love. Don't go," he murmured. "Please, let me explain."

He moved his palms along her sides, gentling her with the touch of his large hands, and all she wanted to do was crawl onto his lap and melt against him. Instead, she forced her body to stiffen. Gritting her teeth at the effort it took to reject him, she pushed away from his chest and the shelter she inexplicably felt there, reminding herself there was nothing safe about this man.

"Let. Go. Of. Me." She spoke through clenched teeth.

Though he loosened his arms and gave her room to step back, she didn't. Staying pressed to him, she told herself it was only to hide her face from the other bar patrons until she'd better regained her composure.

Ford's voice held a note of uncertainty. "I'm screwing this all up." He cupped the side of her face in his palm and caressed his thumb over her cheek, his eyes searching hers. "I'm out of my element here," he whispered. His eyes became distant. Dropping his hand from her face to her shoulder, a moment passed before she saw him mentally return to the conversation. "I don't normally consider how I make people feel."

She furrowed her brow and he clarified. "People do what I want because I have all the money, or they want…other things from me."

He blinked and Evie got the distinct impression he didn't like admitting that. He'd never shared that much with her before. But he was trying, for her. She forgot to be mad at him.

Her softening must have reflected in her face, because his voice turned strong again, resonating that confidence she'd always heard in it. "Mr. Northland apologized to me because he was hoping to keep me as a client. Once they had actual knowledge of your violation, the firm had to fire you. I don't think they had a choice due to their current policies. His apologizing to me and blaming you were simply tactics to allow me to save face and persuade me to stay with the firm."

Evie crossed her arms over her chest. "So?"

"So I fired them, just like they did to you." He screwed up his mouth. "I just wish I had a recording of my own to show them. It was an admirably dramatic touch."

A smile played on her lips as he continued. "Besides, I only deal with the best and any firm who would let someone like you go…" Ford made a disgusted noise. "You should have been listed on their books as an asset. They were paying you a quarter of what they pay their attorneys and you can run circles around most of them." Putting his hands on her hips, he pulled her close again and she let him. "Why did you never go to law school?"

"I couldn't afford it."

"Do you want to go now? I'll pay for it. It's the least I can do."

"No! I'm not going to take pity money from you." His face fell and Evie's heart fluttered with regret. "But thank you," she said stiffly. "That's a nice offer."

"I didn't offer to be nice. I offered because you should get the education you need to be paid what you deserve. Then you could be my attorney." He smiled slyly. "See I was only thinking of myself. I really am a selfish bastard."

She smiled against her will. He was incorrigible.

"Evie." He touched her hair, pressing his fingers gently against her scalp. The touch brought last night rushing back to her conscience. "You can do better. That law firm doesn't deserve you. And you haven't been happy there for a while. I can tell." He searched her face. "John, I'm assuming?"

You could say that.

She lowered her eyes, refusing to answer.

"You've lost a bit of your usual sparkle." He tilted her chin back up. "And I've grown uncomfortably attached to that sparkle, so now your problems are affecting me."

Evie pulled back from him with a huff, muttering, "You're unbelievable."

"C'mon, I'm teasing. But I can help you, if you'll let me." He cupped her cheek and she leaned into his palm. She couldn't help it. It felt good to her.

"Fine." Resigned, she plopped back down on her stool. "I wanted to finish my drink anyway. They don't let you take these things to go." Anchoring both hands around her beer, she took a deep breath and tried to help him understand. "I needed that job. There is no back-up plan. Without that job, I'm in trouble."

A pang of fear iced through her. Pausing for a swallow of liquid courage, she gathered herself. "I was finally getting somewhere. I was starting to pay off my loan and then I was going to save some money for a fresh start." She neglected to clarify that her loan was from John, and that he was currently blackmailing her about the circumstances under which he'd given it to her.

Shoving her drink aside, she dropped her forehead onto the bar. The worn and overly-varnished wood felt cool against her flushed skin. She didn't care if she looked pathetic. She felt pathetic.

"Just leave me alone," she mumbled against the bar. "Don't you have a State Dinner to attend or lunch in Paris, or something?"

"Probably." Ford's reply was soft and sounded as dejected as she felt. And then she felt bad, as if she'd been mean. But c'mon. Lunch in Paris? Tough life. Poor Ford. Why he would be so broken up about his fabulous life was not something Evie had the time or patience to ponder right now. She had actual problems.

She sat back up with a sigh, allowing her shoulders to slump as far as they damn well felt like slumping. Neither she nor Ford spoke for a good five minutes, staring straight ahead and working with dedication on their respective cheap drinks. Finally Ford offered an obvious point. "I would be an important client for any law firm."

"Yes." She tilted her head toward him and spoke softly this time. "All the more reason for me not to give you a blowjob in the law library. Don't you think?"

"I disagree, Evangeline. I rather think it would give you more incentive to do so. Your firing was very short-sighted. Honestly, I think you deserve a promotion for what you did."

Evie's mouth dropped open. "What kind of business world do you live in? Are these sorts of perks common for the elite and I'm just naively unaware of it?"

He laughed and shook his head, biting his lip as he thought for a moment before speaking. "No, unfortunately they are not."

She shook her head, trying to look disgusted, but he had a way about him that was so much damn fun, even in these circumstances. It was refreshing to hear someone speak his mind unapologetically. She couldn't help but like him.

His smiling face gentled. "Seriously, Evie. First time, I swear." He raised his hand in a mock vow. "And wonderful. And all I needed."

Her lips curved in a smile she couldn't bite back. This only encouraged him.

"In fact it was absolutely fucking fantastic," he purred, leaning closer.

A thrill curled low in her belly. When Ford spoke to her in such a crass way in that velvety, graceful voice of his, the juxtaposition made her want to take off her panties and shove them into his pocket in invitation.

71

He licked his bottom lip, his eyes on hers. The self-assured way he seemed completely aware of what he did to her was unsettling. She'd never known a man who could read her mind and body like he could. She shifted on her stool, her pulse reflecting apprehension or lust—she couldn't tell them apart at the moment.

He trailed a finger down the back of her arm, her nipples pricking hard at the stimulation. "I've never received such tremendous customer service before last night." Ford's teasing grin spread wide across his handsome face.

She bit the inside of her cheek. He was so damned distracting. "Ford, you're not helping."

"Fine, then I will help." His tone sobered. "How's this?" He ticked his thoughts off on his fingers. "It was wrong for your firm to fire you over what was clearly a personal matter between you and me after hours. It was ugly of them to play you the tape and humiliate you. It was stupid of them not to just cover this up or at least consult me first before firing you." He leaned his head in to catch her eyes with his, looking genuinely sincere. "And I can get you a job with any firm you want in exchange for my business."

She narrowed her eyes, processing his suggestion. "Okay," she said slowly. "I get it." Maybe Ford could fix this for her after all, without her feeling she owed him something in return. She needed a new job and he needed a new law firm. And she did do excellent work for him, so he should want to use her again. "You would do that? Barter your business for a job for me?" She narrowed her eyes, trying to think of any problem with the idea she might have missed, but her heart had already become buoyant and she loved the plan more every second.

It could work.

"On one condition, love." He scooted his stool closer to hers, turning her again so her knees were between his. He brushed her hair off her shoulder, touching her neck and letting his fingers linger there. The touch wasn't blatantly sexual, yet it wasn't casual either, and it sent her pulse soaring. The flesh warmed between her legs.

Then a light bulb went on. "Oh," she said in recognition, "you want another blowjob." Of course.

"No," he said simply.

"More than one? Oh my god, how many? Or no, it's sex. You want sex." Well, twist her arm... She'd wanted to screw Ford ever since she'd met him. Wanted to screw him worse than any man before, in fact, and that was saying something.

"No, no Evie. Well yes, actually, I'd love a repeat of last night, or more, but that's not what I'm proposing. I want to hire you. And if you work for me for a year, I'll help you get any job you want with any law firm you want. Or I'll pay for you to go to law school."

The rock sinking in her stomach nearly pulled her off her stool. Everything with Ford came with rules...rules that benefited him. "A year! Ford, I need a job at a law firm. Why would I want to work for you?"

"I'm offering a great opportunity. Be my assistant for a year. I'll double your pay and match your benefits. You'll get the best business experience, make more money, and when you're done, I will help you get a job anywhere you want one. I have a lot of influence."

Now her pulse was soaring for a different reason. The jackass was manipulating the situation under the auspices of what was best for her—a call he didn't have the right to make—so she hated to admit the idea had merit. She could pay John back faster than she could while working at another firm. Her mind wandered through scenes of Ford bending her over his desk, her legs over his shoulders on a private plane, sneaking off to a deserted hallway during a cocktail party at his mansion.

It could be fun.

She really did enjoy Ford, even when he was being a manipulative bastard. But could she work for him without John finding out? She just needed the time to get the money together to repay the bastard. She didn't dare try to skip out without giving John the money she owed him. She was not going to spend her life looking over her shoulder in fear.

However, though Ford was offering her a way out from under John's thumb, she didn't appreciate being left without a choice. John had tried to control her life and she'd be damned if she was going to let Ford do the same.

"And what if I don't want to work for you?"

"Then I wish you good luck in your future." He downed the rest of his drink. "Though I don't imagine it'll be easy to find another job, given your...situation."

Evie gasped. "You ass! You're the cause of my 'situation'. So it's work for you or nothing?" She crossed her arms. "I wouldn't be surprised if you did this on purpose." she hissed.

At that Ford looked at her, and for a heartbeat, shock and confusion warred on his face. Then he laughed. And kept laughing. She glared and waited.

Finally he caught his breath. "So let me get this straight. I got you to give me the best blowjob I've ever had in my life in order to get you fired on purpose so you'd have to come to work for me?" His deep laugh rumbled through her while she frowned at him, trying to ignore the manly timbre of his mirth. He looked up at the ceiling. "If only I could get all of my dirty work accomplished that way!" He leaned forward, his voice conspiratorial. "I'd be evil far more often."

He put his hand under her stool and scooted it closer to him, his deep green eyes seemingly sincere. "Love, there is no master plan. I honestly do need an assistant. I've needed one for a long time. I've just never found anyone I'd want to work that closely with. Honestly, I can't stand most people except you and Charley."

She and Charley. Ford Hawthorne, the rich, gorgeous, unattainable guy in the social pages. How had she gone from being his paralegal to occupying one of two spots in his inner circle? Except she felt the same about him. Their connection was organic and unexpected, but undeniable.

Plus, working for Ford would look great on her resume. She pulled back from him, her posture stiff. "What exactly would you want me to do for you?"

"We'll work out the details as we go, but it would be a live-in position. I want you to be available at all times. I often work odd hours."

"Live in?" she squeaked. "As in, at your estate?"

Holy hell. It was the perfect solution to her problem. Not only would John not know where she was, but Ford's estate would have high security. She would be safe as long as she stayed there. Plus, not having to pay rent, utilities and food, she could actually pay John back in — she did the math quickly in her head — less than three months.

"Your work would be mainly arranging my travel, assisting in negotiations, business paperwork, personal shopping, maintaining my schedule, and the like."

"The like", meaning living at Ford's luxurious mansion, maybe having some mind-blowing orgasms and getting to see Ford naked, perhaps often? And she did trust him to come through with a great job for her when it was all over. Besides, she didn't have much of a choice. Ford didn't know the danger it had put her in when she'd lost her job, nor did he realize he'd now offered her the perfect solution.

"Fine," she said simply.

"Really?" He grinned, dimples calling to her.

"Really."

"Excellent!" He smacked his hand on the bar. "We'll work out the details as we go along. Could you possibly move in as soon as tomorrow? I can send a team to pack your things."

"Don't bother. Everything I own worth keeping will fit in my car. I'll be there in the morning." The sooner the better so John didn't find her.

"Excellent," he said again, still beaming. "I'm looking forward to our arrangement."

"See you tomorrow, boss," she sang as she hopped off her stool, grabbed her purse, and swished out of the bar.

Her new, rich employer could pick up the tab.

CHAPTER EIGHT

EEPING ONE EYE on the road, Evie pulled the note out of her purse and glanced at it again, even though she had every awful word memorized. She wanted to throw it away—or better, burn it—but she'd been exposed to the world of criminal law long enough to know it was evidence. And if anything happened to her, the least she could do was ensure John would be caught and held responsible.

For what felt like the millionth time, her mind replayed the moment she'd found it.

She'd left the bar feeling optimistic. She'd gone from half-drunk hopelessness to a way out of her situation with John, better pay, a better home and a drop-dead sexy boss. Plus Ford had told her she'd given him the best blow-job of his life. There was an extra kick in her step at that revelation.

But when she'd arrived back at her car, her footsteps had slowed to a halt. There was a note on her windshield.

She'd glanced around, the parking garage full of cars waiting for their working occupants, but no person in sight. Heart pounding and ears straining for any sound of footsteps approaching, she'd pulled the note out from under the windshield wiper, keeping her eyes peeled all around her. Backing away quickly, she'd circled to the other side of the car to make sure no one was hiding there to ambush her. She'd even dropped down to look under it, but she seemed to be alone.

Pressing the unlock button on her key-chain, she'd jumped when her car happily chirped its horn. Sidling slowly up to the driver's side door, she'd peered into the interior to ensure it was empty. After confirming it was, she'd yanked the door open, jumped in and slammed it behind her, jamming the key in the ignition and hitting the door locks with fluid precision. Throwing the car in reverse, she'd backed out of the space and squealed the tires as she'd careened toward the exit of the dark parking garage.

After driving eight blocks through the sunny, city streets, she'd pulled over and lifted the note from her passenger seat with a shaking hand.

Eves, you made a BIG mistake. Call me immediately. We need to fix the mess you made of things. Call me or I will find you. –John

The only bright spot since that moment was the maniacal happiness she'd felt when she'd remembered the firm had confiscated her only cell phone. He couldn't reach her if she kept running.

She couldn't go home, not with John looking for her, so after a night in a crappy hotel bed, she was on her way to Ford's. The pictures of the dead girls John had used to threaten her with the day she'd broken up with him flicked through her head over and over, like someone else's life flashing before her eyes.

I'm taking care of things. It's going to be okay.

Just once she'd like someone else to tell her that.

Though she'd set every lock and even pulled the cheap hotel desk in front of the door, she'd still spent the night jumping at every sound coming from the too-busy hallway. She would be grateful to get to Ford's.

The estate was twenty minutes outside the city, set among sprawling acres of tall, pine forests. Turning into his driveway, she stopped at a large, black, iron gate that blocked the drive. The gate attached to an equally tall gray stone wall flanking the estate to both sides, so high that driving up she couldn't get a glimpse of the house. Parked at the gate she could just see the house down the drive, fronted by a lush green lawn.

She opened her car door, looking for a buzzer or camera, when a wiry man dressed in head to toe black and carrying a clipboard stepped out of what she'd thought was a "just for show" guardhouse. Fancy apartment complexes had similar guardhouses, but she'd never seen one actually house a live guard.

"Ma'am, I'm going to have to ask you to stay in your vehicle." His gravelly voice twanged heavily in a Southern drawl and his fitted but rugged clothing looked like a soldier's. Topping his uniform was a beret-style hat snugged precisely down behind his ears. The effect was intimidating, as if he was a member of some bad-ass military unit.

"Oh!" She paused halfway out her door. "You surprised me." She sank back into her car and shut her door, then rolled down the window to squint up at him.

He circled her car like a predator, his thumbs looped on his belt, fingering the big, black gun strapped to his hip. She wanted to leap from the car and hug the man, but not at the risk of getting shot. He couldn't know how his severe attention to his job made her heart sing, because soon, she'd benefit from that protection. Finally, his initial inspection complete, he came to her window.

"Name?" His strong jaw barely moved with the question as he studied his clipboard.

"Evangeline." He raised his eyes to her slowly, eyebrows high. His face was heavy with impatience, as if there was a line of people behind her and she was wasting his time. "I'm...Mr. Hawthorne's new assistant?" She flashed what she hoped was a dazzling smile that screamed "harmless" in an effort to speed things up. The sooner she got beyond that gate, the sooner she could relax.

He took a deep breath and mashed his lips together, crossing his arms and looking out into the distance.

"Uh, can you open the gate for me now?"

What was the guy waiting for?

"Your *last* name, ma'am. Evangeline what?"

Her temper flickered, fueled by her impatience. Was this guy serious?

"Mister," she said sweetly, tilting her head and blinking her eyes, "I'm guessing I'm the only Evangeline on your list who has permission to come in today. So I'm that Evangeline."

He glared down at her and clenched his square jaw. "License," he snapped, showing his palm. She dug it out of her purse and handed it to him with a heavy sigh.

"Do you really not know who I am? Maybe you should call Mr. Hawthorne."

"I know who you are. It's my job to know everyone who comes and goes." He handed back her license and turned to walk slowly around her car.

He rapped on her trunk to indicate she should open it. After he was satisfied that all of her items were harmless, he checked her back seat and finally came around to her passenger side and opened the door. Her gym bag was in its usual place on the seat, and he gapped it open to look inside, rummaging around. Evie sighed, officially sick of guards rummaging in her stuff.

Suddenly he jumped back from the car, gun drawn. "Out of the car! Now!" His voice was hoarse with stress.

Damn—the knives.

She pushed her car door open and slowly emerged with her hands in the air, not taking her eyes from the man in black. "Those knives are throwing knives. It's a hobby, that's all." Her voice cracked. She'd never had a gun drawn on her before. Staring at the black hole at the end of the weapon, she felt like all the blood had drained from her.

"Don't move." His voice was icy. Training the gun on her with one hand, he fished a cell phone out of his pocket with the other. Without looking, he pressed a button and held the phone to his ear. "Sir, your new assistant is here, and she is heavily armed." He nodded his head. "That's right. Knives. Lots of them—yes, knives— she says they're a hobby." After another pause he pressed the button again and slipped the phone back into his pocket.

Evie and the guard stared at each other until she couldn't stand the silence anymore. Now that Ford knew she was out there she'd begun to relax. This man wouldn't shoot her with Ford on his way out. "Can I at least put my hands down now? I'm not planning to hurt anyone." Her arms were starting to ache, but the guard didn't answer. Evie sighed. "Is he coming out here?"

"I am." Ford's deep voice came from behind her and Evie whirled around. He stepped through the door in the wall next to the gate. Wearing gray trousers and a tight black tee-shirt, he looked straight off a movie set. Evie forgot to breathe for a minute. This must be casual wear for Ford. The guard barked out an exclamation of concern and Ford held out his hand to him. "It's okay Boone. Stand down."

Evie squeezed her eyes shut for a moment. How sexy was this man that she'd forgotten there was a gun pointed at her?

Ford put himself between Evie and Boone, clasping her elbows in his large hands. "Evie, welcome to my home," he said warmly. "I apologize for your reception, but Boone is very particular when it comes to my safety, and I of course had no idea you'd be carrying deadly weapons or I would have thought to warn him." He kissed her cheek and cocked his head, eyebrows knitting. "Why, may I ask, have you shown up armed? Are you still angry with me?" He looked entirely at ease.

She laughed uncomfortably, the adrenaline in her system now giving way to a fine trembling. "It's a hobby. I throw knives," she mumbled.

"You throw knives?" He raised his eyebrows. "Like people in the circus?"

"No," she said sharply, jaw set. "Like people do in martial arts. I practice kung fu. The knife throwing is just an offshoot of that."

Moving his hands to her hips, he crooked his mouth up and pursed his lips in that way that drove her crazy. "Martial arts? Knife throwing? Very impressive, love. You are one surprise after another, aren't you?" Evie felt her face flush and looked down, smiling as he continued. "You must show me your skills soon. I can't wait to see what you can do." He turned to Boone. "Let her pass, please. Excellent job, Boone, but I don't believe she's going to harm me after all." He moved back to the door in the wall. "I'll meet you in the front hall, Evie. Leave your belongings in your car. I'll have everything brought to your room." With that, he was gone.

Boone holstered his gun and moved back to the passenger side of her car, peeking into her bag again. He looked up at her. "May I?"

She nodded and he pulled out the suede case, unfurling it and sliding out one of the blades, checking its balance in his hand and inspecting its edges. He nodded appreciatively.

"Miss Evangeline," Boone said as he gently replaced the shiny knife in its holder, tucking the case back into her bag. He took his time, not meeting her eyes. "I'd very much like to see you throw." He glanced up at her, his face turning crimson. "Maybe you could give me a lesson? It doesn't feel right having someone on the staff who can handle a knife better than me."

Evie laughed, warming to him now that he wasn't aiming a weapon at her. "I'm sure that's not true, Boone, but of course I'll show you. It would be my pleasure."

Stepping back, Boone rose to his full height, pushed out his chest and opened the gate, motioning her through with a clipped salute.

CHAPTER NINE

*E*VIE'S HEART POUNDED as she stepped across the threshold into the front hallway of Ford's home. Her footsteps on the polished stone echoed off the walls and ceilings. He'd said to meet him inside, so she'd let herself in. Blinking as her eyes adjusted to the light, she looked around. "House" seemed like a wholly inadequate word for the enormous structure. The mansion was made of pale gray stone that matched the walls surrounding the estate. It was constructed in angles, with straight lines and hard surfaces, but the large windows throughout managed to give the interior a natural glow, softening the stark style of the architecture.

She leaned against the massive door to shut it behind her, and jumped when the loud click of the latch echoed off the glossy marble floors. Feeling as if she was overstepping boundaries, but not being able to help herself, she slid the heavy lock into place before stepping away. She moved hesitantly further into the house, her footsteps magnified in the great hall. The furnishings she could see were tasteful and understated, but a kaleidoscope of beautiful paintings hung on nearly every wall. Originals, it looked like, and of many different time periods and schools of art.

Evie's memory flashed on Ford's comment about possessing rare things. When she stepped through that door, had she agreed to become one of those possessions? The thought caused a flutter of excitement low in her body, catching her off-guard. But before she could give it much thought, Ford strolled into the hall like a welcome breeze, carrying two glasses of champagne.

Kissing her on the cheek again, his lips a gentle brush, he handed her one of the tall, delicate flutes filled with bubbles. She felt her skin warm. "Welcome, love," he whispered, tilting his glass to clink against hers and smiling wide, his dimples causing another flutter in her body, stronger than the first, reminding her why she'd chosen to be there. "You look gorgeous. Do you mind if I tell you that?"

"Not at all. I like that." She looked down, feeling like a schoolgirl talking to a teacher on whom she had a huge crush. The fine material of Ford's clothing skimmed the shape of his body and made her pulse kick up. She'd never seen Ford without a shirt, but the clothes he wore were fitted enough to promise her the sight would be quite a treat.

The house was quiet. They seemed to be alone. In the fantasy she'd had the night before, and again on the drive there, they'd barely gotten the door shut before Ford had shoved her against it, devouring her mouth and neck and tearing at her clothes, pushing her to the floor of the hallway to fuck her before they even made it to the living room. She hoped to get very little work done the whole time she was there, but the Ford who'd greeted her was all restraint, the picture of a gentleman.

Evie didn't want a gentleman. She wanted the dominant guy she'd met in the library, taking exactly what he wanted — her. Why wasn't Ford cooperating?

"Let's sit for a moment and talk, shall we?" He gestured into the large room in front of them, populated with a smart-looking couch, chairs and a supple, leather tufted ottoman.

Sit and talk?

This wasn't going at all the way it had gone in her head.

Adopting a pleasant smile anyway, Evie preceded him into the room. Maybe he preferred to ravage her on the couch? A girl could hope.

She had to step down in order to enter the sunken living room area, taking her feet from the shiny marble of the hall to a soft, deeply-plushed carpet. The flat ceiling soared over two stories above her, an effect emphasized by the lower floor. The back wall was floor to ceiling windows, showcasing a breathtaking view of a resort-style pool and manicured green landscaping beyond. Ford sat on one of the chairs and motioned for Evie to sit on the couch.

She lowered herself to the cushion, disappointment seeping in. Had she misinterpreted his desire for her? Had she just been the woman conveniently available to him that night? Or did it somehow change things now that she worked for him? She wished she knew if that was the case so she could resign immediately, straddle him in his chair and have her wicked way with him. But that wouldn't work…now she needed *this* job. It afforded her protection from John and the financial means to pay off her debt.

Besides Ford had to be the aggressor. That's the world he'd opened up to her—the world she was so eager to experience again. That was the reason her panties were wet just being in the same room with him now.

He finished his drink leisurely and leaned forward, cradling the fragile stemware gently in his large hands. "Evie, love, tell me about these lethal activities of yours. I'm fascinated."

She took a gulp of her champagne, thinking it was the best she'd ever had and not being the least bit surprised at that. "I do kung fu and I throw knives. Neither of them is particularly lethal."

He raised his eyebrows. "No? I would think that knife-throwing would be quite dangerous, especially to the recipient." He smiled and she looked away from his dimples before she started panting and embarrassed herself. She and Ford did not seem to be on the same page about why she was there. They were meant to be fucking right now, not making small talk.

Taking a deep breath, she resigned to chat with him about her hobbies instead of sweating, arching and moaning underneath him. "I wanted to learn some self-defense techniques so I took a class in Wing Chun kung fu."

"Wing Chun?"

"It's a style of kung fu that works well for women because it allows smaller, weaker fighters the ability to take on larger and stronger opponents."

Larger and stronger, like John.

His brow creased. "Sounds serious…a traditional self-defense class wasn't enough? Were you worried about your safety?"

Fingering the stem of her glass, she frowned. She didn't want Ford to think she'd brought trouble with her. She hadn't brought trouble, had she? No. How could John know she was there?

"I...had some trouble with an ex-boyfriend, but it was no big deal." Gulping more of her champagne, she turned what she hoped was a casual smile to Ford. "I'm just an overachiever, you know? Why learn some self-defense techniques when I could learn an entire martial-arts discipline?"

He laughed. "I suppose that sounds like my Evie."

My Evie.

She warmed, licking her lips. "It's mainly throws and holds — ways to escape or subdue an attacker, not really be the attacker. So probably not too deadly."

"Where do the knives come in?"

"Oh." She smiled down at her fingers. Throwing knives was one of her favorite pastimes. "I'd gone to class early one day and caught the tail-end of a demonstration on martial arts weaponry. I convinced my kung fu master to give me private lessons."

"Are you good? I want to know how much danger I'm in if I get you fired from another job."

Her smile grew bigger — she couldn't hide the pride she felt in her skills. "I'm pretty good at it. I practice a lot. It's a great outlet for me." Sometimes, when she'd come to work with a sore arm from throwing and a nicked hand, she'd felt as if she had her own secret fight club, so different from the starched corporate environment of the law firm.

"So how is knife-throwing not a lethal hobby?"

She laughed. "Because of Hollywood, people think it's pretty deadly, but actually it's more of a party trick. I do it for exercise, and it helps me clear my mind. It's really no good for self-defense. See when you throw a knife you rotate it." She put down her glass and moved her fingers one over the other in a circle in front of her to demonstrate. "And to throw accurately you have to be a precise distance from your target. If you don't have the distance perfect, the knife will just hit the attacker at some point in its rotation other than the tip and bounce off." She looked up at him and dropped her hands thinking she was going on in more detail than he was interested in.

"So the chances of accurately hitting a moving person are slim," he assessed.

"Right." Relaxing, she sat back on the sofa. He actually seemed interested.

He continued his thought. "And if you miss him, now you've given him a bruise, pissed him off and thrown him your weapon."

"Yes!" She grinned. "That pretty much sums up the problem, but it's fun and a great stress reliever." If thrown well, the knife hit the wood with a solid *thwack* that always made Evie feel like a bad-ass.

Sometimes, when your life's going to shit, feeling like a badass can be very therapeutic.

"You'll have to show me sometime...I'm fascinated. I've never met a woman who throws knives and can take down a grown man with her bare hands." His gaze held hers for a moment before he continued, his tone softer. "And I do find myself in need of stress relief. It would be excellent if you could provide that along with your other responsibilities."

A shiver went through her and she picked her wine back up and finished it, mainly because she didn't know what to say in response. Were they still talking about knife-throwing?

Ford stood up, taking her empty flute. "This ex-boyfriend would be wise to steer clear of you."

While Evie knew he was referring to her own self-defense skills, his words still made her feel protected. She'd been living every minute with a steady niggling fear in the back of her mind, and driving through Ford's gate, knowing Boone was on guard behind her was like a weight finally off her shoulders.

Ford placed their glasses on a polished wood bar at the side of the room and turned back to her, leaning against the bar and crossing his arms. The pose highlighted his upper-body muscles and Evie couldn't believe she was going to be paid to be around this man. Just looking at him made her pulse flutter. Just being in the same room with him made her want to be on her knees in front of him.

What had he turned her into?

She was absolutely preoccupied with sex whenever she was around him. Constantly in a state of arousal. It was distracting, to say the least.

"We have a busy day ahead of us, settling you in. Come here please, Evie."

She rose on unsteady legs and moved to stand in front of him. Even small commands from him made her nipples hard.

Blatantly, he swept his eyes down her form. "I like what you're wearing. It's not as conservative as what you wear at the office. I prefer you in less conservative clothes while you're working for me." He pursed his lips and hesitated, as if daring her to state the obvious — that he shouldn't dictate her wardrobe unless it was legitimately relevant to the job. "Will that be a problem?"

Evie shook her head, afraid her voice would fail if she tried to answer. Except she had no clothes at all. She only had the clothes on her back and her outfit from yesterday in her duffel bag. She'd bought today's outfit at a large chain store the night before, along with shoes and makeup, since all of her belongings were still back at her apartment.

It was a simple navy knit dress, but he was right — it was more body-skimming and shorter than she'd have worn to the office. She'd found some high-heeled sandals with a strap that wrapped around her ankles, and for underneath the dress, black thong panties.

"I'll have to see about getting some new things," she murmured.

"No, I'll see about getting you some new things."

"Mr. Hawthorne, you can't buy me clothes," she protested. She was going to have a hard enough time understanding the boundaries without him confusing things more by buying her gifts and personal items.

"That's not correct. I *can* buy you clothes, and shoes. In fact I provide uniforms for all of my household staff. Just consider what I buy you to be your uniform."

She opened her mouth to protest further, but he'd made a good point. If he would insist she dress a certain way, the least he could do is provide those things for her. So instead she smiled. "Thank you."

"You might not want to thank me until you see what I'm asking you to wear," he warned, his eyes twinkling.

Oh. She tried to chase the vision of a French maid uniform out of her mind.

"We'll start with a tour." He looked down at her feet, cocking his head. "It's a big house and you don't appear to be wearing your walking shoes. Please let me know if you need to take a break."

Evie tipped one of her feet flirtatiously, showing off the heel and flexing her calf, hoping her legs looked fantastically sexy in the pose. "You're right…these are not walking shoes. The uniform shoes you provide will probably be more appropriate."

Ford swept his eyes slowly down her legs, pausing for a long moment to linger on her heels before adopting his familiar, teasing, disciplinarian face. From the twist of his mouth, it was obvious he was holding back a smile. "Actually, the uniform shoes I provide will be higher heels than those, and they will be entirely appropriate for your duties, none of which will include much walking." He smiled, his face infuriatingly pleasant.

Evie dropped her eyes to her shoes, butterflies swooping around her stomach, her heart suddenly pounding. "I can't imagine a lot of activities that heels higher than these would be appropriate for." She spoke quietly, keeping her eyes down, not certain if they were really talking about what she thought they were talking about.

"I can." Ford reached out and put his finger under her chin, lifting her eyes to his. In a heartbeat he'd moved from flirtatious to seductive, his voice a low purr. Evie stared at him, hardly breathing. Would he kiss her now? Pull her down on the sofa? Take her right there against the bar?

Anticipation crackled through her as she waited for his move. He was in control—that was their unspoken agreement. Everything was up to him. But nothing happened. Was there something else she was supposed to say? Give him a thumbs up? Take her clothes off?

Whatever it was, she'd do it.

"Shall we?" Ford released her chin and gestured politely toward the front hallway as if nothing had happened, as if they'd been discussing how she liked her coffee. Evie's shoulders collapsed nearly an inch as the tension in her body released.

"Of course." She concentrated on keeping her voice as steady as his, and preceded him out of the room.

"Evie, are you really going to be okay in those shoes?" He sounded genuinely concerned and Evie smiled thinly, despite her frustration.

"I wear shoes like this all the time. I'll be just fine. I'm very talented." She called over her shoulder.

Stepping up to walk next to her, he placed his hand lightly on her lower back. "Yes you are, love. Very talented." The statement seemed loaded with double-meaning. Mashing her lips into a thin line, she thought she might scream. This man might kill her.

Had any woman in history ever died from unfulfilled lust? Because she just might be the first.

CHAPTER TEN

FORD GAVE HER a lengthy tour — formal garden out back, pool, wine cellar, library, office, theater, ten car garage and the mansion's massive, gourmet kitchen complete with walk-in fridge for catering large parties. Parties he said he never had.

Even though she'd gone on about how amazing his house was, he hadn't seemed excited to show it to her. His demeanor seemed resigned — resigned to living there, resigned that it was remarkable. The only time he'd perked up was when he'd shown her his car collection, particularly his black Aston Martin Vantage, a car she hadn't even known existed. When he'd shown her his vehicles, it was as if he was ten years old and showing her his best Christmas presents.

As he'd explained in detail what made each car special, she'd heard little of it, too distracted by the spectacle of Ford's face lit with enthusiasm. She'd never seen him like that. He was joyful — alive — and seeing it made her realize the contrast of it to the demeanor she normally saw in him. His typical charm and sexy charisma were effective distractions, but they were masking underlying sadness.

It didn't make any sense. He'd told her he didn't allow people into his life. Why would this man, who could have anything and anyone, reject it all and choose instead to be an unhappy loner? She remained subdued for the rest of the tour, uneasy with her realization. She'd chosen to be a part of his life — what part, she was still unsure of. But what ghosts did he have in his past to haunt him?

To haunt her? She had enough of her own to contend with.

As they made their way back to the living room, they passed a massive mirror in the entryway and Evie caught sight of herself. Her reflection made her heart contract in her chest. She looked out of place in his home, next to all his fine things.

And who was that woman in the mirror? The one playing at some game she didn't know the rules for. She was running, but away from something or toward something, she had no idea.

Guilt kicked her in the gut. How could she think such judgmental thoughts about Ford's secrets with her past, her issues, her secrets?

They passed the staircase without going up. "The tour doesn't include the upstairs?" she asked.

His bedroom, maybe?

"I will show you your quarters after our meeting. Then you'll be free to begin settling in."

Right. Meeting. Because she was there to work.

When they returned to the great room, he settled onto the couch this time and briskly ran through an overview of her responsibilities, their earlier flirtation apparently forgotten.

She remained by the door, shifting her weight from foot to foot. Swallowing, she tugged at the hem of her dress and tucked her hair behind her ear, so thrown by his hot and cold behavior that she couldn't concentrate on what he was saying.

Surely he'd intended to continue exploring the world they'd opened up in the library—the masterful role he'd taken in demanding sexual pleasure from her, the mind-blowing orgasm he'd given her in return. She was there to live out her fantasy, dammit. Weren't they on the same page?

Disappointment lay heavy in the pit of her stomach. Maybe he really did just need an assistant.

"Evie, are you listening to me?" Ford's voice cut into her train of thought, jerking her attention back into focus.

Startled, she met his eyes. She almost blurted it out, just to get it over with so they could at least have the discussion and she wouldn't be left wondering. But she needed the job, unfortunately, so she took a deep breath and chose not to sexually harass her new boss.

But that didn't change the fact that she was confused and he was making her absolutely crazy. "Sorry, I'm not listening."

Ford blinked, seeming surprised at her honest answer. "I thought you were going to be good at this job, Evangeline. Was I mistaken?"

"No, Mr. Hawthorne. You weren't mistaken." She looked down, kicking her toe into the carpet like a sullen teenager. Sighing, she resolved to get to work—actual work. Ford should get whatever time he needed to move things along, if he wanted to, just like she should. But if he kept up with the mixed messages, she might need to set him straight on her tolerance level.

"I will be good at this job." She didn't look at him, certain he'd see in her face the X-rated thoughts keeping her preoccupied. Thoughts he obviously wasn't sharing. "I'm just distracted today, I guess."

Leaning forward, his elbows on his knees, he tented his long fingers in front of his mouth and stared at her silently for a minute. "As am I, love. Very distracted." His voice was heavy and dark.

Her breath caught.

"Seeing you here in my home—I like it. I never have guests, other than Charley, but you seem to fit, and I can't think straight having you all alone like this." Curling his lips in the bad-boy hint of a smile that put his dimples on show, he gestured to the expanse of floor in front of where he sat. "Come and give me a show, Evie," he said softly. "Just walk away from me. I want to watch you move."

She hesitated for only a moment before she stepped in front of him and paused, her heart thudding again. He raised his eyebrows at her—an impatient gesture. "I—I'm sorry, Mr. Hawthorne. I'm not sure what you want me to do. I feel silly."

He took one of her hands in both of his, smoothing his thumbs in a sensual rhythm across her palm. "First, don't ever feel silly in front of me. I will only ask you to do things I'm very serious about. And the things I think about when I'm around you…" He met her eyes. "There is nothing silly about those things."

Evie sucked in a bracing breath, her knees unsteady.

"I will be more clear since it's your first time. It's going to be a treat for me to have you in this house with me. You have an incredible body, and in my own home, I intend to freely enjoy it. So specifically what I'm asking is for you to walk away from me and back so that I can look at your ass and your tits."

Her lips parted and she took a step backward, pulling her hand from his. No mixed messages there. There, he'd been pretty clear.

Her mind raced, trying to hit upon an appropriate response, but even in her anxiety, she couldn't miss the tingling from below, the thrill that swelled to life immediately in her pussy when Ford had clearly — and unapologetically — stated his intentions to ogle her without restraint while she worked for him.

He tilted his head when her hesitation lingered, his brows drawing in. "Evie, is there a problem? I thought we'd enjoyed a mutual understanding in the library — that you liked my controlling ways. Does this not work for you?" His voice dropped an octave. "If you need to draw a line, my dear, you'd better draw it now. Because this — " he gestured to the floor in front of them where he'd asked her to walk, " — this is nowhere *near* my line."

Holy shit. Where the hell was his line?

Evie wasn't sure she could go there. So far she could handle him, but something told her she couldn't see his line with a set of binoculars.

"No." Her voice wavered. "This is fine. I did enjoy the way you took charge in the library. I'll just — " she turned and pointed to the intended path in front of Ford, " — just, there and back?"

Ford nodded slowly, an amusement playing across his lips. "Just there and back, love." His voice was exaggeratedly soothing.

"Okay." She turned, squared her shoulders, and walked. Three steps. Four steps. Knowing the entire time exactly what he was doing behind her. *Enjoying her*, as he'd stated. She could almost feel his eyes roaming over her ass and hips.

"Slowly," he scolded. "Slowly, please." She obeyed, swinging her hips suggestively. If this was Ford dipping his toe in the water, she wanted to make it look warm and inviting.

"That's far enough. Now turn around and walk back," he instructed. But when she turned, shock halted her to a standstill. His hand was in his lap. An obvious erection pressed against the front of his trousers and he was stroking it over his clothes. A ball of white-hot heat sprang to life between her legs and began licking flames up every inch of her skin.

She let out a shaky breath, realizing she'd been holding it.

"Come here." Ford's voice was husky.

Before she'd even consciously made the decision to move, she'd already taken four steps towards him.

When she was standing right in front of him he instructed, "Turn around and lift up your dress. I want to see the panties you wore for your first day on the job."

His hand was still on his cock, massaging it over the fine wool of his pants while he watched to see if she'd follow his orders. Pivoting in front of him, she raised her hem, trying to keep her hands from shaking. Whether from adrenaline or lust, a fine trembling ran throughout her body. He hissed in his breath when she exposed her ass, bare except for the thin strip of black thong.

She peeked at him over her shoulder but he scolded her. "Keep your eyes facing forward until I decide what I'm going to do with you, please."

Her legs trembled and she bit her lip against a wave of lust so powerful it threatened to knock her over.

What was this magic?

He seemed to know exactly what to say and do to make her crazy with passion—things she didn't even know herself.

"Bend over and spread your legs." He said this as if he'd simply asked her to grab him a file or make a call for him. Completely cool. Completely in charge.

In contrast, her heart was doing wobbly back-handsprings. Bending over, she braced her hands on her knees. Could he see how wet she was already?

Her excitement in contrast to his composure was almost humiliating, and yet her pussy throbbed harder still. She longed to turn around, her nerves feeling taut to the point of near breaking.

"Your skin is so creamy. I'd love to see your bottom reddened from a good spanking."

Her eyes widened as a jolt tore through her. Spanking?

"These panties remind me of the ones I took from you that night in the library." His voice had turned soft. She jumped when she felt his finger swipe down the black material covering the engorged flesh between her legs. A whimper escaped her throat before she could tamp it down. How did he seem so unaffected?

"Bend over further." The command in his tone was undeniable.

Evie slipped her hands down her legs and squeezed her fingers around her shins, the position not quite comfortable. Holding herself like that, exposed to his scrutiny, she hardly breathed, waiting to hear what he wanted of her.

In the privacy of his estate, he was being even more forceful than he'd been in the library. So it hadn't been a fluke—one crazy night that she'd look back on and laugh uncomfortably about. No. Evie was loving this treatment and wanted more, wanted it to escalate.

How could she have gone so far through her adult life without knowing how much she loved this? Discovering a new, unexplored treasure trove of her sexuality was like Christmas, and she couldn't wait to be forced to open every present.

Just when she was sure she couldn't hold the position any longer, she heard the unmistakable sound of him unbuckling his belt and unzipping his pants.

She thought her heart might pound out of her chest. Her skin pricked as she anticipated his touch. How many heartbeats before she'd feel his hands on her hips, pulling her back toward him, his hard cock probing to find entrance into her slick pussy? Entrance he would not be denied.

But he didn't touch her. "Turn around and kneel down."

Doing as he instructed, she saw Ford had his pants pulled down and his large erection in his hand. Her mouth watered. She'd been fantasizing about Ford's cock since the night in the library, and there it was—as enticing as she remembered—and even his big hand didn't cover it all. Her stomach fluttered as her heart impossibly beat even faster.

She'd never felt this before, this feeling of wanting to do whatever a man demanded, hoping he'd use her for his own sexual pleasure. Some rational part of her brain suggested that it was supposed to feel wrong to be used. But somehow it didn't, at least not by Ford. In fact it felt more right than anything she'd ever done in bed. It felt so natural, so intrinsic, this desire to fulfill his fantasies. And whatever she did to him—for him—made her hotter than anything any man had ever done to her.

The mixture of lust and confusion swirling in her head only further conquered her. It made no sense. She was a strong, independent woman with more than a small problem with authority, and yet somehow that made his domination over her, and her weakness for it, all the more addictive.

It wasn't manipulation, it was pure and perfect seduction. If John had said or done a fraction of what Ford did, she would have laughed at him and told him to go screw himself. But somehow, Ford knew how to bring her to her knees, which was where she was now, looking up at him.

And she was going to let him do whatever he wanted to her.

He let go of his cock, his jewel-green eyes locked in understanding with hers. Right or wrong, kneeling between Ford's legs and ready to service him, Evie felt free. That's why she'd chosen this. He was completely in charge to do with her what he wanted. She didn't need to think. She was safe—sheltered in this fantasy world behind high stone walls—and she could lose herself entirely in his domineering hands for all the moments he needed her.

He pulled her hand to his erection, the skin of his phallus hot and silky under her touch. She fought the urge to wrap her fingers around his hardness and stroke him. Barely breathing, she waited, trembling, for him to tell her what to do.

"It appears that we have a problem, love." He looked down at her, his eyes dark and sparkling. "What you wore to work today, and that little show you just put on… Feel how hard you made me." His voice grew huskier with every word.

She licked her lips, hungering to take him in her mouth again and show how much she could please him. He pressed his hand over hers, forcing her palm to slide up and down on his solid length.

"Look what you've done," he whispered, his eyes boring into hers. There was no mistaking his excitement. He wrapped his fingers around hers, forcing her to squeeze his shaft. She shivered and bit back a sound of pleasure at his behavior, feeling embarrassed that it affected her so much.

His eyes blazed in delight and Evie could nearly read his mind. He knew exactly how hot this was making her. "Evie, love. You've caused a problem. We obviously can't get any work done now. How am I to concentrate with my dick this hard for you?" He let go of her hand, settling back in his chair. "Fix it. Now. Make me come."

His audacity was astonishing and perfect.

Evie's clit had been throbbing ever since she'd turned around to the sight of him staring at her and touching himself, and at this crude demand she couldn't help but moan out loud. She was on the verge of orgasm and he hadn't even touched her. It was mind-blowing, and she wanted more.

She didn't hesitate. Engulfing his erection in her mouth, she sucked, eager to make him come again. But he stopped her quickly, pulling her off of his cock and raising her chin to look in his eyes. "Do you remember your safe word, love?" he whispered.

She nodded. "Jellybeans."

His succulent lips curved. "Very good girl, Evie." Releasing her chin, his voice dropped low and serious. "Now get to work. Strong lips and tongue. I want to feel you suck and I want you make some noise. Do it right or I'll make you do it again." He sat back to let her continue the blowjob, adding, "And if I decide to fuck your mouth like I did the other night, you will accommodate me. Are you prepared for that?"

Whimpering as a quake of lust racked her body at his crass demands, she managed, "Yes, Mr. Hawthorne."

And with her agreement, he wrapped his hand around the back of her hair and pulled her head back down onto his cock with a satisfied sigh, but not before she glimpsed a look of awe and affection in his eyes. That look told her he wasn't just playing a part for her. Evie was meeting his needs as beautifully and perfectly as he was meeting hers.

In fact, he looked enthralled at her acceptance of his dominance—her desire for it—and his eyes twinkled with what, from another man, might even have been a look of pure love. "I'm-never-going-to-let-you-go" love. "You're-what-I've-been-searching-for-all-these-years" love. But she knew better. Ford had said it himself…he couldn't love her. And she didn't need it—not from a man like him. A man incapable of it.

Confusing thoughts about love dampened her excitement, so she pushed them away and concentrated on the sex. She finally had Ford's beefy cock in her mouth again and she was aiming to please. Without taking her mouth off him, she tilted her head to see his face. He watched her as if appraising her, studying her lips wrapped in a tight O around his swollen cock, her tongue stroking up and down against the underside of his erection, strong like he'd instructed. From Ford's position on the stone-gray leather sofa and her kneeling between his legs, she knew he could see over her shoulders, past the twin mounds of her ass, to her heels splayed out behind her.

Arching her back and pushing out her bottom, she hoped to entice him to touch her. She wanted him to fondle her breasts or lean over and caress her ass while she worked. Maybe spank her? Her stomach fluttered. She'd never wanted that before.

But he didn't touch her. He kept his hands tightly gripping his knees, which made her want him to touch her all the more. She pulled down on his balls and wrapped her other hand tightly around the base of his cock to assist the friction of her mouth.

"God," he moaned as if she were exceeding all his expectations. His lips parted and his eyes closed. Dropping his head onto the back of the couch, he murmured her name.

She sucked deeper, hoping to taste his tangy cum. She loved giving blowjobs. Making a man putty in her hands felt powerful, and it was especially yummy to make a collected man like Ford lose control.

Finally releasing his tight grip on his knees, he tangled his hands in her hair and sat forward, not controlling her moves but not freeing her either. His fingers against her scalp reinforced that he was in control. He pressed his knees to her sides, enveloping her in a submissive position in front of him, holding her there as she pleasured him like he'd ordered.

With every moment, the tingling in her clit grew more and more demanding, distracting her. She'd fantasized about this since the other night at the library—Ford releasing his straining erection from his pants and commanding her to suck him until he exploded hot cum into her mouth. But she needed to come too and no one had ever made her come like Ford had. She couldn't stop thinking about what he'd done to her on the library table. She needed that again.

Ford groaned and knotted his fingers more firmly into her dark blond hair. He guided her head up and down now, easing her pace. "Slower, Evie. You are too good and I want to savor it."

She loved his voice—warm and sumptuous. She could bathe in it. His proper way of speaking made his speech distinctive and elegant. He was all cockiness and sex, sophistication and strength. She'd never met anyone like him and he fascinated her. She wanted to crack open his polished shell and crawl inside. She wanted to belong to him.

He spoke slowly and deliberately, the breathiness of his voice barely under control. "I want to remember what you're doing to me later and I want a long memory."

She imagined him stroking his cock in his bed, naked with the sheets tangled around him, thinking of her. Her excitement was bordering on pain in its intensity and she was nearly ready to explode from how badly she needed to orgasm. But it also felt good, almost euphoric, because she'd never felt it like that before. She squeezed her thighs together, longing to create just enough stimulation to fall over the edge to glorious oblivion.

Ford's voice was tight with the effort of holding off his orgasm. "When we're working, I want to think about how your lips look when they're wet with my cum," he whispered.

Moaning at his explicit words, she couldn't wait any longer to find out if he intended to touch her. She reached between her legs, keeping her other hand caressing his balls as she sucked him, hoping he wouldn't notice what she was doing. He hadn't told her to touch herself and she wasn't sure what the rules were in this game. But she had to.

Pulling the strip of damp fabric aside, she kneaded her fingers against her yearning clit as relief flooded through her. She was going to come in seconds and she was desperate for that release. If she didn't get this man's cock inside her soon, she thought she might just explode into a fireball from the heat of her passion. She needed him like she'd never needed another man.

She breathed deeply as her body responded with near joy at her extra helping hand. Ford's cock smelled deliciously like his cologne, leather and vanilla. He must have sprayed it on his muscled belly, or maybe lower, because the smell wafted to her stronger as the heat between them rose.

They were making a lot of noise in the cavernous room. Ford's moans were growing louder and Evie realized there were steady pleading noises coming from her throat, punctuated by her slurping on his erection. She'd pull him all the way out of her mouth with a wet smack before engulfing him again, and when she did that, Ford pressed his hands more firmly to the back of her head, his breathing becoming erratic.

She increased the speed of her hand on her pussy and pushed her fingers inside herself in between fluttering her fingertips against her clit.

So close.

Ford tightened his fists in her hair and made her increase the speed of her bobbing head. Rocking his hips up, he urged her to take him deeper into her throat.

"Take more. Take my whole cock," he grunted, his voice sounding hoarse as he pushed against the back of her throat, trying to force the deep blowjob she'd given him in the library. She knew this was what he'd been looking for. Relaxing in preparation and flattening her tongue, she was able after a few more strokes to swallow his cock down her throat.

Ford groaned. "I can't believe you can do that. I can't stop thinking about it. God. So good." He rocked himself to the hilt in and out of her mouth. In his excitement, he twisted his fists in her hair, pulling a bit too hard. But the stings of pain mingled with the pleasure she was building as she played with herself, and the heady mixture sent shivers through her.

"Take it deep, Evie." His hips lifted off the couch with his feverish thrusting.

She knew he was moments from erupting in her mouth and that thought sent her over the edge. Her hand worked furiously between her legs until suddenly her body peaked in waves of orgasm. Release, glorious release.

She moaned, her lips still wrapped around his cock as he fucked her mouth, her thighs locked tightly together against her hand. Her vaginal muscles flexed against her fingers. She delicately thumbed her pulsing clit until she'd coaxed from it every bit of pleasure her body could give up.

The sounds she made vibrated on Ford's erection in her throat, and he swiftly plunged twice more into her mouth before he stopped his movements altogether for the space of two heartbeats. She could feel his shaft swelling bigger in her mouth and then he found his own ecstasy. He orgasmed and pulled her face against the root of his cock so his cum pulsed down her throat. Moaning, he called out some yeses and oh gods, then, "Evie, Evie…"

He let up, and she gasped, catching her breath while he continued to move in and out of her mouth as his pleasure died out. Untangling his fingers from her hair, he moved his hands to her cheeks. "I'm sorry, Evie." His words were breathy as he came down from his high. "I held that a little too long. God it felt good. Are you okay?" She nodded and he raised her chin. "Are you sure?"

"I'm fine." She smiled, feeling wrecked from the intense encounter.

"Good." He wiped the tears that had leaked from her eyes before whispering, "Then open your mouth, love." Unbelievably, he fed her his softening cock again and relaxed back onto the couch, his eyes closed. She licked his heated skin clean.

When he grew completely soft, she sat back on her heels, her mind reeling. She felt used in the most delicious way, but she unsure what to do next. Her own need felt satisfied, and yet unsatisfied. She wanted Ford inside her, not just in her mouth, but Ford hadn't even touched her.

He seemed to shake himself back to reality. Opening his eyes, he stood up and pulled his clothes neatly back into place.

"That was excellent." He said it formally, as if she'd just skillfully briefed him on his latest business deal. "Now that that's taken care of, we can get on with our meeting."

"But—" She was not ready to work. "What about me?"

Offering his hand, he pulled her up in front of him. Being this close to his face, looking in his eyes, made her feel dizzy. "Love—" he whispered, "—I believe you took care of that yourself, if I'm not mistaken?" A knowing smile played across his lips.

She sucked in her breath—had he seen her? She must have been so distracted by the wild encounter that she'd not been surreptitious enough. Looking down, she felt her face redden. She'd never masturbated in front of a man before.

"Hey." He lifted her chin, his voice gentle. "I have some hard rules in this house, and one of them is you don't feel shame. Everything we do will be for pleasure, for enjoyment. If you are not enjoying yourself, that's where we draw the line. But don't ever feel shame for doing what feels good. This—" he gestured around the room, "—is a safe place. A haven. For the both of us."

She forgot about her embarrassment when she saw that look again in his eyes. The look that seemed to reflect what she felt for him. He looked at her like she was an oasis—a kindred soul in a world of strangers. Hers. His.

Stop it, Evie!

He cupped her chin in one large hand and slowly, gently, brushed his lips across her cheek, hesitating by her ear. "Thank you," he whispered.

Her breathing was shaky. She wasn't sure she could survive this. She was so horny that if he fucked her for two days straight it still wouldn't be enough.

Pulling back, he looked into her eyes. "I thought I must have imagined how good you were—exaggerated it in my memory—but you were even better than I remember. Thank you."

She didn't know how to answer. "You're welcome"? "Any time"? "As soon as you're rested could you fuck me into oblivion with your big penis"? That last one sounded good.

But without waiting for a response, he spoke again, his tone back to being efficient, matter-of-fact. "I'd like to add that to your list of duties, Evie, whenever I might require it."

Her stomach dropped off a cliff. She stared blankly at him...*excuse me?*

He continued, ignoring her speechlessness. "Yes, I think that makes sense. I find it convenient since you already work here in my home. You're a beautiful, voluptuous young woman, and I quite enjoy the way you suck me off." Ford smiled, his dimples somehow making anything he said seem completely reasonable.

"You have a rare talent in the way you can swallow my whole cock. I've never met anyone who could do that. Being able to truly fuck your throat—to bury myself like that—it's fantastic." Enthusiasm danced in his eyes, and then he continued in the voice she knew all too well—he was negotiating a deal. "I want to do it again. And soon. And I don't want there to be any questions about whether I can, nor when. I'm a busy man, Evangeline. I've hired you to assist in my needs, and this is one of them. I don't have time for games or romance, nor do I have the interest. I just want to use your mouth whenever I desire. Do you understand what I'm telling you?"

She didn't answer, but just stared at him, her blue eyes wide, and it occurred to her she must look scared. With surprise, she realized she was scared. She wanted to be dominated, but with Ford it was as if she'd gone from sand-lot baseball straight to the major leagues. Her heart pounded in her chest, partly with anxiety, partly with excitement. With effort, she relaxed her expression. She didn't want him to think she couldn't keep up with him. This was both their game, not just his.

He moved his thumb to press it across her full bottom lip, which felt swollen slightly from the treatment he'd just subjected her mouth to, and let his eyes rest there for a moment before continuing.

"My Evie," he said softly, using those words that sounded like ownership. "You also enjoyed our encounter." It wasn't a question. His tone was confident. "So we are in agreement on your new duty?"

Her mind raced. This was what she wanted…right? To be Ford's plaything? Isn't that a large reason why she was there, whether she'd made the conscious decision or not? She wanted to explore this fantasy, and she wanted to explore it with Ford — handsome, experienced, dominant, sexy as hell. But making it part of her job? It seemed too formal, and besides, she got paid to do it.

He looked at her, expecting an answer.

"Mr. Hawthorne… I…," she stuttered. No one agrees to give blowjobs to their boss as part of their job…right? But wasn't that exactly what made it so perfect? So naughty? The tingling started again between her legs and she knew she was right. Ford took her hands and smiled that dazzling, dimpled smile. And she forgot everything except how gorgeous this man was and how she wanted him to want her.

Ford's eyes turned gentle and he spoke more softly. "Evie, love, you are young. I know this arrangement might sound a bit…out of the ordinary. But I'm a busy man and I'm willing to make unorthodox arrangements to take care of my needs — with the right woman, of course. And you are that woman. I'm sure of that. You did enjoy yourself, didn't you?"

"Yes, but…"

"And I do compensate you well, don't I?"

"Yes, of course you do, Mr. Hawthorne," she whispered. She lowered her head, dragging her eyes away from his so she could think. The heat between her legs was now screaming at her to *do it, DO IT!*

"Then agree," he said firmly, wrapping his big hands around her wrists and squeezing them, causing her to look up at him again.

"I…don't know that I can. I mean, I'll do it again!" she added quickly. "That's not the issue. I want to do it again, Mr. Hawthorne." She looked down, slightly embarrassed, and added softly, "You're right, I enjoyed it. But as part of my job? It's just…" Yet she couldn't seem to find an argument. She had a quick mind and had been holding her own against experienced lawyers for years, but at that moment Evie couldn't seem to formulate a logical reason why she couldn't provide travel arrangements, personal shopping, and blowjobs for her new boss.

"Yes, Evie, you can. I practice a great deal of discretion and I highly value my privacy and yours. If my assessment of you is correct, the arrangement should suit us both nicely." Ford was in persuasion mode now, and she'd seen firsthand that Ford always gets what he wants, at least in business. Was this business? She wasn't sure.

Of course the thought of sucking Ford's cock upon his demand thrilled her. How often do people get to live out their sexual fantasies? And here was her chance to experience her fantasy of being a sexual plaything with someone handsome and interesting, in luxurious surroundings, with no strings attached. Besides she could leave anytime she wanted if the arrangement no longer suited her. She wanted to do this. She would do this. So it was unconventional—so it was crazy—who cares? No one even knew she was there. A shiver of excitement went through her.

Ford seemed to want to prove he knew what she wanted. He pulled her firmly against his chest and she was very aware of how close his mouth was to hers. She could smell his cologne again and the scent memory flashed in her mind of being between his legs with his erection filling her mouth. It made her knees weak.

"Agree, Evangeline," he growled. "I want this, and you will give it to me. You are going put my cock in your mouth whenever I ask." She groaned low in her throat as his controlling words sent shivers of lust through her body. She was helpless against her powerful longing—for Ford and for his domination of her.

Her nipples instantly tightened and she was sure they showed obviously against the front of her dress. Ford looked down at her ample breasts, the nipples protruding against the cheap fabric. "Your body agrees with the arrangement, Evie." She longed for him to touch her taut nipples, to suck on them, pinch them. But other than his hands on the back of her head a few minutes ago, pushing his erection deeper into her mouth, Ford had barely touched her since she'd gotten there, had not even kissed her. And she was aching for it. So much so that she didn't just want to say yes, she wanted to negotiate for a better deal...like unlimited use of his cock or his tongue for her pleasure.

His mouth was so close to hers, and his lips looked soft and ready. If only he would press them against hers. Maybe if she agreed, he'd kiss her. "Yes," she said softly, her lips barely moving to form the word.

"Yes what?" Ford's voice held the thrill of victory and, still holding her wrists, he wrapped his arms around her waist, pinning her arms behind her and crushing her body to his. "I want to hear you say what you just agreed to. Out loud."

"Yes, I'll suck your cock whenever you want, Mr. Hawthorne," she breathed.

"Good girl, Evie." He let go of her immediately and stepped away without the kiss she was hoping for. Disappointed and a little embarrassed, she blinked and looked around not knowing what to do.

He clasped his hands together in front of himself and smiled slowly. "I like the way that sounded. Say it to me again."

She may as well own it. Taking a deep breath, she looked him square in the face and said matter-of-factly, "I will suck your cock whenever as you want me to, Mr. Hawthorne." Ford breathed in deeply and held his wicked smile. They stared at each other for a moment, and the realization of what she'd just agreed to sank in.

He clapped his hands together, dimples dazzling. "Excellent! We're going to have so much fun, Evie. I promise." He said it like they'd just agreed to have lunch at the Plaza.

She knew she'd done a poor job negotiating, but if she was going to be giving him daily blowjobs, surely it wouldn't be long before they were finally having sex, and then she could get the satisfaction her body was aching for from him.

She took a deep breath. Her ex-boss was probably trying to have her killed, and she'd likely have her sexy new boss's cock in her mouth every day, on his demand. Could her life get any more bizarre?

*****

On the other hand, she hadn't yet met Charley.

~CHARLEY~

CHAPTER ELEVEN

"SHALL I SHOW you where you'll be staying?" Standing in his living room, Ford transitioned back into the gracious host as if he and Evie hadn't just taken a break to have oral sex.

Evie followed him up the stairs, careful not to trip as she ogled his ass. The man had a magnificent rear end. Stopping in front of the first door they came to, he pointed to the closed door. "This is your room. Mine is the last door at the end of the hallway." He nodded toward a pair of heavy, wooden, double doors and Evie's eyes lingered on them. Would she ever be behind those doors? Did she want to be?

Pushing open her new bedroom door, Ford stepped back and graciously motioned her in. "Welcome, love, to your new home."

As she brushed past him into the room, she took in his enthusiastic smile—the look on his face both proud and excited like that of a little boy's with something to show off—and it warmed her. After the night she'd spent tossing and turning in the cut-rate motel room alone, worried and scared, damned if this didn't feel a million times better. It was as if she'd just arrived on Fantasy Island and was getting a tour of the resort. Anything could happen here. All her fantasies could come true.

But the room was so breathtaking that for the span of four heartbeats she forgot all about the hunk of man behind her. It was spacious, with natural light pouring in from six over-sized, paned windows on three sides of the room, softened by wide-open, gray-blue, silk drapes that filled the expanse from floor to tall ceiling.

The gleaming hardwood floor was covered with a large, subtly-patterned, pewter and cream rug, thick and soft under her feet. It was the kind of rug you want to roll around on. Naked. With a sexy man. She pressed a toe of her sandals into the plush depth and pulled her mind back from the tangent with effort.

An over-sized light fixture gleaming with clear glass embellishments hung from the middle of the coffered ceiling...not exactly a chandelier, but more a deconstructed version of one. But what drew Evie's attention the most were the flowers. Four different arrangements—the most gorgeous she'd ever seen—were placed throughout the room, some with roses, some lilies, some lilacs and hydrangeas. The room was exquisitely beautiful and Evie stopped short a few steps in, overwhelmed by what she was seeing.

"I hope it's okay." Ford's voice was laced with that unfamiliar edge of doubt. "I didn't know which flowers you liked, so I just got a variety. I know it must be strange to move into someone else's house, so I wanted to make it as nice for you as I could."

She dumped her duffel bag and purse off her shoulder onto the pristine rug and winced inwardly at how coarse her belongings looked among the finery. "It's just beautiful. So beautiful," she said simply, turning to him. "I love it."

He let out a breath, visibly relaxing, and ran a hand through his tousled hair. "I haven't ever had anyone stay with me before, so I wasn't sure what to do. Most of these rooms up here are empty other than mine. I had this stuff brought in last night and this morning so the room would be ready for you. I tried to pick things I thought you'd like."

Evie's gaze had wandered again, but she turned back to him, narrowing her eyes. "This isn't your guest room?"

"No." Ford looked surprised. "No, this is your room. I made it for you. I don't have a guest room."

Her chest felt heavy with affection and gratitude. No one had ever done something like this for her. But she choked back the feelings of endearment. This was a job, she reminded herself. He was not available for affection. And of course Ford would make it perfect. He did everything perfectly. His maid's room probably had a bowling alley and an art gallery in it.

110

"Do you really like it? I didn't know about your knife throwing. If it's too girly for you, you can change anything you want."

She laughed. "No, I wouldn't change a thing. It's perfect. You nailed my taste." Actually, he'd nailed taste she didn't even know she had.

"Good. Please, look around!" As he gestured around the room he was that excited little boy again.

But she didn't move. As much as she knew she shouldn't ask it, the curiosity burning in her head would not be suppressed. "You really don't have a guest room?"

"No." His voice held a hint of astonishment, as if the idea of letting someone spend the night at his house was preposterous. "I like my privacy," he amended quickly, shoving his hands in the pockets of his trousers and looking around at the sumptuous furnishings.

"Then when someone spends the night, where do they sleep? With you?" She shut her mouth so fast she nearly bit her tongue. *Oh my god, why did I ask that?* Squeezing her hands into fists, her fingernails bit into her palms. *What is the matter with me?*

Cocking his head, he frowned at her and she shuffled her feet under his stare. "Though I'm quite surprised you asked that, I'm going to answer it."

"No. I'm sorry," she blurted out. "I don't know why I asked."

But he ignored her protest. "I rarely bring anyone into my home except my friend Charley." The tone of his voice was thoughtful. "In fact, I haven't slept under the same roof with someone since my parents died. Not even the staff stays in the house."

"Oh." She dropped her eyes, her voice a whisper. Her pulse had picked up tempo and she reached up and smoothed her hair, tucking it behind her ear. "Sorry, I didn't mean—"

"Until you," he interrupted, his voice firm. "No one until you." He looked away, his hands still in his pockets. "I know you are going out on a limb by coming here, Evie. It's an unusual arrangement I've asked for, but it's also a bit of an experiment for me as well."

He didn't bring women home. Strange for a single man. She'd known all along Ford was eccentric. Now she wanted to know why. Why didn't he bring anyone home? And if it was such a stretch for him, why did he decide he needed a live-in assistant? And who was this Charley?

She remained quiet, not knowing how to respond. Sighing, he clasped his hands behind his back and shrugged. "You're taking a chance on me, after all. You are trusting that this job is the right choice for your future."

Right. The job.

She didn't know what to say. "Hopefully having me at the house won't be too much trouble."

He grinned. "I'm not concerned about that. There are strict house rules on discipline, should you get out of line." He winked, his dimples flashing.

She sucked in a breath. "I'll be sure to follow the rules then."

He stared at her a moment before responding and she couldn't look away from the intensity in his eyes. "I sincerely hope you do not follow the rules, Evangeline. I'm counting on that rebellious streak of yours to get you into trouble. And then I'll be forced to discipline you."

Her muscles in her core clenched with excitement at the same time her belly clenched in fear, catching her off-guard with her immediate physical reaction. Even at the distance she was, she could see the darkening of his eyes, could feel the air between their two bodies thicken. He closed his eyes, breaking the spell.

"Please." He nodded to the room, sounding distracted. "Look at everything. Let me know if anything should be changed."

So she turned away too, trying to shrug off the moment. She explored, taking in every lavish detail, trying not to let her mouth hang open. She wondered with amusement if she'd find a glass slipper in the oversized closet.

Catching herself, she mentally clamped down on that part of her brain. No fairytales for her, not after her stupid indulgence with John. Evie didn't scare easily and John had done an excellent job of terrifying her. No way was she getting hurt like that again.

Do your job. Get your money. Square things with John. Disappear.

Start over. That was the plan and she was determined to stick to it. Besides this heart-pounding lust slash business arrangement slash pseudo-sex thing she had with Ford? It hardly had the makings of a fairytale, even if it was set in the closest thing to a castle Evie had ever been in.

Fingering the thick, silky, drapes bordering the windows that were taller than her, Evie nodded practically. These quarters would do quite nicely while she used this job to get what she needed — knowledge, money, safety and maybe some mind-blowing sex. The corners of her mouth curled into a secret smile. Not believing in fairytales didn't mean she couldn't have any fun.

Turning to Ford, she smiled warmly. "You did this all last night?"

"Well, and this morning. Yes."

"Unbelievable." She looked around. The furniture was exquisite. Mirrored nightstands of the sort you might see in the bedroom of a forties Hollywood starlet flanked the bed. A long, over-sized dresser finished in a lovely white glaze stood opposite the bed, topped with a massive mirror that nearly reached the ceiling. Even securing that mirror to the wall must have taken three workers.

"How did you get it done so quickly?" Evie didn't think she could even get her landlord to her apartment that fast for an emergency plumbing situation.

Looking at his feet, Ford chuckled wryly. "Money." He looked back up at her, his tone jaded. "Money, Evie. You can have almost anything with enough of it." He looked toward the bed, his body stilling. "I never stop learning that."

"Of course," she whispered. Even her.

Drifting over to the large bed, Ford picked up one of a multitude of pillows adorning it. The bed itself was maybe the prettiest thing in the room next to the flowers. The headboard boasted tufted upholstery in a cream, blue and silver pattern. The sides sloped in a sensuous line to the edges of the bed, curling a few inches around the mattress before giving way to fluffy duvet. A heap of pillows of all shapes and sizes lay invitingly at the head, all covered in crisp white shams with one lovely dusty-blue striped border to dress them up.

Her new bedroom was nicer than any picture of any hotel room she'd ever seen.

Dropping the pillow back onto the pile, Ford gave it a smack to fluff it. The noise reverberated around the peaceful room and a twang of excitement pulled again between Evie's legs. She bit her lip and flicked her gaze to his face. The vibrant green of his eyes bore into hers and seemed to draw the breath from her, his eyes as magnetic as she'd ever seen them, in the dappled light from the grand windows.

There was a moment of silence as they stared at each other across the room, tension and unspoken things crowding the air between them. Sunlight filtered across his tall frame, touching him everywhere Evie wanted to. Blinking, she unlocked her eyes from his and followed the sun's late morning rays across his body, appreciating every virile line of him. The powerful square of his jaw, the sharp curve of his cheek, the strong ledge of his eyebrows.

And his lips. *Goddamn.* He was almost hard to look at. She couldn't seem to get enough air. Apprehension curled in her belly — sometimes the attraction she had for him scared her. In fact "attraction" was a wholly inadequate word. Fixation. Fascination. Obsession. Thrall... Feeling anything for Ford was a very bad idea, yet Evie took one unthinking step toward him and the bed anyway.

"Stop." His voice was harsh and she froze, her weight on her front foot in preparation for another step in his direction. He glanced down at his hands and then away. "Don't do that. If you're going to live here, I have to be the one in control. It's the only way it will work. We have to be careful." He met her eyes, and his were pained, confusing her. "I cannot let this get out of hand or we might get confused. And neither of us will like what confusion will lead to."

"What?" she whispered.

"Blurring of the lines. Look, I like you Evie. You know that. But I've *hired* you to be here. We both must remember that. And I told you — I don't do relationships. They don't work for me, and trust me —" His voice grew emphatic. "A relationship with me would not work for you either. You're going to have to take my word on that. If things were to move in that direction, away from these clear lines we've drawn, you would leave before the year is up." He looked away again, his voice weaker. "You might leave anyway."

Why would she leave? What did he have in store for her?

He was right, though, and she'd better listen to him, because she was having trouble controlling her feelings already. She was going to move far away after the year was up, and she didn't want anything complicating that plan. Especially a complication as big as Ford Hawthorne, with all of his peculiar baggage. They were on the same team about that. She just needed to remember it.

He gestured to her right, back to business. "I should show you the closet. Women like closets, don't they?" His voice was flat.

Breathing deeply, she turned stiffly in the direction he'd indicated, keeping her flushed face averted from him. She could feel her pulse in her throat.

"I'll see about having your things brought up. Help should be arriving soon, I think." She whirled back around as he looked at his watch and reached for the phone next to her bed.

"Oh, no! No need," she called, waving her hand at him, and he hesitated, the phone halfway to his ear. "Really." She tried to sound breezy. "I'll do it myself. I don't like people touching my stuff."

He blinked and after a hesitation slowly put the phone back on the nightstand. That lovely nightstand. She could get used to these living arrangements and she didn't want anything threatening this new adventure. If Ford found out she had no belongings in her car, he'd start asking questions she didn't want to answer.

To divert attention she briskly strode to the closet and threw open the double doors. At her first glimpse of the room—and it truly was a room—she gasped out loud and her hand flew to her mouth. Cream-colored, built-in wooden shelving and drawers covered nearly every inch of wall-space. Chrome and crystal drawer pulls and hanging bars gleamed everywhere in the light from a twinkling chandelier. A tri-fold mirror promised she'd never leave the room without her ass looking perfect.

It wasn't a closet. It was a dressing room in a high-end boutique.

Realizing her hand was still covering her mouth, she dropped it to her side and peeked at him. He was watching her intently, a proud smile on his face. "It's okay? I did it right?"

Evie nodded, raising her eyebrows. "Oh yes. You did it right."

His dimples flashed as brightly as the sparkling drawer pulls. "Of course I did." He winked at her and he was his arrogant, playful self again.

She ran her hand along a shelf with longing, picturing the shoes she wished she could fill it with. Stepping up to the three-way mirror, she saw Ford move up behind her and peer over her shoulder at her reflection. "I'm glad you're here," he said simply.

"Me too." And Evie felt nothing but pure honesty in both their statements. Satisfaction swelled in her chest. She couldn't remember the last time she'd felt this good. How could she feel so connected to this man and yet held so far away from him at the same time?

After studying her for a moment, he added, "You're so beautiful." He reached up and swept her hair back off her shoulder, exposing her collarbone. "I truly enjoy your company."

Her heart leapt at his unexpected words and touch, and she felt an addictive wave of joy. It felt too close to the stirrings of love. Like pure happiness surging through her veins. It probably wasn't unlike the feeling John got from cocaine, and for one insane moment, Evie understood why a person might do almost anything to keep feeling that good, that happy.

Jellybeans.

Ford's voice cut through her trance. "Now Evie, there's something we need to discuss. Don't lie to me. Your things are not in your car, are they?"

She froze. How did he see through her like that? "No."

"I'm assuming you have things. Where are they?"

"Still at my apartment," she mumbled.

"I see." His tone was disapproving. "So there is some doubt over the length of your stay here? You're not ready to make the commitment to move in yet?"

"No! That's not it." She met his eyes in the mirror's reflection, imploring him to hear the truth in her words.

"Good," he said simply, not asking any further questions. He took her hand and turned her around, pulling a black credit card from his pocket and holding it up. "This is yours. Buy whatever you want. Think of it as a fringe benefit." He pressed the card into her palm.

Just as she took a breath to make a demurral he added, holding his finger up as if he were warning a child, "But Evie, I expect you to buy things I would want to see you in."

He was standing so close that the vanilla-leather of his cologne swirled through her senses. She blinked, unsure how to respond to his presumptuous instructions, but he let go of her hand and left the closet before she could decide.

Following him out, her mind churned over whether she should refuse the credit card, or refuse to buy things based on pleasing him, or just refuse it all. But, really, she liked the idea. She pictured lingerie shopping and her heart leapt. She hadn't had extra spending money in so long. Besides, it was his money. Wouldn't it just be rude to spend it without thinking of him?

He strode toward her bag. "Is this all you have?"

"Um, yeah."

He looked from the bag to her with disdain. "You need to go shopping. Today."

"No!" She heard the panicked edge in her voice and made an effort to dial it back. "No. I don't really want to go out." She was afraid to leave the gated and guarded estate. At least not until she had John's money in hand.

He regarded her with a perplexed look, his lips pursing as he thought. Her stomach sank. He was going to make her explain everything and then he'd know the extent of the trouble she'd gotten into. Could he use it to hurt her too? Would he make her leave?

"Knock knock!" A loud rapping on the door and an unfamiliar, deep voice ripped through the tension in the room.

Ford and Evie both jumped and turned to the door to see a man push it open and enter the room. No, "enter the room" didn't capture it. The man swooped in, exploded, split an atom and created more energy than the room could handle.

Evie stepped backward instinctively, stumbling as her heel caught the edge of the rug. She awkwardly righted herself without taking her eyes off the guy.

He was well over six feet tall and had the bulk of someone who spent a lot of time in the gym, lifting free-weights—tons of them. Or maybe he'd lifted those weights in prison? Whoever he was, he looked out of place. He and Ford couldn't be more different.

Ford had refined, handsome features. This man was gruff, rugged. His tight, worn jeans looked well-used…and were being well-filled, she hadn't meant to notice. A white tee-shirt, also tight, stretched across his barrel of a chest. And his big, black motorcycle boots were stomping on her new, pristine, ivory rug.

She opened her mouth to ask him if he would mind backing his big, dirty feet off her carpet when she caught on to his abrupt change in body language. His now hostile posture screamed "fight or flight"—she recognized it from her kung fu training—and her adrenaline surged.

His icy demeanor was directed at her and the anger on his face looked awkward on him—as if it rarely made an appearance. His wide smile had collapsed into a mash-lipped frown. His shaggy brown hair was casually mussed over big, dark eyes that looked like they might have been warm if he hadn't at that moment been glaring holes through her as if she was there to rob him.

She closed her mouth on her scolding for him to get off the rug, thrown by his response to her.

Ford looked from the man to Evie and back, hesitating. He put a hand on the man's large bicep, wrapping his long fingers around the back of the man's arm. "Charley?"

The man's attention snapped to Ford. "*This* is your new assistant?"

"Yes." Ford's eyes bore into the newcomer's as if he thought he could achieve telepathic communication out of sheer will. "This is Evie."

Ford gestured toward the large man with his free hand. "And Evie, *this* is Charley."

CHAPTER TWELVE

CHARLEY TOOK A step away from Ford, forcing him to release his arm. He tore his eyes from Ford and glared at Evie. "Pleased to meet you, ma'am," Charley mumbled stiffly. He had a slight southern drawl, and he was anything but pleased to meet her.

"Hi Charley. Ford's mentioned you. I didn't know we'd be introduced so quickly." She tried to make her voice sound bright, but she was afraid to move her eyes from him, unsure what was behind his thorny reception.

Charley stuck his hands in his back pockets and looked at his boots for a long, silent moment. He swiveled his head to Ford. "So Evie is smart."

"Very smart." Ford crossed his arms, watching Charley intently.

"And she's got a good sense about business, you said."

"Excellent."

Charley's jaw flexed as he stared at Ford for a few tense moments more before turning back to Evie. "And she is also very pretty." It was an accusation, not a compliment.

Evie's brows knit. Her mind raced through implausible scenarios and discomforting thoughts about the two men. The two *friends*.

"She's beautiful." Ford's voice was patient as he studied Charley.

Charley looked back at Ford, and, apparently not seeing in Ford whatever it was he was looking for, grunted and retreated to one of the large windows, his big shoulders hunched.

Ford ignored Charley's behavior. "I didn't hear you drive up."

Staring out the window, Charlie kept his back to them. "I brought the truck. I thought you might need me to haul away boxes or something."

Ford chuckled. "That won't be necessary. She didn't bring anything."

Charley whirled back to them, eyebrows raised. "She didn't bring anything?"

Ford shook his head.

"Why?"

Ford pursed his lips and frowned. "Yes, Evie. Why didn't you bring anything?"

Chest constricting, her eyes darted back and forth between the two men. She wasn't going to tell Ford why she'd been forced to abandon her stuff, especially not in front of this overgrown anger-management dropout. Planting her hands on her hips, she deflected the question. "Instead, how about you two tell me what the fuck is going on here."

Crossing his arms and rocking back on his heels, Charley actually smiled and peeked at Ford, who appeared unfazed.

"Not very professional though, is she?" Charley asked, a good natured smirk teasing his lips. The positive energy he'd burst into the room with came trickling back as his posture loosened.

Ford stared at Evie, his face serious but his eyes crinkling at the corners. "No. She's not. We're going to need to do something about that."

Evie huffed and crossed her arms. It was a standoff. She wasn't going to answer their question and they weren't going to answer hers.

Ford leaned toward Charley, stage-whispering, "She throws knives too."

Charley raised his eyebrows. "Knives?"

"And she knows kung fu. So you might want to ratchet the

hostility back a bit."

"Yeah." Evie hadn't liked Charley's aggressive reception one bit. It had scared her, and fear always brought out the worst in Evie. "What's up with that, anyway? Were *you* hoping to get the closet with the chandelier?"

Charley's eyes flashed hatred, but it blinked out as his face closed off. Shifting his body away from Ford's, Charley's shoulders rounded a bit. Evie noticed the subtle signs. She'd hit a button.

What the hell?

Averting her eyes, she willed herself not to feel for him, but it was too late. Evie, like anyone who grows up with a volatile parent, learned early on how to read the subtlest body language. She'd seen the way Charley had deflated at her remark, and she'd regretted it instantly.

She chewed the inside of her cheek for a distraction. How did hurting this mountain of a man make her feel as if she'd just kicked a small puppy? Opening her mouth, she tried to find an apology but failed. Despite his tough exterior, Evie had obviously poked him in a vulnerable place. And she really hated being "that person". The kind that hits below the belt.

"Okay, children." Ford's voice carried an edge. "I think that's quite enough, don't you?" He pressed a hand to Charley's shoulder, squeezing. "Evie, Charley came to help you move your things and unpack."

"Oh. That was nice of you, Charley," Evie said woodenly. Charley nodded and straightened his frame, rolling his shoulders back into a cocky stance and refusing to look at either of them.

"Now instead of helping you with your belongings, Charley's going to take you clothes shopping. I want you two to spend the day together."

"What?" Charley and Evie yelped in unison, snapping their attention to Ford.

"Charley." Ford's voice adopted that velvet persuasion that was as irresistible as a purring tomcat. "You offered to help and this is the help I need right now. I have meetings today." Ford looked at his watch. Charley opened his mouth to protest but Evie beat him to it.

"Ford, I don't need Charley to chauffeur me around. If you have a computer I can use, I'll just order some things off the internet. Charley can leave."

"And I don't know anything about shopping for women's clothes anyway!" Charley protested.

A smile tugged at the corners of Ford's lips. "You know what a woman looks good in and you know what I like." Ford stepped toward Evie and wrapped his hand into the indentation of her waist, smoothing his palm slowly down the bow of her hip, following the trail of his hand with his eyes. Evie flicked her gaze to Charley and his brown eyes locked to hers for only the space of a breath, but in those seconds she saw his recognition of why she stood there, not moving, not protesting Ford's too intimate touch. She saw it in the softening of Charley's mouth, glimpsed the understanding through his thick lashes as he averted his eyes.

And suddenly she was desperate not to break the connection with Charley's eyes, even if he didn't want to be there any more than she wanted him there. It was like someone holding her hand when she needed a few extra guts. She could tell he knew Ford's power—knew what she was desperate to understand. So when Charley dragged his eyes from hers to look at his boots, a tug of loss surfaced inside her.

Ford tightened his hand on her hip and turned her slightly. "Charley, look. I want you to look at her." Charley raised his eyes slowly, focusing on Ford's hand, low on her hip.

Lightheaded, she couldn't seem to get enough air. Her heart was hammering in her chest. Ford was blatantly displaying her to his friend. His friend who didn't like her. She should have stepped away, but his fingers felt so...

She lowered her eyes, acquiescing to the show Ford was putting on for Charley. But where she was certain she should have felt shame for not pushing Ford away, instead her flesh tingled as she relished the simple pressure of Ford's fingers into her hip, his attention riveted to her body. She trained her eyes on his fingers, trying to pretend Charley wasn't five feet away, his grubby, black boots on her pale, new rug.

"Look at her curves." Ford's voice rumbled with sex and Evie thought Charley shouldn't be in the room. This was too private.

"Charley, you would know exactly what to do with her." Ford turned his intense eyes to the other man, who stood stock-still, watching them. "You would know just what I would want. Isn't that right?"

Evie and Charley caught eyes and looked away quickly. They both knew Ford wasn't talking about clothes shopping. Was he offering her to Charley?

No. No way. That was crazy—who would do such a thing? Evie thought about Ford's line—the one he wasn't anywhere near crossing.

Thrill—unmistakable sexual hunger—crawled over Evie's skin. It was a feeling she'd only experienced around Ford. Lust, sharpened to a point by discomfort. Goddamn, it was addictive. Feeling flushed, she shifted from one foot to the other. Where was Ford going with this?

Ford moved away from Evie and stepped halfway in between the two fidgeting figures. Crossing his arms, he surveyed their mutual demeanors before taking an exaggerated breath.

"My Charley and my Evie," he sighed. They both looked sharply at Ford, seeming surprised he'd said it about the other. "We are part of each other's lives now and the sooner we make this work, the better. I hate wasting time." Neither of them responded.

He turned his focus to Evie. "I have a laptop prepared for you. It's in the top, middle drawer of the dresser. If you insist upon not going out, you can order things from the internet and have them shipped overnight. And I will pick up some things for you while I'm out."

"Oh. Okay. Thanks." Thank god she'd gotten out of spending the day with Charley.

"Great," Charley said, too loudly. "Then I'll get outta here. Nice meeting you, Evie." He nodded his head to her. "Ford, I'll walk out with you."

But Ford dipped his head and smiled. "No Charley," he said quietly. "I haven't changed my mind. I want you to spend the day with Evie."

Evie closed her eyes. This wasn't happening.

"I'll be gone for most of the day today, I'm afraid. My chef always keeps meals prepared in the fridge in the kitchen if you get hungry. You two get to know each other and when I come home tonight we'll all have dinner together."

Charley didn't protest any further. He shoved his hands in his back pockets and stared toward the windows, his face set.

"Evie, house rules. I don't like visitors, so if there's ever anyone you need to see, I'm afraid I have to ask you to meet them out somewhere, away from the house. Will that be a problem?"

"No." When Evie had moved to the city to start her new life as a paralegal, she'd made the mistake of getting wrapped up so quickly with John that she hadn't made her own friends, not that she ever had any anyway. After she and John had broken up, she'd stayed to herself. With a little sadness she realized there wasn't even anyone she'd need to tell that she'd moved. No one but John would be looking for her. She wrapped her arms around herself.

"Charley's a visitor," she pointed out petulantly, redirecting her discomfort.

"Charley is not a visitor. He's part of my life."

Charley turned reluctant eyes to Ford, his tense muscles — *so many of them* — loosening slightly.

Ford moved to where she stood, taking her elbows in his hands. "Thank you for coming here. I think the arrangement will be good for us. Just what we need." But after this strange introduction, she wasn't sure if the "us" included Charley or not.

He kissed her cheek and lingered for one tense millisecond that caused a tempest inside her. She'd never wanted to kiss anyone as badly as she wanted to kiss him at that moment. Kiss him as if she was poisoned and he was the antidote. She wanted him to assure her that everything about them had not just changed completely the moment Charley had burst through that door.

But there was no "them". She knew that. He turned to leave.

"Wait!" she called as his hand touched the doorknob. "Is there a lock on the door?"

Brow furrowed, he turned back to her. "I'm sorry, what?"

"A lock." She pointed at the door. "Can I lock the door?"

"Yes." He depressed the button of the standard doorknob click-lock and then unlocked it to demonstrate.

"No, I need a real lock. With a key."

A cloud passed over his face. "Are you afraid to be in the house with me?"

"No, of course not. It's just…" How could she explain her need to sleep behind a locked door? She flicked her eyes to Charley, who watched the discussion with interest. Moving closer, she lowered her voice. "Could we talk about it alone. Please." She squeezed her hands together against the urge to squirm, shifting so her back was to Charley.

"No." Ford put a hand on her shoulder and twisted her to face Charley. "Now tell me why you require a lock. You can say it in front of Charley. I want you to feel comfortable around him."

Evie's stomach sank. She'd thought she'd moved in with Ford. How much was she going to have to put up with this other man who seemed to hate her? She regarded Charley with the same disdain he was showing her and spoke through clenched teeth. "I just feel safer if I sleep behind a lock." She looked at Ford. "It's not you. It's the way I've always been," she said weakly, knowing it sounded implausible.

Ford's jaw clenched. "That wasn't part of the plan. I do not want that door locked." He jabbed a stiff finger toward it.

Plan?

"But…" Evie flicked her eyes to Charley, who was frowning at her. Anxiety closed her throat and her eyes burned. This could be a deal-breaker. She wasn't sure she could compromise on it, no matter what the cost. "I don't think I can sleep without a lock," she said quietly, trying to control the tightness in her voice. She touched his arm, imploring silently.

He studied her face. "You're not afraid of me?" She shook her head. "Do you trust me?"

"Yes." She didn't hesitate in her answer and it was the truth, she was surprised to realize. For a moment, he didn't speak. His green eyes pierced into hers as she clasped and unclasped her hands, her palms wet with sweat.

"Alright."

She took a deep breath, finally able to fill her lungs again.

"Tomorrow I'll have a locksmith come and install any type of lock you want, up to and including a bank-vault door if that's what you need, but—" He held up a finger. "You must make a concession for me."

"What?" she asked, her tone guarded.

"You will get three copies of the key. One for you, one for me and one for Charley."

"Charley!" She glared over at the man Ford wouldn't let her be free of. Charley met her eyes and lifted a shoulder as if to say, "I have no idea why I'd need a key."

"Yes, Charley too. Those are my terms. Otherwise the current lock stays."

She closed her eyes. She had to have that lock. "Fine," she muttered. "But he—" she poked a finger at Charley, "—had better never use his key unless this room is on fire and I'm trapped in here!"

"Don't worry, honey. I wouldn't even use it then." Charley cocked his head, an easy smile cutting across his face. Evie made a disgusted noise, crossing her arms over her chest.

"Well then." Ford smacked his hands together. "Look at the two of you. I can already tell you're well on your way to being…BFF's. Is that what they call it?" Ford's dimples punctuated his teasing.

Charley and Evie both huffed, but the message underneath was clear. Ford expected them to make an effort to get along while he was out. "I'll see you both later for dinner and you can give me a full rundown of the day you spent together." Nodding to each of them on his way out the door, he pressed the lock in firmly before winking and closing it behind him.

The door clicked shut and Evie and Charley turned a slow stare at each other, bristling. Charley stepped toward her, his long legs eating the distance in just a few strides. She held her ground against the assault on her personal space and glared up at him. She may have been tiny next to him, but she wasn't going to allow herself believe that. She squared her shoulders.

"So what's your agenda?" he demanded, venom in his voice.

"Agenda? I don't have an agenda! He asked me to come here."

"Everyone has an agenda when it comes to Ford. Why do you think I'm the only person he lets in?"

Raising her eyebrows, Evie swept her gaze meaningfully over the room—her room—and then back to him, allowing the silence to say it all.

The fire she saw in Charley's brown eyes turned to ferocity as he spit out his next words. "So, have you fucked him?"

Wow. Right to the point.

"No. Have you?" she blurted in response.

He rocked back, eyes wide, seeming caught off guard that she'd asked him that. She kept her face carefully set, though she was just as surprised as he was that it had come out of her mouth. Uncrossing his arms, he shoved his hands in the back pockets of his worn jeans, his shoulders rounding in the slight way she'd noticed before.

"No," he muttered before turning away and retreating to the window, effectively ending the confrontation.

Evie squeezed her eyes closed and took a deep breath. There was that feeling again—like she was sorry for defending herself against his attack. He just seemed so vulnerable.

She retrieved the computer from the dresser and flopped on the bed, determined to ignore him. Just because he was there, didn't mean she had to engage with him. Heavy silence stretched through the room, punctuated now and then with her clicks and keyboard strokes.

After a while, Charley clomped around the perimeter of the room, the sound of his motorcycle boots thumping through her head like a hammer as his footfalls struck her glowing hardwood floor. She lifted her eyes when his steps halted near her dresser, and watched him pick up a few of the dainty decorations there before callously tossing them back down.

She squeezed her hands into fists. Those were *her* new things.

Nicer things than she'd ever had. He was baiting her and he'd just about won when he picked up two china balls in pearlized colors from a decorative plate full of them and lay down on the rug on his back. His frame spanned nearly from one edge of the rug to the other.

Resting one oversized boot on his other bent knee, he starting tossing the balls into the air, one at a time, and catching them deftly. She could live with that—she had a plate full of them.

He was big, but lean, and she could see what looked like every muscle of his chest through the thin tee-shirt he wore stretched over his torso. The shirt had ridden up and she could see the cords of a fine abdomen split with a trail of dark hair that disappeared under the top button of his button-fly jeans.

She knew they were button-fly, because whatever he was boasting in them caused enough pressure on the placket to gap it so the edges of the shiny buttons were visible. The chrome winked to her under the lights of the room's modern fixture.

Chewing on the inside of her lip, she thought about how good he looked. Especially sprawled out like that in his rough-and-tumble clothes on her fancy rug, like some kind of a yard-boy sacrifice to a rich cougar. The corners of her mouth twitched at the thought.

He cleared his throat and she flicked her eyes to his face. He was watching her, a smirk curled across his mouth. With horror, she realized he'd caught her staring at—*oh god*, her insides shrank—his...package.

"Don't break my balls," she muttered, trying to deflect.

"Don't stare at mine," he drawled.

Pinning her eyes back to the computer, she felt her face turn scarlet-hot. She ducked her head behind the laptop screen, trying to pretend he wasn't there. But she had no luck. The man's presence filled a room to the seams, and her skin pricked with the sense that she had nowhere to retreat from him.

She blew out her breath. "Why don't you just leave?"

"Because he wants us to spend the day together," he answered simply.

128

"Do you do everything he wants?"

He didn't answer right away, and she heard the *smack, smack* of the balls landing on his paw of a hand three more times before his response came, simple and cutting.

"Don't you?"

She didn't answer the question either.

Determined to not let him ruin her day, she focused on her shopping spree, which was proving to be more challenging than enjoyable. She was finding things she liked, but she couldn't decide if Ford would like them. Short of buying lingerie, she wasn't sure what type of clothing he liked on a woman. And she wasn't just following orders — she wanted Ford to like what she wore.

Charley stopped tossing the balls and lay flat on his back on the rug, his hands tucked behind his head and his eyes closed. After fifteen minutes of silence, Evie assumed he'd fallen asleep, and his lack of consciousness finally eased the pressure of their silent standoff.

After browsing through fifteen pages of dresses on one site — a site she'd always wished she could afford to shop on — she growled in frustration and scrubbed her hands over her eyes. How could she get this done? She had no idea what Ford liked. He'd always commented more on her body than on the clothes she wore on it.

Did he like short or tight? Classy or sexy? Bright or subdued? Pants or skirts? Well, she could probably at least guess that one.

"Having trouble?" Evie jumped and heard Charley chuckle. She slid the laptop sideways and saw that he'd turned to his side, propping his head on one bent arm and looking like he'd never been more content.

Damn, as surly as the guy was, he looked delicious. "Yes," she snapped.

He stood up, placed the china balls back on the decorative plate and stretched.

Hello, abs.

She tried not to look, but there was just so much of him to ignore. He twisted his body, broadening his back, and the position granted her an eyebrow-raising view of a divine backside cupped in faded denim.

It was no wonder he always shoved his hands in his back pockets. Who wouldn't want to grab an ass like that? She focused back on the computer before he could catch her checking him out again.

He wandered over to the bed. "What's the problem?" His tone sounded neutral and she looked up at him, deciding to answer him when she read nothing but supreme boredom in his body language. They were stuck with each other. Might as well make the best of it. And maybe he could help.

She pointed to the page of stylish dresses on her computer screen. "I don't know Ford's taste."

Charley rubbed a hand on the back of his neck, eyes unfocused. When he answered, his voice was heavy with emotion far out of proportion with her shopping dilemma.

"You, apparently." He sighed closing his eyes.

"What?"

"His taste. It's you, I guess." He opened his eyes and met hers, and her stomach twisted at what she saw in his look. Gut-wrenching resignation. She'd felt pain like that and she did not want to be the cause of it.

"Charley..." The reluctant note of compassion in her voice was all he needed. He sat down on the edge of her bed, staring at his hands. "Does he know how you feel about him?"

He laughed mirthlessly. "Who knows? With Ford you can't tell if he's really not picking up on it, or if he's purposely ignoring it."

"But..." How should she say this? "Would he even be...open to that kind of thing?"

"I think so. Maybe. We..." He shook his head and trailed off, looking out the window.

We what?

This was a side of Ford Evie would not have suspected. It might have freaked her out, except that Charley had such a natural appeal to him, much like Ford did, that Evie could imagine most any human being willing to try out what Charley had to offer.

The big man was handsome, not in the pure way Ford was,

but in an unpolished, wild way. He had an energy that seemed to swirl about him, a charisma. But unlike Ford's crystal shell of confidence, Charley had a readable sensitivity, his body and the set of his jaw clearly reflecting his response to the world around him. Evie felt for him. How difficult would it be to go through life being such an open book?

"Well, if it's any consolation, he doesn't want to be my boyfriend either. He made that perfectly clear."

Charley looked at her and his eyes seemed to be searching for the cruelty behind her mocking. She made sure he found none.

She'd never had a man as a rival for another man's affections before, but this thing with Ford was so confusing that more so than a rival, she saw in Charley the only other person in the world who maybe understood how she felt.

A heart-achingly beautiful, sad smile graced Charley's face and he lowered his eyes, peeking at her through his lashes. "You are very pretty. But you're not like the others. That's what freaked me out the most."

"The others?"

"Ford goes out. He dates—I suppose as much as you could call it dating. He makes a social effort—let's call it that." Charley shifted on the bed and pulled one leg up on it, facing her. Just two girlfriends musing about the boy they were crushing on…if your girlfriend were a six foot four hunk of a man who oozed sex and sin all over your brand new duvet.

"He's always with some woman or another, and those women are always two things —" He ticked them off on his fingers. "Women who make good business allies or women who look like runway models."

"And I'm neither of those things?" she asked dryly. While she agreed, this didn't seem a nice thing for him to point out.

"No, that's not—! Sorry." His easy smile lit his brown eyes with the warmth she'd seen promised there earlier. "You're just… I mean look at you." He gestured toward her body. "You're not a fashion-model. A skinny mannequin. You're all curvy. You're like a walking promise of sex."

Evie looked down at her body as if there was a sign on her

front she hadn't noticed before.

"And you're a lot shorter than them. It just threw me. It felt like Ford had made a serious change and I'd been left out of the conversation."

She opened her mouth, hesitating as she picked her words. "I don't know if you just insulted me or complimented me."

"It's a compliment. Trust me. I have never, ever felt jealous of anyone in Ford's life until I walked into this room today and was confronted with you." Charley's lips pulled into a frown.

"There's no need to be jealous of me. You're his best friend. I'm just an employee."

Charley nodded with his eyes narrowed, as if he were trying to believe that.

"You knew I was moving in, right?" she asked.

"Yes, I knew, but you're just not what I pictured. Ford doesn't get close to people. I wasn't worried at first."

"And now you're worried?"

Charley took a deep breath. "Now I'm worried." He was as open with his feelings as Ford was closed tight.

"Well don't be. This is a business arrangement. There will be no relationship. And when the year is up, I'm gone. I've got plans — plans that involve being far away from this state."

"You sound very sure of that."

"I am sure." She had to be at least a thousand miles from this state before she might be able to stop living in fear, even after she paid John everything she owed him.

Charley nodded, but his face looked dubious.

"Maybe I can help you." She put her hand on his knee.

"How?"

"I'm not here for the long term. Maybe I can plant the seed for you." And if she could concentrate on bringing Ford and Charley together, maybe she could better control her feelings for Ford. "Maybe I can even...I don't know...help make the both of you feel more comfortable about coming together."

Charley narrowed his eyes, tilting his head to give her a look of disbelief. It was no stronger than the disbelief she was already feeling for having made the suggestion. What did she even mean by that? Had her attraction to Charley really just caused an offer for a threesome to come out of her mouth?

No. That's not what she'd meant. Was it?

She tried to backpedal. "I, uh—"

"That one." Charley pointed at the computer screen.

"Huh?" Evie had forgotten she'd been unsuccessfully trying to pick out clothes. Charley was pointing at a navy-blue, tailored shirt dress.

"Ford would like that. Make sure it hugs your body and wear it with the top four buttons undone. And heels. The higher the better."

Evie peered at the dress. It hadn't stood out to her. The model wearing it looked very prim in the ensemble. Evie would never have picked that one.

"Really? It looks boring. Why that one?"

"It looks boring on her, but on you?" Charley swept his eyes down her body, lingering, obviously not caring if she noticed where his gaze was concentrated. "On you it would look mouth-watering."

"Why?" The word popped out of her mouth too quickly to stop it. She watched his eyes on her and she wanted to know what was behind the flicker she saw in them. He'd said "mouth-watering" not in the way a person would say, "pretty". He'd said it like he understood it.

"Your tits are…well they're not even fair. Forget those knives you carry—your tits are your concealed weapons."

Evie laughed. "That is the strangest compliment I've ever received. And I'm kinda proud of what you just said."

Charley's crooked smile widened and he leaned forward, energy jumping off him like water on a frying pan. "Your tits are the kind a man wants in his mouth. As soon as he can make it happen. I bet you've never had to buy yourself a drink at a bar in your life."

She furrowed her brow. "I've had to buy myself plenty of drinks. And…do you like women?"

Charley chuckled, shaking his head. "See, this is why I don't go out much. Everyone wants to label everything." He met her eyes again. "I love women. In every way. I just don't draw lines. A sexy person with the right chemistry is who I want in my bed. The equipment's not important. The person is." His grin turned wicked. "And man or woman, no one's getting out of my bed before they're thoroughly satisfied." He winked.

She felt her skin heat. Forget what he'd said about *her* body. He was the promise of exciting sin, the kind you've never tried before but always wanted to.

"You like my tits?" She couldn't help but match his flirtation. The conversation was like reading a dirty book she wasn't quite comfortable with—but she kept turning the pages anyway because she had to know what happened next. Her clit had perked to attention.

"I like everything about your body." He reached out and touched her bare ankle, sliding a fingernail over her skin. "When I came into this room and saw you with Ford, it got my adrenaline riled up. Now all that steam's got nowhere to go. So to be honest, I want to fuck you hard right now, until I've got all that extra fire drained out of my system."

Evie felt her eyes widen. This man could be as direct as Ford.

"Do you always talk to women like that?"

"No." He dropped his head, his crooked smile turning sheepish. "But I'm having fun. Are you?"

She laughed, feeling a surge of friendly warmth for the man. "Yeah."

"And besides, the way Ford talked about you at the end of our conversation—as upset as I was, it got me heated up in other ways."

She looked down, picking at the comforter. "Me too." Giggling, she covered her face with her hands. "I'm sorry. This is embarrassing. I just met you!"

"Hey now, don't be embarrassed." Charley's voice was gentle. He pulled her hands away from her face. "It's Ford. That man has a way when it comes to sex. It's like a super power." He wrapped his fingers into hers and didn't let go, their clasped hands resting on the bed between them.

"Yeah, but I can't decide if he uses his powers for good or evil."

Charley laughed. "Me neither, honey. Me neither."

The phone next to the bed blared to life. Evie looked at Charley who shrugged. She picked it up.

"Hawthorne residence."

At first there was silence on the other end and then the laughter started. Ugly, abrasive. Evie hung up so fast she nearly threw the phone to the floor.

CHAPTER THIRTEEN

"WHO WAS THAT?" Charley shifted quickly to the edge of the bed. He put a hand on Evie's arm, squeezing.

"Nothing. Wrong number—just some pervert." She tried to laugh but it came out all wrong.

"Evie, you're shaking!" Charley gaped at his hand on her arm. Shoulders tensing visibly, he stood up, towering over her. He turned his calculating look from her to the phone. He picked it up.

"Charley please!" She reached for the phone. "Just don't worry about it."

The phone rang again, going off like a bomb between them. She dove for it, but Charley held her off easily with one arm. He clicked it on and held it to his ear. Defeated, she had no choice but to watch it go down. Her stomach sank.

Charley's free hand clenched into a fist, the veins popping along his lean and muscular arm. His jaw flexed menacingly and the phone seemed to be in danger of disintegration from his tight grip. He pressed it to his ear as if he wanted somehow to reach through it and murder the person on the other end.

John.

This wasn't happening. How did he find her? And so quickly?

"I don't know who you are, but I'll find out. And I will rip your fucking head off if you call this house again." The malevolence in Charley's voice made Evie's eyes widen. He was a tough guy, but

137

his persona was far more sweetness than savagery. Until that moment.

"That sounds funny?" Charley barked and then held the phone away from his ear, staring at it. "He hung up. He was laughing." He turned a black look at Evie. "Evie he knew you. Who was that?"

Horrified, she couldn't make her mouth work—and didn't know what to say if she could.

"I'm calling Ford." He started mashing buttons on the abused phone.

"No!" She jumped to her knees on the bed, knocking the laptop onto the rug with a clatter. She pressed her hand over his fingers on the phone, stopping his dialing. "No. Charley please don't call Ford." Her voice was high-pitched, wavering in her panic. She squeezed his fingers and placed her other hand on his chest. His heart hammered under the thin, soft fabric of the tee-shirt.

"You tell me right now what the fuck is going on. I won't let Ford be in danger in his own home." His voice was raw with the strain of emotion.

"Okay! Okay. I'll tell you. Just...just..." She pried the phone from his fingers, clicked it off and laid it down. "Sit down. Let's get this over with."

Charley sat stiffly on the bed, the intensity of his concentration on her face causing her to fidget. She picked up the laptop, which appeared to have survived the fall, and tucked her hair behind her ears.

"What did he say to you?" she asked.

"He—" Charley clamped his lips shut for a moment before continuing. "He said some mean things about you and said he was going to get what you owed him no matter how he had to get it."

Evie shivered. "What mean things?"

"I don't want to repeat them."

"Tell me."

He cocked his head and narrowed his eyes at her. "You really have to know?"

She nodded and he took a deep breath. "He said that being

Ford's whore at work wasn't enough, that now you had to move in and be his whore full-time."

Evie closed her eyes. "What else?"

"Evie, just tell me who he is."

"What else did he say?" She raised her voice, demanding to hear every word John had intended for her. She needed to know what she was up against. Charley fidgeted, his reluctance to repeat the message evident in his tone. "He said, now you understand why he didn't want to marry you." He practically mumbled the last part. "That you're the type of woman wealthy men just use for sex and then pass off to another when they're done."

Evie gasped and bile rose in her throat before she could choke it back. How could she ever have had *sex* with that man? Scalding tears sprung to her eyes. Charley reacted instantly, scooting to her and engulfing her in his arms. "Don't cry, Evie." He rubbed his broad hands on her back, gentling her. "Those things are not true. You aren't a whore."

She choked. "I'm here aren't I? At Ford's?" John always knew exactly how to hurt her.

Charley held her away from him, honest intensity in his chocolate eyes. He spoke deliberately, his tone serious. "I know you're not a whore because I don't often get denied. Nine out of ten people, man or woman, would have fucked me on the spot when I offered it the first time."

Her mouth dropped open and for a moment she forgot her emotions. He grinned and his eyes twinkled with mischief. Balling her fist, she cuffed him on the chest. Hard.

"Ouch!"

"You're an asshole." She was laughing through her tears. "That's your whore test?"

"No! God, of course not! That's just my you-have-a-pulse test. My whore test is much more hard-core. I can give you that one if you want. But..." He made a show of looking around the room. "We're going to need some lube. And possibly some plastic sheeting." He got up and opened one of the dresser drawers. "Do you have a video recorder with a wide-angle lens? And a zucchini?"

Now she was in hysterics, collapsing to the bed and kicking her feet in the air, the power of her fear and anger transferred full-force to her belly-laughs. "Okay!" she shrieked. "Okay. I give up." She wiped her eyes and sat up. "Come and sit down and I'll tell you the whole story." She patted the spot next to her but he lay down across the foot of her bed, propping his head on his hand, his tee-shirt riding up again to expose his washboard stomach.

"Wait." He held up a hand. "First, what happened with Ford at your work?"

"Oh, that." Evie looked down at her fingers, feeling as though she was telling Charley she'd slept with his boyfriend. "We had...oral sex...in the library. I got fired over it," she mumbled.

Charley nodded his head. "You both had oral sex? Like he did you and you did him?"

"Yes." She hesitated. "Charley, I don't know what to say. I'm sorry."

Charley waved his hand. "Oh god, don't be sorry! Ford tells me about his exploits most of the time. I don't have any claim to him. I just wanted to understand. And besides..." The corner of Charley's mouth pulled up. "It's hot to think about."

Evie smiled. It was the first time she'd ever remembered having someone make her feel better when she was afraid. She always shrank away from people in times like these, but Charley made it impossible to deny him, just like he'd said.

She took a bracing breath. She'd never told anyone this story before. "That was my ex-boyfriend. He's a criminal defense attorney."

"He sounds charming, what I heard from him." Charley smiled, his sarcasm obvious.

"He wasn't always like that. He used to be a better guy—I'd like to think he was, anyway. But then he got wrapped up in drugs. You have to put in a ton of productive hours to become partner at a law firm, and apparently John turned to cocaine to help him stay awake and work, sometimes for days at a time. At first he had it under control and I didn't realize it was even happening. I don't take drugs, and we didn't live together."

Charley nodded, watching her intently.

"He lent me twenty-thousand dollars to pay off my student loans."

Charley raised his eyebrows in silence.

"Don't look at me like that! My interest rate had doubled and I thought… It was stupid, but I thought he'd offered because it was a step toward combining our finances. For a future together."

"So that's the money you owe him."

"I still owe him thirteen-thousand, but it's more than that. I didn't know the exact dollar amount of the pay-off of my loan at the time, so John gave me a blank check and told me to just fill it out. I did. Only…I didn't know this, but by then he'd started embezzling money from the firm to fund his cocaine habit."

"Ohhh." Charley nodded. "And that money he loaned you was stolen firm money?"

"Yeah." She sighed.

"And *you* filled out the check in your own hand-writing."

Her shoulders slumped. It sounded so damning in retrospect. "Yes. But when I found out he was stealing, I ended things! And I told him I was going to quit the firm and turn him in."

"That couldn't have gone over well."

"No." Evie chuckled, but it was a bleak sound. "That was the start of my living hell." As much as she hated reliving the memory, she was surprised how easy it was to talk to Charley about it. "That's when he told me I'd go down with him—he'd tell them we were partners. So I told him I'd figure it out—make a deal and testify against him—and his whole demeanor changed. His face just…blanked. He went to his file cabinet and pulled out a manila envelope and threw it at me." Evie shuddered at the memory. "There were pictures of dead girls in it."

Charley's face blackened.

"It was from the file of one of his clients. It was a big case, all over the media. John handled his defense and the man had been found not guilty. John said, 'I got him off for raping and murdering those girls.' He didn't say he'd gotten him off for being accused_of those things. Then he said the man enjoys what he does and owes John a favor." For the amount of times she'd replayed the conversation in her head, she practically had it memorized word-for-word.

"Oh my god," Charley breathed.

"Yeah." Evie's voice had grown unsteady and she gripped her fingers together against the trembling that had started again. "He said he wanted every penny back, plus interest, and that I'd have to stay working at the firm where he could keep an eye on me until I paid him."

Charley whistled, long and low. "This guy's a psychopath."

"I know that now. And honestly, I'm sure he wanted the money, but more so he needed me to stay. I was his paralegal and at that point he'd become so dysfunctional because of the drugs that I was doing most of his work for him. He was using my work to hide his secret."

"And you don't have the money to pay him?"

"No. I wish I did! That's why I took this job with Ford. To get the money together fast and give it to John."

"Is that also why you took up martial arts?"

She nodded, her mouth curling up.

"This guy's dangerous. You need to get the money from Ford."

"No!" Evie grabbed Charley's hand, willing him to understand. "I can't borrow from one guy to pay back another. Can't you see? I learned my lesson. I'm going to take care of this myself. I just need more time." She turned worried eyes to the phone. "But I don't know how he found me."

"Well babe, you're out of time. You are telling Ford. I won't let him be in danger in his own house."

Evie looked at Charley's face, feeling her stomach drop. She saw the resolution there. Charley would protect Ford. "Fine." She sighed. "But he's going to make me leave."

"No." Charley's face grew fierce. "If you think Ford would put you out in circumstances like these, then you don't know him at all."

"Okay." Maybe Charley was right. Hadn't Ford proved it, taking up for her to John that that night in the library? She felt the tension in her muscles ease. She had no defense against John outside of Ford's gates. Behind his gates she felt as if she could breathe again, like she had a chance. "Okay. I'll tell him tonight at dinner."

Charley reached out and covered her hand in his. "I'll be there. I'll make sure it goes okay."

"Thanks, Charley." She wanted to hug him. She wanted to lie down and curl against him, have him throw an arm and a leg over her and shelter her with his bulk until she felt strong again. "Alright, then." Charley smacked his hand on her leg. "Now pull up those websites. Ford's right. I am good at picking out what would look good on you."

CHAPTER FOURTEEN

$\mathcal{F}$ORD HAD BEEN right about a lot of things. Evie had never made a friend as quickly as Charley. He was easy to warm up to—he was like sunshine. Evie had no trouble understanding why Ford kept Charley so close.

After they'd done all the shopping either of them could stand, they'd wandered around the estate, found some lunch and ended up in the home's theater, watching old Eighties movies from Ford's extensive library. Inspired, Charley had jumped up on the couch singing a well-known theme song at the top of his lungs. Evie threw pillows at him, shrieking with laughter.

"I see we've learned to get along."

Evie and Charley snapped their heads to Ford, who was standing in the darkened entryway of the theater room, his lanky body leaned casually against the door frame. She jumped to her feet as if she'd been caught doing something she shouldn't. Charley, quiet now, stepped off the couch, clicking off the movie and raising the lights with the remote. Ford looked back and forth between them.

"Evie, did you have a fun day with Charley?"

Evie glanced at the big man next to her. "Honestly, I had one of the most enjoyable days I can remember." Charley grinned down at her.

Ford smiled. "He has that effect. Charley, do you better understand why I asked Evie to come here now?"

"Yes." His answer was simple, but carried pure honesty, with no hint of swallowed pride given his earlier icy reception of her. Evie's chest swelled with affection for the big, shaggy-haired man. Her unlikely new friend.

Ford beamed at them, his dimples making Evie's knees weak, and shook his head. "You two are noisy."

"Sorry, man. I shouldn't make anyone listen to my singing." Charley chuckled.

"Don't apologize. I liked it. I don't think I've ever come home to noise in my house before. And strangely, it made me happy." He stepped back and gestured them out of the room. "Let's go back upstairs then. I have some things for you, Evangeline."

Before they entered the great room, Ford pointed Evie toward the stairs, explaining she'd find the things he'd brought home for her up in her room. "I've set something out for you to wear for dinner. Please go put it on while I make us drinks."

When she opened her new bedroom door, she saw at least seven shopping bags neatly lined up on the floor of her room. She recognized the name on the bags as one of the boutiques she'd walked by a hundred times in the city while on her lunch break, lusting over the clothing in the window, but not even bothering to go in. Three of her salaries couldn't clothe her in a store like that.

New clothes and shoes! She squealed as quietly as she could, hopping up and down on her toes. Maybe this was the best day she'd ever had. And now she got to go spend the evening with two hunky men. She moved to her bed to see what she'd be wearing.

Laid out on her blue coverlet, she found a sleeveless dress of a silky knit material that draped dangerously low in the front. Evie wasn't sure it qualified as a dinner dress, but it was certainly not a business-lunch dress. There was also a pair of high, nude-colored leather pumps, and thong panties made of lace so fine it looked like it'd been woven by fairies.

And for the price it likely cost, it probably should have been.

The dress was skimpy but somehow still elegant. The pumps had a covered platform, which allowed the shoes to look dressy but ultra-sexy at the same time. Once she'd put the dress on, it was clear why there was no bra with the outfit. There was no way to wear one with the way the dress draped so low. She turned in front of her mirror feeling alluring. The fabric hugged all of her curves.

She headed to the great room as Ford had requested. Pausing before she turned the corner, she took a deep breath, feeling like she was stepping onstage for a strip routine. Given what Ford had chosen for her to wear, the feeling wasn't entirely unjustified. Shoulders back, she walked purposefully into the room, her breasts bouncing lightly, nipples hard from the friction of the dress sliding over her bare skin.

Ford had changed from his work clothes into a loose white linen shirt and tan pants. He looked like Evie's idea of a dream-man she might find at a tropical resort. He was pouring a drink and talking to Charley when he noticed her come in. Cutting his words off mid-sentence, his eyes widened. He set the drink down with a clatter on the bar and looked back at it, swearing, when it splattered onto his shirt. Evie snickered.

"What do you think?" she asked, twirling for them. Charley whistled long and low.

The stain on his shirt forgotten, Ford stood frozen, a smile curving slowly around the corners of his mouth. "I knew you'd look like that in that dress." He shook his head as if she'd done something naughty.

She beamed, though she realized he hadn't actually complimented her. It seemed like a compliment, though, from the smoldering look in his eyes. He came over to hand her a drink. Cupping his hand on her hip, he squeezed his fingers into her flesh and kissed her lightly on the cheek. The mixture of hard and soft, loving and rough, sent a thrill straight to her clit and she wished badly that they were alone. She wanted him instantly and was ready for it with just one, masterful touch.

"Thank you for wearing what I picked for you," he said softly, next to her cheek.

"Thank you for picking it for me," she responded, her voice barely above a whisper.

He stepped back to look at Charley. "Shall we?" Taking Evie's elbow, Ford gestured toward the dining room.

Ford and Charley sat on one side of the large, polished-wood table and Evie sat across from them. They ate the most succulent prime rib Evie had ever tasted while Charley recounted their day. She was grateful he left out the part about John. He'd told her she had to tell Ford after dinner and that seemed to remain the plan.

Evie loved watching Ford and Charley interact. She'd never seen Ford so happy. Charley made him laugh over and over. Ford seemed younger around Charley, more alive. And Charley looked at Ford in a way that almost made Evie jealous. She didn't think she'd ever had anyone look at her with that kind of love.

"How'd you two meet? You're so different—how did you become friends?" She'd wondered this from the moment rough-and-ready Charley had busted into her room.

Ford and Charley smiled at each other, the common memory obviously a good one for both of them.

"You tell it, Charley." Ford gestured toward him with his wine glass.

Charley grinned. "I was working for one of Ford's companies as a delivery driver."

"Are you kidding?" Evie practically squealed. Ford nodded, his fingers tented now in front of his mouth, but she could see the smile behind them.

"Crazy right? I'd just finished my shift and was heading home when I drove by Ford's fancy sports car in a ditch and him standing next to it in the rain looking like a half-drowned billionaire." He paused to wink at Ford. "'Cause that's exactly what you were."

Ford laughed, shaking his head and looking as if he was eternally weary of trying to make Charley behave.

"Our Ford here," Charley reached over and rubbed Ford's shoulder, lingering, "likes to drive his cars way too fast, and on that day, ended up in a ditch, thankfully uninjured."

Our Ford.

Ford shrugged. "I can afford speeding tickets and I like to find out what the things I own are capable of." He looked at Evie and his emerald eyes seemed to see right into her. *You are mine. I'm going to find out everything you're capable of.*

She squirmed in her seat, anxiety and excitement sparking

through her like a transformer explosion.

"So I pulled over in my old pickup truck and asked him if he needed a ride. Ford takes one long look over my clunker and says no, he'll just wait for his driver."

"And he laughed at me," Ford interjected, glancing at Charley with affection. "I could see he was wearing the uniform from my company. I'm the goddamned CEO and he's laughing at me!"

"Oh my god!" Evie was laughing, feeling giddy from the wine. She waved her hand in the air. "Go on! Go on!"

"I was shocked. Livid." Ford looked at Charley, his gaze intense as he spoke of the memory.

Charley took over the story without missing a beat. "I told him, 'I thought everyone was exaggerating, but you really are a pretentious fucking control-freak. You'd rather stand there in the rain than sit your rich, tight ass on the ripped upholstery of my piece-a-shit truck."

Evie gasped. "You didn't!"

"He did." Ford sprawled back on his chair, his wine glass in one hand, his body oriented toward Charley.

"What did you do?" She directed the question to Ford but Charley answered.

"I'll never forget the look on his face. In all the time I've known him I've never seen it since."

"He was that mad?" Evie had leaned forward, her forearms on the table, her wine ignored.

Charley looked thoughtful. "Yes, he was mad, but he was probably more flabbergasted. Flummoxed, even." Charley grinned, looking proud of the word he'd come up with.

Ford shook his head again. "The language of a sailor, the vocabulary of a poet." Charley beamed at him.

"I've never seen him flabbergasted or anything like it." Evie tried to imagine it, and couldn't come up with the image.

"I never have either! Just that one time." Charley threw a long glance at Ford. "I've thought about that day a lot—why he got in my truck." The look on Charley's face was that of a lover. Ford met his gaze with the same intensity. Both of the men remained silent long enough for Evie to shift in her chair. Ford was confusing enough on his own, but the dynamic between he and Charley was absolutely indecipherable.

"I think he felt challenged." Charley's voice was soft and Evie got the distinct impression he and Ford had never discussed this before. "I think maybe he had the impression I didn't think he was man enough to get in my truck."

Ford just smiled and took a sip of his wine, admitting nothing, adding no clarity to Charley's musings. They were quiet for another moment and Evie looked back and forth between them. She could almost see the wheels turning in both their heads. The thoughts. Remembering that day.

"So?" She broke the silence. "What happened?"

At the same time Ford said, "I got in the truck," Charley said, "He got in the truck."

All three of them laughed, but exasperated, Evie pushed on, "And what happened?"

Ford picked up on the tale. "I got in, told him I would accept his ride and I appreciated his stopping to see if I needed help, but after he dropped me off the first thing I was going to do was fire him."

Evie gasped, horrified. "You did not!"

"He did," Charley said.

"Were you upset?"

"Hell no." Charley waved his hand. "I was a delivery driver. It's not like I had some mega-career at stake. And the job market was great back then. I'd just drive for someone else."

"It wouldn't matter the circumstances. Charley doesn't get upset." There was unmistakable fondness in Ford's voice.

But Evie had seen him upset and so had Ford. She wondered how Ford felt about the earlier scene in her room, knowing he was the cause of Charley's distress, bringing her in the way Ford had.

"And besides," Charley added with a sexy curl of his lips, "what was there to be upset about? I had the all-powerful, deadly handsome, enigmatic Ford Hawthorne riding shotgun in my truck cab." Charley looked immensely proud of himself.

"Poet." Ford muttered, pouring Charley more wine.

"Hey, just 'cause I don't run three companies doesn't mean I can't string together a damn good sentence now and then," Charley teased.

"Charley," Ford admonished, frowning, "other than that first moment when I didn't want to get into your death-trap of a vehicle, I hope I've never made you feel anything less than equal to me."

"You never have." Charley's tone was grateful, affectionate. Something seemed to pass between them.

"You two are killing me! What happened next?" Evie slapped the table, making her silverware jump with a metallic clatter.

Charley laughed. "Patience, woman! Well I figured I was already fired so I told him I had to make a quick stop, and I took him to a grungy biker bar. One of the places I like to hang out."

Evie squealed, clapping her hands to her mouth. "Oh my god!" She spoke from under her fingers. "What I wouldn't give to have seen that!"

"Ford demanded to know what I was doing. So I told him I'd just gotten fired and that it was customary to drown your sorrows in drink at a time like that and far be it for me to break from tradition." Charley and Ford both grinned at the memory, both clearly enjoying reliving the moment.

"And then he was really pissed. He whipped out his cell phone and I knew I had about two seconds to convince him to stay. So I told him I was sorry I'd sprung it on him, but that he might actually enjoy himself if he'd come in and have just one drink with me. He didn't answer right away, but I could tell he was surprised at my invitation. He had this look on his face…"

Charley looked at Ford and in a moment Evie was restless again, feeling like she was interrupting something intimate between the two men.

"Ford looked at the building and back at me with a look on his face I'll never forget."

"Horror?" Evie guessed. "Terror? Disgust?"

Charley shook his head. "Heaven. Like that dive bar was the State Fair and he was a five year old cotton-candy junkie."

Evie sucked in her breath. "Really?"

Ford concentrated his gaze on Evie. "I'd never in my life been anywhere so seedy."

Charley's laughter boomed off the tall walls of the room. "You're welcome." He peeked sideways at Ford as he spoke, and his voice softened. "I realized then he really wanted to go in, but he was intimidated. I saw it plain as day on his face. And I'd never seen anything but confidence, charm and sexy on the face of that man. From a distance, of course."

Ford shifted, tenting his fingers back in front of his lips. "Oh please, Charley, don't spare the details," Ford said, his voice dry.

Charley put his arm on the back of Ford's chair, tilting his head to catch the other man's eyes. "It was endearing. I think it was the first time I really saw you—I mean past the you everyone else sees anyway. I liked it."

Evie knew what Charley was thinking—could see it in his eyes. *It was the first moment I fell a little bit in love with you.* She had her own tales like that about Ford.

"So I told him not to worry about a thing, that he was with me and I'd make sure he was comfortable the whole time. I promised him. And he got out of the truck. Four hours and ten shots later we stumbled back to the truck, called his driver to come get our drunk asses, and we've been inseparable ever since."

"So I take it you didn't fire him?" Evie asked.

"No. Not that day."

"You fired Charley?" Evie didn't think the story could get any better.

"I'd never had a friend like Charley," Ford said quietly. "And I was so busy with my businesses that I couldn't spend as much time with him as I wanted to, so I went in one day and fired him and then offered him a job as my driver and bodyguard so he could go everywhere with me."

Charley shook his head. "Always have to control everything. I would have taken the job. I was thrilled to take the job. You didn't need to fire me."

"But I ensured the outcome, didn't I? I like to be sure." Ford pursed his lips, his eyes lighting with the memory.

Charley stared at him. "You get excited just at the memory of manipulating me to your satisfaction. What is it with you and control?"

"It makes me tick," Ford said, his voice low, hitting the K hard and somehow making the word sound dirty. His eyes seemed to darken.

Evie watched the chemistry between the two men sizzle in the air. Ford's posture was casual, proprietary. Charley had leaned forward, his elbows on the table, eyes pinned to Ford. She remembered her promise to Charley to help bridge the gap, and after spending more time with the two of them, Evie was convinced that gap wasn't nearly as big as Charley thought it was.

She smiled slyly across the table at the two men. "Wow, you two have a real bromance going on."

"I'd take a bullet for him," Charley said, no hint of hesitation in his voice.

"Thank god I'll never have to see that," Ford said. "Driving me is not dangerous. It mainly involves a lot of waiting around and entertaining me in traffic. Something Charley's great at."

Charley looked at Evie and had a silent mental exchange with her.

He thinks he's safe. We know he's not. You tell him or I will.

Evie nodded and dropped her head, resigned. But before she could form a word Ford sat forward, excited.

"I have a surprise for you, Evie. You're going to have a lot of work to do tomorrow, sorting through all of your things from your apartment that are now littering a bay of my garage."

Evie jerked her head up. "My stuff? How do you have my stuff?"

"I sent some guys and one of my trucks over first thing this morning to collect your belongings. I didn't think it was right for you not to have them. If you don't want them, I understand, but I wanted you to have the option to decide at your leisure. I feared my rush to have you move in contributed to your decision to leave them, and if it did, I wanted to remedy that situation for you."

"One of your trucks?" Evie croaked.

Ford frowned, nodding.

"With your company's name on it?"

"Yes, Hawthorne Enterprises. Why?"

Charley and Evie locked eyes. Now she knew. "He was having the apartment watched. That's why I left the stuff in the first place."

Charley nodded, pulling a corner of his mouth back in a sneer.

Ford cleared his throat. "Would either of you care to explain what the hell you're talking about?"

Evie sighed. "Ford, there's something I need to tell you."

Evie relayed the entire story, with Charley jumping in to add details here and there while Ford listened, his face becoming more and more ashen. Evie's stomach sank and her words grew slower as she flicked her eyes to Charley. Was he seeing this reaction?

She could see he was. Charley was studying Ford's face, his brows drawn together. Finally when Evie got to the part of the story where John had threatened her with his former violent client, Ford jumped to his feet, the heavy dining room chair screeching along the floor.

"You can't be here anymore," he barked to Evie, his face hard as stone. "You have to leave immediately."

Evie's mouth dropped open, the worst-case scenario unfolding right in front of her. Cold fear crept through her. She looked from Ford to Charley, begging Charley with her eyes to *do something*.

But Charley was fixated on Ford, a mixture of outrage and confusion on his face. "Ford! You can't mean that! She's not safe out there!" He swept a muscular arm in Evie's direction. "We've got to protect her."

For a heartbeat Evie's world tilted. *We've got to protect her.* The concept was unfamiliar yet powerful. Would someone do that for her? Hope sparked a small flame in her chest.

"No." Ford's answer was emphatic. "Charley, she can't be here under these circumstances! Do you understand?" He turned to Evie, his face a mask of horror. "Why you're here… What I've asked you to do…!" He made an anguished noise, running both hands through his hair and turning to the window.

154

"Ford," Charley said gently, reaching a hand out to him, but Ford whirled toward Evie again.

"Evie, what you've agreed to do while you're here! It's not right! Not under this kind of duress. It has to be completely your free choice."

Oh. She understood. "That's what you're worried about?"

"Of course that's what I'm worried about!" His brow creased and he shoved his hands in his pockets, hunching his shoulders. "Goddamnit, Evie! I don't have to explain to you why this is wrong."

Evie couldn't keep the surprise out of her voice. "You love manipulating situations to get what you want! Why would this bother you?"

"Having a fair challenge and winning, that's fun. Having you agree to give me oral sex because you are afraid for your life is something completely different!"

Evie gasped and swiveled her eyes to Charley, who shrugged, but Ford waved his hand dismissively. "I told Charley all about it while you were changing for dinner.

"You what?" Evie felt her face blanch. "I don't want anyone to know that!"

"No." Ford barked, jabbing a finger at her. "That's shame. None of that in this house. It's insulting to my desires and I don't want you to have ugly feelings when you choose to give me what I want." He looked back and forth between them. "I decided when I chose to ask Evie here that in my own home none of us are going to feel ashamed or judged over the things we choose to do. I forbid it."

Evie shrank back, his reasoning muting her momentarily. "I just— Who else are you planning to tell?"

"No one. I was being honest when I told you I'd protect your privacy and mine, but I tell Charley everything. You'll have to accept that."

Charley had caught on to Ford's concern. "Ford, even if you think she's here because she feels trapped, you can't just kick her out."

"Now wait a minute!" Evie protested. "Everyone just hang

on." She splayed her hands in front of her, patting the air. "Calm down, both of you. I want to make something clear. I didn't take this job or —" she held her finger up at Ford and forced the words out of her mouth, " —agree to give you blowjobs because I had no other choice. I most certainly had choices." She ticked them off on her fingers. "I could have gone to the police and faced the consequences. I could have skipped the state and figured out some solution that didn't involve you. I could have just taken the job and not agreed to the oral sex. Right?"

Ford crossed his arms, looking furious. "I don't like it. I don't want to feel like you're doing it because you had no other choice. It's creepy, and quite frankly, takes all the fun out of it for me. I need you to exercise complete free will and still want to do every sordid thing I ask of you, just to please me. That's what excites me. I don't want this." He waved his hands in the air in a gesture of dismissal. "Charley's right, Evie. You can't leave when you're in danger. I wouldn't want that. You can stay and do the job, but it's strictly business between us from now on. *Traditional* business," he clarified.

"No!" The protest escaped her lips before she had time to think and she drew back just as quickly, clamping her mouth tight. It had been so easy to believe that Ford was simply so persuasive that he was seducing her into all of this behavior, but her sudden desperation to continue their activities spoke clearly. She wanted this just as much as he did.

She swung pleading eyes to Charley. *Help me.*

CHAPTER FIFTEEN

CHARLEY'S FACE MOVED from distress to amusement. "Well." Charley leaned back in his chair, stretching. His muscular body seeming completely at ease, his sunny energy as alive as ever. "So Ford, all sexual aspects of your deal are off then? With Evie?" Ford nodded stiffly. "Then I guess you won't mind if I play."

Ford and Evie stared at Charley, Evie in dawning recognition and Ford in confusion.

"Evie," Charley said, his tone light. "Do you mind coming around here please?"

"Not at all, Charley." Evie's voice was that of a coquette. She pranced around the table to stand in front of Charley, smiling broadly. "I've started some training at this 'taking orders' thing, so I'll give it my best shot. What did you have in mind?"

"I don't know, honey," he drawled. "Let's see what you've got to work with to make me feel good." He took her hand and helped twirl her around so her back was to him.

"Stop that." Ford's voice was menacing. "I mean it. Both of you."

Evie pretended not to hear, not even looking at Ford. Leaning against the table, palms flat, she pushed her ass toward Charley who was still seated. "Like this?" she asked innocently, peeking over her shoulder. "Is this what you want me to do?"

"That's a good start babe, but let's just see…" He raised the hem of Evie's short dress slowly, inching it up over her bare ass cheeks until she felt cool air on her lower back and knew her lacey thong was completely exposed. Charley sucked in his breath. "Every inch of you I see is prettier than the last." His voice was low and rumbled through her.

She felt a wave of undeniable sexual thrill at Charley's intimate inspection, and suddenly she'd gone from playing along to… What was she doing?

"Stand. Up. Evie." Ford's words were tight, through what sounded like a clenched jaw. "You two will not do this in front of me." The threat in his tone was clear.

But Ford had taken a step closer, Evie noticed, his hands fisted at his sides now instead of crossed in front of his chest.

"Do you like my panties?" she asked Charley. "Because the man who bought them for me doesn't want to see them." She sighed, bending over further. "You might as well enjoy them."

"Charley, stop this nonsense." Ford's tone was flat, as if he were trying to mask something in it. Evie glanced at him and saw that Ford's eyes were riveted to her bottom.

But Charley cupped his hands, as big as bear paws, over her buttocks and squeezed. "C'mon Ford," he breathed, and her nipples pebbled with the shiver he induced through her. "You aren't interested in instructing her, so I'll take over."

Evie stretched her neck, straining to see over her shoulder as Charley lowered his face to her bottom, kissing first one cheek, then the other, nuzzling, licking. During her day with him, she'd more than once caught herself fantasizing about him. There was a lot of him to fantasize about. And now here he was with his lips on her skin, his hot tongue swirling over her flesh, leaving what felt like a trail of sparks. She forgot to check whether Ford was watching.

"My, my. I do like these panties." Now Charley's voice was husky, and it seemed he wasn't playing anymore either. To Evie's hooded eyes, he was a man now ready for sex, and any reservations she'd had about sharing herself with Ford's friend were dissolving under the growing pressure of his skilled fingers. Charley hooked his thumbs under the sides of her thong. "I think I'd like them better, though, if they were around your ankles." He slid the underwear over her hips and down her legs to where Evie could feel them stretched between her shins, just above her high-heels.

She sucked in a breath. Her pussy was naked now, right in front of this big man she'd only met today. And she knew she was wet. Knew there'd be no hiding the engorgement of her pussy that begged for Charley's touch. This had been meant as only a tease for Ford, but she'd allowed it to get quickly out of hand. Encouraged it maybe. How much wine had she drunk?

For the space of a breath, she considered backing out, stopping Charley and letting Ford call her bluff. But Evie's traitorous mind flashed to the idea of the two breathtaking men fucking her while she was bent across the table, each of them taking turns on her from behind, the silverware on the table jangling with each thrust of the men deep into her, until they'd both had their fill of her body.

Closing her eyes, she felt grateful for the support of the table as her knees weakened. Sexual escapades this crazy were only a fantasy yesterday, but now in Ford's house they weren't just possible, they were probable. A carnal sound rose from her throat as Charley trailed his fingers tortuously slowly up the backs of her legs. When the burly man's fingers neared dangerously close to her damp pussy, she writhed her hips, attempting to direct his touch where she needed it.

"*That's it!*" Ford roared.

She felt Charley jump, jerking his hands from her, and Evie's eyes flew open as she froze in her position, bent nearly onto the table, her heart pounding.

"Charley, back away from the table please." Ford's voice had shifted instantly to emotionless, in charge.

Without hesitation, Charley pushed his chair back so far Evie heard it thump against the wall.

"Stand up and turn around, Evangeline." Ford was under control again, buzzing with force. Not knowing if she should pull her panties up or take them the rest of the way off—and afraid to do either—she turned around, shuffling her feet so the black lace remained stretched between her ankles. Her skin prickled with anticipation. Her silky dress dropped back down over her hips, covering her nakedness. Although she wanted to see what Charley was thinking, knowing she could read him so easily, Evie didn't take her eyes from Ford's.

On some instinctual level, her mind perceived Ford as dangerous, but that self-preservation part of her lost out to the hedonistic part of her that wanted the orgasms she'd only ever experienced from Ford.

The situation had shifted, and Evie was familiar with this dynamic. This was the place where Ford felt comfortable because no one else did. Only he knew what was going to happen. What he was going to ask them to do. This was Ford's wheelhouse—his *modus operandi*—and it felt as disconcerting as it was arousing.

Lust, sharpened to a point by discomfort.

Ford's specialty. Evie's new obsession.

The enigmatic billionaire looked back and forth between the two schemers and Evie seized the moment to peek at Charley. He looked far more relaxed than she felt, though he was gripping the arms of his chair as if he feared someone might press an eject button. She lingered on his frame for only a moment, but noted the tense shoulders, glinting eyes, expanding chest. She dropped her eyes to his lap and felt her eyes widen. Jerking her focus back to Ford's face, she groaned inwardly. He'd witnessed her look and her reaction. Her face grew hot.

With a sexy curl of a smile, Ford followed where her eyes had alighted and she saw Ford react too. His chest broadened as he sucked in a deep breath. He clenched and unclenched his fists once.

Charley's cock was fully erect with the thick head actually poking out the top of his low-cut jeans, his thin tee-shirt dropped behind it and stretched over his taut belly.

"Evie." Ford said her name in his perfect host's tone before he even turned his eyes from Charley. "Our guest seems unsatisfied with dessert." Ford looked back at Charley again, his stare lingering low. "From the look of it, he wants something more."

And suddenly Ford was in front of Evie, his hands wrapped into the hem of her dress. "Arms up." She turned wide eyes from Ford to Charley and back. The look on Charley's face was no help. It was clear—he wanted what Ford was offering.

But Ford? The look on Ford's face was pure Christmas

morning.

"Uh, Mr. Hawthorne," Evie mumbled, shifting on the balls of her feet. She had no idea what he was going to ask her to do, either to Charley, or in front of him, and she wasn't sure if she could do it.

Ford reached around and under Evie's dress in one quick swoop of his toned arm and smacked one of her butt cheeks hard. She yelped. Cupping his hand to her stinging skin, he pulled her roughly against him. She could feel his erection, bossy and unyielding between them, driving the situation, fueling her lust as much as his.

Choking on a breath, she tried to calm her erratic respiration enough to ask, "What are you saying?"

Ford spoke against her temple as if it was a private conversation. She could feel his heartbeat as he pressed against her, or maybe it was her own—she couldn't tell. "I'm saying that Charley is our guest and we owe him something sweet after dinner." He pulled back and looked down at her eyes, his green ones practically lit like lanterns. With his other hand he pressed his index finger over her lips. "And what you can do with your mouth, my Evangeline, is damned sweet."

"I can't!" she squeaked, shaking her head and pulling away from him. "That's not what—we were just trying to make a point!" She threw a desperate glance toward Charley. "We were trying to get you to change your mind, that's all!" Two men? It was only her first night at Ford's home and already things were escalating out of control. She felt panic start to take hold.

"Ford, really, it's okay. I'll just go." Charley stood up, looking pale.

"No. You started this." Ford pointed a stiff arm at Charley before swiveling his head back to Evie. "Both of you did. And it worked. I'm excited about the idea." Evie felt Ford's cock twitch between them. "I want to see the two of you finish what I saw starting there. I don't think either of you were only playing." He looked back and forth between them, his eyes settling on Charley. "I want to watch you with her," he said slowly. Ford's low voice had an effect like a vibrator on her clit. Closing the space between her feet, she pressed her thighs together against the excitement multiplying there.

Charley glanced back and forth from Ford to Evie, looking poised to make a run for it. "Evie?" Charley asked, his brow knitted with concern.

"Charley, wait in the other room for us. I want to speak to Evangeline privately. Take our wineglasses with you, please."

Charley did as Ford asked, not making eye contact again with Evie. Her stomach knotted, sure that she'd angered Ford with her "questioning" of his orders and was about to get the "don't defy me or I will make you leave" lecture.

But when Charley left, Ford cradled Evie's face in his large hands, his touch startlingly gentle, his eyes deep, green pools. "I want to remind you of your safe word, love." He raised his eyebrows and she nodded. "Evie, you must never hesitate to use it, and as soon as you do, everything stops immediately. You understand that, don't you?" She nodded again, not trusting her own voice, her chest feeling too full in response to his concern.

He wasn't going to make her leave. He still wanted her, even after what she'd hidden from him, even after she'd brought trouble into his home, putting them all in danger. He was worried about her.

He took his time, searching her eyes, but Evie knew all he'd find there was lust and affection and the desire to please him. She had avoided trying to analyze it, but she knew it was true nonetheless. "Never resist using your safe word because you think I might get angry. It's set up strictly for your protection, to keep you from getting hurt or going to a place you really don't want to go. Do you understand?"

Evie nodded again, placing her hands on Ford's elbows, realizing the two were practically in an embrace. "Good." Ford's voice was lovely, soft. "Because you do something to me I don't understand. I've never felt it. But I seem to want more and more of you. I want to keep you."

Jellybeans, Evie thought, mentally scrambling to shove away the sudden feelings that welled in her. She was tough and could handle most any pain or stretching of her boundaries that Ford wanted to throw at her, but she didn't know if she could handle the pain that would come from falling in love with a man like him. He would never love her back. She was convinced he didn't know how. So *jellybeans* she repeated in her head and resisted showing any reaction to his statement. The safe word was for her protection, after all.

"You like Charley, don't you?" She nodded. "And you find him attractive?" Ford searched her eyes, seeming to look for the truth there rather than believe her answer.

"Yes," she whispered.

Ford smiled. "How could you not?"

Evie kept her lips still. Did Ford even recognize what he was feeling toward the other man?

"Listen, I'm not oblivious to the obvious concerns here, so I want to put your mind at ease. Charley is clean, as am I. I have billions of dollars riding on my ability to run my companies. I have always used protection and in spite of that I still have my health status tested regularly. You could say I'm a bit obsessed with my longevity." Ford grinned. "And Charley comes with me, so I know we're both clean. I wouldn't let him near you if I thought you weren't completely safe." Ford ducked his head to catch her eyes, driving home the sincerity of his words. "Okay? Do you feel comfortable about that?"

"Yes, thank you for telling me that. I'm clean too."

"You've been tested? Recently?"

She nodded. "When I had the trouble with John, especially knowing he was a drug user, I had every test known to man. And I got retested after six months to be sure. Clean." She met his eyes and looked away again. "And I'm on the pill. I mean, just so you know." She rushed the words out of her mouth. Why had she told him that? Sex wasn't even part of their arrangement.

"Good. Good," Ford breathed. "So now that I've hopefully eased your mind—" Ford dropped his hands to her shoulders, squeezing. "Ease what's concerning mine. You are here of your own free will? You don't feel cornered?"

"No!" Evie implored. "In fact this is the only place in the last six months where I've actually felt safe. Free." Ford narrowed his eyes, considering her. "I promise." Evie squeezed her fingers into his arms.

"I'm glad you feel comfortable here, but John is lucky Charley and I don't go out tonight and find him." Ford looked toward the window. "Psychotic fuck," he mumbled. "We'll discuss him, and why you didn't feel comfortable confiding in me, soon." His tone carried a whisper of threat and Evie shivered.

Ford smoothed the hair off Evie's cheek, tucking it behind her ear. Then he pinched her earlobe, pulling down on it, causing an immediate twinge between her legs. "No earrings," he murmured.

She felt herself blush. "I only have one pair and they didn't go with this. Well actually," she looked up at him, "now I have some in the garage, if I can figure out where your guys packed them." She smiled, a full-faced, genuine smile. "Thank you for getting my things. I don't have much, but I do like the things I have."

He released her ear and smoothed his thumb across her bottom lip, a gesture that always made her weak. "Of course, love. I'm just sorry I tipped off your secret hideaway."

"S'okay. Boone will protect me. He loves me," Evie teased.

"He's not the only one," Ford started and Evie's heart leapt to her throat, causing her a moment of light-headedness. "Charley and I will also protect you."

"Thanks. That's nice." Evie tried to keep her smile from looking sad. For the space of a breath, she'd felt the kind of joy that came only when someone told you they loved you. Someone you wanted to hear it from. The realization she'd misunderstood him stomped on her chest. Evie wasn't sure she'd ever heard the words "I love you" from someone who truly meant them. And she wanted to. Just once.

"Well, love, now that we have all of those things cleared up," Ford said, snapping suddenly back to his uber-confident self. "Let's not leave our guest waiting." He knelt in front of her, lifting first one foot, then the other, to free her thong and tossed it on the dining room table. Clamping his hand firmly over hers, he led her from the room, his long strides causing her to scramble in her heels to keep up. "I'm glad we had a talk about your safe word," he said over his shoulder. "Because I'm about to take you way outside your comfort zone. Let's see what you can do." The last part was nearly a mirror of the language he'd used about his sports cars. She'd been right—he'd been referring to her.

She gulped for air, her heart pounding as though she'd just run stadium stairs. Thankfully he was pulling her along, because after that statement she wasn't sure she could have voluntarily made her legs move toward the room where the other man was waiting for them.

Charley was staring out the back wall of windows into blackness, his hands in his back pockets, his posture restless. He turned as they entered, his eyes going straight to Evie's. Raising his eyebrows in a silent question, she knew exactly what he wanted to know.

You okay?

She nodded, raising her own eyebrows in a look of anxious anticipation.

Ford led her to the tufted ottoman. "Take off your dress."

"But I'm not wearing a bra." Her voice wavered with embarrassment at the idea of undressing in front of the two men.

Ford settled onto the couch in front of her and patted the seat next to him for Charley.

"Of course you're not, because I didn't give you one to wear. Now don't argue, love. You teased our Charley earlier with your backside and there's no teasing in this house. In this house we don't toy, we go all the way." He grinned wickedly at her. "House rules. Now, Evangeline, I've asked nicely. Don't make me ask again. Remove your dress or I'll remove it for you. We want to look at your tits."

Her eyes flew to Charley's. She didn't even know this man. Not really.

Charley shrugged, looking relaxed now and in higher spirits. "He's right. I really do want to see your tits, Evie." He grinned, his wide mouth promising her all the boisterous affection she's seen from him for most of the day. His brown eyes were familiar and understanding, though now lit with a smoldering flame.

They were in this together. She remembered her promise to try and bridge the sexual gap between the two men.

She looked back and forth between them. They were hands-down the two sexiest, hottest men she'd ever met in her life. Throwing a glance to the vast window and beyond, into the black of the night sky, she was reminded that she was separated, quite literally, from the rest of the world by Ford's fortress of a home and the high stone walls beyond that. Anything she did in this extremely private house would remain among the three of them. She could do everything. Explore every fantasy she'd ever had. And she knew the two men would enthusiastically participate, giving her as much as she gave them. And it would be just the three of them, enjoying each other.

She smiled toward the great darkness outside the windows of the room. *Fuck you, John,* she thought. *You want to see a whore? Watch this.*

Reaching trembling fingers to the hem of her dress, she pulled it slowly over her head, wiggling her naked body out of the fitted fabric and letting the silky sheath puddle to the floor. Dropping her shoulders back, she felt a rush of empowerment, of pride. This was her life, dammit, and she was going to live it without apologies. Ford and Charley seemed to epitomize that idea, and she could learn from them.

Neither Ford nor Charley had ever seen her naked breasts, and from the looks on their faces, they seemed happy for the introduction. Her nipples elongated and hardened in the cool air and she had an urge to touch them for the two men, pinch them, but she didn't.

"Lovely," Ford murmured.

"God*damn,*" Charley sighed.

Evie beamed.

Ford looked at Charley. "We'd better get undressed if we intend to enjoy this." The men stripped. Naked. Both of them.

The scene was riveting and Evie reminded herself to study it, remember it. Charley's eyes followed Ford as he undressed, and Ford's attention was also frequently on the muscular, naked body Charley was revealing. Evie's pussy tingled watching the two men. There was something immensely hot about two big men eying each other up for sex. She had no doubt that's exactly what they were doing, whether both of them even realized it or not.

The men settled back on the couch, very close to each other, their bare arms and legs touching along their lengths. Charley seemed to be having a hard time keeping his eyes off Ford's dick. Their mutual excitement from earlier in the dining room had waned, and they were both nearly soft now. Their thick cocks lay like relaxed muscles over their powerful thighs, waiting for her services.

"Make us hard, please, Evie. Use your mouth."

She nearly squirmed where she stood. This was a million times more erotic than she could have imagined. Ford was going to make her pleasure him and his friend at the same time. They were both going to use her until they'd had their fill of her. They were both going to come in her mouth and she was going to lick up every drop.

The wantonness of the idea made her throat tight. It was so wrong and somehow that's what made it feel so good to her. She couldn't ever remember being so anxious and yet so sexually stimulated at the same time. Her heart was fluttering in her chest in an unfamiliar staccato and she was so wet she wondered about needing a towel.

This was crazy.

This was exactly what she needed.

John had called today and scared her again, and nothing was going to take her mind off that better than Ford and Charley's naked, hard bodies. Losing herself in sex with these men. She needed the blissful peace that she'd discovered came hand-in-hand with letting Ford be in charge and serving his sexual demands — and she needed it today more than ever.

Making herself move, she bent in front of Ford and reached for his cock but he stopped her. "Our guest first, love."

"Of course," she whispered and turned to Charley. He spread his legs so she could step between them and she knelt shakily, placing her hands on his thighs. They locked eyes — his warm ones capturing and holding hers. He seemed to be telling her not to worry, they'd do this together. He put his hands over hers and squeezed, nodding. *You can do this,* he was telling her. It was the shot of bravery she needed to touch him.

She swept her eyes slowly down his mountain of a body, reaching out and running her fingertips over his chest and along the trail of hair that grew in the defined split at the bottom of his six-pack abs. The neatly-trimmed trail of hair made a beeline to his cock.

Forcing her hand to keep moving in spite of her nerves, she traced the hard topography of his muscles under his tanned skin until her palm brushed against his penis. It seemed to jump in her hand, asking to be gripped.

Ford was big, but she'd never seen anything like Charley. As he grew harder, she pursed her lips, let her held breath escape.

"Our Charley's got a really big cock," Ford said, his voice growing husky. "I don't imagine you can swallow it, but I'm going to see that Charley makes you try."

Evie flicked her eyes to Ford, her skin feeling hot with desire for him. Could he see what he did to her? Talking like that?

Here we go, she thought. *A new man. A new cock.* It wasn't like it had happened that often.

She wrapped her hand around the broad head of him. A moan escaped his lips and he shuddered. She bent in, sucking him into her mouth. Even semi-soft, she couldn't take him all. She'd need to practice to master a cock like his. She bobbed up and down, coaxing his dick to its full glorious length as he groaned. Popping her mouth off him, she locked eyes with him and smiled. They seemed to enjoy each other in a way she'd never felt with a lover. So easy. So loving.

Now it was Ford's turn. She kept a hand wrapped around Charley's erection as she moved in front of her boss. She fisted Charley, stroking him lightly as she caught the tip of Ford's already hard cock in her mouth. She kept her eyes locked to Ford's as she kissed the head of his dick. The corners of her mouth turned up at the look on his face. He was always so in control, but at moments like these, when he had that look on his face—a look of wonder and almost innocence, as odd as that sounded—it was then she knew she had the upper hand at that tic of time. She was blowing his mind, and she loved it. It brought a high she knew she'd never get enough of.

Closing her eyes, she sucked Ford as deeply as she could,

168

jamming him against the back of her mouth like she knew he wanted before relaxing enough to take him fully into her throat. "Goddamn," Charley breathed in response to her swallowing Ford's entire length, his own dick jumping in her hand. She came up for air and bobbed on Ford's cock twice before releasing him and turning her attention back to Charley. But this time Charley leaned forward, gently placing his hands on her sides. "I want to touch you." His voice was lush in its deep manliness. Without waiting for an answer, he moved his hand to trace a fingernail along the underside of her right breast, causing her breath to hitch. "Can I? Can I touch you?"

Charley was a different sort of creature than Ford. Ford would not have asked permission, he would have demanded she allow him. She liked it both ways and decided she was a lucky girl to be able to have both types of men in her bed, so to speak. How many women get that opportunity?

"Yes," she breathed. There had been a point in the day where she'd stopped being in conflict with Charley and had almost immediately begun imagining him touching her. He had a wide mouth and full, soft-looking lips, and she wanted him to kiss her while his big paws of hands cupped her breasts and teased her nipples.

He wrapped one strong arm around her waist and pulled her up onto his knee, forcing her to let go of Ford. "Ford," Charley's lips were inches from her elongated nipple. "This okay?"

"Of course." Ford's voice was gravelly, as if he'd been lost in the scene and wasn't prepared to speak. "She's as much yours as she is mine, Charley."

And though this had never been discussed, Evie liked the sound of it very much. Not only was Charley a great guy, fun and sexy, but whatever part of Evie's brain that controlled her sexual pleasure felt like it nearly shorted out at capacity under the thought of her *belonging* to these two men, there to satisfy their needs whenever the mood struck. Some part of herself she hadn't known existed wanted them to lay claim to her — own her.

Charley put his free hand on her shoulder and pushed back, tilting her body toward Ford and trapping her in her exposed position, her nipples straining for attention from the two men.

Two men. She'd never done this before. Never thought she would.

Charley covered the hard, pink tip of her right breast with his mouth, sucking and flicking it with his tongue before touching his teeth to it. Evie groaned. In all of the pleasurable escapades Ford had engaged her in lately, he hadn't yet touched her nipples, and she'd been dying for it. She squeezed her hand around Charley's hard cock, communicating her appreciation.

She tried not to let go completely — she wanted to remember this moment because it was so extraordinary. She had one man's unfamiliar mouth on her breasts, the bare scruff on his face scraping lightly against her sensitive skin, and another man watching, waiting for his turn with her.

All she could hear was her own panting and Charley's heavy breathing in between sucks on her nipples. He took his time — sucking, nipping, flicking — moving up to nuzzle her neck and then back down. She let her head fall back and relished what the man was doing to her. Opening her eyes, she sought Ford and found him, his dazzling eyes locked to hers, a look of wonder and excitement on his face. His hand was on his own hard cock, and he was stroking it as he watched Charley devour her tits while she in turn massaged his friend's hefty erection.

Holy shit, it was hot.

"God," she exclaimed, feeling ready to burst at the intensity of the pleasure. She looked greedily at Ford's cock and then back to his eyes. She needed something more, feeling desperate to come like this, with two men. Ford seemed to understand her thinking.

"Charley," he growled. "She's ready for you. Taste her and make her come. I want to watch."

Charley didn't hesitate. He hauled Evie off his lap and tossed her back onto the oversized ottoman as if she was on fire and he was going to smother the flames with his mouth. And that's exactly what it felt like to Evie. She whimpered at the rough handling, feeling as desperate for Charley as he was for her.

Her state of arousal was like nothing she'd ever felt. She was so hungry for orgasm that she wondered if two men were even enough for her this night. Her sexual satisfaction felt like an endless pit that had never come close to being filled, and now she was finally getting a taste of how it might be done.

There was no doubt in her mind — she wanted *fucked.* Fucked by both of them. Two men, ravishing her, demanding more and more from her sweat-slicked body until they were all three exhausted and satisfied.

Charley knelt by the ottoman and wrapped his hands around her ankles, forcing her legs wide. He kissed at her knee and then up the inside of her leg, his tongue setting her sensitive skin ablaze.

There's something about the skin on the inside of your upper thigh — it's a place where a tongue or bare hand only ever is if sex is imminent, oral or otherwise, making that skin extra-sensitive in anticipation.

Charley kissed all the way up, his heavy breathing telegraphing his excitement. He closed his mouth over her entire pussy and she gasped unabashedly as he massaged his tongue against her. Once her moans started, they kept coming, over and over.

"Make her come, Charley." Ford commanded, his voice that of a master. "I want our Evie nice and relaxed when we take turns fucking her mouth." At those raunchy words, Evie called out as a jolt of pleasure thrust through her sex. Charley licked her like he had endless energy to do so, his tongue talented and unyielding, his rhythm expert.

Jumping to his feet, Ford crawled onto the ottoman and swung a leg over Evie's chest, straddling her on his knees, kneeling over her, facing her, his hard body coiled above her. Leaning forward, he braced one hand on the ottoman over her head and grasped his dick with his other hand, pushing it against her lips. "I'm not going to wait for Charley to finish," Ford's voice was tight. "Open your mouth for me."

Evie did as he said and Ford glided his erection between her lips. He hissed in air and stilled while Evie swirled her tongue around the head of him, tasting his pre-cum. He must have enjoyed watching her and Charley together.

Slowly, Ford began to move in and out of her mouth. It was like torture for her, trying to concentrate on both acts at the same time. Charley was coaxing her toward the edge of orgasm while she tried not to neglect Ford's cock.

Keeping her eyes on Ford, she could see he was watching over his shoulder as Charley fucked her with his tongue. Without taking his eyes from Charley, Ford let go of his cock and slid his hand under Evie's head, knotting his fingers into the back of her hair in the dominant way he preferred. Then it felt like he was making her suck him, and she loved how incredibly naughty it felt.

Charley flexed his tongue, directing it up to concentrate on her clit. He pulsated quick strokes against her nub over and over, making her writhe under Ford's body, pure pleasure gripping her as she moaned on Ford's cock.

Charley seemed eager to please her. He pushed two fingers into her pussy and moved them in and out slowly as he nuzzled her, building her closer and closer to ecstasy. He stopped and she heard him ask Ford in a hoarse whisper, "Can I put my fingers in her ass?"

Evie's eyes widened as she pleaded silently with Ford, her mouth full of his erection. Charley had clearly said fingers—plural—and she didn't know if she could do that. Ford picked up on her small panic. "Evie, love." He swept his thumb over her cheek, not slowing the rhythm of his hips as he pressed his cock against the back of her throat. "You can do this. Your ass is very pleasurable with the right preparation.

"Charley, behind the bar there's a drawer with lubricant in it. Fetch it, please, and you're welcome to finger her ass." Ford turned his attention back to Evie and continued shoving himself slowly in and out of her mouth while he explained. "Being stimulated in your ass with a finger, allowing yourself to be stretched, will help in your training, Evie. You must learn to take a man in your ass. I won't be denied any part of your body that pleases me." Ford's voice dropped an octave as that familiar demanding tone crept in. "And I will have your ass as part of this arrangement. That point is non-negotiable."

She closed her eyes and groaned in a mix of pleasure and fear—Ford's signature cocktail. Charley abandoned orally pleasuring her and went in search of lubrication. He was back in an instant, and he came around the side of the ottoman to where Evie could see him and stood watching as Ford fucked her mouth with precise control. Fords jaw clenched and the muscles in his shoulders bunched and relaxed. He seemed to enjoy Charley watching.

"Charley, I'm getting close." Ford's voice was tight. "Have your fingers in her ass when she comes. I want her to associate anal stimulation with orgasm." Evie made a noise of protest around Ford's cock and Ford chuckled, looking down at her. "My Evie, I will have something in your ass every time you come if that's what it takes to make you crave a cock in there so much when you orgasm that you beg me for it." Evie groaned, closing her eyes against the thought.

"Orgasm, fingers in her ass. Yes, sir," Charley drawled.

Evie slurped against Ford's erection, her jaw getting sore from her mouth being constantly filled with cock. Ford finally pulled his erection out, allowing her a small break from his taking his pleasure from her. "If your mouth is full and you want to use your safe word, I want you to grab my arm and squeeze hard. I'll be right here with you. Do you understand?"

"Yes." Evie tried to look brave, in spite of her heart trying to hammer out of her chest.

Ford gave her a look of pure adoration, smoothing his thumb over her bottom lip as he peered down at her underneath him. Then he fed her his cock again with a groan, whispering, "Now suck me."

Charley had his tongue back on her in seconds, and she jumped, squealing around Ford's dick when Charley's broad finger pressed against the pucker of her asshole.

"Shh." Charley pulled his mouth off her to talk her through it, his voice soothing. "It's just one finger and I'm going to make sure you're completely slick. It's gonna slide right in. I won't hurt you. I promise."

She turned what she knew were anxious eyes up at Ford and he stared down at her, his eyes softening. He paused his invading of her mouth long enough to whisper, "You're going to enjoy this. I know you are."

The pressure against her back hole increased as Charley pressed his finger into her. His lips back on her sex, he sucked her clit between his teeth as he sank a digit into her backside. His mouth was a heavenly distraction, and the contrast of pleasure and discomfort somehow only served to spike her arousal even higher.

She whimpered. It felt so forbidden and yet so delicious. Soon she realized she was pressing back against Charley's thrusts into her ass, wanting a taste of what it would be like to actually get fucked in that place. It felt good.

"Ford, she's taking this like she wants more."

Ford narrowed his eyes down at Evie and she felt wild beneath him. The man she'd lusted over for so long was pressing his slick cock against the back of her throat while another man, whom she newly lusted over, fingered her ass. And she couldn't believe how good all of this wanton sex made her feel. She was a carnal goddess.

"One more finger Charley, but gently," Ford warned.

Evie's heart pounded at a dizzying rate as she waited for the extra pressure of Charley's second finger. As soon as she felt it, she jumped again, and Ford shoved his cock hard into her mouth, catching her off-guard. She choked and he pulled back.

"You're okay, love," he soothed. "Just focus on my hard dick in your mouth and on the pleasure Charley's giving you, and soon you're going to have an orgasm different from any you've ever had. No orgasm is as good as one borne from pleasure *and* pain."

She gasped at the intense feelings, thinking there was no way Charley was going to get that second, big finger into her. Everything about Charley was big. Fruitlessly she tried to concentrate on sucking Ford off during the ordeal—trying to make him come—but she couldn't keep her mind on the task.

"Concentrate on my cock, love," Ford said patiently. "Don't forget you're here for my enjoyment. You're going to come only because I'm allowing it."

Charley flicked her clit as he twisted his fingers gently against her bottom entrance, not letting up on his efforts to breach her. It didn't hurt so much as it just felt impossible—so much pressure. She called upon her kung fu training, nearly laughing as she did it. Never would she have guessed she'd use it for this. She settled her straining body, relaxing, believing she could do it—when suddenly her barrier muscle yielded to Charley and his digits slid in deeply.

"Oh!" she cried, her words muffled around Ford's dick in her mouth. "Mmm!" She squirmed under Ford and he held her face more firmly against him, not releasing her from what he wanted from her, no matter what she was feeling. She pressed her hips up, actually trying to draw Charley deeper into her ass.

The feeling was the most intensely erotic thing she'd ever experienced. Reaching her hands under Fords kneeling legs, she tangled her fingers into Charley's shaggy hair, clutching Charley's head between her thighs much like Ford was holding her face against his cock. She pressed Charley to her, ensuring she didn't miss one perfect ministration of his tongue while he finger-fucked her ass.

And then finally, screaming in deliverance, she came, her desperate cries muffled by the hard-on still filling her mouth. Her orgasm seemed to go on and on, convulsing through her, drawing joyous relief from the most primal parts inside her.

When her shuddering was done, Ford climbed off her without finishing himself, and stood next to the ottoman, grinning at her.

"Oh my god!" She struggled for any coherent word as Charley pulled his fingers out of her. "What did you do to me? That was incredible!" She swiped her hand across her forehead in disbelief. "That was the best. The best!"

Ford beamed. "Stimulation balanced with distraction. Add in a bit of pain and you might find a masterpiece of sexual satisfaction."

"So you were distracting me with your dick in my mouth? Is that what you call that?" Evie grinned back at Ford as he helped her to a sitting position.

He licked his lips, heat glowing in his green eyes. "I was certainly enjoying it, but I can honestly say, I was doing it for you." He pursed his lips, looking sinfully handsome. She shook her head at him and turned to Charley.

"Really," Evie touched Charley's arm. He was still kneeling next to the ottoman, looking at her shyly. "That was incredible." His smile was genuine and proud.

"No more incredible than what you're about to do to us," Ford growled, fisting his hand in her hair again and reminding her of the obvious fact that she had two big, naked men in front of her whose hard cocks were now waiting on her attention.

She'd had an incredible orgasm and she was ready for more,

and staring at Ford and Charley, she knew she was about to get all she could handle. But could she get Ford to allow Charley to touch him? She didn't know, but she'd promised Charley, and she was going to try.

*****

~DEEPER~

CHAPTER SIXTEEN

*E*VIE LOOKED BACK and forth between the two men, both sinfully handsome…both naked. Things had gotten a little crazy after dinner. Were they ready for things to get a little crazier? Particularly, was *Ford* ready?

Ford prided himself in pushing Evie past her comfort zone. Maybe it was time for her to give him a taste of his own medicine.

Ford stood in front of Evie, and from her position seated on the ottoman, Evie's face was in line with Ford's erection. Charley knelt on the floor next to her. She caught Charley's eye and looked meaningfully at Ford's cock. So close to the man. Right in front of his face. She saw Charley's chest expand as he breathed in deeply, eyes locked to Ford's naked body.

She steeled herself. Time to help her new friend.

Reaching out, she grasped Ford's hard shaft with one hand and pulled down on his balls with the other. He sighed. Stroking, she watched Charley's eyes follow her hand along Ford's dusky skin, his hardness so ready for release. She looked up at Ford and noted his eyes were on Charley kneeling in front of him. This was the moment.

"Ford, I know you like what I can do with my mouth, but you'd be surprised what Charley can do." She kept her voice soft, soothing. "His tongue is so strong." She felt Ford's cock twitch in her hand and knew he was turned on by the idea. She was too.

She pressed further. "You should let him show you."

Charley sat forward, his eyes pinned up at Ford's. Ford didn't agree, but he didn't refuse either. Evie continued stroking him and nodded to Charley in encouragement. Slowly, the other man tilted forward until his full, soft lips were inches from the engorged head of Ford's erection.

Evie felt Ford grow even harder under her palm and saw a bead of pre-cum glisten on the end of his dick. She tugged Ford's shaft gently forward, toward Charley's waiting mouth, and found Ford didn't need any more encouragement than that. Without breaking eye contact with his friend, Ford wrapped a hand lovingly around the back of Charley's tousled head and allowed Evie to guide him into his best friend's mouth.

Charley made a noise between a whimper and a sigh and covered the hand Evie still had wrapped around the base of Ford's cock with his own, peeling her fingers away from the cock he craved, as if he needed his mouth on every inch of it. Charley held her hand in his, squeezing as he took Ford fully into his mouth. Evie felt him trembling, and he gripped her like he was drowning and she was his lifeline.

Ford reached for the arm of the couch, suddenly unsteady, as Charley flexed his jaw, sucking Ford hard. "Fuck, Charley." Ford's voice sounded confused, astonished.

Ford collapsed onto the couch and Charley moved with him, never releasing the dick he'd wanted for so long from his mouth. He finally pulled off Ford's erection with a pop, immediately lifting the other man's balls with his free hand and drawing them both into his mouth at the same time, burying his head in Ford's lap. Ford closed his eyes and sucked in a deep breath before Charley gave his best friend's sac a break and returned to Ford's hard-on, engulfing it again in his eager mouth.

Ford lifted his hands out of Charley's hair and allowed them to hover in the air above the man's bobbing head as if he was at a loss for what to do. "Charley. Goddamn," he breathed, amazement ringing in his voice.

Charley paused long enough to chuckle, the sound reflecting pure joy. "You've never been sucked off by a man before, have you?"

Ford shook his head, his eyes wide. Charley looked at Evie. "Evie, I think we rendered Ford speechless." The look on Charley's face made Evie's heart bound. She'd helped her new friend get what he wanted most.

"Don't you stop." Ford practically choked the words out, as shaken as Evie had ever seen him. Charley grasped Ford's hardness in his large hand and squeezed, stroking the man's dick like only another man would know how. Ford's fiery eyes were locked to Charley and he whispered urgently, "Can I come in your mouth? Will you swallow it?"

"God, yes. I can't wait to swallow you." Charley's voice was hoarse. "As much as you can give me."

Ford closed his eyes and groaned, tangling his fingers into Charley's hair again, pulling him back onto his cock, guiding him.

"Evie," Ford grunted. "Take care of Charley. I'm not going to last."

Charley, who was still holding Evie's hand, pulled her fist between his legs. He took his mouth off Ford long enough to instruct her. "Just wrap your hand tightly around me and let me do the work. I won't need much."

She nodded, doing as he'd explained, happy to continue watching the two men. The sight of the naked men, both corded with muscles—one heart-stoppingly handsome and the other ruggedly sexy—wrapped against each other in a sexual embrace was shockingly arousing.

She watched Charley's jaw flex as he sucked deeper and deeper on Ford's erection, the scruff on Charley's face a tactile contrast to Ford's clean-shaven balls. Ford's hips came off the couch to meet Charley's mouth, a look of near anguish on Ford's refined features as he kept his eyes screwed tightly shut, as if he was straining to memorize every stroke of his first blowjob from another man.

Her hand could barely wrap completely around Charley's large cock, but Evie didn't let go, knowing he was counting on her to help him finish with Ford. Charley had given her a kind of orgasm she didn't think was possible, and she was going to do her best to make this just as good for him.

Charley thrust into her hand as he began making greedy, virile noises in his throat. The look on Ford's face gave Evie no doubt he was close to coming.

Ford grunted, letting go of Charley's head and digging his fingers into the man's shoulders, pulling him nearly into his lap, as if he couldn't get him close enough.

"Going to come." Ford words were faltering. "In your mouth. Suck my cock, Charley. Swallow my cum."

Ford threw his head back and shouted an incoherent word. Every muscle in his body stood out in relief as his orgasm stripped him of his graciousness and left him savage, a beast sating his basest desires in his masculine friend's willing mouth.

Charley's throat worked and Evie knew he was relishing Ford's hot cum for the first time, drinking it like it was nectar from the gods. Charley thrust into Evie's hand three more long, deliberate strokes. She could see the man's hard muscles working in his buttocks—clenching, releasing, like a machine—as he rocked forward and back. She knew that must be what he looked like when he was fucking. He'd look like that if he was draped over Ford, fucking *him*. The thought made her lightheaded.

Charley paused his movements, snapping her back to the moment, and then his body seemed to turn fluid, and he was coming, shooting a white, hot mess onto the front of Ford's couch. Ford grunted, his stomach muscles clenching like a steel cage. Evie saw Charley's throat still working as he groaned into Ford's lap, a primal sound of a conquest hard-won rising from his chest as he swallowed the last of Ford's seed. Charley shuddered as his own cock spent, each wave of bliss seeming to grip him and release. Grip and release.

The way Charley cradled Ford's thighs when it was over, lapping at every drop of spunk he could coax from the man might have looked like love, but to Evie it was even more epic. Like two titans after a battle of lightning and hurricane in which both had finally surrendered to the other and collapsed to the earth, wound forever in each other's arms.

Evie unwrapped her hand from around Charley's now-sloppy cock, pulling slowly away from the two men. The only sound in the big room was their labored breathing. It had been the most passionate thing she'd ever witnessed, and she realized she was shaking. She saw Ford's eyes open and flutter down to Charley's shaggy head in his lap. Saw his body stiffen ever so slightly, and alarm bells blared in Evie's head.

He's going to panic.

Evie kicked off her shoes and crawled onto the couch, squeezing Charley's shoulder and wiggling in between him and Ford, her breasts pressing against Ford's bare chest. She laced her arms around Ford's neck, signaling with her eyes for Charley to pull himself up next to her. His eyes flicked to Ford, and he too seemed to have sensed the change, because Evie recognized the pain she saw flash across his face. The pain of questioning whether you are enough to be loved. She was too familiar with the feeling.

But Charley *was* enough. He was plenty. More than anyone would need. And even if she had to do it without Ford's help, she'd somehow make Charley believe that. Charley tucked himself next to her, curling his beefy naked body onto the couch, snuggling against her as if she was all he had. He rubbed her bare back and kissed tenderly down her spine, and Evie wondered if he was putting on the show he knew he should—the show that said what he and Ford had just done was for Evie, *because* of Evie, because she'd asked for it. Not because it was what Ford or Charley wanted.

Evie hated that Charley had to pretend what had just happened wasn't perfect and complete without her. Charley lowered his forehead against her bare back and pressed his face to her, and Evie felt his eyes wet. Her chest ached for him and a question flickered through her head—was she so moved because she felt such a connection to Charley, her new friend, or because she understood what he felt for Ford and how much that kind of hopelessness about being loved by him hurt?

She wasn't going to think about that right now. Shoving all her thoughts aside, she concentrated instead on the new and amazing feeling of being sandwiched between two gorgeous, naked men, deciding she could definitely get used to this.

Ford relaxed under her feminine touch, and she moved her hand to his chest, caressing his muscles and just being there with the men. Breathing against Ford, under Charley. How had she gotten where she was? Between these two complete opposites—these complicated and devastatingly desirable men—hiding from a madman and living the life of an unabashed sexual plaything-for-hire in the mansion of a billionaire?

An eventful couple of days, to say the least.

Evie yawned, feeling completely spent and Ford stirred beneath her. "Let's go, love. You've had quite a busy first day. Off you go to bed."

Charley peeled himself off her, reaching for his tee shirt and jeans. No underwear, Evie noticed, smiling. That sounded like Charley — free spirit, free-balling.

"Thank you for dinner, Ford. It was nice spending time with both of you," Evie said as she collected her clothes, tugging her dress back over her head.

"Mr. Hawthorne," Ford corrected.

"Huh?" She looked at him, her head feeling fuzzy from exhaustion and wine.

"I'm your employer, Evangeline. You work for me. I expect you to address me as Mr. Hawthorne."

"Oh." She didn't know what to say. It felt wrong. Like she'd just had a completely different experience than he'd had. She looked at Charley, who met her eyes with fully-understood sympathy and then looked away, down at the floor.

Suddenly her throat felt tight. She couldn't get out of the room fast enough. Mumbling her goodbye again, this time to *Mr. Hawthorne* and Charley, she hurried out, the rest of her things crumpled in her arms. She raced up the stairs to her bedroom and slammed through the door, closing it behind her and locking the click-lock before she collapsed against the frame.

Sliding to the floor she dropped her head into her hands and waited for the tears, but they never came. She took a deep, shaky breath and got to her feet, dragging herself into the bathroom to clean up for bed. She was so confused, she didn't even know if she was supposed to cry. Did she care that Ford was keeping her at a distance? What he'd said made sense — she *was* his employee. This thing she'd gotten involved in was just so complex, she'd need time to get used to the emotions she had to learn to control.

Realizing she still had nothing to sleep in, she crawled under her covers naked. Ford had kept her damned underwear again! Did the man collect women's panties? She thought of her new lacy thong, crumpled on the dining room table for the staff to find. A half-eaten platter of grapes and cheese, a nearly-empty bottle of four-hundred dollar wine, and discarded women's panties. Oh, and cum all over the front of the couch in the living room. And probably a wet spot on the ottoman.

Dinner had really gotten out of hand.

She giggled despite her malaise. Maybe the panties would somehow get washed and discretely returned to her room. She had really liked them.

There was a soft knock at the door.

"Evie?" It was Charley's voice, concerned and pleading. "Evie, can I please come in?"

"The door's locked." She called. She didn't need any more men tonight. She just wanted to drift off to sleep.

"Can you unlock it please?"

She rolled her eyes. "I'm in bed!"

"Please, Evie?"

"I'm naked!"

"I promise I won't come in until you're back in bed under the covers. Please?"

She growled. "Fine. Just a second."

Throwing off the blankets, she padded to the door. "Now you count to five before you come in, okay?" Just 'cause he'd just seen her naked, didn't mean she wasn't entitled to her privacy.

"Okay."

She unclicked the lock and had no sooner turned around than he opened the door and entered the room. She squealed, running and diving back into the bed, her naked breasts jostling. "*Charley*! I said count to five!"

"Sorry." He grinned. "I'm not very good at following directions." He closed the door behind him, blocking out the light from the hallway, and locked it again. "All safe! And nice ass, by the way. Your ass looks great when you're all skittish and jumpy like that. It jiggles."

"I don't think it's supposed to be a good thing to have a jiggly ass."

"Yours jiggles in a nice way. Besides, I like a woman with some ass."

Though there were no lights in her room, she could sense his smile cutting through the darkness as if it were a beacon. She smiled too, hiding it in her pillow. "Go away." She tried to sound angry. "I was sleeping."

He moved to her bed, standing at the foot of it and tapping the wood with his hand.

"You weren't sleeping—you were thinking. And you're not mad. I can hear you smiling at me."

She grinned wider. "You can't hear a person smile."

"Sure you can. A person's voice changes when they smile. And I'm right, aren't I?"

She didn't answer, but just took a deep breath, reluctantly sliding back into her funk. Not even Charley's pleasant company made her feel better for long.

He just stood in the darkness, tapping randomly on the wood of her foot-board until she groaned, "Charley, at least tap a rhythm, for the love of god, if you're going to make me listen to it."

"Can't sleep?" he asked, his voice full of mock concern.

"No I can't sleep! Will you get out of my room?"

"I want to talk. Will you talk to me?" His voice quieted. "You're the only person I have to talk to about this."

She sighed. He was the only person she had to talk to also. "Fine, come sit down."

He bounded onto the bed like a four-year old on Easter morning.

"Hey! You'd better not have your boots on!"

"I don't! Bare feet. Want to touch them?"

"No!" She shrieked and giggled.

He lay down on top of the covers, resting his head on the pillow next to her, facing her. There was enough moonlight coming through her windows for her to make out his profile. He studied her eyes, and then reached out and took her hand. He squeezed it.

"I like to hold your hand," he whispered.

"I like when you hold my hand," she whispered back.

They lay in silence for a minute, Evie feeling a comfort she hadn't known in a long time, maybe ever. She had no idea what to make of the situation. Charley was her friend...but he was more. Her lover? What was Ford? Just her boss? More? She frowned, her peaceful feelings crumbling.

Charley broke the silence. "What?" She didn't answer. "Evie, what?" He tried again.

She shrugged against her pillow. "I don't know. When I don't think too much about all of this with you and Ford, I feel wonderful. Protected, content. Happy. Horny." He squeezed her hand and pulled it to his mouth, kissing her fingers. She smiled.

"So what's the matter then?"

"It's when I try to understand what this is all about—who I am to the both of you, who you are to me. Then it goes all wrong in my head."

"Then don't think about it." Charley's voice reflected his enthusiasm for the idea, and a lop-sided smile followed his brilliant advice. Her mouth crooked up.

"That easy, huh?" She didn't like how jaded she sounded, especially in the face of Charley's simple *joie de vivre*.

The bed shook as he chuckled and she was suddenly back to feeling pure happiness. How long had it been since she'd lain under the covers close enough to another human being for his movements to jostle her? She wanted to curl against his large, hard body. Kiss him everywhere. Tuck her head into the crook of his strong arm and just hide there. Listen to his uncomplicated view of the world and believe him. Let him convince her everything was right and everything would last.

What was wrong with that? It seemed so easy.

"Charley, you're obviously all mixed up about Ford inside. How do you keep from letting it bother you?"

"That's just it—I'm *not* all mixed up. I'm very clear about him. I love him. I want to be with him."

"But aren't I just complicating things then? The distance between the two of you isn't great—after what happened tonight, it may not exist at all. Shouldn't I just go away so you can be together?"

Charley sighed, moving his thumb up and down on hers, not loosening his grip on her hand. He stared at their clasped fingers as he spoke. "I don't want you to go away. I'm so glad you're here. So glad to have you to share this with...share *Ford* with."

Evie raised her head off the pillow, propping it on her other hand, frustration rousing her from her tired state. "Why, Charley? That doesn't make any sense. What am I in this equation other than one more thing to stand between you guys?"

Charley raised his head too, mirroring her actions, and met her eyes. Even in the dim light she could make out the flash of passion under his dark lashes that came with his words. "Don't do that."

"What?" She was taken aback, confident her question was legitimate, even caring.

"Don't try to label things. Don't try to make your life fit in a box you picked off someone else's shelf." There was an undertone of anger in his voice. "This is why so many people are unhappy. This is why I can't be with Ford." He furrowed his brow, hiding his eyes in shadow so she lost her connection with him, despite how tightly he was squeezing her hand. "I feel love for Ford—fierce, passionate, punch-you-in-the-gut kinda love. I really, *really* like being around you. Today has been one of the best days I can ever remember. And somehow being with you and Ford together feels, just, *right* to me."

"Charley..."

"No, don't dismiss me. Listen to what I'm saying. Yesterday I thought one thing, today things are...shifting." He shrugged one solid shoulder and she wanted to cup her hand over the muscles there while he spoke. "And why? Because I respect myself enough to not dismiss what I feel. Maybe yesterday I wanted Ford to myself. Maybe today I want him with you." Charley curled his lips into a rueful half-smile. "It is what it is. It may not be what I anticipated. It may not be what my grandmother hoped for me, but that doesn't make it any less real."

Evie shook her head, dropping back down on her pillow. An

easy smile, now so familiar when she was talking to Charley, affixed to her face. "So what about tomorrow?"

Leaning toward her, he trapped their hands under the weight of his chest and brushed his lips over her cheek and then again across her brow. She felt his chest expand as he inhaled the scent of her hair. Pulling back, he whispered, "Oh, don't count on tomorrow. I might not want either of you tomorrow."

And even though she hadn't even known him for a full day, she knew instantly he was teasing her. Charley was an open book and she spoke his language as if they'd grown up together. "Well, at least we know we can count on your loyalty," she deadpanned. They laughed, locking eyes, and when the moment had passed, Evie dropped her lashes, feeling shy. "So do you think things will be different now? Between you and Ford?"

"I don't know." Charley huffed. "It's not the first time something's happened. And that time didn't change anything."

"It's not?" Evie's heartbeat jumped and she felt herself blush, surprised at how interested she was to hear the story.

The corners of his mouth twitched. "Oh, you want to hear about it?" Evie nodded. "I'm warning you. It's very dirty," Charley purred, grinning.

Evie hit his solid chest with her free hand. "Stop teasing me! And get off my hand. My fingers are asleep."

Charley released her other hand and she flexed her knuckles, trying to get the blood moving. He propped his head up again and casually draped his other hand on her hip, smoothing the covers with his palm. His intimate touch raised a question in her mind.

"Do you think Ford minds you being in bed with me?"

"Nah, remember, 'She's as much yours as she is mine'?"

Yes, she did remember. It had sounded amazingly hot in the throes of passion. Now it sounded...presumptuous. She frowned.

Charley lifted his hand from her hip. "What's wrong? You don't want me to touch you?"

"No, no. I like it." She put his hand back on her hip. She made her own choices. "Now tell me that dirty bedtime story about you and Ford." She tried to keep her mind off the pressure of his touch.

It felt so nice to be with him.

Charley launched right into it. "I tried to kiss him once, when I thought it was the right time, and he shut me down immediately. He just looked at me in his way and said, 'don't.' so I didn't. It was one of the many times I told myself I'd just have to learn to deal with being his friend, nothing more. Then one night a couple of weeks after that—out of the blue—he kisses me. We'd gone riding that day—" Charley hesitated in response to her confused look. "Motorcycles. We ride together sometimes."

"Oh." She'd have to ask more about that later. Ford? On a motorcycle?

"We'd had a great day and when we came back here we were having drinks downstairs. Ford suggests we go outside because it's such a nice night, but that we should refill our drinks first. I follow him to the bar talking about how I was thinking about buying another bike when he kissed me. Out of the blue. We got to the bar and he turned around, scooped his hand behind my head, pulled me in and kissed me."

"Wow," Evie breathed.

"I know. I was speechless. I was almost too stunned to kiss him back. Almost." He grinned.

"And?" she prompted.

"So it was nighttime and we hadn't turned the lights on because the moon was so bright and was flooding through all those windows in the back of the house. It was surreal. I had to wonder if I was dreaming it. But the kiss felt so real to me, and not just like he was 'trying it out', but like he really wanted to kiss me." Charley screwed up his face. "I don't know, maybe that's just wishful thinking on my part."

He shook his head and looked away, seeming lost in the memory. "But the kiss was hot, and I got keyed up pretty quick." Charley shifted closer to her, sliding his hand down her hip and pulling her leg onto his, tangling the covers. "I just remember feeling so ready to see where the kiss would take us."

He took a deep breath, leaning into Evie and ducking his head to press his lips to her jaw, following the bone with light nibbles before placing a soft nip under her ear, making her shiver. His voice softened, and he didn't pull away to finish his story. "I poured everything into that kiss—all the passion I feel for him. And the next thing I know he moved in close to me and our cocks—our erections—were pressed up against each other through our jeans."

Without intending to telegraph how hot Evie was finding the story, she sucked in a long, deep breath.

"I know! That's how I was feeling too!"

"Okay, we have to stop reading each other's minds." Evie laughed. "It's freaking me out." Snuggling up to her, Charley buried his face in the bend of her neck, his laughter tickling her skin. She pushed him away. "Go on!"

"Okay, okay. When I felt his erection against mine, I thought I was going to come in my jeans, right then. I'd wanted that man for so long." Evie nodded at that. "But—and I couldn't believe it—then he broke the kiss, stepped back, and opened his pants. Slowly. Without taking his eyes off me. Like he knew exactly what he was doing to me."

"Oh my god," she whispered.

"He pulled his pants and underwear down over his hips, just to his knees. My cock's aching and ready to burst and he's standing there in the moonlight with this incredible erection and I don't know what I'm allowed to do with it!"

She laughed. "This is a line of thinking I never thought I'd be privy to."

"Shh, now listen," he admonished, a teasing smile on his lips. "I'm getting to the good stuff."

"Oh, sorry." She grinned.

"So I don't know if I'm allowed to touch him or what. So I just opened my pants too, and pulled out *my* cock and we just look at each other for a minute but he doesn't do anything."

"Nothing?" Evie's voice pitched high.

"Nothing other than smolder at me."

"Oh, well that's an action in my book." Evie raised her eyebrows.

"The man can smolder, can't he?" Charley agreed. "So I slowly reach out and touch his cock with just the side of my thumb and he doesn't move away, so I opened my hand and wrapped it around his dick. Then he closed his eyes and sighed, and stepped forward so his cock pushes deeper into my grip."

"Ooh."

"Yeah. Oh. I thought my heart was going to jump out of my chest. Goddamn, I can still feel his hard cock in my fist." Charley bit his lip and moved, pressing his hips against her and Evie felt an unmistakable firmness announcing his excitement over the memory.

"You like telling this story, huh?" she teased.

"I've never had anyone to tell it to before." He buried his face in her neck again to suck and lick her skin down to her shoulder blade. Deftly, he pulled the sheets off her, baring her shoulder and caressing his lips over it as he rocked against her, his cock growing harder. She tried to stay on track. "Thought about the incident a lot?"

He paused to meet her eyes. Without a hint of self-consciousness or apology, and with a rasp in his voice, said, "Only every time I've jacked off since that night."

Evie felt her insides turn to jelly at this honest insight into his most private, sexual thoughts. Her breath caught, and where her clit had developed a pleasant tingling as the story had continued, there was now an increasing pulse of lust. She wriggled against him, her pussy lips feeling swollen and slickened with need. But she didn't know how much of her passion was from Charley kissing her, his pushing his weight and cock against her, or his story. There was something strangely exciting about a man kissing *her*, enjoying *her* body, while he thought about his hunger for another man. While he talked about how much he liked touching another man's cock. Evie was ready to climb on top of Charley and satisfy herself while he finished his story.

Her movement against him seemed to carry a message of invitation for Charley, because he jerked the sheets down roughly, exposing her breasts and covered a nipple with his mouth, sucking hard, groaning. She gasped, arching against him, burying her fingers in his hair while she fought to untangle her other hand from the sheets and reach for the crotch of his worn jeans. He released her, kneeling up to feverishly pull off his shirt with one hand as he unbuckled his jeans with the other. Tossing his tee-shirt to the floor, he peeled his jeans off, sinking to the bed to push them off his feet.

And then he was on her again.

He covered her mouth with his, kissing her deeply, pushing his tongue into her with abandon, making noises of hunger, of need, of pleasure. His hands were everywhere.

They both struggled to pull free of the sheets, her trying to get out of them, him trying to burrow under them. Somehow they managed to kick them to the end of the bed so their naked skin could have full contact, head to toe. Warm skin against warm skin. Bodies wrapping around each other, arching against each other. They never broke the kiss. Charley seemed to want to get as close to her as she wanted to get to him.

He slid his hands around to her ass, pulling her against him as he thrust forward, groaning into their kiss. *Damn.* He felt so good. So strong and hard and naked. His weight against her made it impossible for her to think of anything but him at that moment. She didn't think about her fear of John. Her confusion and longing for Ford. Her plans for the future—or lack of them. She only thought of Charley and what they needed from each other. And it wasn't sex— it was a feeling of belonging, love, connection.

But that connection was definitely going to come in the form of sex, if Evie had any say in it.

She pulled her head back, breaking the kiss, breathless from the whirlwind of it. "Make love to me, Charley," she whispered into the hollow of his neck. "Please. I want you inside me."

"I can't." His voice held something close to despair.

"Yes, you can," she insisted, wrapping a leg behind his knee in a futile effort to keep him there.

"No." He pulled his head back and clamped his hands to her shoulders, pushing up from her firmly. "I can't, and goddammit, stop asking me to, or I will." He reached between them and fisted his cock. "Spread your legs," he said gruffly. She did, wondering how this action reconciled with his refusal to have sex with her. He guided his cock to her pussy and she forgot to breathe, but rather than enter her, he pressed the head of his erection into her engorged lips, finding her clitoris. She was dripping at that point, and her juices mixed with his pre-cum making everything slippery. With small, controlled pumps of his hips, he stroked the broad head of his penis, and then his long shaft, over her clit again and again.

Evie gasped, clutching at him. He was so dangerously close to sinking into her...just one miscalculated centimeter and he'd be inside. She hadn't had a man inside her in so long, and Charley was pressing buttons she didn't even know she had. She arched toward him and Charley pressed his palm into her mound, trapping her hips against the bed as he continued to tease them both mercilessly. "Charley, please!" she begged. "Just fuck me!"

He stopped his tightrope dance, collapsing against her. "Goddammit, I know. I feel the same. But I can't. Ford hasn't had sex with you yet."

"So?" Her voice pitched high.

"So I don't think he'd like it if I had sex with you before he did."

"I don't belong to Ford!" She was surprised at her own willingness to sleep with Charley, knowing he was absolutely right about how Ford would feel about it.

Charley sighed, letting his head drop. His breath slowed as he choked off their frenzied pace with his refusal. "You do belong to him. In this house, we both do." Charley made a frustrated sound, pressing his forehead against her shoulder. "Don't make me argue with you when you know it's true."

Evie growled, pushing at him. "Fine, then get off. Let me catch my breath." She pulled her hair out of her face. "Stop teasing me with your dick and telling me hot stories or I swear to god I'm going to find some restraints and have my way with you once I've rendered you helpless." She smiled in spite of her sudden sour mood. "You've been warned," she teased as she tried to scoot out from under him. But Charley wouldn't let her go.

"Now hang on, hang on." He trailed a hand down her side, tucking it between their two bodies, and suddenly his fingers were pushing between her legs. She gasped as he shoved a finger into her as soon as he found her opening, and followed it immediately with another, wriggling it to force entrance into her. "Just because I don't think it's wise for us to make love, doesn't mean I can't make the rest of my story," he paused, "...highly interactive." He tilted his body off of her and pulled his fingers out slowly, then thrust them back into her, making her gasp as her vaginal muscles clenched with pleasure. "Now where were we?" He moved his fingers in a steady rhythm while he found her hardened clit with his thumb and began circling it lazily.

Evie relayed the information in unsteady bursts of breath, getting lost in Charley's touch. "Umm, you and Ford. Pants down. Your hand around his erection. He, um, pushed into your grip."

"Oh yes. That was a good moment." Charley closed his eyes and sighed, biting his lip as he thrust his fingers into her again.

Goddamn. She wanted to bite that lip for him. Suck it between her teeth for a minute. Maybe five.

"So since he's responding, I figure I'm on the right track. I started to stroke him." Charley's voice was growing hoarse, and he paused to kiss her hard nipples again, sucking first one, then the other, while he kept his rhythm into her. She moved back against him, aiding in his efforts to pleasure her. He found her mouth, kissing her deeply. She didn't know if she'd ever been kissed this much by any man. And she loved it.

"Touch me too, Evie" he whispered. Locking eyes with him, she reached down between them, closing her hand over his erection.

"Tell me what Ford did when you were stroking him off, Charley." She curled her toes at the intense pang excitement those words sent through her.

Charley licked his lips and continued. "Ford moaned, so I squeezed his cock and tugged on it hard, to pull him closer to me. He closed his eyes and just let me work him up and down. I could see his thigh muscles bulging in the moonlight—his body was so tense. His jaw clenched and unclenched, but he didn't try to touch me at all, and I was dying for it. So finally I couldn't stand it any longer, and I reached up and start jacking my own cock too, right in front of his."

Evie squeezed Charley's erection, smoothing droplets of pre-cum around the broad head. Charley started thrusting into her hand, not once neglecting the stimulation he was providing her at the same time.

His voice dropped to an unsteady whisper, as if he didn't have quite enough free lung capacity to finish the story. "At this point we're standing very close to each other, and I don't even know if he has his eyes open or not, because I'm jacking his cock like an inch from my own, and I can't take my eyes off the sight. I'm so excited I don't even think anymore about the consequences. I just want to come and to make him come, so I pulled his erection against mine and wrapped my hands around us both, stroking us at the same time. Rubbing his hard cock against mine…mmm."

Charley broke off, breathing heavily. He spread his fingers inside her and picked up the pace of his thumb caressing against her nub. "Slow down. You're going to make me come," she gasped. "I wanna hear the rest of the story."

Easing back a bit on his rhythm, he continued. "I wanted him to put his arms around me, but he was gripping the bar with one arm and one of the barstools with the other. I could see his arm muscles working his hold on that bar like he was going to take the thing down with his bare hands. I'm pumping us with all I've got, but at that point we were both pushing against each other too. My hands were only doing half the work and the friction between us was doing the rest. I have pretty good control, so I slowed down and held myself off until I brought him there with me."

"Okay, faster now," she whispered and saw him smile when he picked up his pace between her legs, the beautiful and familiar tension there sharpening.

"I felt him start to cum so I looked down and watched him shoot in my hand, all over my dick and my stomach. Now my cock's getting all slippery with Ford's cum, and I'm still stroking it, lubricated and slick with the orgasm I gave him, and that was it. I lost it too. God, I think I said his name at least ten times as I came. Ford made this noise when he came, like a grunt—this strong, deep noise."

Evie nodded frantically. "I know that noise. So hot."

Charley groaned. "I swear to god it's the hottest thing I've ever heard, and I just exploded. I emptied myself against Ford—my cum on his stomach, his thighs, his dick. I felt our orgasms finish together, and I didn't stop until I'd jerked every drop out of us both."

Suddenly, as if the end was too near for both, Charley pushed Evie flat onto the mattress, shifting his weight on top of her and forcing her to let go of him. He spread her legs roughly with his knee and pressed his thigh between her legs, rocking his massive, hard quad muscle against just the right spot, rhythmically, as if he were making love to her. He pinned his hand between her body and his thigh and continued his assault of pleasure with his fingers. Lowering his head, he touched his lips to her neck and kissed downward when a sudden, sharp pinch made her cry out as he nipped her shoulder blade with his teeth, cutting through the fog of her lust.

She felt his lips on her ear, and through his ragged breath she made out his staggered, deliberate words. "What I really wanted right then was to drop to my knees in front of him and lick his beautiful cock and balls clean of both our cum. Swallow all of it, and then beg him to fuck my ass."

Evie climaxed. Charley's last, honest words reminding her of the hot scene she'd witnessed earlier between the two men, sending her shattering under him. She writhed against the hard muscles in his leg as he pulled back, leaning over her naked body, and jerked himself to completion too. Just as the waves of her orgasm faded, Charley shot hot ropes of white cum onto her breasts and stomach, groaning over her in release. A few stronger jets, in the clenches of his powerful orgasm, made it to her chin and hair.

His eyes were closed and he moaned until he finished his orgasm, finally collapsing to the bed beside her, completely spent. And she knew that although Charley was in bed with her, the wetness coating her naked breasts was really mostly for Ford. But she didn't mind, she was thinking of him too.

CHAPTER SEVENTEEN

CHARLEY'S CHIN DROPPED to his chest when he was done, still breathing heavily, still poised over her. Evie looked down at her sticky body, holding her hands out to her sides.

"Sorry. I got you pretty messy." Charley looked sheepish. He jumped up.

"No, it's okay. Just let me —" She gestured toward the bathroom with her head.

"Of course, sorry!" Charley moved backwards, getting out of her way.

After a quick shower, Evie came back to bed, surprised to find Charley not only still there, but awake. He pulled the covers aside for her to crawl in next to him and when she did, he wrapped his arms around her. She snuggled against him, their naked bodies spooning in warm comfort. She felt him kiss the top of her head.

"Your hair's wet," he whispered.

"So."

"So it's going to get the pillow wet."

"So get out of my bed if you don't like it. It's *my* pillow."

"I don't want to get out of your bed."

"I don't want you to either."

He squeezed her and she couldn't remember feeling more relaxed and content than she did at that moment. "What happened next?" she asked.

"Huh? Oh, you mean with Ford?"

Evie nodded.

"Nothing." She felt him shrug. "He acted like it never happened."

"No, I mean specifically, what happened that night. Start from where you left off."

"Oh, well, he grabbed a towel from the bar and we cleaned ourselves up, put our clothes back together, Ford fixed those drinks and we went outside."

"Did he say anything? Did you?"

"No, neither of us said a word. We just went outside with our drinks and sat down on the patio chairs. Then he started talking about the bike I was thinking of buying—just picked up the conversation where we'd left off as if I hadn't just cleaned the man's cum off my balls and stomach."

Evie remained silent for a moment. "That was it?"

"That was it."

"Did you ever talk about it?"

"Nope."

"Never?"

"Never."

"Wow. I'm sorry." They lay in silence again before Evie asked, "Did he give you the towel to clean off first?"

"Huh?"

"Did he clean himself off and then give you the towel or did he hand you the towel first and use it when you were done?"

"He let me clean off first."

"Maybe that was Ford's way of saying thank you—acknowledging that he cared about you and what you did. He probably didn't know what to say."

"Maybe. I never thought about it like that." Charley went quiet and Evie felt her eyelids growing heavy. "Or maybe that's just the etiquette of the sex-clean-up-towel."

"What?" She giggled.

"Well, I don't know. Maybe he learned it in charm school. 'A gentleman always presents the sex towel first to the person wearing the gentleman's semen before he cleans his own cum-soaked skin,'" Charley said in a faux snooty accent. Evie laughed for what seemed like three minutes straight.

"Don't make fun of my boss," she teased when she'd finally caught her breath.

"I'm not." He kissed her head again. "I love him."

Evie didn't say anything. "I'm so tired," she finally managed through a yawn. "I can't believe you weren't asleep when I got out of the shower."

"Can't sleep." His voice grew serious. "But this will help. Being with you." He squeezed her.

"What's wrong?"

"I have mixed feelings about tonight."

Evie's feelings weren't even organized enough to call them "mixed". Her feelings were a chaotic, tangled, colossal mess, but rather than address that, she asked simply, "Why mixed?"

"It seemed like Ford finally crossed a line with me tonight. And it was amazing. But I don't like the way he shut you out at the end. Still, thanks for helping me."

The "Mr. Hawthorne" conversation. She didn't like it either. "You're welcome." She found his hand around her waist and laced her fingers into his, squeezing. "I told you he didn't want to be my boyfriend," she whispered.

"No, he wants to be your dominant."

"My what?"

"It's a BDSM term. Do you know what that is?"

She shrugged again. "I guess I know a little bit about it. Is he into that?"

Charley laughed. "Oh he's *into* that, but he's not in the scene."

"I don't know what that means."

"I just mean he's not a trained Dom. These can be very formal things. He's a natural dominant, but he's never explored that world.

And honestly, I think that's always been the issue with Ford and me. He has a real need for a submissive female. I think it's so intrinsic to his nature that he can't be truly satisfied without it. I think he knows instinctively that he can't just be with me and be completely satisfied."

"So that's what I am?" she asked, her voice small. "His submissive female?"

Charley laughed again, rubbing his thumb over her knuckles. "Well, I'm no expert, but I don't think you're a natural submissive like he's a natural dominant. You are way too mouthy, from what I've seen." She jabbed him with her elbow. "But there's something about Ford that makes you want to submit to him, isn't there?"

She felt herself blush, glad for the darkness. "Yes. But it's more than that."

"Tell me."

"I can't! It's too personal."

"Really." Charley's voice was deliberately flat. "After everything that's gone on today, you can't tell me what turns you on?"

She sighed. "I guess you're right. I just never realized how exciting it is to me to be…like…available for the pleasure of men. For certain men, at least. Is that weird?"

"No, it sounds fucking hot."

"You probably think everything's hot."

"Hey now, no second-guessing your sexual desires, remember? House rules."

"I'm trying! This is all new to me. I've never felt like this before. I've never done these things before. It's Ford. He's just so *in-charge*, and when he demands something sexual from me, something crazy, it's just so wrong, so against what I've always been taught I'm supposed to want. It makes me lose my mind." Her voice dropped almost to a whisper. "And it scares me because I wonder if there's a limit. I wonder if there's anything I wouldn't do if he asked me."

"Don't let it scare you, Evie." He caressed her hand lovingly with his thumb. "Just stay true to yourself and what feels good to you. If it feels good and you want to do it, do it. If it doesn't, don't.

Ford will respect that." He lifted his head to kiss her shoulder. "Are you enjoying yourself so far?"

"I am, but..."

"But what?"

"Buuut..." She drew out the word, reluctant to finish the statement.

"Tell me!"

"You already know. I want to have sex. You wouldn't do it, but Ford doesn't seem to want to have sex with me." Turning her head, she buried her face in her pillow.

"Hey." She felt him lift his head. "Hey. Where'd you go?" Letting go of her hand, he pulled on her shoulder. "Turn around."

She turned around, feeling sulky, and kept her eyes firmly shut.

"Evie, that's understandable. I'd want the same thing." He put his finger under her chin, trying to raise her face to his.

She opened her eyes, protesting his attempt to make her feel better. "But you're a man!"

He frowned at her dryly. "Are you really going to say something so clichéd?" Evie didn't respond. "Tell him. Tomorrow."

"I can't. I'm not supposed to be the one in charge."

"Negotiate it. Every BDSM relationship requires negotiation."

She laughed. "So that's the label I'm looking for when I try to understand what I'm doing with Ford? I'm in a BDSM relationship with him? Because I'm so confused I don't even know if I'm supposed to feel sad or not when he pushes me away. I don't know what's going on." Then, after a breath she added, "And there's something else I don't understand. If you think Ford needs this 'submission' so much, why has he never gotten into—what'd you call it? 'The scene'?"

Charley shook his head. "His parents—his dad especially—did a number on that man. Ford is wound so tight, such a perfectionist, just like his father. But Ford's gorgeous and charming and he's got a wild streak—definitely *not* like his father. Everyone's always wanted Ford—either his money or him. They wanted to be his friend or his lover or his employee, or whatever, but people were always throwing themselves at him. He learned early on how to get people to do whatever he wanted either by dangling money or himself. He learned how to trade on those things and I think it caused him to grow up way too quickly. But the real damage was done when he was sixteen. Ford idolized his father, but he's not his father. Ford is a man of...particular tastes, and he told me he's always known it. Just like I've always known I like men as much as I like women." Charley grinned, the dim light coming through her many windows lighting the swell of his cheek.

"So what happened?"

"He was caught with the daughter of a very influential friend of his father's."

"That can't be that unusual."

"She was sixteen years old, naked and tied to the bed."

Evie gasped, clapping her hand over her mouth. "Oh my god!"

"And Ford was fully clothed, standing over her with a riding crop from his father's stables. It made him look like a deviant. It was completely consensual—in fact that girl was probably the envy of half the girls and boys in school—but it didn't make a difference. The scandal had been set loose. Ford's father spent a lot of time telling Ford what a freak he was, how he'd ruined their family's reputation. How Ford would never have a normal relationship. How women don't want the deviant things Ford wanted."

"Oh wow." Evie imagined Ford, a handsome sixteen year old at that awkward age between boy and man, exploring his budding sexuality, and suddenly being publicly humiliated and brainwashed into believing his natural desires were repulsive and weird. "That must have been terrible for him."

"It was. Apparently he went from being Mr. All-American, Class-President-type to being withdrawn. A loner. His father sent him away to school in England and made him live with the Headmaster there. He wasn't even allowed to live with the other kids. His father was so concerned that Ford might do something to a classmate if left unattended with them. He told Ford he had no idea what perverted things he might be capable of. And he made him see a counselor, hand-picked by his father to 'cure' him of his 'abnormality'."

"Jesus," Evie breathed. "He told you all of this?" Charley nodded. "Why?"

"Because I asked him why he never likes any of the women he dates. I was hoping maybe he was gay, but it turns out he's just a kinky bastard." Charley laughed. "We had a long conversation about it because I could relate, my tastes being not exactly the norm either. Only I had it much easier. But Ford..." Charley mashed his lips together. "Now he makes it a point to only date the most 'acceptable' woman for his 'station'. Women he's not the least bit interested in."

"There are no rich or famous women into BDSM?"

This time Charley belly-laughed, shaking the bed. "Oh, believe me. There're plenty. But if Ford gets the idea they might lean in that direction, he runs. He won't allow himself to explore that part of him."

"Until now?"

Charley shrugged and added quietly, "Yeah, I guess. Until now."

"So why now? Why with me?"

"I've thought a lot about that ever since Ford told me about your arrangement before dinner. That's when I knew he was finally dabbling in it." Charley shrugged. "Maybe he's getting old enough to stop denying himself? Maybe his dad's been dead long enough? But I don't think that's it. I think it has to do with the fact that he's paying you. It's like he's found a loophole in his head. He's using that to keep you at a distance. If you're providing a service, then maybe it's no different than seeing a movie—strictly entertainment. It's certainly not *who he is*. It's not a relationship." Charley shrugged again. "I don't know."

Evie thought for a moment. "So when he insists I'm his employee, maybe it's not because he doesn't feel anything for me. Maybe he's just not ready to accept that he could have a relationship like that?"

"Maybe. And did you catch his statement earlier about how no one is allowed to feel shame about what we do, not in 'his own home'?"

"Yeah. I do remember that." Evie remained quiet for a while

absorbing this while Charley stroked her face. Finally she asked, "So what do I do?"

"What do you want?" He smoothed her hair behind her ear.

Evie huffed out her breath. "I don't know," she said heavily. "I guess mostly I just want to not feel scared anymore."

"John?"

"It's not just John. John's just exacerbating it. I've been scared my whole life. I want to feel protected."

"What happened?"

Evie shrugged. "Typical sad story. I don't really want to talk about it."

"Okay," Charley whispered. "Evie, I think you are doing the right things. You need to be clear of the boundaries. Be safe. Understand the rules and don't break them. If you can stay within the confines of what you and Ford have set up, then you should be fine. Just explore this and have fun."

"Okay." Her voice was slow, sleepy.

"But you need to keep something in mind, especially after what I've told you tonight. Ford is completely fucked up when it comes to relationships. I love him, but I know this is true." He took a deep breath. "It's too late for me." She could only see half of his wistful smile in the faint light. "I didn't have a Charley to warn me. But you do. Will you remember that?"

"I'll try," she whispered. "I'm trying."

CHAPTER EIGHTEEN

*W*HEN EVIE OPENED her eyes to the morning sunlight, Charley was gone. She wrapped the sheet around herself and pulled all the clothes out of the bags, exclaiming happily when she found a robe. She'd just finished her hair and makeup when the phone next to her bed rang. Instantly her heart thudded out of control under the lapel of the fluffy, white robe. The phone rang twice before she had the courage to pick it up.

"Hello?" she practically whispered, fearing she'd hear John's laughter pierce through her again.

"Good morning, Evie," Ford purred. "You put in some long hours yesterday, so I let you sleep in a bit today. But now I need you. Meet me in the library. Wear the red dress and what's in the bag with it."

Evie had been thinking a lot since she'd woken about what she wanted and how to get it. Her approach was simple. Ford is a businessman and speaks that language, so she decided to negotiate adding sex to their arrangement as if it were a business deal. And after all…it sorta was.

She put on the red, silk wrap-dress Ford had indicated and another lacy thong. She knew there'd been no bra in that bag when she'd dumped it on the floor earlier. She knew this because Ford hadn't bought her any bras at all. *No problem*, she thought. Going braless had to help when you're trying to convince a man to have sex with you.

Ford was sitting behind his desk engrossed in papers when

she walked in, pulling the door closed behind her to ensure privacy for her potentially embarrassing conversation. He looked up and his face lit when he locked eyes with her, sending a thrill to her toes. He seemed so genuinely happy to see her that she wondered if all the distance between them was only in her head. "Good morning, Evie. You look lovely. Turn around."

She did, slowly. And when she had her back to him fully, she boldly lifted the hem of the dress to show him the skimpy panties. Her breathing had already practically graduated to panting at this "inspection", and she hadn't yet said a word. When she turned back to him, she kept her face neutrally pleasant.

He came around his desk and leaned against it. "Absolutely perfect, Evie. You know exactly what I want."

"Good morning, Mr. Hawthorne. Could I speak to you about something before we get started?"

He looked interested, crossing his arms and tilting his head, he eyes intent on hers. "Yes of course, Evie, what is it?"

She took a deep breath and plowed in. "I'm feeling...unsatisfied with our arrangement." She thought he'd be angry, but instead he looked amused.

"Oh? In what way? I, for one, find it to be immensely satisfying." His smile dazzled her and she had to mentally drag herself back to her task before she got caught up in him and forgot what she'd come to achieve.

"Well, see, you are getting what you need but I want something more." She clasped her hands in front of her and tried to remain professional, tried to pretend she wasn't talking about what she was actually talking about.

His smiled faded as he grew serious. "But Evie, I'm the boss. You are my employee. I am paying you to do a job. It's fortuitous if that job is fulfilling for you too, but that's not always the case."

"I know, but I'm hoping what I'm proposing will be of interest to you as well."

"I'm listening."

She tried hard to just blurt it out. "What I want... I'm just really feeling like I want to..." She closed her eyes and took a deep breath. "I want to have sex. With you. And we haven't yet, and thus... Unsatisfied." She gestured weakly toward her own body, feeling ridiculous. This officially rated number one in the strangest conversations she'd ever had, and she'd had some weird ones in the past few days. She clamped her mouth shut before anything else could come out of it. She'd said what she needed to.

He looked down, studying his shoes while she fidgeted in front of him. Finally, his voice low and serious, he asked, "What is it specifically you are unsatisfied with, because unless I'm mistaken, you looked very satisfied last night after Charley was done with you. And then of course I know he visited your room again later..."

Her mouth dropped open. Did he really *not* want to add sex to their arrangement? She closed her lips and tried to regroup.

Just tell him.

"I want to be..." She bit her lip, delaying saying the word. "Penetrated. Have sex." Dropping her eyes, she waited for a reaction before slowly peeking up at him when she heard none.

"Penetrated," he repeated when he caught her eye, a smile crawling over his face. "Such possibilities."

Settling her shoulders back in fake bravado, she stood firm, squeezing her hands together so she wouldn't touch her hair and he wouldn't see her fingers trembling. Her nipples were rock hard and her pussy tingled in a lively way only Ford seemed to produce. He'd said "penetrated" in such a loaded fashion, and she responded as if she were conditioned—her mind instantly began creating a pornographic picture-book full of creative penetration ideas involving Ford, Charley and her.

Charley? Did she mean to include him?

"So last night when Charley came to your room, he didn't...?" He trailed off, but there was no question as to what he meant.

She shook her head, feeling her face grow hot. "He said he wouldn't. Not until you did first," she mumbled.

He crossed his arms and leaned back. "That's an interesting bit of information. It tells me you wanted to and Charley said no." Ford cocked his head, keeping his keen gaze trained on her.

She opened her mouth, feeling as though she should say

something. Apologize? But she didn't. Closing her mouth she lifted her chin. *No shame.* She remembered the rule. Yes she'd wanted Charley. Yes he'd said no. She wasn't going to feel badly about that. Ford wasn't her boyfriend—he'd made that abundantly clear.

Ford broke into a toothy, shark's smile. "Charley is a loyal friend. He knows I like to be the first to play with my toys before I share."

Evie's face hardened. It wasn't so much just a reaction to his callous reference to her, but in the wisp of coldness she felt in his words. She might choose to be a plaything—choose to be used by this man and his friend—but only if she was being respected and appreciated while she was doing it. He'd just verbally slapped her—taking an easy swipe at her vulnerable position. Many choice words came to mind, but instead of flinging any of them, she turned in disgust on her five-inch heels and stalked toward the door.

"Wait!" He moved quickly, deftly cutting her off before she could reach for the doorknob. He leaned against the door, blocking her. Crossing her arms, she cocked her hip and set her mouth in a thin line, refusing to speak to him. "I'm sorry." He reached for her but she stepped back, keeping her arms tightly crossed over her body. "I'm sorry," he tried again but she didn't soften.

Dropping his head, he took a deep breath and spoke looking at his shoes. "You're not a toy."

"I'm not a *possession*," she corrected emphatically.

He squinted his eyes, screwing his gorgeous mouth up like he wanted to argue with her, but instead tried, "I'd like to table arguing that distinction for now, but you're right to be upset. I meant it to hurt you."

"And you're an overachiever, remember?" She inserted a hefty amount of acid into her tone.

"Yes, so I succeeded. I get it." He met her eyes but didn't continue.

"Why?" She wished his motivations didn't matter to her, but they did.

Shrugging, he looked uncharacteristically uncomfortable with the conversation. "You wanted to sleep with Charley."

"So?" She spat the word at him, surprising herself with the real anger behind it.

Frowning, he didn't answer right away. "So...I want you to want to sleep with me."

She threw up her arms, exasperated. "I *do* want to sleep with you. That's what I'm in here telling you."

"I know. I know." He held up his hands and looked away. "I'm sorry," he repeated again. "I don't know why it upset me."

"I can help!" she sang cheerfully, holding a finger in the air. "Because you're selfish and arrogant, so your hope is I'll want you so much I wouldn't want anyone else at all."

"That's ridiculous." He seemed genuinely outraged. But she held her ground, planting her hands on her hips and raising her eyebrows. They stared each other down, chests heaving in the heat of the argument. Finally, Ford's shoulders sagged. "Yes, I suppose that sounds like me." He smiled, shifting into charmingly self-deprecating in an instant. He reached out and took hold of her wrists, pulling her forward. She allowed him to move her awkwardly, her body stiff with reluctance. "Evie, forgive me. I'm in unfamiliar territory here." She refused to respond. "Forgive me?" He tried to catch her eye and his dimples made her heart skip, his dazzling emerald eyes warming her to the core.

"Stop." She couldn't suppress the urge that made the corners of her mouth twitch up. "You know your dimples are the equivalent of me taking my top off."

"Is that right?" His voice twinkled in amusement. "I didn't know that." And then his voice was a purr, a sensuous treat like velvet wrapping around her. "Take your top off and perhaps I'll understand the comparison." She laughed and relaxed her stance, and he snatched the opportunity to pull her into a hug, kissing her on the forehead. "Now if you can forgive my ungentlemanly reaction to my jealousy, let's discuss the penetration proposal you've brought to the table."

She shook her head at him. Straight back to business. As soon as Ford had gone so far as to admit he was human, he'd snapped the subject closed. "Fine," she said through gritted teeth. "Let's discuss my proposal. But you'll be disappointed to discover I didn't create a

PowerPoint presentation or conduct a cost-benefit analysis. You're just going to have to go with your gut as far as whether you should fuck me or not."

Keeping her wrapped possessively in his arms, he pulled his head back to look down at her, his grin widening. "Oh, you are very sassy. That kind of behavior is going to be so bad for you in this house, and so good for me." There was no mistaking the naughty wickedness shining in his eyes. "I cannot allow such behavior to go unpunished..." She felt his cock stiffen against her and an assault of sexual sparks hijacked her cool intentions.

She allowed him to lead her back to his desk, which she noticed for the first time was completely clear of any papers or objects. He turned and leaned against the broad edge of the solid mahogany, keeping her hand held in his.

"Make no mistake, Evangeline, I want to fuck you. Hard and often." He paused, letting those words sink in for both of them. Evie clenched her teeth against her need to squirm. This man might actually be able to make her come just by talking dirty to her.

He moistened his lips deliberately and continued. "But there's no doubt that fucking will complicate matters between us. So if we're going do this, we're going to do it my way." It came out of his mouth so effortlessly, and with a smile, and bells rang in her head.

He'd planned this. He had purposely withheld sex from her to make her want it. To make her crave it. To make her come begging for it. And when she did, he'd be in the best negotiating position. She should have known she was in over her head making deals with Ford Hawthorne.

"First, tell me something. I'm assuming you are at least partially here to work toward your future?" She nodded slowly, not sure what his angle was, because with him, there was always an angle. "What is your dream, Evie? If you could do anything, where would you like to be in five years?" He let go of her hand and crossed his arms. Pursing his lips in a very distracting way, he waited for her answer.

Though she didn't understand what her future plans had to do with her and Ford having sex, she had an easy answer to his question. It was what she'd secretly wanted for years. And though she'd never told anyone her dream before, it came tumbling out of her mouth as easily as if Ford was her best friend.

"I want to open my own store, a lingerie shop. That's what I've always wanted to do—work for myself doing something I enjoy." She loved lingerie stores—all the pretty, lacy things, and the way lingerie made women feel pampered and sexy. She'd often dreamed of opening her own boutique.

He nodded his head and looked up to the ceiling, considering her idea. "I like it. You'd be good at it. You have a hell of a mind for business and you certainly understand sex appeal. You may even be able to franchise, take on the mall stores..." She could see the whole business plan forming like building blocks in his head, all the moving parts clicking into place.

"Mr. Hawthorne?" She tried to steer him back to their discussion.

"Right, sorry. Okay Evie, here's my offer. I'll give you $500,000 on top of the salary I'm giving you now for one year of your services."

Her mouth dropped open. "What?" she choked out. "How much?"

Despite her shock, Ford continued in his refined and clipped professional voice. "You heard me. A half a million dollars. And I'll still pay for law school on top of it if you decide you want to be my attorney instead of opening a store." He grinned.

"But why? That's a lot of money." This poor negotiation response was all she could manage to come up with. Then the realization hit her. There was a catch. *Of course.* She narrowed her eyes. "For what 'services'?"

He appeared delighted at her astuteness. "In return you will allow me complete access to your body, all mine to do with what I will, whenever and however I want it, for one year." He gazed at her steadily, as if challenging her to refuse. "And, you will entertain Charley in the same manner. Any way he wants to have you, anytime." He tilted his head, his face ablaze with excitement over his offer, assessing her response.

She shut her mouth. That was some catch. She stepped away from him unconsciously. Now the large sum of money made sense.

"Evie." Ford reached for her. Spreading his legs, he pulled her between them, wrapping his arms around her waist and trapping her against him. She had to lean back to look at his handsome face. He was in persuasion mode, which meant she was in trouble. "Open your mind to the possibilities, love. You would enjoy it. We will be utterly discrete and you will be completely safe at all times. We just want to enjoy you." He lifted her chin to look in his eyes. "I will not harm you or allow you to be harmed. I promise you. You'll be mine and I will cherish you as my most valuable possession."

Possession. There it was again. She opened her mouth to protest but he cut her off. "Yes, possession. I want to own you sexually for a year. That's what I'm willing to pay half a million dollars for. I want to think of you as mine. Please don't look at it as belittling—on the contrary, you would be all I think about. Such an arrangement would mean great responsibility on my part." He moved one of his hands down to cup her ass. "And the idea excites me in a way I've never experienced before."

Ducking his head, he placed one slow kiss along her shoulder blade. "You are intoxicating," he whispered. "I want you completely available to me. Anything I might be in the mood for...tender, rough, Charley and I together. I want that kind of freedom. I've wanted to possess you ever since I met you." He tucked her hair behind her ear. "And you're not a 'thing'. You're Evie, this incredible, brave, beautiful woman who might be willing to finally give me what I've been looking for my whole life. What I need to feel alive. But the only way it works is if you agree to become mine."

She hoped she wasn't somehow letting down women everywhere by liking what he wanted from her, but she did. She liked the idea very much. The idea fanned a smolder deep inside her, in the animal part of her that knew only food, water, air and sex. That part of her wanted this as much as Ford wanted it. This craving of hers, that lived in the primitive part of her psyche and had gone undetected until she'd met Ford, was somehow the perfect complement for his own secret need.

How often did human beings meet their perfect puzzle piece? His yin to her yang? All she knew is it had never happened to her, until now. From a purely sexual standpoint, Ford was her perfect partner, and it struck her what a powerful aphrodisiac that was.

Could she do it? Could she be his for the taking? *Theirs* for the taking?

She tried to force herself to think through it rationally. Since Ford had been one of her clients at the law firm, she'd seen his financials and knew that $500,000 was not really a lot of money for him. But he knew for her it was an obscene amount of money. He was offering it because he wanted there to be no question of her obedience. Or—this thought niggled away at the back of her mind—maybe the money was meant to encourage her to leave when he was done with her, because completing the job and leaving would be the only way for her to get paid.

He continued to persuade, his words muffled as he nibbled at the sensitive skin of her neck. "Think about it, love. Wouldn't you like to be fucked while you're sucking my cock?"

Geez god. Her insides turned to lava at his ridiculously hot, raw sexual honesty.

"Wouldn't you like to give it a try?" He pulled his head back, searching her eyes. She felt his arms tighten around her. "Could you please two men at once with your body, Evie? Wouldn't you like to find out? How many people get the chance to explore such a fantasy with complete safety and discretion?"

Evie looked away, her mind reeling, but Ford caught her chin and forced her to look at him. His eyes implored her. "Imagine how proud I'd be, allowing you to service Charley whenever he visits."

She couldn't help it. She imagined it then. Ford's big cock in her mouth, him with his hands in her hair, thrusting into her throat, taking what he wanted from her. But this time with Charley entering her from behind, holding her hips while his skin slapped against her bottom, amazed that Evie would let them both use her in any way they wanted at Ford's command. Charley, pounding deeply into her until she came, moaning as her pussy clenched against one cock in orgasmic bliss while her mouth was full of another man's erection.

A throbbing grew between her legs at the X-rated thoughts, and she wasn't the only one. She could feel him against her—Ford's big erection, rock hard. He was imagining it too. "It's amazing, really, how the body of one woman could please an entire roomful of men," he said softly. And there was something about the look he gave her that convinced her he didn't think of her as a belonging. He looked at her like she was a goddess, deigning to serve a mere mortal for a year because he was so…Ford.

One year as a sex goddess. One year as a plaything to Ford and Charley. She realized the thought, as crazy as it was, made her weak with lust. She wanted them both and she wouldn't have to choose between them. Her desire to have those two men in her bed ached in her, and all she had to do was say yes and she could satisfy that ache.

Could she really do this?

"I don't know how to—" she started to say, and Ford stopped her.

He stroked his fingers down her cheek, his voice husky. "I'll teach you. I'll show you what we need from you. You'll be amazing." He rocked his hips forward, pressing his hardness against her.

His mouth was very close to hers and she wanted to kiss him like a lover. Then it struck her with an uncomfortable certainty that her delay was subterfuge. As hard as it was for her to accept, she already knew. She'd do almost anything he asked.

"$500,000?"

"Yes," he breathed.

"For one year?"

"Yess." Ford sensed her agreement and moved his hands over her ass and then up her bare thighs, lifting the hem of her dress and cupping her naked buttocks. He ground himself against her. His need for their ultimate union as ravenous as hers.

She gasped, drinking in the feel of his hands on her skin, holding her, caressing her, crushing her to him. She felt light-headed with desire stronger than she'd ever felt for a man. He buried his head in her hair and kissed her neck like he was devouring her, like a man starving, his lips and tongue caressing down her neck, then back up to her ear.

She could hear his hot, ragged breath. Taking his hands off her bottom, he yanked her dress up. Lifting her arms, she allowed him to pull it over her head. As soon as her breasts were bared, he covered them with his hands, molding his palms over them. He closed his lips over her hard nipples, sucking them between his teeth, first one nipple, and then the other.

She choked on her gasp, the feeling of his mouth finally on her nipples, his hands finally all over her naked body—she was nearly out of her mind with pleasure. She couldn't stop herself from calling out, "Oh god!"

I need you, Ford. I need you. I need you. Somehow she managed not to say it out loud.

Squeezing her breasts, he rolled her nipples between his fingers, showing attention to each in turn, teasing them masterfully with his tongue and teeth. She wasn't sure how much longer she could stand up on her own. She'd waited so long to feel him move inside her.

He gripped one hand back around her ass and continued grinding his cock against her, giving her nipples a break from his mouth just long enough to mutter, "Your answer?"

Negotiating under these circumstances was most certainly duress. She had a fleeting thought of arguing it to a judge. "But your Honor, I couldn't think straight. He was sucking on my nipples and pushing his huge dick against me. I was dripping wet. I would have agreed to anything if he'd just fuck me. I can't possibly be held responsible for my decisions."

Funny thought, but she could hardly breathe, let alone laugh. "If I do it," she choked out. "I can stop at any time if I choose."

He stopped ministering to her breasts long enough for a hoarse counter-point. "Agreed, but if you are disloyal to me or neglect your duties or refuse me in any way other than by using your safe word, you'll have to leave immediately. I'll need to find a replacement. I'm finding these services you're providing to be quite essential, after all."

If she chose to leave, she wouldn't care what he did, but she had one last demand...if she could keep her thoughts straight. "Understood. But if I leave, I want the money prorated for the length of my stay. Prorated to the *day*. And I want it in cash." She was struggling to sound coherent.

Ford stopped then and pulled back from her to look into her eyes. A smile spread across his face. No actually, he beamed — beamed with pride? He was panting, but his voice was strong. "I should have known after all the negotiations I've done with you that you'd drive a hard bargain." He brushed her hair tenderly off her cheek. "Fine, Evie, I give. Should you decide to leave at any time for any reason, you'll have that amount prorated, in cash, within a week. Do we have a deal?"

She hesitated, finding it hard to agree out loud to have sex with two men for half a million dollars. On demand. How did she get here? He returned his attention to her nipples. "Your tits are amazing," he murmured against them. Moving his hand on her ass downward, he traced his fingers along the curve of her bottom.

Suddenly he reached down the outside of her leg and tucked his hand under her knee, pulling her leg up until her thigh was braced next to his hip. He ran his palm up the back of her leg and found the wet crotch of her panties. He pulled the damp lace aside with strong fingers and stroked into her folds, easily locating her firm clit and making her gasp. Her need for him was near agony. She felt frenzied with it.

He pressed his fingertips to her clit, kneading it, making her squirm. She couldn't help her reaction — rocking her hips against his hand, making unintelligible mewling noises. Ford's hands were finally all over her, inside her, and she was on the edge of a staggering orgasm.

But abruptly he stopped, and gently but firmly pushed her a step back from him. She stumbled, her knees weak from the rapture he had built within her. He steadied her, making sure she wasn't going to fall, but didn't pull her close again.

Oh no, no, please!

She protested strongly. "Don't, Mr. Hawthorne. Please," she begged. She pressed back up against him, reaching for the waist of his pants and pulling at his belt with both hands. She wasn't sure where the behavior was coming from, but he brought it out in her, teasing her until she had no inhibitions left. She shamelessly sought to free his erection, get it inside her, but he grabbed her wrists roughly and stopped her.

"No!" She felt on the verge of tears, her frustration and longing for him was so powerful. She couldn't take it if he stopped now.

He closed his hands on her arms and squeezed tightly, holding her hard. His face had grown stern, though his eyes still smoldered and his breathing was still labored. "I haven't heard a yes. I won't touch you until we have a deal. You are making me wait for your answer, Evangeline. I've made you an incredibly generous offer and I know you want to do this. Agree to my deal or we go back to you sucking me, only. Unless Charley and I have full access to your body, any way we want you, I won't touch you. Please understand; that's how I need it to be."

He looked down at her and she could feel her body trembling so much she was sure he could see it. He let go of one of her arms and ran his hand lightly down the side of her naked breast, but he didn't release his grip on her other wrist and she wondered if her flesh would bruise. He traced his free hand along her skin all the way to her tiny, Ford-picked panties. Tucking his fingers under the lace again, he stroked the thin strip of curly hair between her legs, wet with her juices. He slid one finger down between her lips, teasing her throbbing clit again.

The juxtaposition of sensations was too much for her—his one hand holding her arm brutishly tight, his other hand pleasuring her, sending flames licking through her. She was on the precipice again. It seemed he barely had to touch her and she was ready to come. She moaned and rocked against his fingers.

He pulled her roughly to him, his lips nearly on hers, his tone not to be denied. "Take my deal Evie, and I'll fuck you like you deserve to be fucked." He touched his lips to hers as light as a whisper, not even enough to be called a kiss, and she moaned again, thankful he was holding her up. He spoke right against her mouth, his voice deadly serious. "Don't take it and you can suck me off and go back to your room. Our original deal."

She was vaguely aware that he'd planned the whole seduction, for lack of a better word, to make her desperate enough for his cock to agree to anything. And it had totally worked.

"Okay," she gasped. "I'll do it. I'll trust you. You and Charley, any way you want it. Whenever you want it. Just please, fuck me.

Please."

He smiled wickedly and she knew that smile. It was his I-always-get-what-I-want smile. His that-was-sure-fun-negotiating-with-you-but-you-should-have-known-I'd-win smile.

"Good," he purred. "Very good, Evie. Let's get started then. I'd like to try what I bought. You do not come cheap, but I'm going to make sure you earn your money." He stripped off his clothes, keeping his eyes on her naked body.

She stood, stunned at what she'd agreed to, watching him undress for her first lesson in sex on demand. Sex whenever he wanted it. A man controlling her and taking her any time it pleased him.

Squeezing her thighs together, her face grew warm at her realization that the idea absolutely thrilled her nearly to orgasm.

CHAPTER NINETEEN

"TAKE OFF YOUR panties. Leave on your heels," Ford instructed curtly. Mute, Evie pulled down her thong and stepped out of it awkwardly as he watched. She felt suddenly shy, but it helped that he looked amazing standing there, all tanned skin and taut muscle, his large erection in his hand, ready to finally be inside her.

He pulled her forward to mold her naked body against his. He felt wonderful—his warm, bare skin against hers all the way down the length of her body. He looked down at her, light dancing in is green eyes, and swept her hair off her cheek, continuing his hand around to cup the back of her head.

His eyes searched hers for an unbearably long moment and she wondered if he was actually going to kiss her. Something unreadable passed over his face and he seemed to have made a decision. He kissed her, finally, and for the first time, which was so strange with all they'd done already, that this would be the most intimate act.

His lips were soft at first, his eyes open and studying hers, quiet and sure. But with the touch of his lips, electricity punched through her and she whimpered and rose on her tiptoes, trying to press her mouth closer to his, trying to kiss him more deeply, her hands around his waist pulling him against her.

She sensed him losing his grip on his constant control when he finally closed his eyes and crushed his lips hungrily to hers, exploring her with his tongue. She moaned into his mouth, her legs unsteady with the passion she felt from him, but his strong arms held her up. It was as if he wanted to kiss her as much as she wanted to kiss him. Could that be true?

Evie was completely swept away in the moment. She loved his lips on hers, his tongue in her mouth. She loved his skin against hers, loved the way he made her feel—she loved him in that moment. All of him, every inch of him. Every fucked-up idea in his gorgeous head.

No one had ever made her feel like he did. It was as if he was methodically pushing her to find the outer limits of her capacity for pleasure.

He broke away from the kiss, breathless, and moved his lips to her neck again. His low voice rumbled in her ear. "Tell me what you're going to do for me. Tell me you'll fuck Charley whenever I ask." He tightened his grip on her. "Say it." His voice was rough, uneven.

She would have said anything. Her voice hoarse, she panted, "I will—I promise. I'll fuck you and Charley whenever you want it."

"Yess," he growled into her hair. "You will." He spun her body quickly, moving her between him and the desk, her back to his front. Leaning over, he pressed his chest against her, caressing her breasts and wedging his erection between her ass cheeks.

His voice came guttural from right next to her ear. "I should have taken you long ago, Evie. I've waited too long for this and I'm not accustomed to waiting for anything I want."

He broke off to suck her earlobe into his mouth, tugging on it with his teeth. She was moaning with abandon now, hardly even aware of her surroundings.

His words were forceful, unapologetic. "I'm not going to take my time, not the first time. I want you too much. I'm just going to fuck you. Hard."

"Do it," she begged. "Please, do it."

She felt him reach one hand down to guide his erection and roughly spread her pussy lips with the head of his cock. The firm tip of his erection shoved against her eager, swollen clit and she groaned his name.

"Use your safe word if you must. I'm not going to be gentle." Ford's voice sounded grim, as if he couldn't help what he was about to do to her. He moved forcefully against her, with a ferocity of need, and she knew what he meant. But she didn't care. She wanted to be fucked hard. It's what she'd wanted ever since Ford had introduced her to the concept of pleasure heightened by pain.

He wrapped an arm around her waist in a vice grip, while his other hand ensured he was in just the right spot. Suddenly Ford drove his cock into her for the first time with a deep and satisfied grunt. He buried it as far as he could in his first thrust, aided by the saturation of her juices. The intimate intrusion overwhelmed her senses.

"Oh god! Oh god!" She practically screamed as her pussy was suddenly stretched to accommodate his girth. She came unexpectedly, her orgasm slamming through her, making her eyes fly open in shock and relief. She'd never orgasmed so quickly before. But Ford kept her on the edge of orgasm so often that it seemed she was never far from falling over into the blissful abyss.

Moaning long and low, she writhed as waves of ecstasy rocked her body. She gripped the sides of his desk until her hands hurt, as she felt her muscles pulsing against him.

"Ah, you like it rough," he purred in her ear. "I do too. Now it's my turn." He thrust into her again, deeper, using his strength to fill her even more. It felt amazing, overpowering. Wrapping both arms around her, he cupped his hands over the tops of her shoulders, completely enveloping her. Pinning her arms to her sides.

Using his grip on her shoulders as leverage, he pulled down firmly, burying himself as deeply as he could inside her, but it wasn't enough for him.

"Take more," he grunted, harsh like the command it was, as he tried harder to force his thick erection deeper into her. Letting go of one shoulder, he smacked her ass. The sting caused her to yelp, distracting her from the intensity of the sex. "You can do better, Evie. Spread your legs. Learn to fuck me like I need it."

She squeezed her eyes shut, feeling the flutter of another near-orgasm at his indelicate words, demanding her to perform the way he wanted. She spread her legs further and arched her back, trying to open herself up more for him. Capitalizing on her adjustments, he buried himself all the way into her. He was much bigger than anyone she'd ever been with.

"Yes. God yes." He sounded more satisfied. "That's it my little Evie," he breathed, "take all of it." His voice sounded close to the edge. "I am going to fuck you so often...so much." He drove his cock in an out of her to the hilt, and the heat was building quickly, impossibly, in her clit again. "I'm going to use your gorgeous body whenever I want it." He pounded into her fiercely, easily, as she was dripping wet from his brutish words and treatment.

The sex was rough and wild. In his need, Ford grunted with every thrust like an animal. He drove so hard into her that he pushed her down across his desk.

He held her down like that, both hands on her shoulders, her cheek pressed against the cool mahogany, and it seemed to excite him to hold her prone and helpless. It excited her too, the feeling of being held down and fucked.

Held down and fucked. It thrilled her intensely, and as he continued to use her aggressively, she came again, barely able to move under him.

The feeling of orgasming while being restrained awoke something in the deepest part of her, and her orgasm was staggeringly powerful. And when she came this time, whimpering, her muscles clutching him over and over, she took Ford with her and he finished with a strong, last grunt, burying his wide, pulsing shaft as he emptied deep in her. He continued to move in and out until he rode out every aftershock of his orgasm.

When he was finally done with her, he didn't pull out but stayed draped over her, catching his breath. When he peeled himself off of her, withdrawing his spent cock, he helped her to stand, running his hands up and down her sides while touching his lips to her temple and cheek. He pulled away from her and gathered his clothes, disappearing into the adjoining bathroom. Her pussy felt empty now, but finally, *finally* well-fucked.

After they'd both cleaned up, with Ford ensuring she had what she needed to feel comfortable, he collapsed into one of the library's over-sized chairs and pulled Evie onto his lap, deftly removing her shoes so she could curl her legs up to snuggle against him. He kissed her on the head.

"You kissed me," he said simply.

"What? You mean earlier? Before..." She wasn't sure what to call it. *Before we made love? Had sex?*

"Before we fucked," he finished for her, without hesitation about his choice of vocabulary. "Yes, before that. You kissed me."

"Uh, technically, I think you kissed me. I just kissed back."

"Okay, so you kissed back." He paused and Evie wasn't sure there was more to the statement, but finally he asked, "Did you like kissing back?"

She pulled away to study him. Was this a trick question? Why was he asking her this? She decided she had nothing to lose by answering honestly.

"Yes, I liked kissing you very much." Deciding to take a chance, she added, "I'd like it better if I could call you Ford."

He looked bemused. "Why?"

"Because when I have to call you Mr. Hawthorne, and I kiss you, I feel like I'm kissing my boss."

"You are kissing your boss."

"I know, but I'm also kissing dead-sexy and charming Ford, and that's who I really want to kiss."

He pursed his lips, and she could see he was trying to hide his pleasure at her admission. "Ford," he tested. "I'm not sure if it will work for me. Let me hear it."

"Ford." She smiled. It made her almost feel like they were friends.

"Hmm, I still can't decide. Use it in a sentence please."

"Okay," she said. "Ford fucked me hard while he held me down across his desk."

"Oh." His eyes lit in a way that reminded her of that excited boy again. Pure and unadulterated elation. "That was a good sentence," he breathed.

"I quite enjoyed it myself — the sentence, that is."

"Of course," he agreed, his face solemn. "Who would enjoy being held down and fucked?" He shrugged a shoulder.

She held up a finger. "By Ford — don't forget that part."

"Yes, exactly. Who would enjoy such a thing?"

She knew they were both teasing, but she felt compelled to make him understand. She wanted to find that sixteen-year-old boy in him and tell him he's not alone and he's not a freak. Tell him that many normal, healthy, successful people have the same urges for sexual dominance as he does. And conversely, the urge to be dominated completely, like her. No matter what his father believed.

Taking his hand, she stroked along his long fingers while she kept her eyes down. "I would," she said simply, her tone sincere.

He didn't answer right away, but reached out with his other hand and raised her chin. She saw confusion in his eyes — confusion and what looked like the stirrings of hope. Funny, because that's how she felt around him all the time.

"What?" he whispered.

The vulnerable look in his eyes gave her courage to say it confidently, with no waver of embarrassment in her voice. "I enjoyed it — really, honestly loved it — Ford, when you held me down and fucked me."

"The fucking part or the holding you down part?"

"Both. Together."

He frowned for a heartbeat in what looked like disbelief, and then pulled her close without another hesitation and kissed her, long and deep. His lips soft, his tongue gentle, probing, almost shy. And he kept his eyes closed tightly, cupping her head in his big hands. When he finally stopped, he rested his forehead against hers, his eyes screwed shut.

Finally he blinked twice before thanking her for her time and helping her to her feet. His mask slammed firmly back in place and the moment was over. She touched her lips as she left the room, knowing the last kiss had been different, and that knowledge sent butterflies of joy and unease swirling through her belly.

*****

Ford had suggested she return to her room and soak in the tub

224

while she waited for the locksmith. He'd made her promise to take a long, hot bath, noting she'd probably be sore from the rough sex, and he needed her to take care of herself. Then he'd sent her away, telling her she'd done an excellent job.

By that evening, Evie had sorted through half of her things and taken delivery of at least ten of her internet orders, happy now that she had the things she needed. A sturdy lock had been installed on her door, with three copies ready for their rightful owners. Evie's was in her purse, Charley's was on the hallway table waiting for him to come over and claim it, and Ford's was hanging from a red ribbon on his door-knob, awaiting his return to the house from his day of business.

Evie had spent the day missing the company of the two men. Thinking about them. Thinking about what Ford had done to her earlier. Finally, after she'd had dinner alone in front of the television, she'd turned off her bedside lamp and reached for her vibrator, hoping to quench some of the need she'd built up that day by thinking about her recent adventures over and over. Her fingers had just brushed the latex ridges of her well-used friend when she heard a noise in the hallway.

Ford. Her heart leapt and she hurried out of her room. He was heading toward his bedroom and his posture looked tired, but Evie hoped to entice him into her room for a gentler repeat of what they'd done that morning. Now that she was "all in", why not make the most of it? Maybe he'd even spend the night holding her. That sounded nice. She didn't want to ask for anything, afraid of his reaction—he was so insistent about being in control—but she was aching for him after thinking about him and Charley all day.

"Ford wait." He froze, turning slowly toward her. Though he didn't say anything in greeting, she plowed on. "Um, before you go to bed…" Evie's hand trembled when she placed it on his chest, caressing lightly. "Do you maybe need anything from me? I wanted to make sure you knew I was still up."

She moved her hand down his firm stomach, toward his crotch, feeling more like a harlot than she ever had since she'd met him. But after what he'd done to her that day, she'd been so hot waiting for him that she could barely stand it until he got home.

However, rather than react to her with the same enthusiasm,

he grabbed her hand and pushed her suddenly against the opposite wall, pressing his whole, hard body to hers. She gasped in surprise.

She could feel his hot breath on her ear as he hissed to her in the darkness. "I decide how and when I want you, Evie. I'm in charge of our situation. Do you understand?"

"Yes," she whispered, her voice shaky. "I-I'm sorry."

And she was sorry, and a little scared at his harsh reaction, but as his body pressed against hers, she recognized the stirring of his cock as it stiffened against her hip. "Fix it," he said and put his hands on her shoulders, pushing her to her knees in front of him.

With his growing erection in her face waiting for her service she whispered, "Okay."

He didn't help in any way. She unbuckled his belt and unzipped his pants, pulling out his erection. His cock bobbed thickly, hard and undeniable, like an accusation. She wanted him to fuck her again, but instead she wrapped her hand around his shaft and leaned her face to it, inhaling his scent. But instead of taking him into her mouth, she pulled up on his cock and ducked her head underneath, sucking his balls into her mouth, first one and then the other. Just like Charley had, only, unlike him, she couldn't fit them both in her mouth at the same time.

She stroked him as she suckled each of his balls in turn. Ford groaned, leaning heavily against the wall. She ran her tongue up the sensitive underside of his erection, flicking when she came to his swollen head, before sucking his whole length back into her mouth as strongly as she could.

Ford gasped then, finally reacting to her efforts. "That's very nice, Evie." He put a hand on her head and stroked her hair while she worked him, seeming to settle into the pleasure. She continued her pattern—soft, fluttering tongue on the head while she pumped his cock with her hand, and then strong suction as she engulfed it in her mouth. She worked his cock and balls hungrily—lips, tongue and hands, pulling, squeezing, sucking, and stroking—and he moaned in response. She wanted him inside her desperately, but he'd made it clear that, according to their deal, they did things as he wanted them, and he hadn't asked for that.

Still, she was growing desperate for release. Pleasing him was only making her frustrated state worse. She pressed her legs together rhythmically, trying to assuage the burning need there, but it was no use. It wasn't enough. For the first time she wished, since Ford wouldn't fuck her, that Charley was there behind her, pounding his cock into her—filling her while she was satisfying Ford. The thought only made her burn hotter.

She had both hands occupied and squeezing her legs together wasn't working. She was kneeling on her heels, so she squirmed, grinding the back of her foot into the crotch of her panties. That helped a little. The beautiful tingling started to grow, but Ford was already to the point of no return. She felt him swell harder and then he grabbed the back of her head and lunged deep into her mouth as his hot cum spurted down her throat. She wasn't quite ready for him this time and she choked, tears leaking out of her eyes, but he didn't stop. She regained control quickly and was able to let him finish without panicking and pushing him away. No one could say she didn't strive to do her job well.

"Yes, goddamn..." He fisted his hands in her hair and pulled a little too hard in his excitement. She swallowed every drop he gave her and when he was finally done, he pulled her to her feet, both hands gripping hard on her shoulders, and kissed her cheek. He rested his face against hers while he caught his breath.

When he came away, he must have realized her cheek was wet. She felt him freeze, his fingers stiffening around her shoulders. She couldn't seem to breathe. Would he be angry? Disgusted at her show of weakness? Slowly he reached up and swept a finger over her cheekbone, wiping the tears from her skin. "Oh, god," his voice was anguished. "Are you okay?" She nodded and looked away, hiding her face and cleaning the last of the tears on the back of her hand.

His face looked hard and he shook his head, appearing to struggle for the right words. "I'm sorry to speak to you harshly, love, but you must learn the rules. It's the only way this will work." He dipped his head, forcing her to look at his eyes. "Do you understand?"

She nodded again. "I understand," she whispered. "My eyes are just watering. I agreed to this arrangement. You didn't hurt me."

He cradled her face in his hands as if she were delicate china.

227

Kissing her damp eyelids in turn, he wrapped his arms around her, murmuring words of support, appreciation. Evie leaned into him, relishing the moment of him offering comfort. He kissed the top of her head. "I've never found what I need," he whispered into her hair. "I know I'm not capable of having a normal relationship. Or I'm not interested in faking it. I'm not sure which anymore."

She opened her eyes and pulled back from his embrace to search his eyes, surprised at the sudden and personal revelation. Where was it coming from?

Moonlight filtered through the window, lighting one side of his handsome face in the otherwise dark hallway. "But you're giving me that, Evie. You're giving me the only thing I've ever found that feels right. I finally know what I need now, and it's because of you."

Evie's head swirled in a headache-inducing mix of love, confusion and fear. This made no sense. What was he saying to her?

"Because you were brave enough to agree to try this crazy idea, now I know I can make a discrete arrangement and hire someone to submit to me sexually. I don't have to try and make it work as part of a relationship I don't want anyway." He laughed, his velvety voice sounding touched with pure happiness. "I don't know why I never thought of it before."

Jellybeans.

Feeling suddenly weak, suddenly very tired, she leaned into him. In spite of his words and the small melt-down they'd started in her chest, she was drawn to him—wanting him to comfort her against the pain he created in her. She wanted to feel connected to him, desperate to believe the swell of emotion welling in her wasn't just her imagination, regardless of his careless words.

She tilted her face up to his, wanting to kiss like they had in the library, but he stilled at her advance and gently pushed her back a step.

"Evie don't. The rules. You must try," he whispered tightly. She felt fresh tears threaten. What was wrong with her? She knew better, and she was paying the price for believing in what she knew she couldn't have. He pressed a kiss to her forehead again. "Go back to your room and wait. I've called Charley over for you."

She jerked back from him. "What do you mean, you've called Charley over for me?"

"I mean your instruction. Your training. You must learn to do what I ask of you, without question. Starting now. Your body belongs to me for this year. Now go back to your room and wait for Charley. I've instructed him to use his key to get into your room when he arrives. And when he comes to you, you will be very, very nice to him." He said the last part firmly, pinching her chin with his thumb and forefinger.

Her heart was pounding, her voice high and edging on panic. "'Be very, very nice to him'?"

"Do not pretend you don't know exactly what I mean," Ford said simply, his moonlit face looking angelic even as the devilish words came out of his mouth.

"You're asking me to—" she choked, struggling to say the words out loud.

"I'm not asking you to do anything. I'm telling you to fuck him, Evie."

"No. Not without you there—at least for the first time. Please! It's so..."

"Evangeline, you will pleasure Charley in whatever way he wants of you or we will end this arrangement. That was our deal. I expect you to be completely agreeable to Charley's demands, subject to one rule of mine of which he's been informed. He's promised to entertain me tomorrow over breakfast with a full description about how accommodating you were to his desires."

"Please don't make me do this alone." Her voice was weak. Why was she always pleading with Ford not to make her do things?

Because he's always upping the stakes.

Ford hesitated and then switched to persuasion. "Evie I know this will take some getting used to—following my orders without question—but I need you to learn. This is what makes me tick. This is what I need from you. I will continue to push you because it *gets me off.* You've been so strong. Please don't give up just when we're getting to the good parts."

The good parts?

Ford scooped Evie back into his arms suddenly and kissed her just as she'd been hoping. Gently at first, his lips pushed against hers, his tongue probing into her willing mouth. The raw feelings that poured from him into that kiss made Evie's heart break a little.

Was it possible she was imagining the emotion from him? Could he really be immune to the chemistry she was drowning in?

But Ford didn't think like other people, and because of that, even Evie — an expert at minute changes in body language — couldn't read him. Pulling back from the sensuous kiss that made her legs feel boneless, Ford delivered a raw and filthy ultimatum in the same reverent voice a lover might say, "You are my everything." Only Ford said, "It's time we got started for real, Evangeline. You will submit to my wishes. You will fuck Charley tonight, or tomorrow when I'm punishing you for disobeying me, I'll let him fuck you anyway, only then it will be while you're tied over my desk. It's your choice."

"Punish me?" Her voice squeaked. "But you said you'd never harm me."

"I'll never harm you, but I never promised not to hurt you. On the contrary, I want to hurt you, Evie. Not much, but some. It's part of what I need from you. And I'm hoping you'll learn to like that part too."

Evie's mouth dropped open and she struggled for a response. Before she could formulate anything coherent he pulled her tightly against him, causing her to gasp. "Do you see how just talking about punishing you makes me rock hard?"

It was true. She couldn't believe that so soon after climaxing he was ready to go again, but his erection was undeniable. Grabbing her hand, he forced it to his crotch, his voice rough with some emotion she couldn't read. "This is what you do to me, being brave enough to try this. And I don't want to stop. I'm not even ready to slow down. No one's ever done this for me before." He touched his forehead to hers, his eyes tightly closed. "You have a safe word, Evie. You have a way out." He forced her palm to travel the unyielding length of him between their bodies. "But your submission to me is your only way in."

She shut her eyes to him, mentally bracing herself against the riptide of his logic, his world. It was too much. She'd wanted to react to his words, had opened her mouth to say *something*. His words deserved reaction. These weren't words a lover should say. She shouldn't be caught in his passionate embrace that felt so right and hear the words, "I want to hurt you."

But he'd shown her the effect those words had on him, made her feel the hard truth of it in his erection. She'd heard the strange emotion in his voice that she couldn't place, and her compulsion to respond to his barbarous confession dissipated like smoke.

Still, she wrenched herself from his grip anyway and hugged her arms against her sides, feeling chilled away from his heat. If she didn't say something now, she might never find the words. Time spent with Ford was like a quicksand of consent and pleasure — though she'd relished sexual satisfaction she never thought she'd experience, she feared there was no way to get out unscathed, no matter how hard she tried to keep her heart reigned in.

"Ford, I'm going to say something very real to you right now, and you're not going to like it but I need you to pay attention because I might not be able to say it again. You keep pushing me and pushing me, and I know you say it gets you off but I think it's more than that. You want to see exactly how far I'm willing to go for you. What I can't figure out is why." She looked up, locking her eyes to his. "If I do these things for you, would it prove I really care about you? Is that what you're trying to figure out? Or are you hoping that if you push me far enough I'll never care about you? Is that what you want?" Her voice gained strength as she spoke the words. "And you know what's the worst part? I don't think you know."

"You need to stop." Ford's voice was dull. He crossed his arms over his chest. "Evie, do not over-think our situation. Don't try to get into my head. I am not bluffing when I tell you it will ruin everything." His voice sounded desolate, lonely. And his eyes told her he believed what he was saying.

"Fine," her voice was wavering. "Fine. I'll try Ford, for you. If that's what you need. I promise. I'll try to do the things you ask and not wonder why. I just assumed you'd be there the first time with Charley."

"Evangeline." He drew out her name and his voice had

gentled. "Please just enjoy it. I know Charley can make you feel good. Do you promise me you'll try?"

"I promise," she whispered.

"Good girl." He wrapped his arms around her. "I missed you today. You and Charley. You're great with each other—a better pair than I ever imagined. And you're great with me."

Warmth filled her and she rested her forehead against Ford's chest feeling so close to him, yet so unreachably far away. "I missed you too," she whispered.

"I'll see you tomorrow, love. You'll be wonderful, Evie. You always are." He kissed her on the top of her head and released her. She watched him disappear into the darkness of his bedroom alone, and heard the hollow click of the door closing behind him.

A moment later, sliding the bolt to lock her own bedroom door, she leaned her head against the cool wood, wondering why she was even making such a big deal about it. Yesterday she was begging Charley to fuck her. But that was on her terms—her decision. When she'd agreed to be loyal to Ford, to do what he asked, she'd thought he'd be there commanding her through all the awkward parts. That would make it easier to follow his orders. Not like this.

But like it or not, Charley was on his way to the house right at that moment to fuck her.

*****

~DARKER~

CHAPTER TWENTY

*B*ACK IN HER bed, Evie stared at the intricately coffered ceiling, wide awake, anxiety fluttering her pulse. She'd agreed to have sex with Ford whenever he wanted, and she'd also agreed to have sex with Charley at Ford's command. In fact, she wanted to have sex with Charley, but not like this. She had assumed that—at least for the first time—Ford would be there, telling her to do it.

If she was fucking his best friend because it turned Ford on, then she wanted Ford to watch her do it. She didn't want to be ordered and sent away, like a member of the household staff, meant to disappear and finish the chore unnoticed by the master of the house.

Her fluttering heart instantly began thudding when she heard the unmistakable rumble of Charley's motorcycle. To her surprise, he was at her door knocking softly in less than a minute. She wrapped her new robe around her naked body and let him in.

"Did you even stop to park your motorcycle?" she muttered.

"Are you kidding? Knowing what was waiting up here for me? You're lucky I didn't launch it straight through the window and land right in your bed!"

She giggled, in spite of her anxiety. "You're ridiculous."

The lights were all off in her room but it was a clear night and moonlight poured in through the big windows.

"Why didn't you use your key?" Evie asked.

"Respect," Charley answered simply and she smiled again. She was trying to be grumpy but Charley was making it hard.

"So you respect the woman who's being paid to fuck you?"

Charley nodded his head, his face suddenly serious. "Of course I respect you. I hope you know that already. But that doesn't mean I won't bend you over the end of that bed and fuck you until you can't stand up."

Evie took a step backward, her breath hitching at his blunt, erotic honesty.

Charley moved toward her in slow, deliberate steps, the way one might approach a horse not yet broken to saddle. "And know this…however long I get to spend in your bed tonight, Evie, won't be nearly long enough for me to do everything to you that I want to do. But I'm gonna try."

Evie recognized the tingling growing between her legs at Charley's frank admissions. There was no denying the easy sexuality he projected or the chemistry that charged the air between them. It wasn't simply a mutual attraction they shared. They also shared a secret neither of them vocalized, but of which both were constantly aware.

They were in Ford's capture, willingly.

They were both compelled with a dizzying surety to do whatever Ford asked of them. And whether that willingness came from a love for Ford, from self-exploration of their own sexual limits, or from simple lust, Evie was certain neither of them knew. What she did know is that they were the only two people in the world who were in this together. And especially now after Ford had forced them to bond, Evie felt sure she and Charley would succeed or fail, emerge happy or broken, together as well.

If they were to share an experience as infinite as love or as devastating as heartbreak, and all for the same man, shouldn't they also be as close as two human beings can be? She realized she wanted Charley inside her as much mentally as she did physically. That intimacy might give them the strength to see things through with Ford.

Charley interrupted her thoughts. "At least show me what you've got on under your robe." He gestured toward her. "Since we're just going to stand here all night."

She shook her head. She did want him, but knowing in her gut that she wanted Charley in her bed, and getting straight to the business of screwing him because Ford told her to, were two totally different things.

"Fine, then let's get some sleep." He stepped around her to the bed and she turned to keep her eyes on him. He casually stripped his clothes off, as if they'd seen each other naked a million times. Evie concentrated on keeping her gaze on his face. "I sleep in the nude, whether I'm fucking or not." He grinned and pulled back the covers. "Now tell me in detail what we did so I can tell Ford in the morning. I don't want your reluctance to screw me to be the cause of you getting spanked. And don't leave out the details men would remember, like how much your boobs bounced and how wet you were." He yawned.

A powerful surge of affection for Charley walloped Evie. He was going to lie to Ford for her. That wasn't a decision a man as loyal as Charley would have come to lightly. Stepping toward him, she let her robe slither off her shoulders, leaving her wearing nothing more than white, fluffy socks.

Charley had no similar concerns about keeping his eyes on Evie's face. He hissed in a breath, a wide smile spanning across his handsome jaw, and shook his head. "You are killin' me, girl." In a graceful swoop, he wrapped one strong arm around her waist and hauled her onto the center of the bed so roughly her breasts jostled. She squealed, clinging to the tanned bicep now pinning her to the mattress.

He leaned over her, his voice was husky and low, his mouth so close she could almost feel his lips brush hers when he whispered, "I don't want you to do anything with me you don't want to do, understand?"

She nodded, suddenly so keyed up to screw this man that she was having trouble thinking straight.

"You are something else," he whispered and kissed her, his lips lingering and caressing lazily, as if he had set aside the whole evening just to kiss Evie. "I love kissing you," he whispered against her mouth. "Now that I decided I don't hate your guts, it seems like I want to kiss you all the time."

Her giggle jarred the quiet moment. "So when you decided

you didn't hate me, is that about the time you decided you wanted to fuck me too?" she teased.

"Oh hell no. I wanted to fuck you even when I hated you. Maybe especially then." He curled his mouth into a wicked smile and lowered it again to hers. His lips were so soft and full, all she could think about was having them on her body. His tongue probed hungrily against hers, seeking her response.

She closed her eyes and let go, hoping her urgent tongue would communicate her impatience for him to be inside her. Without thinking, she made a small, pleading sound in her throat. All day the embers of her lust had been held just short of bursting into flame. It was maddening.

Charley read her whimper as all the encouragement he needed. He crushed his lips to hers aggressively, plundering her mouth with his tongue. Then, with a flat palm, he pressed her face to the side with just enough force to make her pussy muscles clench involuntarily. During her short tutelage with Ford she'd discovered it made her very wet when a man reminded her in bed of how much bigger he was than her.

And that he intended to satisfy himself in her body.

Charley exerted just enough pressure to send her that message, as if he knew exactly how to reduce her to his quivering pleasure slave.

Burying his shaggy head against her neck, he nipped until he found the sensitive spot where her neck meets her shoulder. She gasped. He chuckled, low and throaty. "Is that your spot?" he mumbled against her moist skin. "I bet I can find others."

She pressed her hands against Charley's massive chest muscles, running her palms over them and then down his well-defined arms. He had more chest hair than Ford and his tawny skin gave her the impression he spent a lot of time outdoors. He bowed his back, curling his shoulders in as he worked over her body. But he was positioned off to the side, his erection not touching her, and she wanted to remedy that.

She pushed against him, trying to lift him away from her so she could rake her eyes over him like an overzealous patron at a male revue. A naked Charley was quite a treat.

If Ford was a Kobe fillet, then Charley was all cowboy rib-eye—both probably bad for you, but sinfully delicious. And, she was willing to bet, both thoroughly satisfying. It all depended on what you were in the mood for that day.

And, oh boy, she was suddenly starving for cowboy rib-eye. And Charley was an all-you-can-eat buffet.

She wasn't strong enough to push him off her, but he realized her intention and pulled back to look down at her, his eyes trailing the lines of her body. She wasn't sure how much of her naked body he could see, even in the bright moonlight, but she hoped he liked what he saw.

"Evie, goddamn." He shook his head. "Look at your body. You are so curvy. You're sin in skin." A laugh rumbled through his chest. "I honestly don't know where to start fucking."

Evie giggled at his crass seduction, but an electric thrill of anticipation ran through her to her toes as she began imagining all the places he could start.

He settled onto his hip on the bed beside her and reached out, grasping one of her nipples between his finger and thumb and pinching, just enough to make the hard point stand rigidly at attention. Evie groaned under her breath. Charley seemed to ignore her response and outlined his graphic plan for her as if he were outlining the agenda to a college class, the likes of which she'd never attended.

"First, I'm going to start fucking your tits but I'm definitely going to finish inside you." He cupped his hand around one of her breasts and squeezed. She whimpered, thinking she might explode if he didn't do something to her soon—anything. But Charley continued as if she hadn't responded. "I'd love to shoot cum all over your tits and your lips, but I haven't been inside you yet and I really can't wait to bury myself in you. Hard." Charley smirked, clearly enjoying making his sexy plan. "But what I really want to do, Ford says I can't. I can't have your ass. He wants to be the first to fuck your virgin bottom. Too bad." He slid his hand under her. "I really would love to fuck your ass."

Her pulse leapt at the words, reacting with both fear and lust. It warmed her to hear Ford had claimed her ass as his. It was hardly romantic, but that reality didn't change the fact that she liked his proprietariness about her body. No shame in this house, and dammit, she liked it that Ford thought access to her body was his to dole out and his to keep for himself. Maybe with Ford, that was as close as she'd get to romance.

Charley moved back to her breasts and licked and sucked them both, leaving them very wet. He moved up so he straddled her body, his knees on either side of her elbows. Hoarsely, he instructed, "Hold them together for me so I can fuck your tits."

Evie pushed her breasts together, scrambling her fingers against the slickness left by his kisses, so that Charley could shove his cock into her cleavage. Slowly, he pushed his rigidness between her soft mounds, and he slid in easily, assisted by his own saliva glistening on her breasts in the moonlight. Her generous cleavage enveloped even his big cock, which was larger than Ford's, and that was saying something.

Charley blew out his breath, his face lighting up in one of his trademark smiles made of sunshine. "Goddamn Evie! Ahh, fuck! That feels incredible." He thrust his cock up and down through her cleavage. His hands gripped the headboard above her, and his strong legs pressed into her sides as he rocked against her. Closing his eyes, he seemed to lose himself in the joy of using her that way. She drank in the look on his face — exhilaration, fun and pure lust. The combination, reflected in his boyish good looks, was mesmerizing. It was like having a vivacious Greek god fucking her tits.

Soon she felt his quads start to tremble and his thrusting become more erratic. He pulled his cock out from between her breasts and sat back, taking a deep breath and clenching and unclenching his fists. "Nearly lost it there. Damn, it's hard to stop doing that." She had to smile, but he was serious about making sure he'd be inside her, and she couldn't wait to accommodate him.

He moved back down the mattress until he was beside her again. She could feel his now-wet erection against her hip, distracting her while he kissed her softly. She squirmed, anxious for his slick cock to be in another area. Stilling his kisses, he rolled her on the mattress as if she were a doll. "Turn on your side, Evie, with your back to me. I want you from behind."

She shifted, trying to accommodate him, but she still sucked in her breath when Charley pushed the broad head of his cock against her wet entrance. With a shiver, she realized she was on the precipice of an odd but thrilling milestone. She was one hip flex away from fucking another man because Ford had commanded her to do it. But Charley seemed in no mood for reflection. With purpose, he rocked his hips forward and entered her. She groaned, fireworks exploding in her brain at the moment she'd done what Ford had demanded.

Charley seemed lost in her. He tilted his body, using his weight as leverage to work his cock deeper, pressing her into the mattress. His whisper was husky in her ear. "Ford said I could have you any way I want you. Any time."

She moaned, arching her back and pressing up to meet his next thrust. He took the opportunity to shove hard into her, as if trying to bury every inch of himself. She gasped as the sheer size of his cock stretched her full.

He pulled her hips against his, cradling her with his body. Charley's touch was that of a lover, his affection open and obvious, but the words he repeated were straight out of the mesmerizing, erotic darkness of Ford's world. "Ford said I could have you, Evie. He said I could fuck you." His ragged whisper was punctuated by the rhythm of his strokes.

Charley's crude words reminding them both of Ford's dominance over her, and the long, rough thrusts of Charley's cock were exactly what Evie needed. She reached backwards, pressing her palm against the hard, flexing muscles of his buttock. "Charley!" she practically screamed. "Take me hard!"

Charley growled, rising up and bracing himself on his left arm while at the same time scooping his hand around Evie's waist. He pinned her body under him so she was facing the mattress, her head turned to the side so she could breathe. "You sure you're ready for this?" He spoke into her hair, right behind her ear, his voice tight with his effort for control.

"*Please*. I need to come. Let me."

He braced himself up on one elbow, tucking his hand around her front to press his fingers between her sensitive pussy lips, seeking out her clit. She squirmed when he honed in on it, pinching and stroking. He circled her hard nub, eliciting whimpers and gasps she'd never heard herself make. That expert stimulation plus four more long, heavy strokes of his cock into her later and the orgasm that had been simmering inside her all day was finally unleashed.

The reverberations of ecstasy ripped through her. She curled into herself, tucking into a ball in front of him as she convulsed in pleasure. She cried out Charley's name. Screamed it with all the power behind the release he'd just given her.

She wanted Ford to know how well Charley had taken care of her, since Ford wouldn't.

Though her body felt slack with satisfaction, Charley had not yet had his fill of her. He sat back on his heels, hauling her hips into the air, not even slowing long enough for Evie to relish the orgasm he'd given her. Wrapping his hands around her hip bones, he dug his fingers into her flesh, pulling back on her pelvis for leverage as he lunged into her. With this technique, every thrust buried him in her. "Are you gonna come again?" His words were ragged. "You're gonna come again for me, aren't you Evie? You love this." He punctuated the accusation with a sharp smack on her bottom.

She yelped at the sting and Charley adjusted her backwards so his thighs slapped against her ass making a sound of wild, pounding, driving sex. The exact kind of sex Charley and Evie were having two doors down from the man who'd ordered it. "I'm not gonna let you sleep tonight until I make you come again," he growled.

"Oh, she's going to come again, but I'll decide when." Ford's voice came from the direction of the door and Evie and Charley froze.

"Jesus, Ford," Charley breathed. "You scared me."

Ford strode across the room and Evie realized with a start that he was naked.

And hard.

"How long have you been watching us?" Adrenalin coursed through her body and her voice squeaked, reflecting the instinctual stab of guilt in her gut, though it was Ford who'd insisted she screw the man whose dick was now still halfway inside her.

"Long enough," he answered, his tone completely neutral. "Charley, pull out. I want to be inside her."

Evie's eyes widened, but she didn't speak. She watched over her shoulder, feeling that the scene was unreal—like it was happening to someone else. Charley slid out of her and moved aside. Ford climbed onto the bed and replaced Charley's cock immediately with his own, burying himself in her to the hilt with his first thrust. Biting down on a gasp, she instead made an incoherent noise reflecting some reaction between pleasure and pain.

"My," Ford said, his voice low and dark, "Evangeline, you have been well-fucked already, haven't you?" He grabbed her hips and drove into her mercilessly, her breath hitching with every powerful thrust.

"I enjoyed watching Charley take you," Ford whispered, his voice hoarse. "Did you like what he did to you?"

Her hair tickled her upper back as it tossed wildly in response to her enthusiastic nod.

"Out loud," Ford demanded, his tone harsh. He didn't rein in his pounding stroke.

"Yes," she gasped. "I liked...having sex with Charley." She squeezed her eyes shut, her embarrassment about being forced to vocalize it momentarily overcoming her desire to please Ford. She looked around for Charley, as much for comfort and assurance as anything. He was at the side of her bed, hand wrapped around his erection. She could see his cock in the moonlight, still glistening with her wetness. He slowly handled himself, waiting for his turn with her.

With that thought, her rational brain all but vanished, and she was left with only animal desire to savor this uninhibited, decadent behavior. She'd agreed to be their toy, to play with whenever they wanted her. It was surreal, but as she reviewed the scene—that she was in a room with two men who were taking turns fucking her, who planned to use her until they both came, inside her or all over her—the crass picture made all the overstimulated nerve endings of her pussy snap taut. She cried out as a wave of near-orgasm twanged through her.

So close!

She was seconds from coming again. But just as she neared the edge, Ford pulled out abruptly. Keeping his hands clamped to her hips, he curled his tall body over her to rest his damp forehead between her shoulder blades. His labored breathing matched her own. Evie glanced back at him and pushed herself backwards, angling to come in contact with his cock again.

"No." Ford pushed her forward and flattened her to the bed. She whined, wriggling her bottom under him like a succubus. "No more." He knelt back and swatted her bottom with his open palm, the smack echoing through the room like a firecracker. Evie bit down on her cry of pain as Ford continued. "I only wanted to feel you after another man had been inside you. But I told you I wasn't going to fuck you like you wanted me to tonight, and I meant it. Now turn over."

She eased around, wary of the possibility of another spank. Her fear sharpened her excitement to a near unbearable level as Ford still knelt so closely, his cock hanging heavy and hard above her. But Ford turned his attention to Charley, still standing next to the bed with his unspent erection in his hand. "I came for Charley tonight."

CHAPTER TWENTY-ONE

*C*HARLEY'S POSTURE STIFFENED and he flicked startled eyes to Ford's. His hand dropped away from his cock as he took a step backward.

"Charley?" Ford seemed to search his friend's face, his voice instantly unsure.

Charley blanched and recovered, drawing close to Ford. Evie could see Charley's massive chest expand and contract as if he'd just run a marathon. "I'm sorry," he said, ducking to catch Ford's eyes. The space between the two men disappeared as Charley pressed even closer, speaking to Ford with such purposeful intimacy, as if they were the only two people in the room. "I wasn't expecting to hear you say that, but I'm so glad you did."

Ford's demeanor had gone still and distant as if a wall had come down around him. Charley's small hesitation seemed to have given Ford a moment to second-guess what he was doing.

Evie, who'd forgotten all about her own nakedness and need for attention, tensed. This could be a bad moment for all of them. In spite of all of the frequent and seemingly casual throwing about of cum, sex and orgasms among the unlikely trio, they were playing a serious and delicate mental game.

But Charley didn't allow Ford the chance to change his mind. He molded himself along Ford's side, murmuring to him. Though she couldn't see clearly in the moonlit room, Evie knew Charley's erection must have been pressed against Ford's hip.

Charley slid his bear paw of a hand down Ford's arm to cover the other man's hand with his own, squeezing. Their clasped hands rested casually so close to Ford's cock that Charley's large knuckles must have been grazing Ford's balls. Charley nuzzled his nose up the side of the other man's face before assuring him in a soothing purr. "I'm so glad you joined us. We both wanted you here." His next words he spoke slowly, in between exploring Ford's ear and neck with those full lips. "I want to be with you Ford, if you'll let me." Evie couldn't seem to get enough air.

Ford's eyes slid closed and he leaned into Charley's face, his body seeming to surrender to the magnetism of the larger man. Their clasped hands moved to Ford's erection and Charley immediately untangled his fingers and fisted his hand around his friend's penis. Ford covered Charley's hand with his own for a heartbeat and Evie was afraid he'd remove Charley's hand from his dick, but instead, Ford groaned and thrust his length into his best friend's fist. He turned to Charley and pulled him into an embrace, kissing him with the power of two thunderclouds colliding.

Evie couldn't help it. She fumbled for the switch on the small lamp next to her bed. This, she didn't want to miss. She'd never before considered a man being with another man to be a subject of her sexual fantasies, but Charley and Ford were enough to make her revise her entire masturbation repertoire for life.

There was something about the two men together. Physically, they were both gorgeous, each in his own way, but it was more than that. The attraction between Ford and Charley was real and raw. As if it didn't matter to them what gender they were, that they came from such different worlds, that they were such different people. They were so obviously drawn to each other, interested in each other's bodies—each other's pleasure—and the genuine affection between them made their naked intertwining all the more sexy.

As lost as they were in their deep kiss, the men seemed oblivious that the room was suddenly washed in the dim light of the small bulb. Evie watched transfixed, relishing every second of the forbidden treat. The men's strong jaws worked as they plundered each other's mouths, their arms straining and powerful as they grasped at each other's hard bodies like only two men would. Charley's shoulder muscles rolled as he shoved his hand lower to clamp around Ford's balls, tugging them downward, harder, it seemed, than Evie would have dared, but Ford groaned and his body dipped as he appeared to momentarily lose support in his knees at the rough handling.

Charley held him pinned to his chest, and worked Ford's balls in the palm of his hand. Ford moaned, his head down and buried in the crook of Charley's neck. Evie saw Ford's long fingers trail, hesitantly at first, and then with more purpose, down Charley's back until he could explore the deep contours of Charley's fantastic ass. Soon his confidence in the act — or maybe need — took over, because Evie saw Ford dig his fingers into Charley's flesh and pull his tight butt cheeks apart as he ground against him. Charley made a guttural noise and drew his head back, his eyes burning into Ford's. Evie knew exactly what he was thinking.

"What are you going to let me have from you, Ford?"

When Ford only smoldered back, offering no hints, Charley collapsed to his knees in front of the man and looked up at him, his eyes entreating. Evie could read the absolute devotion and hunger on Charley's face. She knew Ford could too. Unlike the night before, Evie had no participation in this. This was only the two men. Could Ford accept that turn in their relationship?

A shiver passed through her, drawing her nipples into hard points. What would it be like to have a man like Charley offer you all of him, anything you wanted to take? Up to and including what would destroy him. It was beautiful and heartbreaking, and Evie felt her nerves strained to the snapping point as she studied Ford for any hint of acceptance of Charley's love.

Evie had grown so close to Charley, was so connected to both of the men, as if they were hers and she was theirs. And she knew from personal experience what it felt like to offer Ford anything he wanted to take. She knew the secret thought that accompanied such total submission. *"Please let me give you anything you need, no matter what the cost."*

For Charley and Evie, their submission to the elegant, icy, angel-faced Ford was a raw and voluntary servitude. Evie feared in her gut, though she tried to smother the thought, that they wanted to be on their knees for Ford, pleasing him, because they were both desperately in love with the eccentric, imperfect, infuriating man.

Ford stared down at the bigger man bent in front of him and Evie prayed he would accept Charley's offering. A moment stretched wherein it seemed no one in the room breathed. The trio was at a precipice—continue down this road that none of them would have imagined a week ago, or call the whole thing off. Ford was the only one who could decide for them all. They belonged to him, mind, body and soul.

Finally, Ford reached out and ran his hand slowly through Charley's shaggy hair until he cupped the back of his head. Fisting his fingers into Charley's hair, he pulled the man's face to his erection. "Do it," was all he said.

Charley groaned and captured Ford in his mouth, curling his shoulders toward the object of his desire and wrapping his arms around Ford's hips in a sort of deep, fellatio embrace. Hungry, wet noises came from Charley's lips as he savored all of Ford's rigid length he could sink into his throat.

Ford closed his eyes. "Goddamn, you can suck hard." Ford's voice wavered. "Keep doing it. Just like that. Yes..."

Evie realized she was holding her breath while she ogled the spectacle. She eased back, pulling her legs to her chest and wrapping her arms around them slowly, trying to be quiet to avoid disrupting the two men. It was awfully fun to watch.

Her eyes flicked to Charley's penis, which jutted hard in the air in front of him, an exclamation point aching to be addressed. Charley pumped his hips into nothing as he worked Ford's dick, obviously desperate for his own stimulation. It was shockingly hot, watching the two well-muscled men together, Charley's head bobbing up and down on Ford's generous length, Ford's legs trembling in response.

Almost without thinking Evie reached down to help stoke her own growing fire.

She worked her fingers over her clit, pressing downward in matching cadence to Charley's bobs. Charley popped Ford's swollen glans out of his mouth and flicked at it with his tongue, savoring the liquid he was coaxing out of it by swirling his tongue around the broad tip of Ford's cock. Ford grabbed Charley's head with both hands and forced his cock back between the man's lips, looking as if he intended to fuck Charley's throat. He made an animal noise.

Evie's breath hitched and she added her other hand between her legs so she could plunge her fingers into her pussy while rubbing her wet clit. She sighed, content to bring herself to orgasm while watching Charley suck Ford off.

But her sigh drew Ford's attention and he straightened, taking his hands off Charley's head. "Evangeline, what are you doing?" Charley paused looking first up to Ford and then over at Evie, confusion on his face at the interruption.

She jerked her hands away from her hot pussy and sat up straight, feeling suddenly exposed. Her face warmed. "I was…it was just…hot. Watching Charley do that to you."

Ford looked down at Charley with a dimple-heavy smirk. "I imagine it was. It was hot having Charley do that to me." He turned back to Evie. "But I didn't give you permission to touch yourself. We've made a deal and your body belongs to me. Your orgasms belong to me. I say when you can come."

"But I—"

"Don't argue with me." Ford raised his voice, his hands clenching in obvious frustration.

But Evie's temper flared too. She wanted satisfaction just like they did. "That's not fair, Ford. Why do you care if I just—"

"Evie," Ford interrupted her. "I never said I wasn't going to take care of you. I want to take care of you. I will always take care of you, but you have to trust me. You have got to allow me to be in charge. Why is that so hard for you?"

She didn't answer, impatience making her chew at the inside of her cheek. She tucked her hands under her butt, huffing her breath. Somehow, Ford forbidding her to touch herself made her want to find release at her own hand all the more desperately.

Ford turned to Charley. "Please excuse me for a minute. I'd like you to wait on the bed with Evie." Ford touched Charley's troubled face. "Don't look like that. I'll be back to see this through."

Charley eased onto the bed as Ford strode out of the room. Neither Evie nor Charley spoke at first. Finally Evie ventured, "What do you think he has in mind?"

Charley snorted his lips curling into a smile. "With Ford, who knows?"

"That's what I'm afraid of."

Ford returned, carrying what looked like a handful of leather straps. Propping Evie's pillows at the head of her bed, he instructed her tersely, "Lean back on these pillows and put your hands over your head."

Evie exchanged a glance with Charley, who only shrugged. She did what she was told. Her heart pounding, she raised her hands over her head and looked at Ford. He deftly tied a leather strap around one of her wrists and fed the strap through something... Only then did Evie notice the ring secured to her headboard. She flipped her head in the other direction and found one there too. Two dull nickel rings, attached securely to the pretty bed, nearly invisible against the swirling silver and blue design of the upholstered headboard. The rings were positioned at just the right width apart to tether the arms of a woman Evie's size.

She gasped. "You had those added to my bed?" Ford only winked at her, looking wickedly pleased with himself. "I can't believe your presumptuousness!" she squeaked.

Ford moved to secure her other hand, speaking in his infuriating, logical manner. "And yet here you are, love, tied to your bed naked, with two erect men in the room with you, not forty-eight hours after you moved in. And with an agreement to let us do anything we want to you." Evie felt her face flush even redder, half with anger, half with shame.

Ford paused, kissing Evie's hot cheek and down to her neck, his lips managing somehow to erase her negative feelings about his preparations to her bed. "There you go again, breaking my rules. I said no shame, my love. I won't allow it." A smile lit across his face, his dimples turning him into an angel again. "Still so willful and now this? You are absolutely begging to be punished." He ran a finger lightly over her lips, making her pant in response to her heightened pulse. "Soon," he whispered. He sounded delighted that she'd broken his rules, and Evie's stomach clenched in trepidation. What did punishment mean to Ford?

"Now Evie," he persuaded. "Don't think of it as

presumptuousness. We've always had a connection—you know that. We're giving each other a great gift—the gift of exploring our darkest sexual desires. After our encounter in the library, I had a good idea what you needed and I had every intention of making it happen when you moved here. Nothing could have deterred me." He kissed her gently on the lips, his teeth catching her bottom lip and biting with just enough pressure to make her core clench in pleasure. "I always get what I want. Now don't over-think it."

He smiled and his face was so gorgeous—absolute perfection, absolute confidence—but it was his eyes that won her over. It wasn't confidence she saw in his beautiful, green eyes, it was hope. Hope that she wouldn't reject him.

She didn't respond, but pulled on her hands, testing the security of the rings. Her wrists were held tight. Sighing, she settled back and asked softly, "So what now?"

"Now I'll allow you to make a choice. You can have Charley to privately finish what I walked in on, giving you total satisfaction, or you can watch, unsatisfied and with no attention to your sexual needs, while I try things Charley's way."

Evie's eyes flew to Charley's. They exchanged a wordless, "holy shit".

Evie didn't hesitate. "You with Charley."

"Evie..." Charley's voice sounded anguished at her sacrifice.

"No. Ford says I get to choose. That's my choice."

Ford handed a longer leather strap to Charley. "Tie her ankle." Charley met Evie's gaze and she could not mistake the love and gratitude burning in his wide, brown eyes. He bent to secure her ankle to a similar ring in the foot-board, squeezing her leg affectionately when he was done. Ford tied her other ankle to a fourth ring.

The pillows propped her head and upper body up at a comfortable angle, giving her a clear view of the end of her bed. Taking a deep breath, Ford met Charley's eyes across the bed. Charley stared back at the man. For a moment they looked like any two men considering how to tackle a challenge together. Except these two men were naked and semi-hard, and their "challenge" was how to fuck each other.

Butterflies swooped in Evie's stomach and her breathing grew shallow. She could only imagine what Charley must be feeling. But the silence between Charley and Ford began to stretch a few beats too long. Evie grew uneasy. Someone had to make a move before everyone's bravery crumbled.

"I don't get why I have to be tied up for this. I'm not even participating," she whined, hoping to snap Ford back to his in-charge, dominant demeanor where he was so comfortable. It worked.

Ford's posture straightened and his eyes flashed toward Evie. "I've asked you not to touch yourself and I don't trust you." He raked his eyes from Evie's wrists, down her naked body to her exposed pussy. Her legs were forcibly spread, preventing her from closing them or covering herself. Or stopping the two men from each taking her in turn.

She whimpered at the thought, praying Ford couldn't see the juices that evidenced her excitement trickling to her thighs. "Besides," he murmured. "I like you tied like that." His voice grew more sure as he finished addressing her. "It gets me off, and that is reason enough."

Now radiating the confidence that was so attractive on him, Ford turned back to Charley. "From what I've experienced so far, I'd say things are about to get very hot."

With that, Charley's posture visibly relaxed and he grinned at Ford. "You have no idea," Charley drawled, shaking his head.

Ford pursed his lips and narrowed his eyes, looking every inch the sexy, natural dominant that he was. "I'm no expert on how this works, but I suppose we'll need some lubricant.

"Got it!" Charley whirled around and snatched his jeans from the floor, pulling a tube of something from his pocket.

Ford and Evie both raised their eyebrows. "Do you always carry lube around in your pocket?" Ford asked, bemused.

"Only when I'm coming over here." Charley looked back and forth between Evie and Ford. "Hey, a boy can hope, can't he?"

Evie laughed but Ford only put his hand out to Charley, his lips twitching. "Come here."

Charley crawled onto the bed, locking eyes with Ford and moving on hands and knees until he was in front of him. Charley was careful to avoid Evie's tethers.

Charley knelt up when he reached Ford and opened the tube of lubrication, squirting a generous amount into his palm. He slathered the lube onto Ford's cock, working the billionaire to rigidness again. He didn't take his eyes from Ford's face as he stroked and squeezed him.

Ford closed his eyes and blew out his breath, sounding as if he was searching for control of his body's response. "I loved that night when you made us both come. Your hands are so big."

Evie realized Ford was referring to the one and only encounter he and Charley had together before Evie came to live there. He'd never acknowledged it, according to Charley. This was big.

The same thought must have been going through Charley's head. "You liked that?" he asked Ford softly.

"I've thought of that night many times."

Charley closed his eyes and took two deep breaths. When he opened them his whole being looked as if a burden had been lifted from his shoulders. He stretched up to Ford's face, kissing him softly on the lips. "Me too," Charley whispered, his voice thick with emotion. "So many times. And I can give you other things you'll like too." He licked his tongue across Ford's lips, and his best friend stilled, closing his eyes. Charley spoke against the corner of Ford's mouth, so softly Evie almost couldn't make it out.

"I can give you tighter things. Hotter things."

Ford opened his eyes and grasped Charley's shoulders, locking eyes with him. "I want that. Tonight, Charley." Ford's voice was hard, sure, and Charley moaned, catching his own cock in his other hand and squeezing himself in response to Ford's words. Evie bit her lip. This was fucking intense. But Ford grew suddenly serious. "I've never done this before. You will tell me if I do something you don't want me to do?"

Charley shook his head, pulling on Ford's cock in time with his own, and answered in a hoarse whisper. "The only thing I don't want you to do tonight, Ford, is stop until you come as deep in my tight ass as you can bury your cock."

"Jesus," Evie whispered. She was trembling as waves of excitement crashed over her with nowhere to release their energy. She pulled her restraints tight.

Ford groaned, practically leaping to the other side of the bed and positioning himself behind Charley. He put his hands on the man's massive shoulders and took a breath before looking down and very purposefully wedging his erection between Charley's ass cheeks. Charley closed his eyes. Ford slowly stroked forward along the crease, pleasuring himself and lubing Charley's bottom at the same time.

Charley groaned, throwing himself forward on all fours and gripping the duvet with murderous strength. He pressed his hips back to Ford, but Ford stopped to retrieve the tube of lubricant Charley had dropped on the bed. He slathered more slick gel onto his fingers and then pressed those wet fingers against Charley's sensitive opening. Evie watched Ford's forearm muscles solidify and roll under his tanned skin as he worked his fingers against Charley's asshole, spreading the lubricant and making Charley's cock jump.

"Is it okay if Evie's here? Mine and Evie's first time was private. Do you want ours to be private too?" Ford asked Charley the question with a tone of genuine concern, though Evie saw one of his fingers disappear into Charley's ass without waiting for an answer. Charley shuddered at the penetration, his face a mixture of heat and heaven.

Evie's eyebrows rose. That question sounded caring, emotional. Ford didn't usually play in that world. She was shocked he'd even thought to ask.

"No." Charley's voice was hoarse. "She's part of this. I want her here." Charley wrapped one of his hands around Evie's bound ankle, squeezing. Her heart leapt with affection for the man.

"Good." Ford said. "I want her here too. I want her to watch me satisfy myself in your ass." Ford pushed a second finger into him and Charley arched his back, meeting the thrust of Ford's fingers. Ford looked up at Evie. "Pay attention, Evangeline," he growled. "I will have your ass soon too. And so will Charley."

Evie gulped in a breath, fear and desire coalescing into a state of desperate excitement. The bossier and cruder Ford got, the more her body rocketed to a higher plane of lust. The corner of Ford's mouth curled as he considered her reaction. He locked eyes with her while he continued to work his fingers into Charley, who was moaning softly now. For a moment, Ford's dimples betrayed the hardness he seemed to be trying to project. He quickly turned his attention back to Charley, muttering, "One more, I think," and sank a third finger home.

Charley dropped his shoulders to the bed as if supplicating himself, leaving his ass high in the air. Ford's arm muscles stood out in relief, evidencing the strength at which he was stretching Charley's asshole, preparing him to accommodate Ford's large erection.

Ford leaned over Charley murmuring softly as if they were the only two lovers in the room. "Charley, you and I don't have the same kind of relationship as I have with Evie." Ford's voice wavered, but with effort or passion, Evie didn't know. "If you need me to stop at any moment, just tell me and I'll stop immediately. I don't want to hurt you unnecessarily."

Charley half-moaned, half-chuckled into the softness of the feather duvet. "I've done this a few times before, Ford. You're not gonna hurt me."

"If that's truly the case—" Ford sounded as if he were speaking through gritted teeth, "—then I'm going to go as hard and deep as I've been wanting to in your ass."

Charley made a choked noise that sounded as full of anticipation as it did passion. Blood pounded through Evie's body and she realized she was straining against her leather straps just to get closer to the men. She had a perfect and unobstructed view of what they were engaging in, and saw the very moment Ford pulled his fingers from Charley's ass and replaced them with his erection, poised at Charley's entrance. Ford held his cock at its wide base to guide it and wrapped his other hand around the side of Charley's sinewed hip to use as leverage.

Evie bit her lip and whimpered when she saw Ford's arm and butt muscles contract as he committed to his first thrust into Charley's ass. In spite of his promise to pound Charley hard, Ford eased himself in, his face a picture of awe, ecstasy and bare restraint.

The head of his cock disappeared into Charley's hole. Slowly then, one inches, two inches... Ford's legs were visibly trembling with his apparent effort at control.

Charley moaned low and long when Ford's entered him. As hot as the scene was, the look on Charley's face broke Evie's heart a little. She saw love, pure and vulnerable, on Charley's rapt expression. And she wondered if he could handle having sex with Ford. She was concerned about Charley's heart, not his body.

Could Charley get over this intimate act if Ford could never love him back? Could Charley resign himself to casual sex with his best friend? What if Ford decided it was a passing whimsy and he wasn't interested in having sex with Charley again? Evie was hopeful about her ability to keep her emotions out of the sex she had with Ford, but Charley, who was already in love with Ford, was in a more vulnerable state.

Charley pushed backwards impatiently, sheathing Ford to the balls in his ass. Ford and Charley both grunted—satisfied, animal sounds. The virile sound of two powerful men having sex. Evie had never heard anything more primitive than those grunts. Or anything hotter.

"God Ford, you're inside me..." Charley trailed off, squeezing his eyes shut. "Feels so good."

Evie seemed to forget all propriety. She moaned and writhed against her ties, straining to get to the men, to get in on the feral lovemaking. But her restraints did not give. The two men were so engaged in their moment they didn't even seem to notice her reaction.

Ford put his free hand around Charley's other hip, lower so as not to block Evie's view, and pulled himself slowly out to the rounded tip of his cock before plowing back into him. Both men grunted again. Ford began rocking in and out of Charley slowly, seeming to take his time to explore the sensations of being inside a man. He stared at his cock disappearing again and again into Charley's hard, muscular bottom, as if mesmerized. Ford's chiseled face looked hungry but determined, as if he could stay there in Charley's ass, fucking him for countless hours while Evie watched, until neither man could stand up.

"I hope you're ready to take me hard, Charley," Ford's deep voice was gravelly, and strained with the effort of his control. "'Cause I'm gonna give it to you hard."

"God yes," Charley sighed. "Fuck me hard, Ford. Fuck me any way you need it." Charley rocked his hips back, slamming his ass into Ford's pelvis and burying Ford's substantial cock inside him. "I want you to love my ass, Ford. I want you to love to fuck it."

Damn, Evie thought. *These two talk dirtier than I do with either of them.* She craned her head to get the absolute best view of Ford sinking again and again into Charley.

Ford dropped his chin, his shoulders bunching with effort as he picked up his pace until his thighs smacked sharply against Charley's ass. That sound nearly drove Evie out of her mind. Ford was driving his cock relentlessly into Charley's backside. The two men shook the bed with the power of an earthquake. Evie wondered if Ford was really letting go—having sex rougher and more powerfully than he'd ever been able to with a woman. Charley was built like a tank and could certainly take a hell of a hard fucking.

"You're in me so goddamned deep..." Charley made a sound that Evie would have thought was a cry of anguish if she hadn't been looking right at his unmistakably rapture-filled face right at that moment. "Can't hold out, Ford. Too good. Gonna come," Charley gasped almost incoherently in between poundings.

Evie felt her eyes widen. No one and nothing was touching Charley's cock, which bobbed under him, heavy and flushed red. He was going to come just from Ford fucking his ass? With no contact to his own cock at all? Was that even possible?

"You will not stop until I'm completely done in your ass," Ford growled, reaching around Charley and squeezing his hand around the base of Charley's dick, preventing him from release.

"Let me come while you're in me. Goddamn, let me come!" Charley pleaded, his eyes shut. This time the cry he made truly was one of anguish. The hand he'd wrapped around Evie's ankle squeezed so hard she cried out, afraid he might break her bones in his frenzied state.

A moment later Ford released his seed inside Charley with what looked like the power and heat of a mighty volcano. He slammed his dick home in the man's ass two more times, and with a wild yell of triumph, shuddered as he buried himself in Charley's tight hole and came. He released his tight grip on Charley's erection and didn't even bother to stroke the other man. But it didn't matter. Charley didn't require it. As soon as Ford released his grip on Charley's manhood, Charley cried out and orgasmed with a sound of tortured relief, his cock jumping as he orgasmed into the air, with nothing touching his gorgeous erection at all.

Evie moaned, her clit feeling as tortured as Charley's face had looked before Ford had released him. She clenched her vaginal muscles, trying to coax the relief she desperately needed, but she couldn't. Not with her legs forced so far apart. Ropes of Charley's hot, wet cum landed on her leg in pulses as Charley nearly sobbed with the intense release the orgasm drained from him.

Ford grunted as he bucked the last of his seemingly never-ending load into Charley's ass. Finally, Ford collapsed against Charley's back as Charley seemed to lose his strength too and sank to the bed. They didn't move for several heartbeats, and all Evie could hear was their labored breathing.

Each man looked exhausted, as if each had given all he could and taken all he could take from the other, their cocks generous and greedy at the same time. Ford had demanded complete satisfaction but had also managed to give what had looked like unending pleasure to his friend.

Finally, Ford sat back, allowing his softening, wet cock to slip out of Charley's now well-fucked ass. Charley groaned sleepily at the loss. "Don't move," Ford ordered, then got up and padded to the bathroom.

Charley turned his head without lifting it from the bed and opened his heavy eyelids just enough to find Evie's eyes. He smiled sheepishly, and they didn't need to say anything. Evie knew what he was feeling.

The. Best. Ever.

Evie had known that feeling every time Ford had pushed her further down his sexual rabbit hole. Charley kissed her shin, letting his eyes slip closed again. "Glad you were here with me," he whispered. "Someone else saw it so it must have been real."

Evie smiled. "I saw it this time, Charley," Evie whispered back. "It happened, and it looked really, really good." Charley just smiled, resting his cheek on her leg.

Ford returned looking fresh from a quick shower and carrying a warm washcloth and a towel. Moisture highlighted his mop of hair and his naked skin was beaded with droplets that caught the light. Charley raised his upper body and reached for the washcloth but Ford shushed him and pressed him back down to the bed. He took his time, cleaning Charley gently, thoroughly, asking if he was okay, if he needed anything.

"Not that I'm complaining about the sponge bath, Ford, but I'm fine. Promise," Charley assured him.

After Ford cleaned the cum that had splashed onto Evie's legs, he stretched onto the foot of the bed next to Charley, a smile playing across his refined features. "Sorry I was so rough on you."

Charley laughed. "Thanks for saying that, but no you're not. How long have we been friends?" Ford raised his eyebrows, shrugging one shoulder in mock surrender to Charley's words. "You love to push. You're never happy until you see how far you can take things."

Ford's dimples flashed to life, highlighting a wicked smile. "You do know me, don't you?" he murmured, toweling Charley's backside completely dry. "I'm proud of you, Charley. Impressed. You took that like a man."

"And that's exactly how I wanted it."

"Um, guys, I hate to interrupt, but…tied up here. And my butt's falling asleep." Evie pushed her shoulders into the pillows shifting to get the blood flowing again in her backside.

Ford smiled up at Evie—a radiant, satisfied smile, so beautiful on his expressive lips—and Evie felt a wash of affection for the man. As quickly as it came, Evie felt sick to her stomach. She liked him. Liked him in a way she shouldn't. Liked him a lot. And he had kissed Charley in a deep and passionate way. He'd poured himself into that kiss. Why wouldn't Ford kiss her with the same abandon?

She didn't want to feel jealous of Charley. After all, when the job was over and she was gone, she hoped Charley and Ford would stay together and be happy. But she couldn't help the feeling of disappointment that crept over her that she'd never had a kiss like that from him.

Ford spoke to Charley. "What do you think? Has she learned her lesson? Should we let her go?"

"Yes," Charley grunted, sounding half asleep.

"I don't know. She's really bad at following my rules…"

"C'mon, stop playing with her. Let her go." Charley's voice was thick with exhaustion and muffled against Evie's shin.

Ford relented and untied her ankles, massaging each one thoroughly and checking her over to ensure she was okay. When he was satisfied her ankles were now comfortable, after many assurances from her, he got up and returned the towel and washcloth to the bathroom.

Evie watched him and for the millionth time marveled at what the man looked like naked. Ford eased back onto the bed next to Evie, his cool skin sliding down hers until he was positioned against the entire right side of her body, his leg thrown over hers. Instantly her nipples pricked into hard pebbles and goose bumps broke out on her arms.

He held his head propped on one elbow and plucked gently at the hard, rosy tips of her breasts. "Do you regret your choice?"

"Which one?" She'd made more potentially regrettable decisions in the past few days than ever in her life.

"Charley and I instead of Charley and you." Evie shook her head and Ford studied her face, letting the silence settle around them both like a blanket. Charley's breathing was deep and regular and Evie knew he'd fallen asleep. "You're awfully quiet for someone with no regrets," Ford finally whispered, pinching a nipple hard enough to make her suck in a breath.

"Can you please untie me?"

"Not until you tell me what's on your mind."

She looked away, knowing he wouldn't relent. "The way you kissed Charley…you don't want to kiss me like that," she whispered.

"I don't want to?" he repeated, trailing the tips of his fingers around her nipples, keeping them puckered hard. "I wouldn't agree with that statement. I choose not to. That's more accurate."

"Why?" Evie met his eyes again, surprised at his admission.

Ford took a deep breath, looking suddenly weary. "It's important we don't confuse things. We're not in a relationship. If I kiss you like that, I'm afraid we might end up…confused. I'm being cautious for both of us."

"So you want a relationship with Charley?"

Ford furrowed his brow and shot her a look of disbelief. "Charley's my best friend. We already have a relationship." He shrugged. "What we choose to engage in with each other when we're screwing around won't change that."

"Oh." Her chest felt tight. Charley was already too far gone in love with Ford to prevent certain heartbreak when Ford refused to admit their relationship was anything other than friends, no matter what they did in bed.

Ford gave her nipples reprieve and moved his fingers to her mouth, brushing his thumb across her bottom lip. Shifting, he lifted his upper body so his face was close to hers. He met her eyes and he looked…hopeful? She held her breath. "Evie, you're clear on our situation?" She nodded. "I like what we've created here. I won't have any threats to our arrangement."

She shook her head, just as determined as he was to have no confusion, ignoring the ache it caused in the pit of her stomach. No way in hell was she walking away in a year dragging her mangled heart behind her again. She was just going to move on to the next adventure and not look back.

He untangled himself from her and slid off the bed. "I'm going to untie your arms." He made his way around the bed, releasing her restraints. She groaned with the freeing of each of the bonds, rubbing at her numb wrists. When he'd completely untied her, he curled back into bed next to her, careful not to disturb Charley, who was sleeping at their feet.

He caressed first one wrist, then the other, pressing into her dented skin with his thumbs, soothing her. "You did well, Evie. I'm proud of you." Lifting her hands, he kissed each of her inner wrists in turn, his lips on that sensitive skin making her core warm again. "Did you enjoy watching?"

She nodded. "Why couldn't I participate, or take care of myself, or…something?" She searched his eyes, as if the answer could be found there.

He smiled, pressing her fingers to his lips and kissing them. "To teach you patience. To teach you to let me choose the time and place of your pleasure. That's what I want. It's why I hired you." He tilted his body over hers and leaned close to her face. "What if I kissed you?" he whispered.

"What if?" she answered.

"Could you remember the rules?"

"Could you?"

He smirked, pursing his lips and making her want to devour him. "Fair enough. Then let's do something really crazy."

He shifted, pressing his body weight against her side, his naked skin feeling like heaven against her own. He touched his lips to hers, slowly at first, exploring. Raising her head to meet his mouth more firmly, she pressed into him. He cupped his large hand around the side of her face, slanting her head for a better angle to deepen the kiss. His tongue parted her lips and she met it with her own.

Increasing the pressure, Ford's kiss became more proprietary, more insistent to let him in, let him do what he wanted. Her heart leapt in her chest as he pulled back unexpectedly, touched his lips to hers twice, and then resumed his deep exploration, as if to own her completely with his mouth.

The heat she'd built up while watching the two men had not yet been sated, and her pussy throbbed for his touch. Without meaning to, she whimpered into his kiss, and when he finally left her mouth to travel lower, nuzzling at her neck, she moaned.

"Those noises you make when I kiss you," Ford breathed in between nibbles at her collarbone. "I love those noises."

"Will you let me come now? Please, make me come." Evie gasped, hardly able to speak with Ford's teeth now teasing her nipples, gently threatening to bite.

"I told you to trust me, Evangeline. I'll always make sure you're taken care of. For all the pleasure you give me, I'll match it with yours." Ford whispered those words against her stomach as he licked his way down her body, just as he had in the law firm library, to deliver on his promise better than anyone ever had.

CHAPTER TWENTY-TWO

EVIE WOKE UP alone. The morning sun sifting through the windows warmed her face. Feeling far too comfortable to get out of bed, she stretched and groaned as her sore body protested. Scene by decadent scene, she pieced together the end of the evening the night before. Her stopping Ford in the hallway. Charley's visit at Ford's behest. Ford joining them in bed, and then…

Evie squeezed her eyes and wrinkled her nose as the more tender parts of her body woke up at those thoughts. *Damn, that had been hot last night.* Crazy, but hot. Watching her current "lover" have sex with her other current lover — both of them men — while she was tied up and made to watch, wasn't something Evie could even have imagined doing a week ago. Let alone enjoying it. But she had. Oh, she had.

What was Ford doing to her?

But she was self-aware enough to know that Ford wasn't changing her. He was revealing her.

Being under Ford's control — under his spell — was a no holds barred sexual revolution. But were she and Charley willing partners, or just pawns in Ford's master game? She clenched her teeth, staring at the ceiling and wondering if there was anything she could do to help protect Charley. For a man so big, she feared he was particularly vulnerable with his heart in the hands of man like Ford Hawthorne.

She could handle having her heart jerked around — she'd had

practice. But after seeing the absolute gut-wrenching honesty of Charley's love for Ford evident on Charley's face as he'd knelt in front of Ford, silently offering to suck his cock, Evie's stomach flip-flopped.

Throwing off the covers, she groaned as she pulled herself to sitting. First thing…a long, hot bath. After that she'd do her job in as carefree and enthusiastic manner as she could, giving the men fun and sex to distract them until maybe Ford would naturally slip so far into love with Charley that he'd realize he never wanted out.

There was only one problem with her plan. How did she get two of their threesome to fall deeply in love while somehow keeping all those same emotions from gaining purchase in her own heart? She padded naked to the bathroom vowing not to think about it. She'd worry about that later.

The house was mostly quiet except for the occasional sound of a staff member working. Ford's household staff was so unnoticeable that Evie suspected they were being purposely stealthy. Their invisibility was probably specified in their job descriptions. Ford had a way with creating unique job descriptions.

Feeling less achy after her bath, Evie completed the to-do list of work items Ford had left for her in a note addressed to, "My fantastically dirty girl" and ending with a paragraph of appreciation for what she'd done with the men the night before, in graphic detail, yet written as eloquently as Ford speaks. She had to sit down after reading the to-do list and fan herself with it.

The doorbell rang, startling her out of a daydream about Ford and Charley. She stood slowly, uncertain whether she should answer it or not. Boone was standing guard at the gate, but that didn't keep her knees from going weak as she tiptoed toward the massive, wooden door. Three thumps on the door echoed through the entryway, making her jump. She looked around instinctively, but no one seemed to be coming to answer it.

Should she let it go unanswered? She took a step back, deciding to do just that when she heard Boone's voice, muffled through the stone and wood fortress of a house. "Evie? It's Boone." Feeling relief wash through her, she unbolted the door and hauled it up, squinting against the sudden sunshine at the military man. The sun filtered through the peach-fuzz of hair on Boone's closely-shaved head, making him look like he had a halo.

"Miss Evie," he said, tipping his head and touching his beret. "I hope I didn't catch you at a bad time. I apologize for not calling ahead like I usually do, but I was headed up this way to check the grounds when this came for you." He held out a flat, cardboard envelope.

She took it, wondering what was in the parcel. She'd ordered a lot of things off the internet during her shopping spree, but this didn't appear to be a package—more like just papers. Who would have sent her papers? There was no return address on the envelope.

"While I'm here, would you like me to check the house, ma'am?"

She shook her head, smiling at the serious man. "Oh, no. Everything's fine here." Distracted, she tore off the obligatory strip to open the envelope and gapped it to peek inside. She could only see the corner of a photograph, but she didn't need to see any more to know what she was looking at. To have the floor drop out from under her. To have her fingers start to tremble.

"Ma'am?" Boone's tone of voice instantly hardened and he leaned forward to look into the envelope.

Evie pulled it behind her back, affecting a casual stance. She didn't want Boone to see the picture of the dead girl. A copy of one of the many John had threatened her with in his office the day she'd broken up with him and threatened to come forward about his embezzlement. She was embarrassed to be mixed up in something so crazy, so psychotic. Though she knew Boone would think of nothing but protecting her, something about the mess made her feel dirty, like she was tracking mud into Ford's pristine life.

She smiled at Boone, hoping to brush off the incident, though she knew his highly-trained guardian instincts had already been triggered and she wasn't fooling him. "Thanks Boone, for bringing this to me. It's always good to see you." She moved to close the door. The stiff-postured man stepped back to allow her, but his laser-sharp eyes didn't leave hers until she'd closed the door between them, breaking the eye contact.

When the door clicked shut, she turned and leaned against it, letting her breath out in a whoosh. She squeezed her fingers around the envelope until it creased, her heart pounding in her chest. Without looking down, she slid a hand between the two thin sheets of cardboard and slowly pulled out the photograph. With dread, she lowered her eyes to it. Scrawled across the horrifying image were the words, "WHERE'S MY MONEY BITCH?" Evie frowned, noting his grammar was missing a comma because he didn't have an Evie to proofread his work anymore.

The thought made her laugh until she doubled over. Stuffing a hand against her mouth, she tried to stifle her giggles. She sounded a bit hysterical. She felt a bit hysterical.

Her fist seized around the picture, crumpling it in a death grip. Numbly, she headed for the kitchen where she remembered seeing a trash compactor. It wasn't the same as an incinerator, but crushing the evidence felt better than tearing it up and throwing it into the nearest garbage can. Crushing it felt a little like burying it, which is exactly what Evie wanted to do.

The compactor growled to life three times, crushing the envelope and picture until Evie felt a little better. Boone was on guard, and armed. There were high stone walls around the entire estate and the house had state of the art surveillance and security. John could scare her, but he couldn't actually hurt her. Filling her lungs with a deep, cleansing breath, Evie held her hands out in front of her until they stopped visibly trembling.

She was protected at Ford's, plus she wasn't helpless. She could protect herself. Maybe throwing knives had no real self-defense value, but all her practice had taught her how to yield a blade better than the average person. Still, she hoped it would never come down to her, John and a knife.

*****

The last item on the list Ford left her was to meet him in the great room at 4pm for cocktails. She'd been tingling all over for forty-five minutes by the time she stepped into the large room at three fifty-nine. He was standing at the bar, his back to her, and her heart bounded like an excited puppy. She drank in the way his broad shoulders stretched the finely-tailored white dress-shirt, his tapered waist, and his incredible, athletic butt.

She looked up from her ogling just in time as Ford turned to her and smiled. "Evie, love, I've been looking forward to seeing you all day." He came forward to greet her, the look in his eyes making her feel as if she were naked. "It's hard to work with someone like you around, knowing I could have you any time I wanted." He handed her a martini.

"Ford." She tipped her head and smiled as she took the glass. "You were at the house today? I never saw you."

"I mostly work at home in the library. I find it preferable."

She fought back disappointment to find he'd been there the whole day and had never come to see her. "Please remember," she tilted her head up, hoping to God her sultry smile was just that, and not something laughable. "While you're working, I'm always available to provide you company."

He pursed his lips and clinked his heavy bourbon tumbler to the lip of her delicate martini glass. "Of course you are, Evie. I've ensured that, haven't I?" Swirling his drink once, he swallowed the last of his bourbon and set the glass down with a thump onto the bar. Evie noticed the tightness across his back.

"Is everything okay?" She wanted to touch his shoulder and feel his muscles bunched beneath her fingers, soothe his worries away, but she didn't, not knowing how to read his mood.

"I met with my new lawyers today." He didn't look at her, but tapped the bar as if impatient, staring at the wall. "Rumor has it John was fired."

Evie snorted. She couldn't help it. "Ah, well, they finally figured out he wasn't doing his own work."

"I'm sure you're right," Ford said grimly. "Which is exactly what worries me. He'll blame you." He turned and looked at her, the set of his brows giving his eyes a mixture of worry and ire.

Ford was right. If John had no job, there was nothing to stop him from spending all his time obsessing on revenge against Evie. That must be why she'd gotten the picture. If she didn't pay John back soon, he might come looking for her. She had to get him his money, fast.

Something twisted in Evie's gut and she dropped her eyes from Ford's angry look. Was he mad at John, or at her? *Oh God.* She'd brought this problem to Ford's house. "I'm s-sorry," she stammered.

He blinked, pulling his head back. "Sorry? This isn't what you need to be sorry for." His voice was icy. "This is not your doing. What you need to be sorry for is hiding things from me. Things that involve your safety." Ford held up the crumpled picture of the dead woman that Evie had disposed of in the trash compactor earlier, his large hand thankfully covering most of the gruesome picture.

She averted her eyes, setting her martini glass on the bar. "How did you find that?" she whispered.

"Boone informed me you'd received something in the mail that'd upset you. I looked for it in the trash on a hunch."

"You picked through the trash?" Evie was genuinely amazed.

"Evangeline, I'd bathe in trash if it meant protecting what's mine." Her eyes widened and the words sent a shiver through her, as much due to the intensity of his message as to his reference to her as "his".

"I'm sorry," she said again, stepping closer to him, hoping to disappear in his shadow. Somehow his vow to protect her made her feel shy.

He narrowed his eyes at her.

"I'm sorry for hiding it from you," she rushed to clarify. "I shouldn't have. You need to know the danger I've brought to your house so you can protect yourself, or so you can..." Her words faltered and she dropped her eyes, hating that her posture made her look meek, but afraid she'd cry if she looked at him as she said her next words. "So that you can ask me to leave."

Ford grasped her shoulders, crumpling the picture in his grip. "Ask you to leave?" His voice was gruff. "Look at me," he commanded, and she raised her eyes, gritting her teeth against the tears—not because of his reaction or the real possibility that he'd kick her out, but because she was fine in any situation as long as she didn't have to think too much about it or share it with others. With her unusual aversion to fear, admitting she was in a truly scary situation and facing it was hardly one of her strong suits.

"You aren't going anywhere. I won't allow it." He searched her eyes, seeming to realize her heightened emotional state and his grip on her softened. Pulling her against him, he wrapped her into a strong embrace and kissed her hair.

Closing her eyes, she exhaled, feeling the pressure of the stress and anxiety lift from her like a vice being released. She pressed her face into his chest, drinking in the safety she felt there like an addict.

"If he wants to hurt you," Ford whispered into her hair, "I'll simply need to keep you closer at all times." He moved a hand down her back, pulling her against him all the way down, stirring heat to life in her core. "And since my work necessarily takes me away at times, I'm going to have Charley move in."

Evie pulled away to look up at him. "Really?" she asked, a huge grin spreading on her face. She loved the idea of having Charley under the same roof. Like Ford, she couldn't get enough of the man.

"Yes." Ford smiled, looking like the dashing businessman he was in his expensive dress attire, only his flashy dimples adding a hint of playfulness behind the polish. "You'd like that?"

"I'd love it!" Evie practically squealed, bouncing in his arms. "Both of you living here together twenty-four seven? Oh—" She sobered. "Can I handle you both that often?" she teased.

"You will, love. You will. If you have to practically live in a warm bath or on the massage table, you will. If I have my way about it." He pursed his beautiful lips into a bad-boy smirk. "And I always have my way, don't I?"

"You do, Mr. Hawthorne. And that's just the way I like it," Evie whispered, her voice coy as she twined her arms up around his neck to rake her fingers in the hair at his neck.

He kissed her, his tongue dipping through her parted lips to caress hers like a lover. She felt his passion and need for her in the kiss, and it occurred to her that she was happy. So happy. And what was so surprising to her is that for a moment, Ford seemed to feel the same. Happiness was an emotion that seemed foreign to Ford. Smiles from him weren't rare, especially given that he knew the power of his dimples and unleashed them strategically to manipulate those he could, but his smiles had no depth. His smiles looked right, and they looked pretty, but they rarely seemed to reach his eyes. Behind his eyes, she'd only ever seen loneliness.

Until lately. She melted even more in his arms, basking in how right it felt. This gorgeous feeling, his lips on hers...it couldn't be false. It couldn't be.

Ford groaned as he broke the kiss, pressing his cheek against her forehead. "Mmm, Evie. I like the idea too. The three of us together, in bed together—inside each other—it is good, isn't it?"

She smiled up at him. "It's better than good. It's perfect. So does this mean we'll be sleeping in your room?" she asked, knowing she was pushing him, but feeling that if he felt a fraction of what she felt in his arms that surely it would all be okay. Surely his loving response would come as smoothly and easily as her descent was going in falling for the unavailable, screwed-up man.

But she knew better, even though her fantasies made her forget sometimes.

His smile faltered, a shadow seeming to pass over his face. He stepped back from her, placing the ruined picture face-down on the bar with a thump, as if the matter was now closed. "No, of course not. We'll each have our own space as we do now. I've got plenty of extra bedrooms in the house." He waved a hand toward the ceiling and the rooms above them. "Would you like another drink?" His posture pulled up straight and the distance between them formalized again with the snap of the bar towel he'd picked up and shook out before wiping under the tumbler he moved to the bar sink.

"No. No thank you." She opened her mouth to say something to hurt him, to push him. Something about her asking Charley to stay in her room and they'd enjoy each other's "space" without Ford if he needed his privacy so badly, but she quashed the rebellious urge at the last second. It wasn't his fault. He had his issues just as she had hers. And he'd given in on the lock situation, not trying to change her. She'd return the favor. Besides, spending the next year spooning in bed each night with the two men was a sure-fire path to a broken heart when she had to move out. Best to keep things at that glaring arms-length he was now maintaining between them.

The two fell into an awkward silence, then Ford's eyes lit. "I have something for you." He reached behind the bar and produced a small, robin's egg-blue box, adorned with a white ribbon.

Evie gasped, taking a step back and jabbing a finger toward

the jewelry box. "What is that?"

Ford knitted his brow, his face clouding. "Well, whatever it is, I don't think it's going to bite you. You'd think I'd just pulled a small rodent from my pocket."

She laughed, hating the shaky sound of it. "I'm sorry, Ford. That was rude. I'm not used to getting presents. It just caught me off guard." And she didn't like the idea of getting jewelry from Ford, especially after the reminder of their status she'd just been smacked with. Gifts of jewelry were too personal, and she had emotional confusion to avoid.

"Then you must *get* used to getting presents." Ford's voice was staunch. He held out the box until she took the gift gingerly, staring at it as if she didn't know what to do with it. "Open it." His tone held a hint of impatience.

She fingered the satin ribbon. The box was so pretty she didn't want to open it. Wishing she could take a picture of the package while it was pristine, she slowly pulled off the ribbon, trying to memorize how it'd been tied so she could recreate it later.

"Evangeline, if you don't want it, just say so and I'll return it." His posture stiff now, Ford looked every inch of his over-six-foot height. The stance might have been intimidating if it wasn't for the insecure look in his eyes that humanized him. The look was so out of place on Ford's face that she had the sudden urge to hug him.

Women in his social circles probably casually and quickly opened packages like this as if they were as commonplace as a greeting card. Looking down, she said quietly, "No, Ford. I want it. I've just never gotten anything from this store before." She slid the ribbon between her fingers, relishing the way it slinked against her skin, the thick feel of it speaking to its quality. "The box is so pretty. I wanted to take my time opening it."

"Oh." He relaxed his frame, rubbing the back of his neck. "Wow. This is not going at all like it had in my head." Smiling, his eyes crinkled and his infectious charm came roaring back. "I suppose if you're going to get used to getting presents, then I'm going to need to get used to giving them graciously." He gestured toward the still-closed box and added gently. "Please. Take your time, love."

She set the ribbon down in a neat pile on the bar and lifted the lid on the box. A smaller, but just as blue, velvet box nestled snugly inside. She extracted the velvet box, her excitement growing with each successive round of packaging. She tilted the lid open. A pair of sparkling earrings nested on a white, silk pillow inside. They might have been silver, but Evie was certain they were the finest white gold. Each had a petite, teardrop gemstone of pale blue dangling from a silver ball. They sparkled like mad in the late sun coming through the wall of windows at the back of the room. Evie swallowed. They were exquisite.

"Whoa," she breathed. "Ford, I don't know —"

"Put them on," he insisted.

"How did you know I needed earrings?"

"You weren't wearing any yesterday." His smile was indulgent. "And since you brought nothing with you, you need everything."

She laughed. "But you got my things for me." Delicately pulling out one of the earrings, her heart leapt as the gems somehow sparkled even more than they had in the box. As much as the baubles brought her joy, she couldn't help the unease that shivered up her spine while admiring them. She had to be honest with him about her confusion. Mixed messages were dangerous in the insanely intimate game they were playing. "Ford, I love them. So, so, so much." She couldn't take her eyes off the small, brilliant jewel in her fingers. "But I don't understand this gift. It seems…romantic."

Without answering, Ford cupped his hand around hers, carefully plucking the earring from her fingers. He moved in close to her again, enveloping her with his scent. Every sense in her snapped to attention, as was usual whenever his body was so near hers. Reaching up, he tucked her hair behind her ear and touched her earlobe, pulling on it gently. She reminded herself to breathe. Why did every touch from him seem backed by live wires of electricity?

After securing the earring in her ear, he tapped the jewel so it swung and then met her eyes again. "I'm pleased you brought that up, and there's no need to worry, this small gift is not meant to be a

272

romantic gesture." Evie registered her pang of disappointment and screamed at herself in her head, furious for feeling it.

And another thing occurred to her—small gift? The earrings probably cost two months of her old law-firm salary, maybe more.

He picked the second earring from the box and secured it in her other ear as he continued, her cheek tingling as the backs of his fingers brushed against her skin. "I have a lot of money, and as I told you before, I don't get close to people. So I never have anyone I can spoil other than people who are only around with the hopes that I might spoil them, and I despise that."

He put his hands on the outside of her arms and stepped back, inspecting how the jewelry looked on her as he continued. "But now that you're working for me and living in my home, I have someone I can spoil without worrying about unfortunate consequences or misunderstandings."

He grinned at her. That heart-achingly, beautiful smile lighting his face. He did look truly happier than she'd ever seen him, and because of that she tried to shake off her misguided feelings of sadness. He wasn't doing anything wrong; she was. She knew the rules—she was just having a hard time getting her heart to obey.

These are not true feelings, she insisted in her head. *It's typical self-destructiveness, plain and simple.* She'd dealt with her patterns of self-annihilative behavior her whole life, but she'd hit rock bottom with John, and this time would be different. She'd emerge from this house in a year with a clean slate, a new job and an unbroken heart.

"They look beautiful on you. When I saw them in the window, I went right into the store. They were made for you."

Taking a deep breath, she smiled. "I love them, and I'm glad you like them on me." Her protective inner voice hit its stride. *He's not trying to make me happy. He's adorning me in what he wants to see me in for his own pleasure. Be honest with yourself.*

Giving her expensive presents was about him, not her. She could work with that.

He pulled her to him and wrapped his arms around her again, kissing her forehead. "You have no idea how nice it is to have someone to buy something for. I've got all this money and no one to share it with—well, no one I want to share it with, except you and

Charley."

She was concentrating hard on not melting in his arms, afraid her heart might crack open and ooze love all over them both, creating a terrible mess. Remaining emotionally neutral around a man like Ford—the kind of man who pushed every button she had—was going to be twice as difficult if he planned on being so unusually affectionate, as he was today.

"So you've never bought earrings for Charley?" Her voice was muffled against his chest and he released her, stepping back. She looked down, smoothing her blouse in an effort to hide how shaken she was—how shaken she always was—by his embrace.

His laughter boomed in the large room. "No, no earrings for Charley. Charley would prefer a gift of..." Tilting his head, he appeared to think for a moment. "A tattoo. A new pool cue. Bail money."

They both laughed, and when the happy noise died down, he touched her cheek once before turning back to the bar to pour himself another drink. He took a sip, his eyes moving around the room and falling on one of the room's comfortable, over-sized chairs. He sauntered to it, setting his drink on the table between the chair and couch so he could remove his tie and dress shirt, laying them neatly over the back of the sofa. He paused then to look her over, his eyes seeming to assess her outfit—a fitted skirt and blouse. When his eyes fell to her shoes, the tallest heels she owned, they lingered there as he instructed, "Take off your all clothes except your panties and heels and put on my shirt." He picked up the still-warm dress shirt and handed it to her. "Now, please."

She raised her eyebrows and couldn't hide her smile. It was almost funny the way he commanded things in such detail—like his mind never stopped working on what he could ask her to do next. But she'd agreed to the arrangement, so she did as she was told, though she left the room to change her clothes.

When she returned wearing only his crisp, neat shirt, which was three sizes too big for her but smelled deliciously like him, and her panties and heels, he whistled long and low from his spot in the chair. "Look at you...my, my, my." He shook his head. She felt sexier than she'd ever felt, draped in the shirt that smelled of him. This arrangement made her think of herself as a sexual creature in a

274

way she never had before. It was powerful.

She picked her martini back up and wandered the perimeter of the room, wanting Ford to watch her. His place was gorgeous, but she realized that, like her room, there were no pictures of family or friends. There was a picture of Ford riding a camel in front of pyramids, a picture of Ford on a small sailboat, looking like a Kennedy, a picture of Ford skiing on top of the world, a helicopter in the background, but none of him actually with anyone. "Can I ask you something?" she asked.

"Yes of course."

"Where are your pictures of family and friends?"

"I haven't got any."

"Pictures?" She looked at him.

"Family or friends." His lips crooked into a wistful smile. "Except Charley, of course, who took all those photos."

Her gaze sharpened and she scrutinized his face, realizing he wasn't kidding. This would explain the loneliness she sensed in him. She moved to the large ottoman that doubled as a coffee table and sat down facing him. In three gulps she finished the rest of her drink and he raised his eyebrows, but she set down her glass and ignored his look.

"You really are serious that you have no one in your life except Charley." She pulled her legs onto the ottoman and hugged her arms around them, knowing the position gave him a perfect view of the satin crotch of her panties, barely covering her flesh. She watched his eyes. He noticed.

In a matter-of-fact voice, he said, "I am an only child. My parents were very busy and I was with nannies or off at boarding school most of the time. We hardly had a relationship. My father died of a heart attack when I was eighteen, and my mother drank herself to death soon after."

"Oh. I'm sorry." She tried not to sound as taken aback as she was at his intimate and sad revelations.

"Don't be, she'd been working on it for years and she finally succeeded." He took another sip, staring at his glass. Evie realized they had that in common too—few friends and family, bad parents or no parents. In fact, other than Charley who was now both their friend, Evie and Ford were both alone in the world.

"I'm not so different from you, I guess."

"How's that?" he asked.

"Want to know why I need a lock?"

Ford's eyes sparkled with interest. "Yes I do. Very much." So Evie told him, with as little passion as he'd recounted his history to her, of her life with her mom, how she never felt safe or cared for, and her reluctance to have any friends for fear of exposing them to her real situation. Any sorta-friends she may have developed as an adult were taken care of by John. After things went sour with him she was afraid to make a connection with anyone, for their own safety.

"So we're both alone, you and I," he said when she finished.

"Alone with Charley," she clarified and they fell into silence as Ford seemed to mull over the story of her past.

She looked around the cavernous room, realizing how quiet the house was—how empty it must have been before she moved in. When she looked back at Ford, he seemed so disconnected from the world, sitting in the large, fine, leather chair that probably cost as much as her car, fingering his glass with that reflective look on his face. She longed to reach out to him, to make him feel warm, even if he couldn't return the affection. But she didn't. She'd made enough mistakes already.

He continued with his own story as if he'd never paused to hear hers. "I came into a large inheritance before I was even twenty. I used the money to start my first company. That probably kept me out of trouble, having so much responsibility so early. Lots of rich kids get lost when they have nothing to do." He sipped his bourbon and looked past her, out the window.

"I'm still surprised, though, that you don't have a larger circle of friends. I mean, c'mon, you're Ford Hawthorne. People know you. You're in the papers. Why don't you have a million friends?"

"Just Charley." His smile, though weak, was real. The mention of Charley made him come alive.

"But not only are you fabulously rich, which would make lots of people come out of the woodwork to be your friend anyway, you're also handsome, charming, outgoing, and...fun, I guess...in your own way. People must be interested in being your friend." Ford raised an eyebrow at her somewhat-compliment and smirked, shaking his head.

He sighed, as if deigning to finally say the truth out loud. "It's not that people don't like me. I don't like them. I don't have a lot of patience and I'm selfish. I want what I want when I want it, and I have no desire to reciprocate in kind. That makes for a very one-sided friendship, and frankly I don't wish to put forth the effort it takes to maintain quality friendships. Except for Charley. He understands me."

Evie tilted her head, trying to discern emotion in his face. Anger? Regret? She couldn't read anything. "It sounds like you've got it all figured out. So why not change?"

"People were hired to take care of my needs my whole life." He shrugged. "That's how I learned to relate to the world, I guess. Those were my expectations. I'm not making excuses. I know it's unacceptable. I've tried changing, over the years, but I can't sustain it and, frankly, I don't enjoy it. So instead I have an extensive network of people I know and spend time with occasionally. None of whom I'd really call a friend." He finished his drink and stared down into his empty glass for a moment, apparently lost in his thoughts, before placing the whiskey tumbler gently on the side table.

Evie again fought the urge to touch him, to make him feel her warmth, how real she was. She had a crazy urge to assure him she'd never leave, but that was ludicrous. She would leave. He would make her leave.

She gripped her fingers together to stop from reaching for him. Ford had just drawn her a blueprint of exactly how he'd hurt her, and exactly why he could never give her what she needed. The thought cooled her mood toward him.

"Do you like yourself?" she asked, causing him to raise his eyebrows.

"Now that's a very loaded question," he answered, his voice soft but tight.

"Sorry." She dropped her head, embarrassed she'd let the question tumble out before she'd considered its impact. But he pulled back a corner of his mouth in resignation.

"I don't know. It's not important whether or not I do, is it." He said it as a statement.

"Of course it is! It's the most important thing."

He smirked, his beautiful lips inclining her to defend him further. "Why's that?" he asked.

"Because this is your life, no one else's. No one needs to approve of you, agree with you, believe in you, but you."

"And society agrees with you on that philosophy?"

She guffawed. "Since when do you care what society thinks? You just gave me a whole speech about how you didn't even want to be part of it."

He frowned. "Yes, I did, didn't I?"

"Besides—" Now she did touch him, reaching out and laying her hand on his. "Everyone's crazy. It's one big crazy contest out there to see who's the biggest weirdo." She jerked her head toward the front door. "Trust me."

He laughed, the sound genuine, causing Evie to mirror his smile.

They sat in silence for a minute, their smiles fading until awkwardness set in, and Evie slid her hand back to cup her shin.

"Are you lonely?" she asked quietly, pushing her luck on the personal questions, but she'd never before caught Ford in such a sharing mood, and she couldn't help herself.

"Yes and no. If you call this lonely—" he gestured around the large room but she knew he meant his life, "—then I've been lonely all my life, so I've had a long time to get used to it. Honestly, I don't even know what I'm missing. So I simply indulge myself in whatever I want. I concentrate on running my businesses, which takes a lot of time. I read. And now I have a new pet project which occupies my thoughts constantly." She raised her eyebrows at him. "You."

Oh. She reached her hand to tuck her hair behind her ear and caught Ford's eye. He nodded to her hands which were wrapped again around her knees. "What happened to your blue nails?"

She laughed. "I don't have blue nails all the time. I like to change things up."

"I don't." He frowned. "I like things consistent, predictable."

"Well, I'm sorry, Mr. Hawthorne," she said, smiling. "You have enough of my body already. You can't choose my nail color too. I'll decide what I wear on them."

He grinned at her. "I could buy your nails too, you know."

"No, actually, you couldn't. Some things are simply not for sale," Evie said with a haughty tone, inspecting her fingernails in an exaggerated fashion.

"So you'll let two men share your bed, doing filthy things to your body, but the color of your nail polish is where you draw the line?"

"My nails and my hair. If you want a redhead, you're outta luck. But you can have everything else. You and Charley." She grinned back at him and he sat forward, wrapping his hands around her calves, rubbing his fingers up and down her smooth legs.

"I will have everything else. And it's good to know you have limits," he said, his mouth curling up wickedly at the corners before he dipped his lips to her legs to graze a kiss against her knees.

She asked the question she'd been wondering ever since she'd first laid eyes on Ford at the law firm. "What about girlfriends?" She tried to sound more casual than she felt, and she couldn't ignore the niggle of distress that told her she cared about his answer.

"Ah, girlfriends!" Ford looked up from his attentions to her knees, his eyes sparkling now. "Evie, I will continue to answer your very personal questions but first you must take off that shirt. Perhaps it's all this talk about friends and family, but now I *am* feeling a bit lonely. I want to feel your naked body while we talk."

She stood up in front of him, trembling slightly. The answering of his every sexual whim was still new and challenging enough to her to kick up her nerves whenever he issued an order. She unbuttoned the shirt slowly, letting it slide off her shoulders. Her nipples were instantly hard from the exposure to the cool air. He stared at her standing naked except for her panties and heels and then reached for her, placing his hands on her hips and pulling her to him. He rested his forehead against her bare midsection and she touched his hair hesitantly. Twisting his head, he rested his cheek against her palm.

He made what sounded like a contented sigh and then reached around her, scooping her into his lap. He wrapped his strong arms around her, snuggling her body against his. She couldn't help how nice it felt.

"Now, the subject was girlfriends, correct? I discovered early on that I had a particular talent in gaining the interest of women. I took advantage of that talent. Often." He pursed his lips into a rakish smile and she caught her frown before it showed. Jealousy...and he wasn't even hers. "I suppose perhaps that's one of the reasons I don't keep friends—I've been able to find all the companionship I desire from new women, when I want it." He stroked his hand absently down her arm.

"But you wouldn't consider any of those women your friends?" She looked up into his eyes and found his face very close to hers.

"Oh no, I wouldn't." He brushed her hair off her shoulder and kissed the bare skin there. Her nipples tightened again and came to attention, seeking his touch. "I don't have relationships. I lose interest quickly. Frankly, I have a terrible problem in that I'm bored with people most of the time. I'd rather just be by myself. Perhaps that makes me an asshole, but it's the truth. And I understand and have accepted the consequences of that—hence my lack of photographs with friends."

Ford buried his nose in her hair and breathed deeply. "You smell wonderful." He nuzzled the words into her neck. The thrill of being so close to him grew in her, even as he continued to explain to her why it was so very important she keep her emotional distance.

He leaned back, ending his explorations just in time, before Evie started panting in his lap. "Besides," he continued, "as I said, I'm selfish and demanding, and I don't enjoy thinking about the feelings of others, other than how I might use those feelings to get the things I want." Evie raised her eyebrows in surprise at his unapologetic confessions.

"I know that sounds terrible, but in my defense, I'm basically a good person. I try not to hurt people." He shook his head with a wry smile. "And don't try to talk to me about it. I'm not willing to change. I'm old enough to know that about myself, and women don't put up with my selfish behavior for long. God, when it goes bad! The drama. I can't stomach it."

He was an asshole and he embraced it, and Evie realized she kinda liked that about him. At least you knew what you were getting. He was completely self-aware and didn't try to be something he wasn't. He was simply Ford, take it or leave it.

"And all of that is why this arrangement is so perfect for me, so freeing. I can't believe I never thought of it before!" He laughed, dimples flashing, and looked at her with what seemed to be pure affection. He trailed his fingers up and down her back. "I like you, Evie. I find you to be very interesting. You're smart, sexy, and different from most of the women I've met. You can be challenging, but I like that. And this thing we're doing is so exciting. I don't think I've ever had so much fun."

"You've never done this before?" She frowned, confused. He seemed to know what he was doing. She'd assumed she wasn't the first to have had this arrangement with him.

"No, never." He squeezed his arms around her. "And I can't believe I haven't. I don't have to pretend with you. I can tell you what I want you to wear, and what I need and when I need it. It's perfect. And I don't feel like an ass, because I've made a business deal with you, and you're getting what you want too." She knew he meant the money, but she wondered if what they were doing wasn't somehow perfect for her too. There was no doubt she was enjoying it a hell of a lot.

"But sleeping with me is a problem? Like actually sleeping? You left last night, and then what you said earlier about everyone maintaining their own space..."

He shrugged. "I prefer to sleep alone."

"Did you make Charley leave my room last night too?"

Nodding, he confirmed. "It didn't feel right, leaving you and Charley there together without me."

"You and I are here now, without Charley," she pointed out.

"Yes, but you are my employee. That's to be expected."

She bit her lip, nodding, and then asked a different question. "I did what you asked last night. Were you pleased?"

"Oh yes." He stroked the skin of her arm.

"Did you enjoy Charley?" she asked. The question held so much weight in her mind that she had trouble forcing her tone to sound light.

"I always enjoy Charley. Though last night I enjoyed him in a way I never had before." Ford smirked and looked over at the pictures Evie had been studying earlier. "The fun we could have been having all those years... Well, there's time now. And there's you to play with. I have so many ideas." He pursed his lips, his dimples signaling the wicked scenarios she knew were percolating inside that gorgeous head of his.

She narrowed her eyes, her stomach tightening with trepidation. "What are you going to make me do next?"

Ford laughed. "You enjoyed yourself last night. Why do you ask with such concern in your voice?"

"Because everything with you is about upping the stakes. I'm not sure if you know a limit."

"Evie, you are more than just my sexual companion." Warmth flooded through her at those words. "I care about you and I won't ask you to do anything I know you won't like or be good at." He pulled her into him and tucked his head to her neck, his lips exploring down and back up, his tongue tasting her skin.

A chill tingled through her and the inner walls of her pussy contracted with a pang of excitement. He made her so hot she couldn't think straight. She was ready to come and he'd barely touched her. She never knew when, or if, any affection was coming from Ford, so when she got it, the sensations seemed magnified tenfold.

He spoke in between kisses, his face buried in her hair. "That doesn't mean that I won't stretch the limits of your comfort zone, Evie. On the contrary," he nipped at her tender skin, "I intend to stretch many parts of you." She could feel his lips pull into a smile against her skin, and he moved up to her ear, sucking her earlobe into his mouth. *Goddamn.*

He stopped kissing her and held her face to look at him. "Remember though, no matter who I share you with, at the end of the day, you're mine. I take you home. I take you to bed if I choose. I decide if I'm going to share you. I intend to keep you happy and well-fucked, because you. Are. Mine. Do you understand?"

"Yes, of course," she whispered, knowing she was lying to him. There was no question at least some of her heart already belonged to Charley.

"Good girl, Evie. I knew we could make each other happy with the right arrangement." He touched her hair, stroking her as if she were a cherished pet. "When I asked you what your dreams were, you gave the right answer—a future for yourself. I was worried you'd say something else and ruin everything."

"What were you afraid I'd say?"

"Well you're obviously attracted to me or you wouldn't have agreed to our deal. I believe you enjoy spending time with me and living in this house."

"I do."

"I was afraid you might make a reference to becoming more in my life—like my wife or my girlfriend."

Evie sat up and laughed, trying to emulate his detachment. "Oh no, I wouldn't have said that."

Ford's brow furrowed and a cloud passed over his face, but as quickly as it had struck, it was gone and his face was a mask of playboy-casual again. What had it been? Confusion? Hurt?

"Does that bother you?" she asked, her voice incredulous.

"No, of course not." He shook his head and the teasing glint came back to his eyes. "I can't help but be curious. Why are you so sure about not wanting that?"

"Hey, I understand our deal and I respect it. Besides, I'm not looking for a romantic future." Her thoughts touched on John and she wondered when she'd ever be ready again. "But there are other reasons too."

Ford trailed the back of his hand from her neck down to her breasts and brushed his fingers over her hard nipples. She sucked a quick breath in through her teeth as she felt the thrill to her toes.

"Tell me, love" he said softly, and he traced a finger around one of her stiff nipples.

She tried to remember what they were talking about. "First, you're too old for me." She rushed the words out, her breath coming faster.

"Old? I'm thirty-six!" Ford widened his eyes at her in mock shock.

"Yes, but I'm only twenty-six!"

He caressed his hand over one of her breasts and then moved it to her ass. "Yes," he said, his eyes devouring her body. "You do appear to be only twenty-six, young lady. What else?"

"I couldn't marry you. You're too controlling, and you know I don't respond well to men in authority." He tore his eyes from her breasts and looked at her blankly. Then he got her joke and they both laughed until there were tears in their eyes.

She felt Ford's cock stiffen under her ass, and his voice had gone soft and breathy. "Actually, that's exactly why you would marry me, love, if marriage held any interest for me. You love it when I'm in control. You love this arrangement as much as I do."

He licked his lips and his demeanor changed as his voice became deep and commanding. "Young lady, now that you've thoroughly insulted your employer, I'm going to have to show you what a bad girl you've been and what bad girls get in this house." His eyes glinted with the promise of his intentions.

CHAPTER TWENTY-THREE

"WHAT DO BAD girls get, Mr. Hawthorne?" Evie asked, being coy.

"Bad girls in this house always get a thorough fucking," Ford growled, putting emphasis on the "fucking" part, and she moaned at his sexy threat and ground her bare ass cheeks against his lap, anxious for him to free his stiff cock from his pants. His cock felt very ready.

He cupped her breasts and caressed them, then sucked one nipple into his mouth, teasing it with his teeth. She groaned, "Oh god, Ford, don't make me wait!"

He took his lips off her breast long enough to snarl, "I will do what I want when I want it." He stood up and practically dumped her onto the lusciously soft carpet. Standing over her, fully dressed, and looking down at her half naked form, his crass words made her entire body come to life with heat and longing. "You are right, Evangeline. I am controlling. And now I intend to fuck you until I've had my fill, as per our deal." Oh god. Her pussy was dripping. She was so ready for him. He was right—she enjoyed this as much as he did.

He kicked off his shoes and removed his undershirt, then dropped to his knees and reached one hand out to massage her breasts, pinching a nipple hard. She gasped at the twinge of pain that somehow made her burn hotter for him. He continued rubbing her breasts with one hand while he quickly unbuckled and unzipped his pants with his other, releasing his cock without bothering to pull off his trousers in his haste.

Evie reached out and tugged down on his pants, helping him remove them. She stared at his erection marveling how every time with Ford made her feel as if she'd never wanted a man so badly. She was practically writhing on the carpet in her need.

"Ford please," she begged. "I want you inside me." His cock was swollen with excitement that echoed her own, and her pussy throbbed for the feel of him plunging into her. He leaned over and yanked her panties down with both hands, making her breath catch.

"Spread your legs," he commanded. She spread them dutifully, and he crawled on top of her. His weight on her naked body felt so right. His breathing was rough and he moved quickly, wrapping his strong arms around either side of hers, pinning her arms to her sides, his hands gripping her shoulders.

"Evie, pet, you are so wet. You like what I'm doing to you, don't you?" He moved a hand to his cock and rubbed her clit with the head of his erection. He was breathing so hard with excitement that she almost couldn't understand his next words. "You like sucking my cock when I tell you to? Fucking my cock when I tell you to? Fucking my friend when I tell you to do it?" His voice was a hoarse whisper.

"Yes." Her eyes locked to his. "I like it very much." He moaned low with pleasure and without taking his eyes from hers, found her warm, wet entrance and shoved his erection into her as far as he could push it. She screamed in pleasure with the feeling of being so suddenly filled up. He moved a hand to her breasts and squeezed them, caressed them. He worked into her with long and slow strokes, lowering his head to lick and suck on her nipples.

"Oh, oh Ford, oh god, Ford!" She couldn't seem to stop calling his name. She wished she could fuck him twenty times a day—the feeling was so amazing she never wanted it to stop. The excitement in her core was building rapidly, with every slow and deliberate thrust of Ford's searing-hot cock.

"Evie," he said in between licks to her breasts. "You feel amazing. You're going to make me come. I'm going to fill you with it," he promised and increased the speed of his thrusts, moaning as he did. She was sighing and whimpering, just at the edge of her own orgasm.

A visceral excitement seemed to overtake him then, and he stopped caressing her breasts. He seemed no longer concerned about her pleasure, only his own, as he roughly sought his release using her body. But he didn't need to be concerned about her pleasure at that moment. He was pounding her hard with his thick cock, and that was exactly what she needed. Her pleasure built quickly to the edge. It took only four more thrusts. His weight pressing her down, rubbing her just the right way, his cock filling her up completely, the animal sounds he made as he pumped into her, the thought of Ford using her to get off...and a powerful orgasm crashed through her. There was just something so forbidden about it.

She called out incoherently as waves of intense pleasure pulsed through her body, her pussy gripping his cock over and over. He moaned loudly at her reaction and came too, pounding his cock into her clenching pussy, his fingers digging into her shoulders painfully as he made that delicious, manly grunting noise he made when he came. He kept moving his cock into her at a slowing pace until he was spent.

He stayed there, half on top of her, body wrapped around hers, as his breathing slowed. It felt so good, the soft, plush rug under them, their naked, sweaty skin touching. Her breathing slowed too, as she relaxed in his arms.

"Evie," he whispered. "I could lay with you like this forever." He snuggled against her more firmly and kissed her on the mouth. It felt very natural, as if he did it without thinking. She smiled into the kiss, her eyes closed. She couldn't believe he'd said that.

He must have realized the same thing, because she suddenly felt his body go rigid and he pulled his softening cock out of her and jumped up as if late for an appointment. He went behind the bar, turning his back to her as he cleaned up and pulled his pants back on, zipping his fly. "Evie, that was..." Ford's tone was stilted. "Uh...thank you. I'll let you know when I need you again. You may go now," he said brusquely, not looking at her.

She huffed as she got up to dress. "Why do you do that?"

"What?" he asked, his head down as he shoved his shirt into

his waistband, made a frustrated noise and yanked it back out, tucking it in again more carefully this time, until he was satisfied.

"We were enjoying each other, and then you just...freak out." She eyed him from the corner of her eye as she dressed, knowing she was pushing her liberties in questioning him.

"I don't know what you mean," he said, picking non-existent lint from his shirt and pulling his cuffs straight.

"Fine. But I had fun and I think it would have been nice if you'd have lingered, is all." She kept her voice light, not wanting to push him too hard, but feeling disappointed he'd decided their time was over so abruptly. His mood swings were impossible to understand.

When he didn't address her statement, she turned to leave but his words stopped her. "I won't be home for dinner this evening," he said, not looking at her.

"Working late?"

His voice softened, suggesting a hint of reluctance. "I have a date."

Though he said it gently, she felt as though she'd been kicked in the gut. Then she felt the same emotion over again as the shock of how much she cared about his stupid date struck her. "Oh," was all she managed, and she hated how disappointed the small, loaded word sounded coming out of her mouth.

Jellybeans.

"I'm calling Charley to tell him to pack a bag and come over. You two can have dinner together. I don't want you left alone anymore." This cheered Evie a bit. She loved her alone time with Charley, and he'd help take her mind off Ford's date. Ford strode to Evie and took her chin between his thumb and forefinger, forcing her to look him in the eyes. "Make sure Charley gets whatever he wants." The glint was back in Ford's eyes.

"That won't be a problem. Your chef seems to have ingredients for anything." She smiled sweetly.

Ford scowled at her, but Evie could see the amusement peeking through. "That is because the chef is good at his job. As long as everyone around here remains good at their jobs, there won't be the need for..." Ford's large hand traveled down her back to her ass, caressing a cheek before sharply smacking it and pulling her against him. "...repercussions," he finished, his smile wicked.

"Of course," Evie breathed, knowing her face was flushed.

"Off you go." He released her, turning his attention to his phone.

She left the room slowly, her mind awash with a confusing swirl of emotions—fear due to the picture from John, happiness from the intimacy she'd shared with Ford, jealousy about his date. She climbed the stairs to her room feeling lonelier every step she took away from Ford, and she couldn't help but wonder if Ford felt the same.

*****

~THE PUNISHMENT~

CHAPTER TWENTY-FOUR

ITH THEIR FORD out on a date, Evie and Charley ate pizza in her bed and watched TV, something Ford would never have done. That little rebellion made Evie feel a smidge better about being left at home while Ford was out on the town with another woman.

Charley entertained her with inane observations on everything from fashion to plot twists. Evie couldn't remember a time she'd laughed so much. Charley was in a great mood, nearly walking on air after Ford asked him to move in, though he'd given Evie an extended, arms-crossed lecture when he found out about her hiding the picture from him and Ford. When he pointed his finger at her she'd finally cut him off.

Craving an after-dinner treat, Evie went to the kitchen to find something for the two of them to share. Going into the walk-in fridge by herself always gave her the creeps, but she was rewarded for her bravery when she found a cheese platter arranged with five different types of luscious cheeses. After locating crackers and a sharp knife she grabbed two wine glasses and a bottle of zinfandel. She studied the label for a minute and then shrugged. It could have been a $15 bottle or a $1500 bottle. Either way, she decided Ford wouldn't miss it. Balancing the glasses on the platter and tucking the wine under her arm, she headed back to her room.

The route back to the stairway led her past the library that doubled as Ford's office, and when she heard his voice she pulled up so short she nearly sent the wine glasses tumbling. She thought he'd already left for dinner.

Ford's biting voice sounded angry. Curiosity overcame her and she slowed her steps, realizing he was on the phone. She wanted to keep walking so as not to eavesdrop, but Ford sounded so angry, and she'd never heard him lose his cool. Fear gripped her stomach at the sound. Whatever he was talking about, or whomever he was talking to, was really upsetting him.

"No I got your message and I'm calling to tell you that you will not step foot near my house, ever.

"No, no need. I will take care of it tomorrow, and after I do, I expect you will cease all contact immediately. And hear me on this—I better never hear your name again." Ford's words seethed with hatred. She heard the phone clatter to the desk and then his angry footsteps neared the door. Ducking into the darkened doorway of a nearby room, she held her breath. He was so livid that she didn't want him to know she'd overheard him.

His footsteps disappeared down the hallway and she heard the front door open and slam. Soon after the tires of his sleek, black Aston Martin Vantage peeled out of the driveway.

Damn. She took a deep breath, trying to slow her heartbeat, and crept into the hallway and back toward her room again. She didn't know Ford could get that rattled. She wondered if she should tell Charley, but Charley was Ford's bodyguard. Surely he knew if Ford had gotten a threatening phone call. And if he didn't…Evie didn't want to get in the middle of that. If Charley didn't know about the call, there was clearly a reason Ford didn't want him to know.

She remained quiet through the rest of the movie they'd rented. Charley stage whispered through the entire climax of the film but Evie didn't mind—she was too preoccupied to pay attention anyway. Her thoughts didn't wander far from the phone call she'd overheard. Could it have been John?

She volunteered to return the snack to the fridge, hoping to run into Ford again, but this time all was quiet in the mansion's wide, dim halls. Still troubled, she made her way back to her room to find the lights dimmed and Charley under her covers and naked, as far as she could tell from her quick inventory of men's clothing strewn by the bed. "Should I take it you're looking for dessert?" she asked wryly.

"What?" He affected offense. "I just want to cuddle!" He threw back the covers on her side to offer her a spot, revealing his thick cock, already rigid and ready.

"With that?" Evie pointed to his huge erection. "You expect me to believe you just want to cuddle?"

"Just cuddle! Naked. And hard. And repeatedly." He patted her spot in invitation. She shook her head in exasperation as he continued. "I call it 'sticky cuddling'. It's just like regular cuddling, only stickier. Hop in and I'll teach you the finer points."

Evie laughed so hard she bent over, bracing her arm on the bed. She needed Charley—he was the perfect foil to Ford. She waved a hand at him. "Stop! You're a nut-case," she gasped as tears streamed down her face, but she pulled off her robe and climbed in naked next to him, still giggling and wiping her eyes. As much as she thought she should feel strange about putting out on demand for Ford and his friend, Charley made it too fun not to enjoy it, and Ford... Well, Ford was a walking multiple orgasm with whom she hoped to collide at every opportunity.

She and Charley stared at each other silently after she'd caught her breath. Evie never felt more content than she felt when looking at Charley lying on the same pillow as her. "Are you happy?" she whispered. "Living here. Plus, you and Ford...you made love."

"We had sex." He corrected her.

"Right. Well, maybe. Did you like it?"

Charley reached out and took her hand, tangling her fingers in his. He closed his eyes, a look of pure satisfaction softening his features. "Incredible. Better than I thought it would be."

"Really?" She figured fantasy nearly always trumped reality.

"Because you were there. In my fantasies it's always been just Ford and me."

Evie blinked, shock slowing her response. She frowned. "You wouldn't have rather been alone with him?"

"No, not now that we have you. With you and Ford I get everything I want."

Her pulse kicked into higher gear and her stomach twisted with the realization of it.

Goddammit, he's right.

With him and Ford, she had everything too. A loving, loyal, affectionate soul-mate and a dark, edgy sexual master. She wanted them both—needed them both. Closing her eyes, she sucked in her breath. She was totally screwed.

"What's wrong?"

"Nothing," she mumbled.

"Evie, tell me."

"No, it doesn't matter."

"If it makes your face look like you just ran over four baby ducks being pulled in a cart by ten kittens, then, yes, I'm guessing it matters. At least it matters to me."

"Wha—" She couldn't even come up with words, so instead just shook her head in disbelief, giggling. "I've run out of words for you, Charley. You're a complete wacko."

"We already know that. Now tell me what's wrong."

"I don't want to talk about it."

"Tell me or I'll get Ford to spank it out of you."

"What?" Evie punched his massive shoulder with their clenched hands without releasing him. "You're not into that, so you'll just have him do it when you need something?"

"I never said I wasn't into it. It's just not my thing like it is Ford's. Now stop stalling and tell me."

"No," she whispered.

"If you tell me, I'll tell you a secret too."

"I like secrets," she grinned. It seemed Charley could always make her smile, no matter what her mood.

"You're a filthy whore," he whispered, his eyes glittering with good humor. "My favorite kind."

"That's not a secret," she whispered back, deadpan. "I kinda am." They both burst out laughing and he reached around her, flipping her easily to spoon her backside against his rigid cock and wrapping a tree-trunk of an arm around her protectively.

"That's one of the reasons I like you so much," he said softly as he rained kisses on her cheek and neck. "But I've got a lot of other reasons too."

She really loved Charley—the things he said to her, his tough vulnerability, his charm, his body. As Ford had pointed out, Charley really was something special. "I was thinking I'm screwed," she blurted out.

"That's not a secret either," Charley whispered from beneath her ear where he was nibbling on her lobe. "You've been screwed a lot since you got here...by Ford, by me." He ground his erection against her bottom. "And you're about to get screwed again. Remember, Ford says I can have you whenever I want." He murmured the words against her skin, and she felt his cock jump. "Speaking of that, can I have your ass yet?"

"No, you can't. And that's not what I meant. I was just thinking that you are almost everything I've always wanted in a man."

"Almost?" he asked the question plainly, without any pretense of the insecurity or offense she'd have heard from most men.

"Ford sorta forced me to discover something about myself—that I crave a...I don't know...an almost cold control from a man, sexually."

"You didn't know that before?"

"No." She shook her head and pulled their clasped hands to her mouth so she could kiss his fingers, loving his warmth. "That's why I'm screwed."

Charley's chest rumbled as he laughed. "You're gonna need to explain that one. I might like to have sex with men, but I'm not one of your girlfriends. I don't speak 'girl-talk'."

Evie gasped, trying not to laugh. "You're a dick sometimes, you know that?"

"Sure I am. Now explain."

She closed her eyes. He really was hilarious and endearing in a way she'd never experienced. And he felt so familiar. It was as if they'd been friends and lovers for half their lives. So she felt comfortable enough to try to explain.

"It's like Ford's a puzzle-piece that completes my picture, but I hadn't even known I was missing a piece at all until he showed me."

She frowned. "No. That's not right. He doesn't complete my picture — it's not like without him I'm less than whole. Ford's a catalyst. Like I can have good sex and a good relationship, but you add Ford and now it's something more — it's explosive and mind-blowing on a whole other level. It's like he's the vinegar to my baking soda."

Charley hugged her close, laughing so hard he shook the bed. "The 'vinegar to my baking soda'? I can almost guarantee you no one has ever called Ford that before." His voice softened. "But I know what you mean. He's magnetic, in the best and the worst way."

"He's a little dark and I like that."

"Darkness is good?"

"It is on Ford. It's part of his dominance. I'd feel like I was missing out now if I didn't have it. I want that controlling, ownership flavor Ford brings to the table. Even when it feels like he's using me just to pleasure himself, it totally does it for me."

Charley pressed his hardness to her bottom again. "I know it does. I've seen what it does to you." He pulled her shoulder back, kissing along her collarbone and making her shiver. "So I'm still not getting why all this means you're screwed."

She smiled weakly. "How am I supposed to find all that in one guy? I've been out there. There is no other Ford, and there's certainly no other you — not on this planet anyway." She laughed.

"Well," he murmured against her skin, "who says you need to go find it elsewhere?"

"The deadline says so — a year is all he wants. No more. Not to mention he's been clear he can't have a relationship, and he doesn't want one."

Charley stopped kissing her and was quiet for a moment. The only sounds she could hear was their breathing. "He told me in the past that he couldn't have sex with me either. But he did. You can't know what the future holds, and neither can he. No matter how all-powerful he thinks he is."

"You're so optimistic, Charley." She twisted her body, wanting to look into his eyes when she said the words she knew would hurt him — wanted see his reaction so she could punish herself with the memory of it later, over and over as penance for saying it. But it had to be said. She loved Charley. She'd come to realize Charley may be the only real friend she'd ever had, and as such, she'd do anything to protect him, even if that protection had to be against their own Ford. For all his size and muscle, she didn't think Charley was as strong as she was.

"But Charley, even after you got what you'd been wanting from Ford all along, what do you have? Are you closer to what you want? Or are you just one step closer to total annihilation by him?" She swallowed the sick taste in her throat as she watched his face crumble from the high of a step closer to his dream of love to the low of oh-god-maybe-you're-right. "Charley, I'm so sorry to have to say that." She reached up and touched his face, cupping his solid cheekbone in her palm, feeling the scruff of a day's worth of stubble.

Pressing his lips into a thin line, his eyes bore into hers. She could see the war in him, raw on his face. But then he blinked twice and his face visibly softened though his voice was hard. "You might be right, Evie. You might be almost certainly right and I might be the biggest idiot ever, but I will never apologize for loving someone and opening myself up for them to love me back. No matter how badly they could hurt me." A subtle shift took place in the set of his eyes, and suddenly Evie thought he looked sorry for her. "Evie, love is an amazing, rare thing, and even if it's not reciprocated, that doesn't mean it's not still worth everything. To love someone—really love them—it's worth all the heartache in the world. And it should never be denied or ignored. A connection like that might never come along again." He twisted his mouth into a wry smile. "I won't ever regret loving Ford the way I do, even if it means someday I have to heal from what I let him do to me. Even if it kills me. It'll still be worth it, to love like that."

Her heart seemed to skip a beat as she realized in many ways she was doing the same thing, only far more literally. Letting Ford hurt her and healing later. Both of them taking what they needed from the other and dealing the consequences down the line. She blinked at Charley. She hadn't been giving him enough credit—maybe he was infinitely stronger than her. Infinitely braver.

Charley narrowed his eyes, seeming to understand her mind was working overtime. He hesitated before adding. "At least I'll know I gave everything to try to nurture a real love. And that's the best I can hope for, I think…to have loved someone enough to have been destroyed by it. I guess I'd feel lucky. Some people never find someone capable of inspiring a love like that."

A wide smile broke across Evie's face and a tear slipped down her cheek. "God, I always feel like I want to protect you, but you don't need any protection, do you?"

Charley wiped her face with his thumb, his calloused skin rough against hers. "Evie, my being open to love doesn't make me weak or blind to what's going on here. I know the danger. I'm making choices with open eyes and I'm prepared for the consequences. I'm ready to live with my decisions, no matter how they turn out for me. I just needed Ford to give us a chance, and you're helping him do that."

She moved her hand to his mouth, tracing a finger along his upper lip. "You are really, really special. I wish I had a tenth of your courage and heart. I really do. But I can't do it like you. I can't just willingly walk into the lion's den and hope my love's enough not to get mutilated. Especially not with Ford. He's done and said everything he can to make sure I'm crystal clear on what a moron I'd be if I fell for him. I don't think there's much more he could do to try and warn me off of him."

Charley was quiet again. Then, his voice barely above a whisper, he said, "Maybe there's something to that? Has it occurred to you maybe he's trying to push you away a little too hard?"

She shook her head, mussing her hair against the pillow. "Don't do that. Don't encourage stupid ideas. And besides, what about you? If that was the case, why would he push you and me together? Maybe he's hoping you and I will just run away together so he can be alone and miserable like he wants."

"I don't believe that." But Charley's body had stiffened and Evie could feel the anxiety prickling off him. "I don't think you should either."

"No?" Evie pulled away and propped her head on her hand, her elbow on the pillow. "Charley, he's on a date tonight. He left you and me together with instructions to fuck while he's on a date with another woman. How stupid do we have to be to think there would ever be any chance for...for... What? What is there? All three of us? Together? What is that? Pinning down Ford is one thing, but calling the three of us some kind of relationship is another. There are just too many impossible hurdles that no sane person would take on."

The usual light in his warm brown eyes dimmed and Evie's gut clenched again. It was one thing for her to be hard and cynical. It was another thing for her to take hope away from this wonderful, loving man in front of her. "Charley, I'm sorry. That doesn't mean there's no chance for you and him."

"No. I think I'm the only one here who sees what's happening. There really is no chance for Ford and me. There never was."

"Charley, that's not tr—"

"Until you came along."

She shut her mouth. Opened it. Couldn't think of the right words and so just went with, "Huh?"

He wrapped his arms around her again and pulled her to him, his body radiating heat like an electric blanket. She felt she could stay in his arms and just let the world go by forever. Instead of answering, he kissed her, slowly at first, his lips soft and caressing. She was reluctant to kiss back, feeling she didn't deserve his kisses for hurting him, for diminishing his optimism about true love. But soon, she opened for him and their tongues slipped to find each other. Her body and her emotions responded in unified pleasure and joy at Charley's body heat and his sexy affection.

When he broke the kiss, leaving her breathless, he whispered, "Evie, you're not the only one who discovered what you were missing." She searched his eyes, trying not to interpret his words. She was in too deep already and her self-preservation instincts were screaming at her to not hear what he was saying. "I think Ford does love me, and I think he wants to be with me, but up until now it's been impossible. I can't ever be everything he wants, because Ford needs a woman he can dominate. He needs that sexually. It's in his bones. But the right woman. A rare kind of woman he could actually love. I think that's the only way Ford will ever, ever open himself to feeling love—if it's even possible." He grew quiet for a moment and neither of them spoke. Finally Charley added, "I was sure that woman didn't exist because Ford never likes anyone. Ever. Until you."

Evie chewed on the inside of her cheek. "So what were you missing that you found?" she heard herself ask, dreading the answer for the hope it might bring. Hope she couldn't afford to have for an entire year, only to have it destroy her.

"I found you." He smiled and kissed her softly. He spoke in between kisses. "I didn't even realize how incredibly lonely I was trying to love that man by myself until you came along. You're funny and brave and crazy and smart. And you have tits, which I love." He laughed, brushing her nipple with his thumb. "And you accept me straight-up, which feels like a miracle to me. I didn't know there was such a thing as someone like you. I didn't even know I needed you until Ford forced you into my life. Now I don't want to live without you. I don't want Ford without you. I want all of us, together." He swept her hair back over her shoulder. "That's my secret. I'm falling in love with you. It seemed important," he whispered, "so I thought you should know."

She felt as if she'd been sucker-punched by the odd-couple of happiness and terror. Her chest tight, she struggled to breathe. Or at least not throw-up on him.

Charley smirked. "Okay, really, we haven't known each other long, though it's been intense. I didn't expect you to pledge your undying love right back to me, but looking a little less horrified might go a long way toward soothing my ego."

Evie choked on sob and a laugh at the same time. "Oh god, Charley. I'm sorry." She wiped her cheeks. "I'm horrified because you're right and I have no idea how it's come to this. It feels like you and I have always been friends, even though I just met you. I've never felt a connection like this with anyone else, except Ford. You're so good, and ridiculous and fun and...hot. I just want to crawl in your lap and never leave, unless Ford wants me to come and suck his cock, I guess."

Her laughter bubbled in spite of her tears and Charley laughed too, snuggling her close. He pulled her leg up onto his thigh, effectively spreading her legs and pressing his cock against her pussy. "That sounds like a perfect plan," he whispered, his voice growing husky. "I like the sound of it. I like seeing you with Ford knowing I can join any time. It's fucking hot."

"Charley, this is going to end badly," she whispered.

"Maybe," he acknowledged, tucking his head into the crook of her neck and raising chills on her arms as he nibbled her skin there. "Maybe. But I'm gonna love every second of it until it does."

"You're the brave one," she whispered, rocking against him, her core tingling to life against his firm penis. "Or maybe you're the stupid one."

"Nah," he whispered back, reaching under the covers to cup one of her breasts. "I'm the good-looking one."

She burst out laughing. "Okay, stop!" she gasped. "No more funny stuff. And no more talking about our doomed romance!" She reached down, wrapping a hand around his hardness. With a squeeze she elicited a groan from him. His strong jaw clenched and unclenched. "Let's just fuck until we forget all about love."

"I think that's a terrible idea, Evie," he admonished and rolled on top of her, crushing his mouth to hers and tilting his body just enough to reach between them and direct his cock to her entrance. He rubbed the broad head of his dick in between her pussy lips before pulling his hand back up. Breaking their kiss, he pushed two fingers into her mouth. "Suck," he demanded. She did. He moved his hand back to her sex and shoved both fingers, now wet with her saliva, into her at once. She gasped, her hips rising involuntarily, driving his fingers deeper.

"You're so unromantic," he grumbled. "But if fucking's what you want, that's what you're gonna get. No foreplay. No more kisses. I'm just gonna fuck you." He pulled his fingers out and impaled her sex immediately with his thick erection, causing her to cry out at the intensity of his size forcing into her. She was tender from her body seeing so much use lately, but the pain was good.

Goddamn it was good.

She couldn't believe how quickly her body responded to him. Almost instantly she was wet enough to allow his thrusts to slide in and out easily, and he took full advantage, kneeling back and hooking his arms under her thighs, pulling her legs wide as he buried his cock in her, pulled shallow, and then buried it again with a grunt. She gasped, her fiery orgasm exploding so quickly she only had time to utter, "God, you feel good! I'm going to—" And she was off the cliff and flying, her orgasm shattering through her as she writhed under the big man.

Her vaginal muscles contracted and released in her climax, milking his cock until seconds later Charley finished too, with an incoherent sound, pumping hot cum into Evie. As his thrusts slowed with his waning ecstasy, she heard the door latch click and jerked her head toward the sound to see Ford in her room, closing the bedroom door behind him.

CHAPTER TWENTY-FIVE

*S*TARTLED, EVIE JUMPED, her heart leaping to her throat. Charley, however, spared only an exhausted glance toward the door before collapsing on the bed next to Evie, his spent cock sliding from her. Ford stood at the door with his hand on the knob, quietly watching the pair before crossing in front of the bed, heading to Evie's bathroom without a word.

Light stretched into the bedroom and across the bed when Ford turned on the bathroom light, bathing Evie and Charley in a dim spotlight. Leaving the light on, Ford returned, carrying a towel. He tossed it on the bed. "Looks like I've already missed the fun," he said. "Too bad." Strolling to the window, he turned his back and stared out into the night, thoughtfully giving them a moment to clean up privately.

Charley picked up the towel and pressed it to Evie's thighs. She took over, cleaning herself of his cum before handing the towel to back to Charley and pulling the sheet up over her naked body.

Disparate thoughts warred inside her—annoyance at Ford's interruption of her loving time with Charley, excitement that Ford was home from dinner and in her room, perhaps seeking sex from either she or Charley, or both, meaning his date likely hadn't gotten any. Since Evie was there only to provide carnal pleasure, jealousy about Ford's orgasms seemed the only emotion she was justified to feel.

"Ford?" Charley said, getting the man's attention. Ford turned to look at them and then dropped his head. Evie saw his chest expand as he took a deep breath before moving back to the bed. He was dressed in the clothes Evie assumed he'd worn to dinner—a thin, turtleneck sweater that looked fantastic stretched over his athletic chest and shoulders, and elegant, dark pants. The indirect light illuminated his face so that it nearly glowed, making him look like an angel.

But Evie knew better.

He looked devastatingly handsome, standing there watching them silently, and she both loved and hated him in that moment. "Did you just get back from dinner?" she asked when she couldn't stand the silence any longer.

"I've been back for a while," he answered softly. He looked away, as if trying to organize his thoughts. Finally he turned back to them, his eyes hard. "I wasn't going to come in here," he said emphatically. "Yet..." He lifted his hand, palm up, and then let it drop in a gesture of futility. "Here I am." His last words sounded defeated.

He focused on Evie and frowned, reaching out and pulling the sheet off of her.

"Hey!" she complained, grabbing at the fabric.

"Evie, stop." His tone was sharp and she stilled, unsure of the mood he was in and what it meant for her and Charley. "I won't fight you for what I'm already entitled to." She slowly loosened her grip on the sheet and allowed him to pull it down to her knees, exposing her diamond-hard nipples and her pussy, still damp with her juices and his best friend's cum. She didn't take her eyes from Ford's, her heart pounding during what suddenly felt like a stand-off.

Ford stripped naked on the lower half of his body, never moving his glaring eyes from hers. Evie lay perfectly still. Frozen. Watching him. Was he going to just crawl on top of her and fuck her? Use her like his living sex doll just to get off, after he'd treated another woman to a proper date?

Evie had agreed to the deal, and Ford had every right to come home and do what he wanted with her under their agreement, but she couldn't get her mind right about it. Her feelings were all over the place. She was angry, annoyed, jealous...yet her body betrayed her.

No matter whether it was right or wrong, Evie wanted him to do it. She wanted him to ditch his elegant date to come home, tear off Evie's panties, shove his cock in her and get off. She wanted him to do it, and the proof was a clear as the juices spilling onto her thighs, the tightness twanging in her pussy. All she had to do was squeeze her thighs together and she was nearly there already, and he hadn't even touched her.

It was simply the truth of it, and she was as unsettled by it as she was turned on.

She looked down at his nakedness, visually tracing the curve of his quad muscles with the agitation of an addict. She felt Charley shift next to her and she was sure he was relishing the sight of Ford's body just like she was. Ford sat on the edge of her bed and she could see his penis, heavy and thick, as it rested on his thigh. She couldn't stop staring at it in the dim light, feeling anxious, like it was a bomb set to go off at any moment and she was too close to it. He put his hand on her bare knee and his eyes swept over her. Even his intense gaze on her naked skin made her breath catch. She felt Charley scoot closer to her, his heat comforting on her gooseflesh.

"What do you normally wear to bed, Evangeline?" Ford raised his hand and ran the back of his fingers over one of her breasts, brushing her nipple and sending a thrill through her as her skin rejoiced at his touch.

"A nightie," she breathed. "I like lingerie."

"You will not wear a nightie to bed in my house. You'll wear only panties. I like removing panties." He raised his hand to her chin, tilting her head to look at him. "I want you ready for fucking whenever I might feel like taking you. Do you understand?"

"Yes," she whispered and everything inside her twisted with a twang of pleasure so sharp she had to bite down on a moan. What he'd just said to her was... Well, she didn't know what it was, but it was not romantic. Yet, even so, she was instantly throbbing at the idea of going to bed nearly naked every night in case Ford decided to pay her a visit in the dark to use her body for his own pleasure. Ford's dominance over her was like a drug, and she couldn't get enough.

He put his hand back on her leg and slid his palm up her thigh until his thumb was millimeters from her sex. The feel of his fingers so close to where she wanted them was immediately all she could think about. Charley kissed her shoulder, mentally bringing her back to the room, and suddenly she felt awkward lying between the two men, naked, exposed and wanting Ford as she was. "Did you have a nice dinner?" she asked to fill the silence, her voice wavering.

"Yes, thank you for asking." He leaned over her and found the curve of her neck with his lips, tasting her, and she couldn't stop her small moan. "My dinner companion was lovely—educated, cultured, tall, attractive."

A pang of jealously punched through Evie at Ford's description of the woman. Charley found her hand and squeezed it three times. She tried to find comfort in that but she couldn't stop her traitorous brain from picturing the lady at the table of some fancy restaurant, sitting across from Ford. Rich, expensively dressed, a mane of shining hair, perfectly coiffed, laughing throatily at Ford's clever wit, crossing and uncrossing her long legs, touching his arm... The other patrons must have thought they made the perfect couple.

Jellybeans.

Teeth gritted, Evie reminded herself that Ford was there now, in bed with her and Charley, trailing kisses down *her* neck, not the long, elegant neck of his dinner date.

Ford spoke between kisses. "I, on the other hand, was terrible company. I could only think of you and Charley, here, alone, enjoying each other without me. And you Evie," he nipped at her neck, causing her to suck in her breath, "craving my direction. Wanting me to tell you what to do to me and to Charley." Charley shifted, pressing against her, and she could feel his cock against her hip, slowly thickening again. "All I could think about the entire dinner with this beautiful woman was when I could politely excuse myself and come back home to both of you."

Her anxiety burst like a bubble at his words and a thrill rocketed through her. She tried to resist responding, but her lack of self-control easily bested all the warning bells going off in her head. Being with Charley was so easy—teasing with Charley was so

306

easy — that maybe she'd momentarily forgotten that being with Ford was not easy. In her giddiness at his admission she ribbed him as she would the other man. "Ford, you like us. I didn't think it was possible, but you wished we were your dates tonight, didn't you? You know, that can be arranged. I like nice dinners. Don't you, Charley? Imagine how they'd talk!" Her voice was teasing and she turned to Charley at the end of her words. That's when she knew she'd made a terrible mistake.

Charley's face blanched and he shook his head once almost imperceptibly before he nervously looked back at Ford. She turned back to him as well, her stomach dropping. She hadn't been able to resist making the point to Ford. She knew she was right, though she'd tried to keep the accusation light. Ford would be sensitive to such an idea, but if he could push her past her comfort zone, then dammit, she could push him too.

Ford sat back, his face hard. "Honestly Evie, it ruined my night. That's why I wasn't going to come in here tonight. I don't enjoy feeling beholden to people. What I enjoy is doing whatever the hell I want, whenever the hell I want to do it. That's how I arrange my life — to ensure just that."

Evie didn't respond. She'd pushed him too far, too fast. No matter how strongly she believed it was true, clearly Ford wasn't ready to admit it. "I'm sorry. I didn't mean to upset you. I was only teasing."

"And that's exactly the problem. You're too familiar. I'm greatly concerned at how quickly you're feeling — " Ford seemed to search for the words. " — settled into my home and my life." He swept a glower at Charley and then back to her. "I am not your boyfriend, Evangeline, and neither is Charley. I am your employer — your temporary_employer — and Charley is my best friend with whom I share your services. That's the extent of our entanglement. Are we clear?"

Charley's fingers dug into her palm as he squeezed her hand too tightly. Tears at Ford's words pricked in Evie's eyes but she'd be damned if she'd let him see them. His bucket of cold water over her head was one thing, but hurting Charley, who genuinely and deeply loved Ford, was another.

"Mr. Hawthorne," she made certain her voice was steady.

"You're absolutely right about where I fit in here, and you have my apologies. In fact, I'm thankful you set me straight. It wouldn't be smart for me to get confused about what's happening here. But still..." She took a deep breath, her inner rebel not willing to let the matter go unpushed. "I can't help but suggest that you take Charley on a date sometime. You might be surprised how much you enjoy it."

"Evie, don't," Charley said under his breath.

"A date? Charley is my best friend. Enjoying each other when we're sharing you doesn't change our relationship. Our friendship is no different now than it was before you came."

She closed her eyes, feeling sick, knowing her actions had provoked him to say those words out loud. Her heart broke for Charley and she mentally cursed herself. Why had she pushed Ford? She knew she couldn't win against him. She felt Charley's chest expand against her side as he took a deep, slow breath. He pushed himself to kneeling and reached out to place his hand on Ford's shoulder. "That's right Ford. Nothing's changed. We have the same fun we had before. No worries." Evie blinked and swallowed, taking a moment before forcing her eyes from Charley to Ford again, feeling miserable.

If Charley was taking care of everyone else, who was taking care of Charley?

Ford looked from his friend to her, the moonlight reflecting off his cheek, throwing his handsome face into sharp relief. He gazed at them quietly for a long time. She couldn't read his eyes and she didn't want to. Crossing her arms over her chest, she turned her head away.

Finally Ford spoke. "I'm sorry, both of you." She jerked her gaze back at him, utterly floored by his apology. "I don't mean to be so harsh. I just..." He shook his head, looking back to the door. "I wonder sometimes if we should continue this, especially when it starts to confuse even me. Maybe we'd be smarter to call it all off." His voice sounded tired.

Her stomach twisted at the words, and she fought rising panic, but her heart skipped when he looked back at her. His eyes were boring into hers, and she saw his own desperation not to end it. His own panic at feeling the way he did. So unsure of what was going on inside him. She could see it in the way the moonlight lit his pale eyes, and the emotion she found in them was deeper now, somehow, than before, as if tonight his eyes were open right through to his soul.

He was floundering in territory he didn't understand, and he was looking to Evie to help him.

Her lips parted, and her chest rose, as if even the breath in her body was drawn to him, but she refused to uncross her arms and reach for him, hold him, assure him it was okay to feel the way he did. She beat down that feeling inside her, angry at herself for even having it. She wouldn't help him. She wouldn't help him hurt them.

But she knew deep down Ford was lost. Maybe more lost than any of them, only he had no one to talk to about it.

"Evie," he whispered simply, his beautiful voice sounding bare and heartbreaking, and she felt as if that one word encompassed an entire conversation he didn't know how to say out loud. Without breaking eye contact he lowered his face to hers and she didn't even hesitate to open her mouth and welcome him.

Everything in her wanted everything in him.

She had no right to feel the hurt and betrayal she was feeling. She was the one breaking the rules, after all. But she didn't uncross her arms. She held them barred in front of her heart like a physical shield against him as he kissed her.

The sweet and heady smell of bourbon on his breath mixed with the vanilla-leather scent of his cologne and permeated her mood, nearly succeeding in moving her brain from thinking to simply sensing. He ran his tongue over her bottom lip, the wet stroke strong and sensuous. She felt Charley shift next to her, and then a kiss on her shin and the rasp of his five-o'clock shadow. Charley squeezed her ankle and kissed her again. She knew he was telling her — maybe begging her — to let it go.

She was too easily persuaded. *Absolutely screwed. Totally fucked.* It was beyond her control.

Giving in to her need for the man, she unfolded her arms and wrapped them as far around Ford's broad shoulders as she could, shouting at herself in her head for her stupid and overwhelming love for this fucked up man. He was rich beyond belief. He could give her anything in the goddamned world except for what she really wanted.

Ford made a noise of raw need when she broke down and embraced him, and his kiss grew deeper. Without taking his mouth from hers for a moment, he climbed on top of her, straddling a knee on each side of her naked body. She felt Charley move back up to her side and out of Ford's way. Ford broke the kiss and knelt up, grabbing Charley under his jaw and pulling him up to his lips roughly.

Charley opened for him, and Ford tongued his friend's mouth as deeply and passionately as he had Evie. Charley's body tensed, sexual energy pouring off his massive form as he pawed at Ford's sweater, pulling it up to explore the man's incredible abs and chest. Evie saw Charley was hard again, this time for Ford.

The men broke the kiss only long enough for Charley to pull the sweater over Ford's head. He immediately dipped his face to kiss Ford's now-bare chest, and when Charley trailed his tongue to the billionaire's nipples, Ford groaned, closing his eyes for a moment, lost in ecstasy. Evie watched, fascinated, as Ford reached down and wrapped his hand around Charley's large dick. He swirled his thumb around the head of Charley's cock, who pulled back, shaking his head and staring wide-eyed at Ford's fist around his erection. "Fuck," Charley whispered in awe.

When Ford's thumb was wet with Charley's pre-cum, he hooked it into his own mouth, tasting the other man. Ford made an appreciative noise deep in his throat at the tang, and Charley sat taller, his frame stiffening. "Ford," his voice was huskier than Evie had ever heard it. "If you've got a plan, you're gonna wanna get on with it, 'cause if you do something like that again, I can't be held responsible for what I'm gonna do to you."

A groan rose from Ford's chest and he cupped his hand around the back of Charley's neck, forcing the man to bend over, pulling Charley's face to Ford's cock like the order it was intended to be. Keeping one hand clamped behind his best friend's neck, Ford grasped his erection and fed Charley his now-rigid shaft, inch by inch. Since Ford was still straddling her, Evie had a front-row view of the scene unfolding in her lap. Ford shifted, sitting back so his weight was on his heels. Her eyes widened as Ford forced Charley to take nearly all of his length before the larger man gagged, and only then did Ford release him.

"Not as deep as Evie, but I like your mouth for other reasons," he purred to Charley, pulling him up and kissing him again until both of the men groaned with sounds of lust. Breaking off, Ford turned his attention back to Evie, hunching over and kissing her. His breath was hot on her mouth and he smelled like Charley. Ford going from kissing a man to kissing her...it did things to her, and her body reacted at once. She wanted Ford to do things to her—lots of naughty things.

She felt Charley grasp her hand at her side, squeezing it three times again before lifting her hand to guide her fingers around his erection. She obliged immediately, squeezing his cock and stroking him while Ford's tongue reminded her why she'd missed him so much while he was out at dinner.

"You're trembling," Ford whispered, moving his face back to meet her eyes. "Are you that aroused?" He searched her face, his voice deep and husky.

"I want you that much," she sighed, giving herself over to the longing.

Ford slid down the bed and adjusted until he was kneeling between her legs. She could make out the profile of his erection, large and hard, and it only made her aching worse. "Ford," she reached her free hand out to him, lifting herself, then looked to her side at the hand she still had wrapped around Charley's cock. "Charley," she whispered. She wanted them both. Needed them badly. Ford pushed her back down onto the bed and spread her legs wider.

He ran his hands down each side of her torso to her hips, where he stopped and pressed his fingertips into her skin as if to remind her with that little bit of force who was in charge. Her breath hissed in when he moved his hands between her legs and ran his fingers down her folds, sneaking his fingertips in and finding her excited clit. She gasped at his touch, pressing her hips upward, wanting a stronger, steady, rhythmic touch. Charley caressed her breasts and she remembered to stroke him.

"Where is your lubricant?" Ford asked, his voice gravelly, snapping Evie back to her senses immediately. *Lubricant?* Why did he want that? Her heartbeat kicked up. She was intrigued by the idea of anal sex, but she'd never been able to do it, and she hadn't realized he'd want to move into something that...advanced...so quickly. Unless it was for Charley?

"I...I don't have any," she stammered, her heart pounding.

"I've got some!" Charley sang, making Ford chuckle.

"You both wait here. I'll be back in a moment." Ford left the room.

Evie looked at Charley. "Do you think it's for me or you?"

Charley shrugged. "If it's for you, just relax and enjoy it. I promise it feels good."

"I'm not sure it's that easy," she stage-whispered. "I'm not the ass-whore you are, apparently."

Charley laughed, throwing his arms around her and rolling her to her side to kiss her face, forcing her to let go of his phallus. "Oh you will be, Evie. I can't wait to help make sure of that," he teased her between pecks on her cheeks, his smile stretching across his scruffy face. She heard Ford's footsteps on the stairs and she and Charley sat up. "You have a safe word," Charley whispered. "And don't you be afraid to use it. I can give that man all the ass he wants." His crooked smile made her feel at ease. "And remember, I'm right here." He took her hand and squeezed it three times again. "I love you," he said, squeezing her hand once with each word, explaining the secret meaning.

"Oh," she breathed, her insides melting to liquid. And there was no question in her head how she felt about him. She'd never loved someone so easily in her life. She squeezed his hand back four times, saying, "too" with the last squeeze before lifting their clasped hands to her mouth and kissing his fingers.

Charley's smile could have lit a city block in a blackout. "I can't believe you said that," he whispered, his voice awestruck.

"I didn't say it. I squeezed it."

"Did you mean what you squeezed?"

"I never squeeze anything I don't mean," she answered

solemnly.

A grin broke wide again across his gorgeous face and he shook his head. "You're right," he said. "We're completely fucked."

"I know."

He leaned over to kiss her quickly as Ford came back through the door, and she could feel Charley's heart thudding against her arm. He felt electric, so alive with happiness he could have shot off fireworks with the energy he was putting out.

Ford had a large tube of lubricant in his hands. "I picked up supplies on my way home from dinner, when I was thinking of what I wanted to do with you two at home, waiting for me." He smiled as he looked at them, his dimples causing her already warm insides to turn to lava. "Look at you two," he said softly. "How did I get so lucky?" Without waiting for a response, Ford moved seamlessly into dominant mode. "Charley, come stand next to me."

Charley scrambled into position next to Ford while Evie drank them both in—naked, bodies like gods. Their softened cocks hung like thick muscles against their thighs. Ford pointed to the floor at their feet. "Evangeline, on your knees. Suck us both."

Her vaginal muscles tugged hard at Ford's outrageous demand. She locked eyes with him, and maybe it was the new understanding between her and Charley, but suddenly she was determined to impress him. Lowering herself slowly off the bed, she crawled naked to Ford and Charley, not breaking eye contact with Ford. Kneeling up in front of him, she finally dropped her eyes to his cock, which was stiffening in front of her.

She leaned forward, catching his penis in her mouth without touching it, and easily sucked his whole length between her lips. He wasn't fully erect yet. She grasped Charley's also-hardening penis and used it to pull him a step closer to her. She wrapped her other hand around the base of Ford's shaft and pulled them both to her mouth. They shifted closer at her coaxing until the heads of their cocks touched. Stretching her mouth as wide open as she could, she tried to fit the tips of both their now-solid erections into her mouth at the same time. The feat wasn't possible, but both men groaned as she tried.

She stroked them both while she licked and sucked sloppily

313

from one man's cock head to the other, pressing the two men's dicks together and working them both at the same time.

"That's good, Evie. That's very good," Ford praised, his voice sounding tight with excitement. "Now Charley, go lie back on the bed." Charley did as he was told, settling himself in the middle of the bed, his shoulders on Evie's pillows. Ford offered his hand to Evie, helping her to her feet. "Climb onto Charley, love," he said. Ford moved to the side of the bed and wrapped his hand around Charley's cock, which jumped at his touch. Charley closed his eyes, relishing Ford's touch.

Evie crawled onto the bed as Ford instructed. "Straddle him," Ford demanded. "Ride his cock for me." Evie moved up Charley's body as Ford stepped back and she guided Charley's erection into her already-well-fucked pussy, slickened once already by Charley's cum that night. She slid easily down onto his substantial length, but she couldn't concentrate on the man beneath her. She looked over her shoulder, eyes locked to Ford. What would he ask of her now?

Ford climbed onto the bed behind Evie, cupping one hand into her waist and fisting the other in her hair, making her gasp. He used his handful of hair to force her head back around to look at Charley beneath her. "Do you like having his cock in you?" he asked as he lowered his head to her neck, nipping along her skin.

"Yes," she breathed. She met Charley's eyes and held, but she knew they were both thinking of Ford and what he had in store for them.

Ford put both hands on Evie's waist and scooted up close behind her, also straddling Charley's legs. He spooned his naked body against her back, wedging his erection between her ass cheeks. Then he pulled her upwards, lifting her along the length of Charley's dick, making her ride the other man. Up and down. Up and down. He held her hips, moving her on his best friend's cock, and at the same time causing her ass cheeks to slide up and down against his own firm shaft.

"Charley," Ford whispered. "Does she feel good to you?"

"God yes," Charley sighed, and Evie's pussy muscles clenched around him in a wave of pleasure.

Ford continued to move Evie between them, rocking her on

her knees, and Charley wrapped his big hands around her thighs, squeezing as he groaned. Ford was getting Charley off—creating the rhythm, controlling Charley's pleasure—but he was using Evie's body as his instrument. It was dirty and ingenious, and so very Ford.

"You know what you both feel like to me?" Ford's voice was soft and he continued without waiting for an answer. "You both feel like home to me. I missed you two so much tonight." Ford paused her movements to nuzzle the cradle between Evie's neck and shoulder, sending chills over her. She looked at Charley, wondering if he'd caught the strangely intimate statement from Ford.

Charley squeezed her thighs again, his face reflecting only bliss and satisfaction and lust. But Ford's words had jolted Evie out of the ecstasy she'd been slipping into. She and Charley felt like home? What did that mean?

But the moment was gone as quickly as it'd arisen. Ford released her waist, wrapping his arms around her chest like steel bars and pulling her back against him as if to prevent her from escaping. He spoke against her ear. "I'm going to take your ass tonight," he said, his voice dusky and aggressive. "It's time you learned to please me that way. I want you fully available to me, any way I want to have you."

In an instant, she forgot all about Ford's odd statement and whimpered, as much in excitement as fear. She'd never had anal sex, but she trusted Ford. He could teach her, couldn't he?

He released her, leaning back, and she locked eyes with Charley again, whose erection she was still impaled on. Charley's lips curved in a slight smile and she knew he was looking forward to this as much as Ford was, leaving only Evie in a state of anxiety.

The cold of Ford's lubricated fingers jolted her attention back to him. He spread the lubricant between her ass cheeks, slathering her thoroughly. In a moment, there was no mistaking the broad head of his cock that he touched to her entrance. She jumped, trying to shy away from him, but he held her in place with one arm wrapped around her midsection.

"Shh," he gentled. "Not yet. I'm only getting you used to the idea."

She tried to settle, telling herself to relax. He placed his cock there again and rocked it up and down, rubbing against her, moaning as he enjoyed her hot, wet crevice. The pleasure of being stimulated there while still filled with Charley's erection struck her like a gong reverberating through her body. She felt Ford's arm around her waist trembling, and she knew it was from his excitement about taking her virgin ass.

Charley reached up, tweaking her nipples with one hand, rolling the hard tips between his thumb and forefinger. With his other hand he ventured lower, finding her clit with his thumb and pressing against it, circling around it. She sighed as his ministrations helped elevate her pleasure above her anxiety.

"That's it, Charley. Touch her. Make her feel good. I want her so hot that she begs me to fuck her ass." Ford spoke huskily against her ear. "I will have your ass, Evie. You're going to be so good at this that soon I'll take my pleasure in your ass any time the mood strikes me. And Charley will too."

She moaned at his promise, pressing back against him. His words were raunchy and hot. Ideas flitted through her head about what it would be like for the two men to take turns fucking her tight bottom.

"God, I can't wait to have that ass," Charley moaned, closing his eyes as if imagining it. He thrust upwards, bouncing Evie on his cock.

Ford pulled back and touched her with his fingers again, his control intense as he stroked the perimeter of her second entrance, teasing his fingertips into her. She whimpered, wanting him inside. He worked his fingers in one at a time.

She gasped at the feeling of her asshole being stretched open by two fingers, and then three. The nerve endings in that area were so sensitive, she'd never experienced such strong sensations of pain and pleasure at the same time. Ford had taught her the heights of excitement she could expect when he mixed these two feelings— opposite ends of the spectrum—and she was already squirming in her excitement.

When he'd gotten three fingers worked fully into her and she was gasping and panting between them, Ford asked if she was okay.

She nodded and whimpered, not trusting her own voice. "I'm going to use my cock now," he said, and she moved to lift off Charley's dick. But Ford pulled her back down immediately, ensuring Charley remained inside her. "No, no," he admonished. "You're going to do both of us at the same time."

"Ford, no!" Her voice was panicked. "It's too much! I can't—not my first time!"

"You can. You have your safe word, but you won't need it. You're going to fuck both of us until we empty inside you." Ford bit her earlobe, eliciting a whine from her. "You have no idea how many times I've imagined this." His voice wavered, turning Evie's blood to lava as she sensed Ford's extreme level of excitement.

For her.

She groaned, gripping her fingers to Charley's chest muscles. Charley winced but continued touching her, murmuring words of lust, words of encouragement for what seemed like an impossible task. While Ford held her from jumping away, he placed the head of his cock against her slickened hole and pushed just a little. His cock was much bigger than his fingers, and the difference was obvious. She relaxed and tried instead to concentrate on how good his fingers had felt stretching her out, and how this hard length would feel even better.

"I'm going to leave it just like that Evie, so you can get used to the sensation." His voice was tight with the effort of his control, and she felt safe in his instruction. He reached around her and cupped her breasts, pinching her nipples to take her mind off the large cock pressing into her ass. She moaned and bravely pushed back against him, realizing that as long as he didn't force it, he would not gain entrance until she was ready. Her muscles there were quite tight.

He ran his hands over her back and shoulders, murmuring sensual things to her, complementing her skin and her shapely body. Charley did the same in front of her, rhythmically stimulating her clit with his thumb. All the while Ford kept a constant pressure between the head of his cock and the entrance to her ass, not to be deterred from getting what he wanted.

Panting with the pleasure growing in her over this taboo act, she wriggled against Ford, hoping her muscles would relax enough to allow him entrance. She wanted to please him. As she worked to open herself up to him, his excitement at finding himself so close to being inside her tight hole seemed to war with his control.

He leaned into her in an impatient, bossy move, tilting her over Charley's chest and causing her breath to catch. "Let me in Evie," he whispered. "I want to fuck your virgin ass." He pressed slightly further into her and she moaned at the overwhelming feeling. She wanted him inside her, wanted him to have sex with her there, but she couldn't seem to do it. "Let me, Evie," he commanded, his tone growing hard. "You will learn to make your ass available to me."

"You can do it, Evie. Just relax. Ford will feel so good in your ass, trust me," Charley whispered and pressed up into her, flexing his cock in her with his own memories of Ford fucking him there.

Between Charley's expert technique on her clit, her pussy still stretched full of his cock, and Ford's raw, dominant words, she was close to climaxing. But she wanted to experience an orgasm while completely filled with the two men in her life. She wanted both Charley and Ford inside her at the same time.

She suddenly couldn't wait any longer to feel what it was like to have Ford in her ass. Pressing herself backwards she let her head fall back, begging the man behind her in a hoarse voice, "Fuck my ass, Ford. I want you to be the first man inside me there." She closed her eyes and made one last heroic effort to will her muscles loose.

"I want to," Ford said, his voice betraying a hint of anguish at the control being asked of him.

"Just take it," she ordered through gritted teeth. It was all the permission he needed. Ford grunted and pressed hard into her taut opening, now demanding admission and finding it. Her muscles finally allowed him to slide past and he was in. Eased by the lubrication, he slowly worked his hard length into her impossibly tight bottom until his balls pressed against the skin of her ass cheeks. All the way in.

The act was intensely intimate in a way that transcended the simple physical closeness of their bodies, their sexes. When they moved, they could each feel it, inside and outside. When Ford pulled back and then thrust, all three of them were rocked by the force of it. They were truly, all three, making love to each other, together as one.

Charley groaned. "I can feel you moving inside her," he whispered. Then his tone grew purposeful. "Take her, Ford, I want to feel you stroking against me inside Evie. I want to feel you come inside her there."

Gasping at the sensation of having a man in her virgin hole, Evie reached for Charley's fingers on her clit, moving them like she needed them. "Oh god...oh god..." It seemed to be the only words she could remember how to say, drowning as she was in the deluge of sensation the men were creating in her. Ford pulled his cock shallow and then thrust into her bottom again, making her call out with pleasure.

He didn't hesitate any longer. He buried himself in her over and over, sending her screaming and quaking past the point of no return. Her orgasm exploded through her as Ford took her ass just as he'd fuck her pussy. She cried out, her body pulsing against both men inside her in a climax more intense than she'd ever had. She bucked between Charley and Ford, feeling both enveloped by them and completely possessed by them as they enjoyed her body, and she begged them not to stop.

Wrapping his hands around her hips, Ford pumped his cock into her ass hard enough to drive her flat against Charley's chest. Charley's moved under her, grunting animal sounds as Evie was jostled with Ford's rhythm on Charley's cock. She squeezed her fingers against Charley's chest, holding on, relishing every wave of intense sensation that Ford forced into her.

"I can feel you, Ford. I can feel every stroke against my dick. It feels— Oh god, I'm there!" Charley gritted his teeth, a guttural noise of release coming from deep in his throat.

Ford finished too, at that pinnacle of heat. "Ah, fuck yes! That's it—" Ford grunted that sound of pleasure that Evie heard in her dreams. "God, I'm coming so deep in your ass..." Ford and Charley both emptied in her, not stopping until they'd spent every drop, filling her with their cum.

The trio collapsed to the bed, the men's softening cocks slipping from her. They were tangled together, arms and legs wrapped into each other like a complicated knot she had no interest in undoing. She felt completely full and empty at the same time, in the best way. Happy, content, without complication. The intensity of the act had cleared her mind—the adrenaline and pleasure burning the worries from her brain like cobwebs against a candle flame.

The act had confirmed what she already knew—she trusted and believed in these two men. The safety and belonging she felt as she lay there wrapped into them was what she'd longed for all her life. Sighing, she tried to memorize the feeling of being cocooned in total bliss, held between these two gorgeous men as the trio recovered from the pleasure they'd all shared.

Evie didn't have much experience in the feeling of belonging, but she imagined it felt much like she felt now, nestled between Ford and Charley. Not because they'd just fucked her in every way a man could fuck a woman, but because she had what felt like a rock-solid footing with the two men—a surety of inclusion in their threesome. They felt like a family to her. Ford and Charley had been friends for a long time, but Evie sensed that the pair hadn't truly solidified into a comfortable union until they'd become a trio, body and soul, with her.

Shifting her body to snuggle deeper into the hollow between the two men, she thought about what Ford had said and now understood it to her soul. Wrapped in the two men's arms felt like home to her too. The home she'd never had, the friends she'd never kept. Even when she'd been with other men, even in bed, even when she'd thought she was in love, she'd always felt alone. But for the first time, she no longer felt alone, not when she was being held by Ford and Charley.

She couldn't imagine them moving on without her, but a wisp of sadness crept through her, because she knew Ford would want to do just that. Neither she nor Charley would be able to stop him from trying to move on at the end of the year, of that she was sure. Her gut twisted. Was Ford even capable of having the same feelings she did? Could he embrace them? She wasn't sure he was could. But, maybe.

No. Stop it.

Her heart was breaking even as she was letting herself think it. She couldn't torture herself for a year. And it would be torture, because she could see the future, stark and clear. She'd have to learn to live without them both. As much as she'd tried to prevent this from happening, it had happened anyway. And so fast. Her heart had recognized its fillers even if she hadn't, and it had filled its empty spots up to bursting with Ford and Charley.

Ford sighed and untangled himself. He sat up, stroking her head. "Evie. You never cease to amaze me."

"Mmm." She was exhausted. "Stay with us." She grabbed his wrist and looked up at him, hoping to see her feelings reflected in his face. She knew Charley would stay if Ford would let him, and she wanted to spend the night held in both men's arms.

"Yeah, stay with us Ford." Charley added, wrapping his arms around Evie and snuggling against her.

For a long moment, Ford didn't respond. The dim light painted his face in shadow and Evie couldn't read his expression. Finally he sighed deeply. "Evie, your bed is a mess." He picked at the sheets. "All wet. So much cum." There was a moment more of silence where Evie's heartbeat kicked up. Finally Ford finished, "You can't sleep here."

Ford stood and began gathering his clothes. "Well, c'mon. Both of you. You'll have to sleep in my bed tonight."

CHAPTER TWENTY-SIX

EVIE PADDED DOWN the dark, silent hallway toward Ford's room. The men were already in bed. Evie was the straggler, needing more time in the shower than either man. Nervous and excited about the invitation into Ford's room, she'd freshly shaved her legs and after the shower had made sure her hair was completely dry. She had a hunch Ford wasn't as cavalier about wet pillows as she was. Wearing only a robe and panties, ready to crawl into bed nearly naked and curl up with the two hot men, Evie hesitated with her hand on the doorknob.

She couldn't bring herself to open the door.

Heart hammering with anxiety, she turned and paced to a nearby chair, set in a hallway alcove. What was wrong with her? There were two gorgeous men in that room probably spooning each other right at that moment, and she had an invitation to snuggle in between them for the night. Her toes curled in pleasure at the thought, yet she couldn't go in.

Sinking into the chair, she pulled her legs onto the seat and hugged her knees. She'd never been in Ford's room. She'd never slept with Ford.

She laughed silently as soon as she had the thought. She'd *slept* with Ford but she'd never gone to sleep with Ford. She'd been bedded by Ford but she'd never been in Ford's bed. Smirking, she dropped her head back until the hard, top rail of the chair supported her neck, and stared blankly into the dark corners of the ceiling where no light reached.

She waited...waited for the blazing thought she hoped would come—the one that would provide the clarity that would organize all the confusion swirling in her head. The thought that would allow her to open that door to Ford's room, and to those two men...but it never came. Closing her eyes, she felt another wave of unease and realized her heart was still pounding. She was having an anxiety attack.

Great.

She was supposed to be throwing caution to the wind, indulging her decadent side—*no shame*. But it was all just making her more anxious. Throwing caution to the wind required a certain amount of cavalierness to consequences, and Evie wasn't made that way, at least not in matters where her heart was at stake. Mashing her lips to a thin line, she cursed Ford silently for his charm, his mysterious magnetism. If she could just bring herself to like him a little less every day, things would be perfect. But the balance wasn't heading in that direction.

Why was she surprised? Some small part of her knew she'd been falling in love with the man a little bit more every day since she'd started working for him way back he was just her beautiful, eccentric client at the law firm. Though back then, the only thing at stake had been her job.

Now it seemed everything was in danger—her heart, Charley's heart, and with the threat of John lurking in the background, maybe even her life. She unfolded out of the chair, and her robe fell to cover her knees again. She stared at Ford's door. Imagining crawling into bed between those two big men and their hard bodies and warm, muscular arms nearly overcame her self-control, but she hung her head for a moment before resolutely turning back toward her room.

A quick search of a hall closet netted a set of crisp white sheets. Back in her room, she stripped the ruined sheets off her bed, and along with them, the wonderful smell of the two men and the raw scent of the sex she'd had with them. After remaking the bed neatly with the fresh linens, she crossed back to her bedroom door and threw the bolt on her lock, feeling her stomach settle when she heard the heavy rod slide solidly home. Safe, for now. With a tug she double-checked the security of the door, and satisfied, crawled into her bed alone.

*****

The next morning she dressed slowly, feeling sullen and sore, even though she'd soaked for a long time in a hot bath. She'd never had this much sex in her life, and last night... "Geez, god," she said out loud, shaking her head at her reflection in the mirror. Her pussy was already waking up again at the memory of what she'd done the night before.

Knowing she was going to have to answer for not joining the men in bed as she'd been instructed, she made her way slowly to Ford's office. Might as well get it over with and hear what he had to say.

Ford glanced up from his work long enough to give her a quick smile, and then in his "all-business" voice he said, "Evie, good morning. Take off all of your clothes and leave on your heels. I'd like to get started right away this morning." She hadn't even had coffee yet.

Feeling uneasy, she did as he said.

Without even sparing her naked form a glance, he gathered the work in front of him and put the pile into a desk drawer so that his desk was completely cleared off. She couldn't remember if there were normally items on the desk, like a clock or paperweights, and she had an unsettling feeling he'd cleared it off just for this occasion.

He patted the desk in front of him. "Bend over." Being on the opposite side from him, she leaned over it towards him, keeping a wary eye on him.

"All the way over, Evangeline." He grabbed her wrists and pulled them to the front corners, forcing her to lay the upper half of her body flat on the huge desk's surface. She gasped, as much in response to the treatment as to her naked skin being suddenly plastered against the cold wood. Her bare nipples puckered hard at the feel of the cool, dark mahogany. Wondering what was going on, she lifted her head and looked at him to read what she could in his body language. He seemed matter-of-fact, cold, and she knew he was definitely not happy about her choice to disobey him the night before.

"Have I done something wrong?" she asked, hoping to gauge

how angry he was.

"Many things," he said simply, and her stomach did a little flip-flop. She stayed still, waiting, her heart now pounding with anxiety. Ford opened the top right drawer of the desk, extracting long, thin strips of leather out of it. He took one of her hands and tied a strap around her wrist, then opened the heavy, top desk drawer and dropped the excess into it. He slammed the drawer shut, trapping the lashing and pulling it tight. He did the same for her other hand.

She tested the slack. He'd effectively immobilized her hands. Her pulse fluttered and she felt her hands grow slick on the wood as her palms began to sweat.

He came around the desk behind her and spread her legs with all the care of an arresting officer. He wasn't gentle, and without meaning to, she let out a small whimper that exposed her fear. He didn't react—he just used the lashings to tie her ankles, just above her heels, to each of the corner legs below her on her side of the desk. He stepped back, she assumed, because she couldn't feel him touching her anymore. She couldn't turn her head enough to see directly behind her.

She wriggled, but due to the size of the desk and the technique of Ford's bondage, she was firmly secured across the desk, her ass facing the door, her pink, flushed pussy lips exposed to anyone who might come in.

She could lift her head, but otherwise couldn't move. Ford was still behind her somewhere. Her heart pounded in her ears as she strained to hear a clue of what was coming. She had no idea what Ford was doing or planning. He strolled back around the desk, stopping right in front of her. Though she couldn't lift her head up high enough to see his face, she could see the crotch of his pants in front of her nose.

This also meant that she couldn't miss how the fabric of his trousers stretched over what was obviously a massive erection. Ford was ready to go, and she was...well, he could definitely have his way with her, whether she was ready to go or not. She couldn't stop him, or anyone else for that matter, from taking her any way they liked, for as long as they wanted, or as many times as they wanted, until Ford chose to let her go. She shivered.

With some shock Evie realized her utter helplessness and humiliatingly exposed position was making her very wet.

"Evangeline," Ford started quietly, and his voice sounded neutral. She hated not being able to see his eyes—read his body language—especially when she was stuck in such a vulnerable position. He stroked her hair gently off her shoulders and let his hand trail down her back. She had her chin resting on the desk and when he leaned over her, the crotch of his pants, and thus his large erection, pressed against her cheek all the way to her forehead. As disconcerted as she was, she had an urge to nuzzle her face against his cock, but she wasn't ready to let on how much she was enjoying what he was doing to her.

He leaned back. "Why didn't you come to my bed last night?"

"I felt more comfortable in my own bed." She felt awkward trying to talk while tied chest-down on his office furniture.

"It was not a decision I made lightly. I've never asked anyone into my bed before. Ever. It was very rude of you."

She felt her cheeks flame, but it was anger—sudden and hot—that made her blood rush. She'd really wanted to come to his bed last night, and damn him for making her feel as though she couldn't—for making it mean something. She'd missed out on spending the night with the two men, and it'd been Ford's fault, not hers.

He began pacing around the desk. "And I saw that you used a set of my personal sheets on your bed."

Evie's eyebrows rose and her rebelliousness kicked into high gear, fueled by the pettiness of his last statement. "I didn't know they were your *personal* sheets, and besides, you ruined my sheets." She'd curled into a ball under those clean sheets last night and hadn't been able to get warm. Sleep hadn't come for hours, her thoughts jumping like firecrackers, sizzling from sex act to sex act, burning into her brain as she thought of the two men down the hall waiting for her, warm and naked. But she couldn't have them—not really. Not the way she wanted them.

The emotional exhaustion of her troubled night washed over her in a black wave and she lashed out without thinking.

"Actually, I shouldn't just blame you for ruining my sheets.

Most of that cum was Charley's. He did me twice in my bed last night. You only did me once."

The smack on her ass came so suddenly and was so sharp that she flinched violently and cried out.

"I better never hear you talk like that, Evangeline. It's disrespectful to Charley and me, and worse, it's terribly disrespectful to yourself. You are not a whore, and I won't allow you to talk about yourself as if you are!" His last words had risen in volume to a shout.

Tears sprang to her eyes, not from the pain of the blow, though not insubstantial, but from the shock of it. That, coupled with her overflowing frustration level and Ford's raised voice, overcame her defenses and fat teardrops rolled silently down her cheeks.

Ford either didn't see them or chose to ignore them. "It's time I dealt with your behavior. You've kept secrets from me, you continue to be willful about what I ask of you, and you struggle with treating me with deference. Such behavior is unacceptable." Ford's voice rose again, and the ire Evie heard in it made her uneasy. She was, after all, defenseless in her position.

"Acting as I want you to act and satisfying me sexually must be your first priorities." He paused for a long time, and when he spoke again, his voice sounded as if he now had his emotions under tighter control. "I'm afraid this is my fault. You trusted me to guide you in how to perform your role and I've been lax in addressing your mistakes with the punishment they merited. I will to make up for that today. Do you understand my intentions?"

"Yes," she answered cautiously, her anger being edged out by fear.

"Evangeline," he snapped, and his voice had the tone of correction. "This is your punishment position. When you're in it, you will address me as Mr. Hawthorne or sir." Ford sat down at his desk chair in front of her so she could see his face. His jaw was clenched tightly and his mouth pressed into a thin line, but his eyes sparked with something wild.

Leaning back in his chair, he folded his arms across his chest. It gave the impression that he was in no hurry, as if he had all day to stare at her, prone and bound naked before him. The idea chilled her. How long would it be before being held in this position became very uncomfortable?

Ford's eyes wandered over her for a few moments before continuing in his coldest, business voice. "When you agreed to this arrangement, our deal was that we did things my way or you leave this house. It's always your choice to continue, but if you refuse my wishes, you must leave immediately and forfeit the rest of your money. So I ask you now, with the understanding that you have no idea what I intend to do to you…do you trust me?" He lowered his voice to a wicked tone that sent shivers through her body. "Will you stay and take your punishment?"

He leaned forward so his face was close to hers. She could feel his breath on her cheek. She could smell his vanilla-and-leather cologne, which always made the scent-memory of sucking his cock for the first time in the library flash through her head. She studied the way his long eyelashes framed his dark green eyes, the curl of his strong lips, arching into those sexy dimples, his mouth so close to hers. Breathing heavily, he was so keyed up that the energy seemed to be jumping from his skin.

She knew why. According to Charley, though Ford desperately craved the kink she was providing him, he'd never let himself explore it before. Had he ever even done this? Tied someone up since that fateful time when he was sixteen and caught in the early days of his kink? Charley had clued her in. Ford needed her— not just to be at his sexual beck and call—but to be tied to his desk, braving his dark punishment, submitting to his strong will, and enduring whatever pain he wanted to make her feel for him. This was the fire he was missing.

Evie was sure she could do it. Even though she was frightened, she trusted him, and she could endure almost anything. But what Ford didn't understand is that nothing physical he could do to her would hold a candle to the pain he was capable of causing her heart. Her and Charley's. Ford might enjoy bondage and corporal punishment, but in matters of the heart, he was being a true sadist and he wasn't even aware of it.

She was mindful of her own breathing, heavy now, and the blood rushing in her veins, heating between her legs. With a deep breath she had one of those thoughts that whispers through a person's mind, but no one never says out loud.

I'm not sure there's anything I wouldn't let this man do to me.

Would she stay and endure her punishment? "Yes I will, Mr. Hawthorne," she whispered. "Punish me."

He wanted to hurt her, or at least he wanted her to *let* him hurt her. She didn't understand it, but she did know one thing...her thighs were trembling as much from lust as from fear. She thought of the sight of Charley kneeling before Ford and offering him anything. This act was her kneeling, her offering to Ford. It was what she was willing to give for him, and for them.

Ford's face softened and he leaned in and cupped his hands around her cheeks. Her skin was wet with tears, and she knew he couldn't miss them. She could feel his hands shaking. He pressed his lips to her forehead in a maddeningly slow gesture. She wanted him to just let her go, push her to the floor and make love to her with urgency, his body weight on hers making her feel very small, making her feel enjoyed, used, relished.

When he pulled back, his lips curled into a smile, then parted, and suddenly she wanted a kiss from him so badly she was ready to beg for it. Her heart pounded, and she waited. Time slowed. He didn't move, and she couldn't move, her restraints holding her across the desk. The only sound was their breathing, heavy and quickened. He pressed his thumb across her bottom lip. She implored him with her eyes, waiting, pleading for a real kiss.

"Please," she whispered finally, as the tears came again. "Please kiss me first. ...Mr. Hawthorne." His eyes looked into hers, and they seemed to be searching, for what, she didn't know. Then she watched in sickening defeat as a cloud passed over his face and instead of kissing her, he rested his forehead against hers.

"Evie." His voice was a whisper of anguish. "What am I going to do with you? Why do you make this so difficult?"

She could ask him the same thing.

Taking a deep breath, he sat back, pulling his face far away from hers and the moment was over. Disappointment stung in a sharp jab, and she dropped her moist eyes.

Dammit.

She was furious with herself for her emotions. She had to

concentrate on the sex he wanted and just give it to him. That was the only reason she was there. He was not interested in her heart, only her body. And she knew better than to get involved.

She steeled herself with great effort to be professional. She'd done this a million times during arguments with lawyers in her job as a paralegal—no room for emotions at work, even in heated situations. Besides, if Ford thought even for a minute that she was interested in being his girlfriend, or more, he'd probably throw her out. He'd told her before there was no room for that in his life, which was why he was paying her for the convenience of satisfying his sexual needs with no strings attached other than money, which he had plenty of and no hang-ups about sharing it.

It was no different than paying his chef to cook his meals. Sex, submission...they were just Ford's needs, and she was just another service-provider paid to meet those needs. Evie was merely a well-paid member of his household staff, not unlike his housekeeper or his gardener. That depressing thought allowed her to smother her emotions with relative ease.

Ford had leaned back in his chair again, his hands folded together casually. "After this day, I'll ask you to assume your punishment position whenever you've angered me or haven't done your best to fulfill my needs." He raised one eyebrow. "Or maybe just when I feel like using you like this—tied to my desk." He paused, maybe to wait for her to protest, but she remained silent.

His voice took on a note of irritation. "Recall last night when I pulled the sheet off you so I could look at your naked body and you grabbed at it, pulling it back up?" Evie nodded as best she could in her position. "In this house you are mine. Your body is mine. Whether you are in your bed or my bed, you are mine. If I want you naked, you will be naked. If I want to look at you, you will show yourself to me without hesitation. I won't have you acting like a petulant child when I want access to your body of which I am entitled. Do you understand?"

"Yes."

"Yes what, Evangeline?" he thundered, sitting forward, tension rolling off his body.

She flinched at the aggression. "Yes, Mr. Hawthorne."

PIPER TRACE

"Last reminder. You have a safe word. Use it if you must." Ford opened a bottom desk drawer and removed a wooden paddle, showing her both sides without explanation. Her eyes widened and her heart started hammering. He was serious! He wasn't just going to spank her—which already was outside the realm of her experience—he was going to paddle her. With an actual paddle!

Standing, he disappeared from her view and she could hear him behind her. She started to panic, squirming and begging him. "Don't hit me with that! I promise I'll do better. Ford, please!"

"It's 'Mr. Hawthorne', Evangeline, and yes, you will do better after this." He smacked her naked bottom hard with the paddle.

She yelped at the harsh sting. "Motherfucker! That hurt!" she shouted.

Ford actually laughed, sounding pleased. "Filthy language, young lady. I'll add one more for that." SMACK!

"For—Mr. Hawthorne, no more!" she gasped, shocked at how the all-encompassing bite of the paddle took over every thought in her brain, dominated the attention of every nerve in her body. Every cell in her seemed to focus and center on the small, burning spot where the paddle had last landed.

"You are here to please me. Your body is for my use." SMACK!

"Ow!" she yelped again. "Okay. I promise. Please let me up!"

"You need to understand what I expect." SMACK! SMACK!

"I promise! I won't forget, Mr. Hawthorne. I'll do better. You'll be pleased." She was breathless now from adrenalin and pain, and she was begging him with all sincerity.

His voice dropped an octave. "I will use you any way I want." This time the smack came lower and a bit softer. Somehow the change in his voice and the gentler blow shifted something elemental in her. Tears of a different kind—cleansing somehow—sprang to her eyes and she half-whimpered, half-sobbed his name. She felt him stroke his hand carefully over her bare ass, the nerves in her skin jangling. He seemed to be exploring the warmth she was sure was blooming there on her abused skin.

"Shhh, Evie love, I'm almost done." Now his voice was

332

soothing, but he didn't stop paddling her bare bottom. Only his blows were softer now, almost enjoyable, and he sometimes paused to caress his hand over her tender skin. Surely her ass cheeks were red and hot to the touch. It might be hard to sit for the rest of the day. Tears now streamed freely down her cheeks.

"I'll satisfy you, Mr. Hawthorne." Her voice shook with the effects of the adrenaline and the surge of emotions pouring through her with every smack. The emotions were chaotic. She struggled against her restraints but it was no use. She had no choice but to accept the pain he was causing her. It was no worse than she'd expected when she'd consented, but it was difficult to bear nonetheless.

Ford came around to the front of the desk and dropped to his knees in front of her. He wiped her tears. "Is it over?" she asked, her voice tremulous.

"It's over if you need it to be," he whispered. "I know this is hard, Evie. I understand if you can't do it. Please use your safe word if you need to."

"But you're not done?" she asked quietly. The thrill of excitement that blazed through his eyes told her his answer before his simple "no" was uttered.

She closed her eyes. "Then take whatever you need. I want to give it to you."

"Evie." He said her name like he was making love to it. He took her face in his hands, wiping her tears with his thumbs as he kissed the corner of her mouth and across her lips with such love and gentleness that she was afraid it might break her heart. "I can't. I can't finish." His voice was barely a whisper. "What if I love it so much I never want to let you go?"

Jellybeans.

"Please," she begged, in an effort to make him stop torturing her with affection and turn his attention to back to punishing her instead. "I want you to do it." She locked eyes with him, willing him to see the truth in her words. "Take what you need from me. That's why I'm here. I can handle it. I want to show you I can handle it." She closed her eyes, steeling herself. "I want it." And she did want it, she realized, slipping a little closer to heartache.

He stood back up and took a deep breath. His voice hardened an octave lower. "Look at you, my pet. Bound, legs spread. You are completely available to me like this. I can have you any way I want you. I could allow anyone to use you." There was no ignoring the large erection jutting against the front of his pants. He wasn't going to let her go, he was going to fuck her while she was tied up and helpless.

And Evie badly wanted him to do it.

She saw his hands reach down, unzip his trousers and pull out his large, hot cock inches from her face. He put his hands on the back of her head and pressed his erection against her cheek. She could smell the pleasant scent of his skin mingling with his cologne. She didn't know what he wanted her to do, and she didn't want to disappoint him for fear that he'd pick up the paddle again.

"What do you want me to do to you, Mr. Hawthorne?" she asked shyly as soon as he pulled back.

"Nothing. I'm going to do it to you."

He held his cock down and brushed it roughly across her lips and cheeks, smearing his tangy pre-cum over her face. Then he said in a dark voice, "If I feel teeth, I'll punish you even more harshly," and he shoved his cock roughly into her mouth and throat. She gagged, which was unusual for her, but she was not used to having her throat abused like that without having some control of the depth herself. Her reaction did not stop him. He hesitated for only a moment before he shoved harder, deeper, seeming determined to punish her and to take his pleasure in her mouth. She concentrated on relaxing her throat and quickly was able to accommodate him.

He rocked his hips back and forth, fucking her mouth while she was helpless but to accept his thrusts. Then, as quickly as he'd begun the assault, he stopped. He pulled out from between her swollen lips, and with relief she tried to catch her breath. "Enough?" he asked.

She shook her head, swearing. "I can do it for you," she whispered. "I can keep going."

Brushing her hair from her wet face, he fed his cock to her slowly this time, and she opened her lips obediently, the thought of doing anything but please him nowhere in her mind. Her thoughts were empty except for Ford. Her soul belonged to him.

"God, you are what I need. And you're mine." He breathed as he wrapped his hands into her hair and pressed forward until his erection hit the back of her throat again. "Swallow me now." She relaxed her throat and this time, with the benefit of his warning, it was even easier than normal, given the position of her head. The effects of the adrenaline coursing through her body from the spanking had her feeling as limp as if she'd just had a two-hour massage.

"God, yes," Ford muttered, as he pushed into her until his balls touched her lips, and held himself there for a heartbeat too long, causing her to gasp for air when he pulled out. He let her take two gulps before fucking her mouth slowly, deeply, pausing just long enough to allow her to adjust her breathing.

"Do you want to swallow my cum?" he asked softly, stroking her hair while he fucked her face. She nodded on his cock. "Not yet, pet. Not yet. I need more from you. I need you to surrender to me completely."

She already had. She was beginning to understand how cathartic the experience was. Her mind was focused down to one simple thought—serve him. Ford pulled out of her mouth and picked up his paddle again, making his way back around the desk while she caught her breath.

This time she didn't wince at the first blow. She squirmed. Her stresses, her frustrations, her fears, they were all gone. No, not gone. Rather, for a rare moment she was totally present. There was nothing but this man and how he made her feel. Heat bloomed from where his paddle connected, over her buttocks and into her pussy, spreading to her thighs and her breasts.

That heat carried a powerful aphrodisiac, and she felt her excitement dampen her thighs. Ford paddled lower and his thumps became gentler as they landed on her exposed sex. Now when he paused to caress her hot skin, he caressed her pussy too. She moaned without restraint.

"Shh, don't cry Evie. Don't cry. We're done." She hadn't even realized she'd been crying again, but her knees buckled with relief when she heard him put his paddle down beside her. The massive desk held her, always in the same position.

He smoothed his hand over both her sensitive ass cheeks, moving from one to the other, making her jump. "Your pretty bottom looks cruelly treated, love." She whimpered as the adrenaline leached from her body. A limp, euphoric feeling replaced it.

Ford pressed into her tender skin and his fingers traced her pussy lips, now wet with the juices of her unexpected, yet complete, excitement. He cupped her pussy in his hand and kneaded his fingers against her, causing her to gasp and then moan, low and long. Her nerves were at attention, super-sensitive after the firm spanking.

"I'll take the pain away, love. I'll kiss it and make it go away." His voice was silky. She felt him kiss her pink bottom. He trailed his lips downward until he hovered just over her sex. She felt his breath on her.

"Yes," she sobbed. "Please, Mr. Hawthorne!" She struggled against her restraints, squirming to get his lips where she wanted them. He obliged, and closed his mouth over her, licking up through her folds, his tongue searching for her hard clit.

"God!" she choked, barely coherent as his tongue found its target. After so much pain, the pleasure seemed intensified, swelling through her until she felt her body couldn't contain it. Like ecstasy might pour from her fingers and toes and puddle on the floor under her restraints.

"I love how you taste," he murmured and then plunged three fingers into her wet entrance at once, drawing a cry from her. He fucked his fingers into her hard while he sucked on her clit, and when she realized she was going to come, she didn't even have time to finish the thought before she plunged off the edge.

Evie orgasmed with such completion that it was as if Ford had made her come apart with his paddle only to heal her completely with this beautiful orgasm.

And it was a wonderful, worthy trade.

She bucked against her restraints with the force of the climax, her back bowing. The spanking had built such tension in her that when her orgasm released it, it was like a wound spring set free in a torrent of pleasurable twangs. Without the sturdy desk, she would have collapsed.

Ford took his fingers from inside of her, and she couldn't see where he was behind her. She laid her head on the desk and just breathed. He came back around and she could see he was now naked. His erection swayed with his movements, and as exhausted as Evie was, she wanted him. She heard the clatter of wood against wood when he picked up the paddle and dropped it back into the bottom desk drawer. Relief flooded through her — the spanking was really over.

CHAPTER TWENTY-SEVEN

ORD UNTIED EVIE'S wrists and then went back around and untied her feet. He put an arm around her waist and a hand on her shoulder and pulled her up against him. She crumpled into him and he guided her gently to the floor in front of the desk, spooning her on the soft carpet. "Shh," he murmured. His hands were everywhere, caressing her. "You did so well, Evangeline. You were so brave. I kept pushing and you just kept giving, until I got everything I needed."

He rolled her gently to her stomach on the soft carpet, smoothing her hair from her face. He left for a moment and when he returned she smelled something pleasant, but she couldn't seem to open her eyes. When he began massaging cream into her tender buttocks, she knew it was some sort of balm for her abused skin.

She hissed when he started, feeling a sting, but soon her skin felt soothed under his gentle touch. He pressed his body against hers, holding her and touching her as if he couldn't get close enough to her. She felt him kiss her eyelids, her cheeks, her neck. It seemed like he took hours, kissing and caressing her skin where he'd spanked her, and she thought she'd endure any punishment for this raw, concentrated affection from Ford. She hadn't even known he was capable of such tenderness.

The way he touched her, and the way he took his time, making love to every inch of her body with his lips, tongue and fingers, she knew with total clarity that Ford could love, genuinely and completely. He could love her and Charley. He might not know it, but she knew.

With Evie still on her belly, he spread her legs, and she whined as her body protested. "I'm sorry, love," he said grimly. "I know you're tired and sore, but I'm going to fuck you now." He moved on top of her and she felt him reach between them and position his rock-hard cock. He entered her from behind with a groan that sounded of pure elation.

Twisting their bodies to the side for leverage, he pulled shallow and then buried himself in her again. He cupped her ass gingerly in his large hand and she flinched under him. "I know," he murmured. "I know I did this to you." He thrust his cock into her harder, grunting and wrapping his hand around her hip to slide his fingers between her legs from the front. "You're skin. It's so red where I hurt you. And god it makes me so *fucking hard.*"

He shoved into her again, the movement stinging her red skin. Her hiss of pain turned into a moan when he pressed his fingertips against her clit in a slow caress. "To mark you like that, and then fuck you while I look at what I've done. Goddamn." He grunted again, pushing himself deep inside her. "It's so exciting to take you like this." His voice was losing coherency. "Come inside you while you're stinging from my punishment. Claim you."

She whimpered, pressing back against him in spite of the burn of her skin. He played his fingers across the hood of her clitoris until she made mewling noises and writhed under him. He stopped touching her, and as if lost in his own pleasure, pushed her flat to the floor and pounded into her. With that delicious sound he made when he came, he finished in her, his final thrusts sending her also spiraling with him. She cried out in a voice that didn't even sound like her own as her orgasm showered sparks through her body, making her forget about any pain.

Ford held her against his chest, rolling to the side and spooning her, not pulling out. They lay on the soft carpet for a long time, their breathing synchronizing. Finally he pulled his softening cock from her and went to the bathroom to clean up. Returning with a towel, he helped clean her gently before pulling her up onto his lap on the library sofa.

She finally opened her eyes so she could see his handsome face. He was staring at her with a look of complete contentment. His face was so captivating, so charming. She touched his cheek. It didn't look like a face that would enjoy the cruel things Ford did…the things that pushed her to the limits of pleasure.

"I don't ever want to let you go." He said it as if the thought surprised him. Taking her face in his hands, he kissed her slowly, his lips soft like a lover's. "I feel more free and accepted right at this moment than I think I've ever felt in my life. And god you made it so good…"

A wave of love for him had her mentally groping for her safeword, but she couldn't even think it. This time—just this time—she'd let herself bask in this feeling of love from him. She'd earned it.

She snuggled into his embrace and he stroked her hair, pulling it off her face where it had slipped over her mouth. The look in his eyes seemed to reflect how she felt, but she was too wiped out to ponder over whether it was real.

"Evie," he whispered, and pressed his forehead to hers, not needing to say anything more.

"I know," she answered. "I know." They were both fighting and they were both failing. Her stomach twisted as she wondered if he'd make her leave. He didn't want this. He fiercely didn't want to fall in love with her.

"Are you alright?" His voice was quiet, and sounded suddenly tight, strained. She looked up at him, because she didn't understand the sudden shift in emotion in his voice.

"Yes," she said simply. "I'm alright."

"Are you going to leave?"

Leave?

"No, of course not. Why would I leave?"

"Why *wouldn't* you leave? How can you stay, knowing that's what I want to do to you? Why would anyone want that?" His voice was anguished and he wouldn't look at her.

She took his face in her hands, forcing him to look at her. "I don't understand everything in this world, but I do know that you have pleasured me over and over, including during that punishment. And I can give you want you need. I can." She kissed him. "Charley and I are strong enough to make you happy. You just need to believe. No shame in this house, remember? Someone in charge told me that was the rule."

He lowered his face and kissed her, his lips barely touching hers. She parted her mouth in anticipation of more and he kissed her again, a little more completely this time, his tongue stroking softly against her bottom lip. Melting into his strong arms, she was too exhausted to fight against the feelings she knew she shouldn't be having.

"I have to go," he said, his voice sounding of regret. "I have to take care of a problem—a buzzing fly that needs swatted." She detected a note of irritation and thought about the heated phone call she'd overheard him having. Were the two situations related? Could Ford be in some kind of trouble? "Listen," he said, "if you go out, make sure you have your ID on you—Boone will not let anyone into the estate without identification."

"But he knows me now, right?"

Ford smiled. "Evie, I only hire people who do their jobs very well. If I say check all ID's, Boone will check all IDs."

She smiled too. "Well, I'm not going anywhere."

Ford hugged her close and then patted her arm. "Up you go, then, tough girl."

She climbed out of his lap and found her clothes, pulling them on gingerly. Ford straightened his own clothes and grabbed a thick envelope out of another desk drawer. Her stomach flip-flopped when he'd reached for the drawer, but she'd relaxed when he drew out the envelope rather than the paddle.

"Charley went home to grab more of his things but he should be back soon. I will see you later, Evie," he said, and kissed her cheek. He slid his hand down her hip to brush her bottom with his fingertips. She flinched away and Ford made an appreciative noise. "You were excellent today, love. Strong and brave, but accommodating. You were absolutely perfect. Absolutely what I want." He smiled and kissed her cheek again. "You are so beautiful," he whispered, and turned to go.

"Oh," he paused, as if he'd just remembered to mention it, "Evie, don't put the cheese platter back in the fridge with the knife still on it. That makes me crazy. Makes me want to reprimand you so that you remember to be tidier." He glanced back at his desk to drive home his warning and then grinned, his eyes twinkling wickedly, before he turned and left. Her heart sang as she watched him go. She didn't move until she heard the front door slam, and then the high whine of his car's engine as it pulled down the long driveway.

She'd endured the lesson to his satisfaction. Who knew something so...aggressive? Sadistic? Could be so enjoyable?

When she returned to her room, she stripped off her clothes again and checked out her butt in the mirror. Her skin was mottled in pink and red, and it felt warm to the touch. She ran her palm lightly over it, but it didn't hurt. Emboldened, she poked at herself but found she really wasn't too tender. He hadn't done any real damage. Nothing that wouldn't go away in a few hours mostly.

Looking at the bed, she thought about crawling into it to ease her exhaustion, but a glance at the windows reminded her of what a nice day it was. She was at a mansion with great security and a pool, and no work to do today—Ford hadn't left her any instructions other than to rest and take care of herself.

So instead she picked out a bikini—a traditional string one, with strategically placed triangles covering all her good parts. It was turquoise with white polka-dots, and it was one of her favorites. She added white, wedge sandals and an over-sized hat and inspected herself in the mirror, turning around. The small bikini bottom didn't cover all the pink marks on her ass cheeks, and she was glad. If Ford saw the marks visible under her skimpy bikini bottom, he might not be able to keep his hands off her.

Chewing on her lip, she smiled at her reflection. Being with Ford and Charley was great for any body issues she had. She couldn't help but to think of herself as a sexy woman, because she was constantly being used for sex or being forced to think about the next time she'd be used for sex. And it didn't feel odd—it felt as though she was a goddess.

She adjusted the triangles on her top. She wasn't bean-pole skinny by any stretch. In fact she was fairly curvy. She tugged at the triangles again but there was simply no more fabric to be had. Shrugging, she turned from the mirror to pack a pool bag. Her choice of swimsuits probably wasn't in good taste, but hey, she had a private pool and two handsome men who might catch her wearing the too-small bikini and decide they just had to have her. Yes...they. She giggled at the wicked thought and headed for the pool.

*****

~THE SUNRISE~

CHAPTER TWENTY-EIGHT

*E*VIE SMOOTHED ON sun block before she reclined on one of the cushy chaise lounge chairs by Ford's Mediterranean-style pool. She quickly fell asleep, eventually waking up blinking into the sun. Stretching her body languidly, she felt the heat seep into her to the bone.

She was more relaxed than she'd been in months. The spanking session Ford had subjected her to earlier had been as stress relieving as a full body massage. Who knew? She thought about the potential spa treatment possibilities and laughed out loud.

"Evie's Spanking Spa", let us paddle your worries away, you bad boys and girls!

She sighed and kept giggling to herself sporadically, thinking of her spanking spa. She imagined pitching the business plan to a man in a suit down at the bank in an attempt to get a loan, and dissolved into laughter again. He'd probably want a free spanking before he loaned her the money. The giggles eventually faded and she just lay there, feeling good, feeling the sun beat against her eyelids. Her contentment bloomed, and it dawned on her that she was happy.

It struck her as odd that she would feel so genuinely happy, and yet there it was. She had a bizarre job with an eccentric boss; she was in a pseudo-relationship with that boss and his best friend, where apparently it wasn't outside the realm of possibility to get tied up and spanked if she didn't perform well. Her job was fifty percent executive assistant and fifty percent sex toy—well, maybe more like twenty-eighty—and she got paid obscenely for it. And somehow all of that madness solved the scariest problem she'd ever

345

had…John and the money she owed him. Life worked in mysterious and sexy ways, sometimes.

Evie was living life outrageously, deliciously, rolling life around in her mouth and savoring it, devouring new sexual experiences until she felt full to bursting with ecstasy. Lust and orgasms were fun, but lust and orgasms in an opulent setting with two incredibly hot and interesting men? Fun wasn't close to a good enough word.

Her belly grumbled and she remembered she hadn't had breakfast, not even the coffee her body normally required. She was surprised she didn't have a headache from the lack of caffeine. Maybe spanking cured addictions too? It was a panacea! She giggled at the thought and gathered her stuff to go find something to eat. Maybe Charley would be around to have lunch with her.

As she neared the garage on her way back into the house, she heard the whine of Ford's Aston Martin coming up the driveway. A smile spread across her sun-kissed face. If she could get where he could see her, she'd be able to greet him in her tiny bikini as he returned home. Surely he'd be pleased with that. He might even screw her right there in the grass.

Geez, she was turning into a damned harlot.

Ford was maneuvering into the garage just as Evie came around the side, and she could tell from his face that he hadn't seen her. Her smile fell like a brick when she saw the back window of Ford's sleek car. The window was shattered. A chaotic spider web of broken glass emanated from one point…a hole in his window the size of a walnut. She was no expert, but that looked like a bullet-hole.

What the hell?

Her stomach seized, her earlier relaxation and carefree mood replaced by a cold dread. The dread was a familiar feeling she'd been living with ever since John had threatened her in his office months ago.

Had John tried to hurt Ford? She heard the car door slam and then Ford's voice. He was angry—yelling into his phone. She instinctively did not want him to know she was witnessing this, so she ducked back around the corner of the garage and listened. Her chest tightened above the knot in her stomach as she thought about Ford being in danger. She couldn't live with herself if Ford was dragged into her mess with her psychotic ex.

"I want it stopped NOW!" Ford yelled into the phone, his voice so angry she flinched. Her heart pounded as she yanked off her hat so she could flatten against the outside garage wall.

"You have what you want." Then there was a pause. "Well you can't have that! You listen to me...you better never fucking come near—hello? Hello? Fuck!" Ford slammed the phone to the driveway with such force that it shattered, and he kicked at the pieces as if he were angry the phone had the nerve to break.

Ford stood still for a moment gazing in the direction of his gate. He put both hands up to the sides of his head, his fingers laced in his hair in a gesture of despondency. Evie could only see him from behind, so she didn't know what his face looked like, but his posture was all tension. The bad feeling in her gut intensified.

He stalked to the side entrance of the mansion, slamming the door so hard the window rattled. She let out a breath she didn't know she'd been holding and realized she was trembling. Easing slowly off the wall, not taking her eyes from the side door to the house in case Ford decided to make a reappearance, Evie slipped into the garage.

She didn't want Ford to catch her snooping around if there really was a bullet-hole in his car. She went to his beloved Aston Martin, the first car in a row of eight cars, one motorcycle and a boat, and opened the door on the driver's side to look at the rear window. Sure looked like a bullet-hole to her. She turned her head slowly to the front, visualizing the path the bullet would have taken through the car, not wanting to believe what she was seeing.

And there it was.

Vertigo slammed into her as the world tilted. She grabbed for the door frame to steady herself until the lightheadedness passed. Then her eyes focused on it again—confirmation. There was a hole shattered into the dashboard of the car. A plate that used to house knobs for climate control now hung off the dashboard in pieces, one of the knobs shattered, leaving only a metal stick protruding from the ruined faceplate. Broken plastic lay scattered across the car's console.

She looked down at the driver's seat and did the mental calculation. Ford had come within five inches of that hole being in his neck instead of the dashboard. When he'd left the house that morning, he almost hadn't returned. Instead of black plastic spread throughout the front seat, it would have been blood. Ford's blood.

Ford was a force of nature. She couldn't imagine such a strong life-force being snuffed out. Shaking, she backed away from the shattered interior of the car.

John had done this.

Could he be so disturbed that he'd try to hurt Ford because he took her in? She was sure she knew the answer to that question. Her gut clenched again. This was her fault. She'd brought this to Ford's house.

Dejected, Evie trudged from the garage. Maybe Ford would tell her what happened.

Evie went into the same side door Ford had gone through and checked the library for him. He was there, leaning back in his desk chair, looking out the window with his hands tented in front of his mouth. When she peeked her head in, he smiled, tight-lipped. Almost as if he couldn't help it—as if his mouth didn't want to make the gesture, but it broke through anyway.

"Evie." His voice held a hint of what sounded like trepidation. "You've been to the pool. Let me look at you." He gestured for her to come into his office. She entered cautiously, afraid of what Ford would tell her. She searched his face for some hint of what happened to him and his car, but she saw nothing more than his body tension, a sign that he was feeling troubled under the surface.

He was hiding his unease, so she knew not to bring up what she'd seen. She stood in front of his desk and he twirled his finger to indicate she was to turn around. She rotated and looked back over her shoulder to watch his face. He whistled low and long, his eyes twinkling.

"That bikini bottom looks so good on your ass. It's just small enough to show your gorgeous curves. Come here."

She went around his desk to stand directly in front of his chair. He put his large hands on her hips and turned her around again.

Dipping his fingers under the edges of her suit, he slid the sides of her bikini bottom into the crease between her butt cheeks, exposing her skin with his improvised thong.

"Look at you," he murmured. "I can still see the marks on your skin from your spanking. This pretty suit doesn't quite cover them." He caressed her still-pink skin. "Does it hurt?"

"Just a little," she answered, though really, it was fine. He smoothed the fabric back into place and turned her around again to pick her up, as if she weighed nothing, and set her on his desk, facing him in his chair.

"Did you go swimming?" He spread her legs and pulled his chair up between them.

"No, I just relaxed in the sun. Maybe next time we can go swimming together?"

"No." The word came out as a chuckle. "I don't use the pool."

"You don't?"

"No, never." He ran his hands up and down her smooth, tanned legs.

"Why not?"

"I'm scared of the water." He gave her a crooked smile, looking up at her sheepishly through his eyelashes.

"But you have a pool. And a boat!" she said, incredulous.

"I have those because they are things rich people have." He grinned at her. "Actually, I do like to sail, but I always have a life-jacket close at hand."

"I didn't think you were scared of anything."

He glanced up at her again, and it was a moment before he answered, his searching gaze seeming to delve into the depths of her blue eyes. "Some things, Evie. I've discovered there are some things I'm very afraid of."

She frowned. His cryptic answer further dragged down her already-troubled mood. She was sure he was referring to her and Charley somehow.

Wrapping his arms around her waist, he buried his nose between her breasts and inhaled deeply. "You smell like sunshine and coconuts," he mumbled into her cleavage, smelling her suntan lotion. Her nipples peaked at the close proximity of his mouth. He must have noticed her reaction because he closed his lips on one of her hard nipples, over the bathing suit material, and sucked. She felt the pull on her skin and the friction of the material, and her breath hitched.

He stood suddenly, and took her face in his hands, kissing her urgently. The kiss went on, long and hard, as if Ford was kissing her out of need and not simply desire. He broke away finally and they were both gasping. He yanked her bikini top up and her breasts popped out from under the fabric, nipples hard and yearning to be sucked. He moved to kiss her neck and worked both of her breasts with his hands, caressing and squeezing them.

"Oh Ford," she cried without meaning to—he was acting with an uncontrolled ardor she normally didn't see. Noises were coming out of her mouth without thought, as Ford laid her back across his desk for the second time that day. He leaned over her, pressing his crotch to hers, grinding against her with their clothes still on, and lapping at her nipples.

"Evie, god, Evie, you were so good to me today. You feel so right." He spoke passionately in between kisses to her nipples, like it was important that she understood his words.

She was glad he was pleased with her. He reached a hand down between them and pushed the fabric between her legs aside, finding the wetness there and delving into it, making her squirm.

Moving back up, he kissed her mouth again, and she welcomed his strong, hot tongue, relishing the intimacy of it. Ford rarely treated her to this many real kisses.

Without breaking the kiss, he deftly untied the side strings on her bikini bottom and she lifted her hips so he could pull it off her. She heard the metallic sounds of his belt buckle being unclasped, then his zipper being pulled down. He braced himself over her with one hand and she felt him use the other to guide himself to her wet entrance.

He shoved his cock into her, and she groaned, arching her neck, lifting her shoulder blades off the desk at the feeling of pure pleasure she felt from Ford inside her. Scooping his hands around her ass to pull her towards him, he used the counterforce to bury himself in her. She gasped, grabbing at his hips, lifting her heels into the air, trying to pull him deeper, though it was impossible. She just couldn't seem to get close enough to him.

"Wait." His voice was husky with excitement, and he pulled out of her. "Turn over. I want to look at your spanked ass while I fuck you." She levered herself to her feet and turned around, bending over his desk as she'd been positioned that morning.

He entered her again like he couldn't stand not being inside her, but he held still in her while he touched her tender bottom, tracing the pink marks on her skin, his breathing heavy. Soon, with a moan, he began thrusting again.

He rocked against her urgently, as if she hadn't just made him come only a few hours before. As he sank into her, he kept repeating, "Yes, yesss." Her pleasure built quickly with each stroke. Ford was ravaging her with such fervor he seemed to be barely in control, and Ford was always in control.

In a ragged voice, his lips right next to her ear as his hips slammed against her ass, he asked, "When you were tied to this desk and I punished you, did you want me to fuck you before I let you go?"

"God yes," she answered truthfully, without hesitation. "I wanted you to fuck me just like this—from behind. I couldn't see you back there and I couldn't stop you. I wanted you just to take me while I was tied up." Her voice jumped in rhythm as his thrusts jarred her body, but he had heard her and it was enough for him. She felt him grow larger inside her and he pounded deeper, his fingers digging into her hips.

She knew they were both thinking of him taking her while she was tied up and helpless, and the thought made them both come, him only a moment after her. The reverberations of her orgasm were still pulsing through her as his cock started pumping cum deep inside her at the point of his own orgasm.

When he was finally done, he leaned over her, holding himself up with his arms, catching his breath. Slowly, he pulled out, and she grabbed the beach towel out of her bag and used it to clean up. He used the other end of the towel to dry himself while Evie arranged her bathing suit back into place. The hem of his shirt had gotten wet, she noticed, since he'd been in too much of a hurry to take it off first. He touched the spot and cursed, excusing himself to the bathroom.

When he emerged, looking as if he'd had a stylist in there with him, he came to her and embraced her for a long, quiet moment. "You're too easy to be with," he said into Evie's hair, and it sounded ominously like an accusation to her. He pulled back to look in her eyes. "I couldn't forgive myself if something happened to you," he said, causing her stomach to twinge with worry. He'd done a good job of distracting her from what she came to ask him about.

A dark cloud seemed to pass over his face and he pulled back, dropping his head with a sigh. "I, uh... I'm going to work out." He straightened the cuffs of his shirt, his attention seeming suddenly rapt to anything but her.

Evie chewed the inside of her cheek. Ford was fidgeting. Avoiding eye contact. She'd never seen him fidget.

"What's wrong?" she asked, her voice edgy with concern, her own eyes pinned to his averted ones.

"Nothing. Why don't—"

"Ford," she cut him off. "Talk to me."

"No." His voice was sharp and resolute. "The only thing you need to know—" his eyes caught hers and the intensity in them made her gut twist with fear "—is that I will not allow you to be harmed." He blinked twice in quick succession, his eyes going unfocused for a moment before he seemed to return to her. He was seriously distracted.

She didn't like the look on his face. His jaw was like steel, and his lips were mashed in a grim line. He seemed resolute about whatever had just played out privately in his head. Whatever it was, it didn't make her feel any better.

He offered a hand to help her off his desk. "Charley might be around. I saw his truck out front, but not his bike. If you can find him, show him how you throw knives. It'll really freak him out."

She smiled in spite of her unease, knowing Ford's attempt at lightheartedness was a front for whatever he was really feeling. She didn't say anything else to him, but took her time in gathering up her bag.

They met eyes again as she turned to go, and again Ford couldn't seem to hold her gaze, dropping his beautiful emerald eyes and running a hand through his hair in an uncharacteristically anxious gesture.

Evie closed the library door behind her reluctantly, vowing to find Charley and take him out to the garage to look at Ford's car, but her biker man was nowhere to be found. She slowly climbed the stairs back to her room, so many thoughts snarling in her brain that she didn't know what to think about first.

After showering, she grabbed a short, silky robe and wrapped it around her naked body, too distracted to pick out an outfit. Dropping heavily onto her bed, she stared out the window for a long time, mulling over the idea of asking Ford for enough of her salary in advance to pay John back immediately.

She hadn't wanted to do that, and she knew it would cause an issue with Ford. He'd give her the money—she was sure of that—but it would change things. It was important to Ford that she had the free choice to leave at any moment, and if she borrowed money, she'd be beholden to him. She didn't think Ford would continue their...relationship, for lack of a better word, if she owed him money.

And she wasn't ready to give that up. Charley and Ford were giving Evie the only real happiness she'd had in years, maybe ever. To feel loved and desired and safe...well, she just couldn't bring herself to change things.

She pondered how to get the money without altering their deal, but after an hour she gave up in frustration. If Ford gave her the money it would change the delicate balance between them, and Evie didn't want that to happen. She had more than herself to think of—Charley was a part of this too. If she altered her relationship with Ford, who knew what effect it'd have on Charley and Ford. And she was *not* going to be the cause of Charley's fresh heartbreak.

She left her room in search of both men, seeking comfort and an answer that wasn't there. But she wanted to see them, needing to be reassured of her safety and theirs.

Instead of turning right out of her room and heading for the stairs, as had been her plan, she went left toward Ford's room, her heartbeat racing. If he was in there, he might be angry at her for seeking him in his private quarters. Her eyes lingered for a moment on the spot in the hallway where Ford had made her suck him before demanding she fuck Charley alone. She shivered. So many things had gone on among the three of them. They'd been connected in ways that were beyond her wildest imaginings only weeks before. No wonder their feelings had grown so intense so quickly.

At least they had for her and for Charley. How could Ford remain unaffected?

She rapped hesitantly at his door, entering when she heard a distant, "Come in." Ford was in his bathroom. She'd never been in his room before, so she followed the direction she'd heard his voice.

Upon entering the bathroom, she was struck by two overwhelming sights. The first was the architectural masterpiece that was his *en suite*. If Evie could imagine what the master bathroom might look like in the penthouse floor of a luxury Las Vegas hotel suite, she still couldn't have come up with the reality of Ford's bathroom.

First, it was huge—half the size of her last apartment, it seemed. And second, there were mirrors and marble everywhere. Even the intricately coffered ceiling had been fitted with mirrors. The room was partitioned into two areas, the first being a dressing area with thick, marble counters on both sides of the room, topping drawers that lined up under the stone slabs, adding order and linear aspects that were repeated over and over in the parallel mirrors. The effect was an elegant, breathtaking space of a caliber she'd never seen.

Yet all that shine and glitz was overshadowed by something else...the other sight that had swamped Evie's senses with pleasure the second she'd stepped into the room. Ford, leaning on one of the counters on closed fists, wet from a shower. A towel was slung low around his waist and water beaded on his skin. His hair tousled in a messy, sexy way she'd never seen, shiny and wet. He looked at her through the reflection without turning, keeping his muscled back to her.

He held her eyes, his expression heavy, before dropping his gaze back to his own reflection. His eyebrows fell into a scowl, and his mouth tightened with disgust as he looked at himself.

She leaned against the door frame, not saying a word, and instead just drank him in, content to stand there. Finally, he glanced up at her again and, catching her eyes, he watched her watch him.

He was clearly troubled, and she assumed his unease was due to the bullet hole in his two-hundred thousand dollar car, so he caught her off-guard when he said, "Evie, don't look at me like that. Please. Not you." He averted his eyes again.

She blinked. "Look at you like what?"

"Like you might do anything for me." The words came tight through his clenched jaw. He looked down at himself and straightened, crossing his arms across his tanned, chiseled chest. "You're in danger, and I think we both know that you being here is only making it worse now. Yet, I can't seem to bring myself to make you go, for your own safety." He took a deep breath, flexing his jaw. "I want you to do it."

He met her eyes, his words harsh and demanding. "I showed you the things I want. I want to *hurt* you. You can't want that! You don't deserve that." He closed his eyes and took a deep breath before continuing, his face miserable. "I let you see all of me —" His face darkened and he glowered, looking away. "But still you won't leave. Even after what I did to you. After what I've made you do with Charley..." He cut his words off, dropping his head. His posture highlighted his straight shoulders and corded back, bunched with tension. "Is it my money? Is that why you're staying? Because being with me isn't worth five-hundred thousand dollars, and it's certainly not worth the danger I'm putting you in."

Evie closed her eyes in a slow blink. "I'm going to try not to take offense at what you just said, due to your complete lack of skill in having a relationship with a woman, friends or otherwise," she said dryly. "Ford, you have problems alright, but your sexual kinks aren't one of them. Your biggest problem is your hatred for yourself."

He squinted his eyes and frowned, his face a confused scowl.

She continued before he had a chance to deflect her words. "You don't ever let people know the real you because you think you can't be accepted — that you're not worthy of love. And since you only let people see the shallow stuff — your looks, your money, your body—you think they only want you for it. It's a self-fulfilling prophecy."

He raised his eyebrows and pulled the corner of his mouth back in a skeptical expression, and she could see him mentally shrug off what she'd said as bullshit. "I appreciate your theory, Evie, but I have a hard time believing it. That's not the reason I don't get close to people."

"Why then? Because you're bored? I don't buy it." She let her voice harden. "I've known you for a while and I've never seen you as happy as you are now with Charley and me. You need this—you need people around you. Why do you do this to yourself? What's so wrong with you that no one can love you?"

He raised his voice in response to her heated words. "You don't understand. You didn't grow up like I did. People being paid to love you, to care for you. Everyone knowing before you walked into a room who you are and that you are to be coddled and sucked-up to. It makes a person feel inhuman."

He pulled himself tall again, turning around now to face her, leaning his towel-covered ass against the polished marble counter. "The ironic part is that people act like that because they think you're special, or they're told to treat you like you are, but it doesn't make you feel special in the long run. It only ever made me feel worthless."

His shoulders seemed to hunch at his admission and his voice lost its edge. "After years of that it made me feel like I wasn't worth honest emotions, real reactions, true judgments. And then I guess no one seemed real anymore."

She crossed her arms, mirroring his hostile posture. "No, you're right." She pressed her lips together and nodded sharply. "I don't know what it's like to have everyone fall all over themselves to take care of me and make me happy. In fact I'm not sure I've ever had one person want to do that for me in my entire life. Ever. So you're right. I don't understand."

He closed his eyes, his voice pained. "I'm sorry, Evie. I wish things had been different for you." He shook his head, looking away, silent for a moment. "Our lives have been so different and yet, in a vital way, so similar. We've both felt so alone."

"I did feel alone." She paused. "Until..." She trailed off, unsure if she should finish the thought.

But he'd caught it. "Until what?"

She shrugged, but his voice took on the tone. "Until what, Evangeline?" He was suddenly angry, his face reddening. "Until what? And don't lie to me." The volume of his words had risen again, and now his crossed arms rose and fell as his chest heaved. "You can't mean until me. You can't mean until I paid you to have sex with me and then hurt you, because that's bullshit."

She closed her eyes before speaking, reluctant to let him in on her special, private memory. "Until you took my hand in the library," she whispered finally.

He blinked and his body stilled. He looked at her blankly.

"When John called and was berating me. When he said he was going to come to the library, and I was scared. You know how I hate to be scared now, but you didn't then. And yet you took my hand. You put your arm around me. You somehow knew I needed something, and you were there for me. You took up for me. Protected me."

She sighed. She was in this far...may as well finish her confession. "And then later when you spoke to me like you owned me. Like I was yours. And you trusted me enough to share your most private sexual desires." She softened her expression, knowing he'd have a hard time accepting what she was saying. "Those memories. Those are when I didn't feel alone anymore."

She watched him for the rebuke she was sure she'd get for being too familiar, too attached to him. For layering feelings that he didn't have for her over his actions. But he just sighed heavily, dropping his crossed arms to fist his hands together in front of him, staring grimly at his fingers.

"I don't know what I'm doing anymore," he said, looking away as if he was talking out loud to himself. "I had a plan, but I don't recognize what this has become." He pulled his hands apart and cupped his elbows, his forearms crossing protectively over his bare midsection. He looked suddenly vulnerable, and he raised his eyes back to hers as if seeking for her to make everything make sense for him again.

The silence expanded, but she forced herself not to speak. She'd laid herself bare and she wasn't going to help him now through the frightening stillness. He was going to have to fill it.

Finally, he closed his eyes, his velvety voice coming tight from his throat. "When you did everything I told you to, when you let me do anything I wanted to you and you not only stayed, but you made me feel like it was okay, that's when I knew you were mine." She drifted toward him, drawn closer by his honest words, his beautiful face in profile as he spoke without looking at her. "But that's when this problem started."

"Problem?" She bristled, stopping in mid-stride and refusing to come any closer.

"This need. I want you around me all the time. I *want you,* not just to control, but just to be with me. I want to take care of you in every way." He shook his head, scrubbing at his eyes before running his hand through his damp hair. "But I had to pay you so I could have that feeling. I thought paying you would make it right for me—for both of us—but it didn't. It's just another thing that makes me feel worthless." His posture stiffened and he refused to look at her again, his shoulders hunched in on himself. "I can't understand why you're still here."

And then he did look at her. Glared at her, and then broke her heart.

"*I can't love you.* I can only hurt you." He spit the words out with precise enunciation, as if she might not understand them unless he spoke slowly. "I *want* to hurt you, Evie. Do you understand that? I want to. It gets me off." He looked up, shaking his head as if trying to rid it of his feelings. "And now you're in real danger and I'm not even strong enough to stop needing you in my life. In my bed."

"I think you mean 'over your desk'," she mumbled, and then smirked in spite of her mind swirling madly with his words, some that filled her with joy and some that cut through her like a searing hot knife.

He dropped his hands to either side of his hips, clutching the edge of the counter hard enough to whiten his knuckles. He looked disgusted with himself.

She stepped toward him again, coming right up in front of him. All of his body language screamed *back off*, and she ignored it. She made her voice soft. "Do you really think I'm only here because you pay me? Because you're rich? Because of how you look?" He didn't answer, but tilted his head up enough to look at her from under his lashes, his face bleak.

She dropped her arms loose to her sides in an open posture to contrast his closed one. "I'm not going to pretend I don't like the way you look, because I do. I like it a lot. But none of those things are why I'm still here."

She reached out and touched his shoulder with just one finger. He flinched away almost imperceptibly, but she noticed it, as in tune as she was with his body. She pressed her fingertip more firmly against his bare skin and traced her nail down his arm, leaving a white scratch line. *Making* him feel her touch. This time he didn't pull away.

He closed his eyes and inhaled deeply, his solid, masculine frame easing its tension under her fingernail scrape as if in surrender. Leaning forward, she molded her body against his to speak directly next to his ear. "But none of those reasons are why I let you do those filthy things to me," she said, her voice sultry.

His lips parted and a soft moan escaped. Dropping his head toward her, he gripped her shoulders first, as if thinking about pushing her away. Then scooped his arms around her in a vice grip, hugging her for a long moment. She could feel his hot breath against her shoulder through the silk of her robe, his embrace so complete that he didn't even raise his head to get an unhindered breath.

Finally he pulled back and met her eyes, his green ones seeming to plead with her to make him believe. And she noticed a flicker of fire had started to light the malachite flecks of his irises, causing a twinge of desire to flutter low through her. She had a flicker of her own—a small oven bursting to life with one heated look from this man.

He stood up straight, lifting her easily and turning to place her on the counter. He spread her legs, shoving her robe up high on her thighs when he did so. He pressed himself to her, and there was no denying his mood had shifted, his agitation morphing into something erotic.

Now he was in the dominant position. Slowly, as if he knew the carnal effect he had on her, he licked his full lips. "So tell me then," and his voice had become his familiar commanding one. "Why would you let me do those filthy things to you?" he whispered, his questioning words sexy and low. But then he seemed to catch himself and pause, searching her eyes. It was as if he'd only then realized he wanted a real answer and not just naughty talk to stoke his fire. "Why do you let me use your body the way I do?"

Evie didn't even know where the words came from, she just let them fall from her lips, honest and unfiltered. He deserved to hear the truth. "Because I love how it makes me feel. Because I'd never known what it was to feel safe and truly connected in trust with another person until I gave myself over to your will. And you taught me how a little pain can make the ecstasy that much more satisfying." Hesitantly, she touched his cheek, marveling, as always, at how intoxicatingly gorgeous he was. She leaned her face closer to his. "Because of your confidence and your drive, and the way you hold your mouth when you're teasing me. Because you're mysterious and distant, and yet fierce in your need for me. The way I feel utterly cared for by you. And because you brought me Charley."

A smile flickered across his face and he dropped his eyes, as if he couldn't hold her gaze while she spoke of him in that way. He pulled his hands from her hips where they'd been resting and grabbed her wrists. He kissed her fingers one at a time, his lips and tongue lingering over her fingertips, sending shivers through her and stoking that fire into an inferno, one finger at a time.

"And because you always give me as much pleasure as I ever give to you, maybe more." Her voice was starting to reflect a breathy quality as her respiration kicked up along with her lust.

"As I take from you," he murmured against her hand, turning her wrist out and trailing his teeth against the soft underside, gently biting. Every nip got slightly more aggressive, reddening her skin, and every stitch of pain reminded her that she was his.

His bites seemed to have a direct effect on her pussy, which grew warmer at his treatment. Her core ached with a need she knew only Ford's mastery could sate, and that both terrified and thrilled her.

"What?" she mumbled, losing her place in the conversation as Ford's lips worked against her skin.

"As I take from you," he repeated. Halting his gentle assault on her wrist, he met her eyes again. "You said I always give you as much pleasure as you give me. I corrected you. I take my pleasure from you. I take it."

Ire flashed in her, and she fought the urge to shake him. Leveling her eyes at his smoldering ones, she chose her words precisely. "Make no mistake. You may 'take' it, Mr. Hawthorne, but you take it only because I give it to you freely. Because I want you to use my body for your sexual satisfaction in whatever way you need it. *You*." He blinked, looking lost. "And not because of your money, or your face, or your body or your cock. But because you're Ford. And you're my Ford, *our* Ford, Charley's and mine. And because you make me feel like no one else I've ever been with."

His face softened, revealing a vulnerability that made her heart hurt.

"I hope you heard her." Charley's deep voice reverberated through the room and Evie and Ford whipped their heads around to see Charley step into the doorway and lean casually against the frame, taking up nearly all of the opening with his bulk.

The ease that comes along with Charley seemed to spill through the room ahead of him, his lopsided smile radiating a warmth that was even bigger than him. He stood slowly, meandering toward them with his hands in his pockets, his eyes on the floor at his feet as he walked.

"I hope you're listening to her," he repeated more firmly, his soft brown eyes pinning Ford's as he drew up next to the counter. Ford dropped Evie's wrist and reached for Charley, pulling the man over to lean against the counter next to Evie. He rested his hand on Charley's hip.

"Charley Baker," Ford drawled affectionately, his lips curling. "Welcome to our honesty session." He smiled wryly at Charley. "I'm stumbling through it, blind and stupid."

Charley crossed his arms, his eyes boring into Ford's. "Honesty session, huh? I was wondering what all the shouting was about. You don't often raise your voice."

Charley looked at Evie, seeming to check that she was okay, and Evie leaned to kiss him chastely, warming at his concern for her. He turned back to Ford. "It doesn't matter how honest she is with you if you don't believe her." He shook his head. "Don't ask her to tell you the truth and then disrespect her by dismissing it."

"I know," Ford's voice was thin. Charley moved to the side of them, forming their group into a triangle. He covered Ford's hand on his hip with his own, his uncomplicated demeanor a stark contrast to Ford's devastatingly handsome, sharp features. Ford's analyzing, jewel-colored eyes were locked to Charley's. Ford's muscles were still tightly wound, and his hands were molded proprietarily to each of Charley's and Evie's bodies.

"I'm going to simplify what she said, Ford. She said you are worth loving and wanting." Charley draped his arm around Evie, hugging her to his side, and met Ford's eyes with a laser-steady stare. "You aren't perfect. None of us are, but that doesn't make you not worth loving. It's why you're worth loving, with all of your imperfections, infuriating quirks and your kinky needs."

He tilted his head, his eyes imploring Ford. "Now you can believe that or not, but your worth is the reason this gorgeous, strong woman..." Charley seemed to pause in his thought, turning his attention to Evie and pulling her head against his to kiss her hair before continuing, eyes still locked to hers. "This brilliant woman, who fucks with the energy of a tidal wave, and makes us both feel a little bit like gods when she makes us come, allows you—" he turned those painfully honest eyes back to Ford before finishing, his words slow and sexy, " —to do those filthy things to her."

Silence hung in the air after his last words before he added, "And Evie loves it. And you and I love it. And it's *perfect*. Don't diminish this incredible thing we've found by pretending it's not real for any of us, including you."

"You're right." Ford's voice sounded broken, his eyes bright with emotion. "You're right." Ford's eyes went back to Evie's. "I'm sorry, love." Evie realized she was holding her breath. She shifted what she was sure were startled eyes to Charley and something passed between them. It was a breakthrough. There was a crack in the wall and Evie and Charley were going to bust it the rest of the way through.

Charley seemed to understand that he needed to keep Ford off balance — take control to prevent Ford from slipping back behind his protective shield of power, comfortable in his role of always being in charge. Evie and Charley silently agreed, communicating in this matter as clearly as if they'd spoken the words out loud. Turning back, Evie saw Ford's eyes were still trained to her, a depth in his look she'd never seen before.

"Show her," Charley growled, an impressive simulation of one of Ford's own sexual orders. "Show her you believe you are worth everything we want to give you." Ford pulled himself to his full height at the command, not taking his eyes from Evie's, and banded his strong arms around her, enveloping her in his manly, clean scent, fresh from the shower. The emotion she felt in his embrace saturated her senses and brought tears to her eyes.

His own eyes sparkling, Ford brought his lips to hers, kissing her so softly at first, whispering, "Evie, god Evie," between kisses. And then, "You're mine? Really mine?" against her ear, his voice growing husky.

She nodded, closing her eyes, her lips parting. "You're ours?" he amended, his words spoken through his teeth as he bit down gently on her earlobe, eliciting a gasp.

"No," Charley said firmly as he moved around behind Ford, pressing his body to the other man's, causing Ford to mold more firmly against Evie. Charley lowered his head, sucking on the skin at Ford's neck as he reached around his friend to find the tie on Evie's robe. He yanked it loose, allowing the silky garment to fall open. Ford groaned and moved his hips, and while the movement caused him to rub against her in a yummy way, Evie was pretty sure from the way Ford had let his head fall back onto Charley's shoulder, that it was Charley's cock he was actually grinding against.

Her eyes flitted up to the mirror behind Charley on the opposite wall, and she saw Charley wrap his paws of hands around each side of Ford's hips and gyrate against his best friend, Charley's ass moving in sensuous circles as he rubbed his jeans-clad erection against Ford's tight ass.

"No," Charley repeated. "Evie's not ours."

Ford's eyes opened as he raised his head and looked at Charley through his reflection in the mirror, the look on his face suddenly predatory. "Why not ours? Why isn't she ours?" His voice was a rumble, thick with emotion.

Charley reached up and sliced his fingers through the side of Ford's thick, nearly dry hair, almost palming the other man's skull. "Because we are yours, Ford." His tone was that of an avowal, an oath of devotion. Then he repeated softly, "We are yours. Evie and I. It's never not been true. In your heart, you know that." Charley shifted back to Ford's side, and keeping the man's head tilted, he nipped at Ford's jaw before moving to his ear, sucking his earlobe between his lips.

Ford made a long, groaning noise that told Evie he liked the sound of that. Releasing Ford, Charley reached to catch Evie's chin between his thumb and forefinger, forcing her head to his. He kissed her deeply, his tongue plundering her mouth, as if he was making a point. Without breaking the kiss, he brushed the silk robe off her shoulder like it was in his way.

Charley tugged her robe down and Evie pulled her arms out of the garment, leaving her completely naked. With the same hand he found one of her breasts, plucking her nipple until it was even harder, making her pussy muscles contract in pleasure in response to each small pinch.

Pain was usually Ford's territory, and Evie found herself newly breathless at Charley's takeover. She whimpered and he pulled back with a chuckle. "Ford's not the only one who can make you squirm, little Evie."

Ford nuzzled Charley's cheek, his tongue reaching to touch against the corner of Charley's generous mouth, drawing a small moan from both men. Their gazes locked together and they shared a current of mutual adoration and heat before Charley closed the gap and claimed the other man's mouth with his own.

Evie saw the muscles in Ford's body tense hard in an instant when Charley moved his hand from her breast to trail his long fingers down the taut muscles of Ford's bare abdomen until he reached the towel, tented with Ford's erection. In an instant the towel was on the floor and Charley's fist was around his best friend's thick cock.

Ford was making a predatory noise as Charley tongued his mouth, a noise a lion might make as it satisfied itself on raw meat from the hunt. Evie watched their powerful jaws clench and unclench as they seemingly devoured each other while Charley stroked Ford's hard cock. Finally, Charley broke the kiss, his chest heaving.

Ford looked back and forth from Evie to Charley. "You are both mine," he said, his voice a hoarse whisper of excitement.

"Yes," Charley affirmed. "But not tonight." His face had a wicked light in it Evie had never seen. He physically turned Ford back to Evie, sandwiching the billionaire between him and her. He spoke to Ford's reflection in the mirror. "Tonight you are both *mine.* And I'm going to do whatever I want with you." The center of Ford's eyebrows dipped as if he wasn't sure he liked the idea, but within a few pounding heartbeats, Charley was naked and hard behind Ford, his clothes in a discarded pile at their feet.

Evie sucked in her breath as she took in Charley's fine ass in the mirror behind him. With a thrill, she realized she could see the trio from every angle, the three of them, naked and wound together, were reflected in perpetuity from every surface of the room except the marble. She had an unlimited-angle view of whatever escapades Charley had in mind. They all did.

Reaching around Ford, Charley closed his fist back around Ford's erection, dipping his head to nibble down Ford's neck to where it met his shoulder. He wrapped his free arm around Ford's other side, pinning the man against him and caressing one of Ford's defined pectorals, flicking his finger over Ford's hard nipple.

"Mmm," Charley groaned, not lifting his head from Ford's skin. "So clean. You smell like soap. Did you clean yourself thoroughly? Everywhere?" Ford grunted, frowning with his eyes closed, but his lips dropped open, belying his increasing panting. "Did you think of me when you did? Did you think of what you did to my ass with your stiff cock when you soaped yourself there?" Ford shuddered, his body melting against Charley's, as if in affirmation.

Evie held her breath, feeling like she was one with Ford in enthralled anticipation of what Charley wanted to do.

Keeping his pumping hand working on Ford's shaft, Charley moved his other hand to flatten his palm against the base of his friend's neck. Holding Ford's pelvis in place with his tight grip on his cock, Charley forced Ford's shoulders toward Evie, bending him slightly at the waist until Ford braced his hands on the counter on either side of Evie and pressed his cheek to hers.

"I've been an accommodating friend to you, Ford." Charley's voice, low and powerful normally, carried an even more resonant timbre than usual, causing sparks to spread through Evie, raising gooseflesh on her arms. "I've given you everything I can give another man, and I think it's time for you to let me have some fun."

Evie's scalp tingled. Was Charley talking about what she thought he was talking about?

Charley began kissing down Ford's spine. Evie watched as Charley's head dipped lower and lower, slowly revealing more and more of Ford's finely shaped back until Evie could see the trimmest part of Ford's waist, right where his muscles bulged again to form his athletically-shaped butt.

Charley released Ford's cock and knelt, pulling his best friend's ass cheeks apart with both hands. Evie tore her eyes away from the spectacle when she felt Ford's body stiffen, and her eyes met his startled ones.

She could almost see the raw, roiling emotion he kept tightly reigned in, and at that moment she felt more a part of their union than she ever had. She felt responsible to protect both men, yet at the same time she felt protected by them. This connection they had — this act they were about to share — couldn't happen without her.

It was love she felt, and not just love toward both men, directionally — no. What she felt was the feeling of being *in* love with them, and them with her. It swirled all around them and through them in a never-ending loop, reflected in each of them back out to the other two, just like the multiple mirrors reflected their naked, entwined bodies infinitely in every direction she looked.

Evie had never been in love before, and that fact was never clearer than it was at that moment, now that she was being bathed in a torrent of the unbelievable feeling.

Ford's body twitched, and Evie glanced to the side, seeing in the reflection that Charley had pressed his face into the crease in Ford's ass. When he pulled back to get a better grip, she saw Charley's tongue snake out, reaching to pleasure Ford by flicking against his asshole. Ford sucked in a breath.

"God, Ford. I love your ass," Charley whispered, before pressing his face to it again. Evie took Ford's face in her hands to settle him—he was completely out of his comfort zone. Not only was he letting someone else take charge—something that, alone, she wasn't sure Ford could handle—but he was also being tongued in a sensitive place by another man. Evie was certain from his expression that Ford didn't know what to think. He was too wrapped up in his own head to enjoy it.

She cupped Ford's jawline in both her hands, his skin smooth under her fingers from a fresh shave. Tilting his head, she kissed him, licking his bottom lip and sucking it into her mouth before pushing her tongue into him, just as she knew Charley was doing. He responded hesitantly at first and she pulled back just enough to whisper, "He won't hurt you. You know he won't. He just wants to love you. All of you. Let him love you, Ford."

Ford closed his eyes and took a deep breath. Evie knew he was trying. She kissed him again, reaching down to squeeze his cock between them. "Let him love you," she repeated. She scooted forward, wrapping her legs around Ford to rest her feet on Charley's shoulders. She rubbed Ford's cock to her wet pussy, then positioned him at her entrance before using her legs to pull her hips against him, sinking his erection inside her.

Ford groaned, dropping his head to her shoulder, and Evie saw in the reflection how his hands splayed out on the counter on either side of her, practically clawing at the marble. She gyrated her hips, using her leg muscles to work her body in a hot caress on his cock, almost forgetting she was doing this for him, with the pleasure it gave her. She felt him bend a fraction further, opening himself a bit more to Charley, who grunted, bobbing his head more enthusiastically as he laved the sensitive rim of Ford's ass.

She pulled Ford's face to hers again, and this time there was no hesitation. He kissed her as if she had the secret to happiness inside her, and he was determined to find it with his tongue.

Ford moved his hips, an action that both helped Evie to fuck him and Charley to stimulate his ass. It was incredibly erotic, and Evie's skin felt like it was on fire from the pleasure coursing through every cell in her. Ford groaned again, resting his forehead to hers, and this time the noise he made held more urgency.

Charley pulled back for air, reaching for his discarded jeans and pulling out the small tube of lubricant that he carried with him that had always made Evie and Ford laugh. Now Evie was so happy he had it.

He stood, squeezing some of the substance onto a finger before smoothing that finger into the crease of his friend's backside.

Ford flinched. "Charley, this is—I don't think—" Ford stammered, and Charley wrapped his free arm around him, pressing his body to Ford's while the fingers of his other hand oiled Ford's ass between them.

"Shh, you can," Charley whispered. "Open yourself up to me. To us. I want you to do something you never thought you could do, maybe then you'll believe new outcomes are possible." Charley's arm around Ford's chest tightened. "But you have to want it."

With those last words, Evie watched in the mirror to the side as one of Charley's thick fingers bent and pushed into Ford, causing Ford to shudder and thrust into Evie, his cock feeling somehow harder and more swollen.

"I want you to fuck her," Charley said, his voice demanding, with tremors of excitement obvious in his words as he fulfilled what Evie knew was a long-held fantasy. "Fuck her and think of me fucking you, because that's what I want to do tonight."

"God," Ford moaned, closing his eyes again. "You're inside me. Try another." He licked his lips as if they were dry.

Charley's mouth curled into a wicked grin as he locked eyes with Evie but spoke to Ford. "Oh you'll take another Ford. You're going to take three of my fingers, maybe four, until I can stretch you enough to at least fit the head of my big cock in your ass. You're mine tonight." He bit Ford's ear, causing him to grunt in pain, but Evie noticed Ford's cock jump inside her.

He was learning the pleasure of pain as well.

Charley pulled his finger out and added more lubricant.

Slowly, he sank two fingers into Ford, who groaned at the intrusion, panting as if he was climbing a mountain. But his groan of discomfort turned to whispered, "oh god"s as Charley used his fingers buried in Ford's backside to pull Ford's lower body backward and forward, causing him to fuck Evie with the motion.

Ford reached back, wrapping his hand around Charley's large erection and stroking it as best he could in his position, seeming to want to feel what could be inside him—what Charley wanted to fuck him with.

"You're so hard, Charley," Ford croaked, his voice tight with a mixture of trepidation and out-of-control lust.

"Hands on Evie's breasts," Charley commanded. "You feel so good, I'm afraid I might come all over your back if you touch me, and that's not going to happen. Tonight I'm going to come *in* your ass, Ford, even if I can just get the tip of my cock in your tight, virgin asshole. You're going to take at least that much of me tonight."

Evie moaned along with Ford now, impressed and turned on out of her mind with the way Charley was turning the tables, "forcing" Ford as Ford usually did to her, and insisting Ford take him into his ass. It was incredibly hot.

Ford did as he was told, moving his hands to Evie's breasts, caressing her and tweaking her nipples as she writhed against him.

"I want you to pull out, bend over and make love to Evie's pretty pussy with your tongue while I get you ready for me," Charley detailed to Ford, who again, without hesitation responded to the order. Spreading Evie's thighs wide, Ford bent at the waist, immediately plunging fingers into her and wriggling his tongue against her hard clit.

"Spread your legs," Charley demanded, and Ford spread them. Evie made a mewling sound as Ford's enthusiastic lapping brought her to the edge that quickly, as the amazing visual took place right in front of her and was reflected all around her. She dropped her head back, realizing with a zing of excitement that she had a bird's eye view of Charley's assault on Ford's ass from the mirrors on the ceiling. She decided this was the greatest room on the planet.

In a heartbeat, Charley had two fingers sunk back into Ford and was working up to a third. Ford moved his hips against Charley's fingers, his heavy cock bobbing in the air, unstimulated. As distracting as Evie thought Charley was being to Ford, the man never paused for a moment trying to make her come with his tongue.

Charley's oversized biceps bunched as he pushed his fingers into Ford, twisting his hand, trying to loosen his best friend's ass so he could bury his huge cock in the man. "Remember fucking me, Ford?" Charley asked, his voice gravelly with desire. "Remember what it felt like to pump your hot cum into my ass?"

Ford paused in licking Evie long enough to choke out the words. "Yes—God I loved fucking you."

Evie made a noise of desperate excitement at the words—thoughts of her two insanely hot men sucking and fucking each other sending her over the edge the second Ford's tongue caressed her clit again. She cried out, pulling Ford's hair as she held him against her, making him continue to lick her until she'd rode out every wave of the orgasm.

"There you go, Ford. Now I wanna come. Stand up." Charley pulled his fingers out and Ford stood with a sigh of relief. "Enter Evie again. I want the three of us to make love together. We can fuck each other separately all we want, but the three of us together will always be making love. It feels so goddamned right, doesn't it?"

Ford held Evie's eyes as he positioned his cock and shoved into her wet pussy again, shutting his eyes briefly for what looked like a private moment of bliss at the feeling of burying himself in her.

This time Charley slathered lubricant on his erection, working quickly, as if he was afraid the moment might pass. He centered himself behind his best friend, and both Evie and Ford's eyes were pinned to the side wall reflection as Charley scooped one hand around Ford's hip and positioned his cock at his best friend's asshole with his other. Charley's gorgeously defined butt muscles clenched as he pushed toward Ford and the fulfillment of the fantasy Evie knew he'd had for years.

Ford screwed his eyes closed in what looked like intense

concentration and Evie kissed him. She kissed his mouth and cheeks and eyelids, and Ford, distracted with his focus on Charley, let her lavish affection on him without response. "Let him in, Ford," she whispered. "Let Charley make love to you. Let *us* make love to you."

"I want to," Ford's voice was tight as he spoke through gritted teeth.

"Let me in," Charley urged.

And then Charley made a noise of satisfaction and Ford grunted. "How far are you in?" Ford asked, his voice breathy with excitement and pain.

"Just the tip," Charley answered. "But it's enough." He leaned forward, sucking at Ford's neck. "If that's all you can take, man, it's enough. I'm so fucking hot for your ass that you let me squeeze the head of my cock in and out of your tight hole a few times and I'll fucking empty in you. Then I'll turn you around and suck you off while my cum leaks out of your ass."

Ford choked on a breath at Charley's filthy words and Evie's core clenched, nearly spasming in another climax at the raw, dirty talk.

"It's not enough." Ford shook his head, his coherence suffering from the intensity of the situation. "I want to give you what you really want, even if it hurts. Not just part of me, but all of me."

Evie felt Ford tense as he tried to push back onto Charley and failed. She watched his face go from determined to pained to defeated. His brow furrowed and Evie touched his forehead, murmuring to him. "No, no. Don't force it. It won't work. This isn't something you can will into making happen. You just have to surrender yourself to his cock. Decide to let the man have you. Let him have anything he wants. Give yourself to him completely. It's the only way."

Ford's eyes opened and his jewel-green eyes held hers. "He can have me," Ford said, as if trying to do what Evie had suggested. "He can have my ass." His voice trembled and she felt his body relax. "You can both have me," he whispered, and he shut his eyes and pushed back toward Charley, grunting a sound very similar to the incredible manly sound he made when he came, and Evie watched, wide-eyed, in the reflection as he sank inch-by-inch onto Charley's rigid cock.

"Goddamn," Charley marveled, as he watched his dream unfold before his startled eyes. "Goddamn," he repeated, his gaze pinned to Ford's ass.

Evie reached down between her and Ford and touched herself, almost ready to explode again at the X-rated love-making happening in front of her. Ford was too distracted by his ass being filled with Charley's cock to rock against her, and she wanted to orgasm with them, when they did. It felt like the perfect thing to do when the three of them made love.

"Finish in me, Charley," Ford whispered tightly. "I can't hold out with you in there. I'm gonna come."

Charley pulled back slowly, gently, only about halfway before thrusting again, pushing Ford into Evie, mashing her fingers against her clit and shifting her to another plane of excitement. She watched him in the mirror, seeing the tenderness in Charley's entire, massive frame, his concern for the man who'd finally let him inside.

"God, I'm almost there, Ford. I just want to savor this." He pulled back again, a little further this time and thrust forward harder, this time wrapping his arms around Ford's chest and pinning Ford back against him while he held himself still as deep as he could go inside him for a heartbeat. "So tight," he whispered. "So hot. So good wrapped around me. I've always wanted to be inside you."

"Charley, I can't wait." Ford's voice was anguished. "I want to feel you come in my ass."

Charley released him, pushing him against Evie. Ford kissed her, wrapping his arms around her in an embrace that said he needed her, and reached between them, shoving her hand out of the way to replace it with his. "I can take care of you too," he murmured.

Evie dropped her head back, watching Charley piston himself fully into Ford, crushing the man to her rhythmically, and jostling her on Ford's cock. Charley's skin smacked against Ford's ass and echoed around the small room.

Watching Ford get absolutely fucked by Charley pushed every

button Evie had and sent her pleasure reeling. Ford seemed to have passed the point of no return when he locked eyes with her, whispering, "Come for me now, pet."

She did as she was told.

Charley dropped his head onto Ford's shoulder, curling his back toward Ford and pushing himself as deeply as he could one last time into the other man before he cried out. "I'm coming," Charley choked. "I'm coming your ass. Oh god, Ford!"

In spite of the look of concentration on Ford's face that Evie knew came from trying to delay his release, the sensation of Evie's pussy clenching around his cock and Charley emptying cum into his ass in small, quick thrusts were more than enough to overcome the billionaire's control, and he grunted that noise that gave Evie chills as he released, gripping Evie's head between his hands as he claimed her lips with his during his own orgasm, making erotic noises of pleasure into her mouth.

"I can feel you coming," Charley breathed, seeming barely able to talk as he finished his last in Ford.

When Ford pulled back from the kiss, there was a moment of stunned silence as the three of them held their embrace. Evie tried to memorize their reflection, noting how perfectly they seemed to fit together in this complex and naughty way. She couldn't believe Ford had done it.

"Thank you, Ford." Charley nearly sobbed, kissing the man's neck. "For letting us make love to you. For showing us you can believe."

Slowly, they detangled, Charley grabbing Ford's discarded towel to help them clean up the worst of it until Ford suggested they simply step into his gigantic shower. They took their time, soaping each other, laughing, embracing, and kissing—all three of them, the way it should be—until they emerged, cleaner, and with a better idea of how happy they could make one another.

CHAPTER TWENTY-NINE

$\mathcal{E}$VIE WOKE EARLY, the sun still hours from rising, and her mind went immediately to the day before. She, Ford and Charley had spent the rest of the afternoon and evening just being together.

They'd eaten, watched movies, laughed, snuggled and had no more discussions of John, relationships or the insanely hot thing Ford had let Charley do to him. It was as if the encounter in the bathroom had physically and mentally exhausted them all, and they'd gone to bed early. Ford had suggested they all stay in his room, and this time, Evie had happily complied.

She shifted her body, feeling safe and comfortable between the two men. Ford's arm was draped over Evie, and he'd held her while they slept. It was an amazing feeling, having Ford Hawthorne wrapped against her all night. Smiling to herself, Evie remembered what Ford had told her about never before having shared his bed with a woman, and here he was spooning her all the way to her ankles, as if he didn't want any part of him not touching her as they slept. Maybe he really was opening himself to the idea of change, the idea of love.

Charley was on her other side, sleeping much more expansively than Ford. He was on his back, one arm under his head and the other thrown over the side of the bed. His hard-muscled leg was hooked over Evie's and Ford's from his knee down, and Evie was snuggled against his chest, one hand resting on the top middle of his abs, right where that trail of hair started in a delicious path from his pectorals to his cock.

Being between the two men reminded Evie of when they'd both been inside her, filling her, loving her, finding release in her. She wondered if she could get that on the agenda for the day. She'd love a repeat. In fact she'd love a repeat of most everything they'd done. Thank god they had a year together.

A year.

A cloud settled over her. How could Ford put a time limit on their relationship? How could he not want this to go on and on forever, as she and Charley did?

She moved her fingers, toying with the hair on Charley's chest. She didn't know what was more insane—the idea of the three of them trying to make a go of it, or the idea of the three of them not. But then her mind touched on the bullet-hole in Ford's car, and a sick feeling twisted her gut.

She was in love with Ford and Charley. She was never more sure of that than that moment, and though she tried not to think about it, Ford's request that she be strong enough to leave them kept resurfacing in her head like a drowning swimmer coming up for air.

It would just figure that she'd finally fall in love and she'd have to leave. It looked as if John had found a way to get revenge on her without even realizing how deeply he would hurt her. She'd never recover from this. Never stop loving Ford and Charley and wanting this amazingly special thing they had back.

But none of that mattered. Ford had come five inches from getting shot the day before, and it was because of her—she knew it. She couldn't let him or Charley bear the risk she'd brought with her. If she left, John would leave them alone.

Maybe she could get a job somewhere, even if it was outside of the legal profession, and then get a loan from a bank to pay John back. Maybe then she could come back.

But would they want her? After everything that had changed, would Charley and Ford's relationship even survive after she left? She hoped so. If anything, she wanted them to have a happily ever after.

Charley stirred under the touch of her fingers, and reached up to cover her hand in his, squeezing hers three times with his private message.

"I love you too," she whispered back, wanting to say it out loud for the remaining time she had left to say it to him.

Ford squeezed his arms around her. "I love you both," he said, his voice gravelly with sleep.

Charley's hand squeezed reflexively around hers and her eyes flew open to the dim light of the moon seeping through the windows. She and Charley froze and she knew he was straining his ears just as she was straining hers, to ensure they hadn't imagined it, or maybe, to hear it again. Charley's heart pounded under her palm.

Her own heart had become a ping-pong ball in her chest. Shock punched through her. She opened her mouth to say something, but closed it again, afraid to say anything. Afraid that if she spoke or reacted in any way that Ford might take it back—deny it. Claim he'd just been talking in his sleep.

Evie stayed quiet. Neither she nor Charley spoke. They just let those words hang in the air like wisps of smoke. Like if they breathed, the words might dissipate and be gone forever. In her mind, Evie replayed them again and again, and each time they sounded just as good as the first time.

Ford loved them.

Was it possible? Was he even capable of it? Did he realize what he'd just said?

But he'd said it so easily, so simply, as if he'd said it to them a hundred times—as if it had always been true. She bent her head and kissed Ford's arm, and he hugged her tighter, pressing his semi-hard cock against her bottom, giving her a small thrill. But she soon heard the deep, rhythmic sounds of his breathing and knew he'd fallen back asleep.

Finally, she fell back asleep too.

Ford loved them...

*****

As soon as Evie opened her eyes again, this time to the morning sun, she remembered Ford's sleepy declaration. Happiness flooded through her and she smiled and stretched like a cat.

She was naked and happy. It was a new day in a new world—

a world where Ford loved them.

He wasn't snuggled against her anymore, and she rolled over to find him, hoping they could wake Charley together and the three of them could make love again. But she found Ford awake, sitting with his back to her on the end of the bed, his head down and his shoulders curved into himself. It must have awoken her when he'd moved to sit up.

She opened her mouth to say good morning, but stopped. There was something about his posture. Something about the tightness across his shoulders. She could read body language like an expert, and Ford was not happy.

She realized Charley wasn't in the bed. "Ford?" Her voice was hesitant. "Where's Charley?"

He turned his head halfway, treating her to his handsome profile, but didn't look at her when he answered. "He went to get pastries." Ford held up a note he had crumpled in his hand. "He left a note that he was getting food so we could spend the day in bed together, celebrating." Ford's tone was flat. Evie's skin prickled. Something was very wrong.

"That sounds nice," she ventured.

"He signed it, 'love you both'." Ford balled up the paper and whipped it into the corner of the room.

Evie stopped breathing. Slowly, she reached out to touch his shoulder, but as soon as her hand made contact with his skin, he flinched away from her and stood. Alarm bells, all too familiar, went off in Evie's head.

"Ford?" she asked hesitantly.

"We're not spending the day in my bed. I don't want either of you in my bed. This is my private space." His voice did not sound loving. This was not the Ford she thought she'd wake up to on what she thought was a glorious morning.

"Okay. Fine," Evie said, a hint of annoyance showing through in her voice. He'd invited them into his bed last night.

Turning to face her, arms folded tightly in front of him, Ford's tone turned accusatory. "Charley and I have been friends for years, and everything was perfect. Now Charley's confused. This is your doing. He would never push things like this on his own."

Evie sat up and scooted her back against the headboard. Uneasiness gripped her, and she hugged the pillow against her body, covering herself. "Everything wasn't perfect before, Ford. Charley was in love with you, and you were lonely. Now things are changing for the better."

Ford paced to the window, arms crossed in on himself. "I should have known better than to try this arrangement. Everything was fine before, and now everything is a mess."

Shit.

Ford was freaking out. Evie had been afraid he might, given how far they'd pushed him out of his comfort zone the day before. Clearly, they'd pushed him too far, too fast.

He spoke with his back to her. "You'll have to explain it to him when he gets back." Ford looked at his feet, keeping his arms crossed tightly. "Explain there won't be a repeat of yesterday and he's not to say he loves you or me, not in front of me, anyway. That's not what this arrangement is about."

"Ford, that will break his heart!" She felt sick, picturing Charley's eyes when she told him. She couldn't do that to him.

"You have yourself to blame for that."

She ignored his ludicrous statement. "So he loves you. What's the big deal? There are worse things in the world than having a man like Charley love you. Don't say it back if you don't want to, but don't tell him he can't feel it." Now her words were loud with her growing anger.

Ford turned his head to her, his face grim. "It's more than that. Yesterday was a mistake," he stated flatly. "This is all a mistake." His tone was cold as ice.

"You were *happy* yesterday. I saw it. Charley and I both saw it."

He turned back to the window, uncrossing his arms and resting his forearm against the window molding. He clenched his fist and struck the wood hard, making her jump, but after a moment of silence, his shoulders fell as he dropped his head. He looked exhausted.

Finally, he spoke without looking at her, his voice soft and deadly serious. "It won't work this way. Can't you see that?" She saw his back expand and his shoulders rise as he took a deep breath and turned around, his jaw set hard. His eyes flashed anger. "Don't you understand that you're ruining things? We can't make it work like this!" Ford gestured across the bed, sheets mussed from their group-sleep, but Evie knew he meant the three of them, together, in a relationship.

"Ford, c'mon," Evie tried. "I know this is hard for you, but last night you said you —"

"I know what I said!" Ford thundered. Evie flinched as if he'd struck her. Then he seemed to catch himself and started again in a controlled calm that was no less scary. "I know what I said. I was half-asleep. It was another mistake."

"Well, I won't tell Charley your love for us is a mistake," she whispered, her voice tremulous.

"Fine." He stalked back to the bed and met her bright eyes with his cold ones. "You don't want to talk to Charley? You want to stay and see where things go? Fine. On one condition. That you do your *fucking* job."

Ford shook his head and looked at the floor, not her, to speak his next words. "Just do the job, Evie. It's a simple job, really. Fuck me and do what you're told."

"Jesus, Ford," Evie whispered, but Ford ignored her.

This time he looked her in the eye as he stabbed her again with his short summary of all that he wanted from her. "Fuck me and do what you're told!"

His words hurt exactly how he'd intended.

Evie's eyes stung with tears, her stomach tight with hurt and anxiety. She'd been so close to happiness, and she wasn't ready to give up that ending, no matter how unlikely. She'd been prepared to leave last night, for all their goods, but then he'd said he loved them, and it changed everything.

Now she didn't want to go. Now she was ready to brave anything for the chance they could be happy together.

"You don't love us?" she asked as she hugged herself, her

voice small.

He turned away to go back to the window. He didn't answer her question. "Evie, you understand you are not here to be my girlfriend or my wife? Or Charley's either. Did I not make that clear?"

He turned back to her, arms still folded in front of him. He looked so striking standing there next to the window, the morning sun streaming through the glass, highlighting the masculine lines of his nearly naked, perfect body.

Those thoughts made her ache.

He continued with his punishment of her, "You are here for me to fuck, not to love. Are you somehow unclear about that? I only want to use your body. I don't want anything else from you. I don't *need* anything else from you, Evie."

She cringed from his words as they stung her. Fat tears she frantically wished would disappear broke free and rolled down her cheeks, oblivious to her willing them away.

Ford returned to sit on the bed, and took a deep breath before continuing. "When the year is up you will leave and I won't see you again. I'll get a new girl to take your place. Tell me you understand that." He turned a fierce look to her and waited. She realized he was going to make her answer him, no matter how cruel it was.

She opened her mouth but knew if she spoke, the pathetic sobs she was barely controlling would burst forth, so instead she just nodded her head, staring blankly straight ahead, avoiding his eyes.

"Get out," he said flatly, pointing at the door. She couldn't leave fast enough. She had to get out of that room and away from Ford. She scrambled to the end of the bed to get her robe, and he turned to watch her go—Evie, sobbing now, and naked.

"Wait," he roared and slammed his arm across the bed, grabbing her around the waist from behind. He pulled her back against him hard, pressing his skin to hers, and she choked out a moan of despair, not pleasure.

"Ford don't," she begged. "You're hurting my heart." She screwed her eyes shut and sobbed, just letting the words spill out. "I don't want to love you. I don't. I can't help it." She tried to struggle out of his grasp. "I can't help it."

"Evie. God, Evie." It was as if he was trying to envelope her with his arms, make her a part of him. Like he couldn't get close enough. He made a noise of frustration that almost sounded like he was in physical pain. "I'm sorry I can't be what you want." He spoke against the curve of her neck, his voice thick with emotion, and she cried as silently as she could, wanting him to let go of her, and yet praying he'd never let go.

He moved his hands to her shoulders and she heard him inhale slowly. He seemed to steel himself, and then his fingers tightened almost painfully into her skin. He pushed forward and shoved her to the bed, face down.

"I'm sorry," he repeated, and now his voice was flat and emotionless again. Completely controlled. "This is the only thing I know how to be." He placed one hand on the back of her neck, pinning her down, and one hand on her hip, lifting her butt in the air, molding his body to hers. He was hard.

He was going to fuck her. She almost couldn't believe it. After telling her he couldn't love her. After breaking her heart. He was going to fuck her and come in her while her face was wet with the tears he caused.

Her chest constricted in sorrow, as much for Ford as for her and Charley. This wasn't all Ford was, but he was desperate to convince them it was. He wasn't going to let them succeed. He would destroy their love. He hated himself so much that he believed he was a monster, and he was going to prove it to her.

She knew he wasn't. Charley knew he wasn't.

Could she convince Ford of that if she stayed?

She couldn't think. She couldn't think.

Ford reached down and shoved a finger into her, making her gasp. His next words were a declaration. "I'm no one anyone could love."

He moved, and she turned her head in the sheets and watched as he opened a bedside drawer and took out a bottle of lubricant. They'd only used lubricant when he fucked her ass, but this time he smeared the slick liquid over his cock only because he knew she wasn't ready for him. And he didn't care; he was going to take her anyway.

Why didn't she leave? Yet she couldn't make herself make the decision, knowing if she refused him now, it would be the end of everything. She wasn't ready to make that choice. And so she chose to stay, and she prepared herself for what she knew he'd do to her.

He came back to the bed, the hard line of his erection jutting in front of him, more than ready to fuck her whether she was ready or not. "Are you staying, Evie? Does this deal still work for you?"

If she left, she'd break Charley's heart. She couldn't do that. She needed to talk to Charley first. Evie had gone from the high of realizing she was hopelessly in love with Ford, a love she thought he returned, to him crushing her heart, all in the span of a few hours. She didn't know what to do.

"Get out of my bed and leave now if you're not still willing to fulfill your duties," Ford demanded. She looked up at him for a long moment and saw his eyes were as full of pain as hers. He seemed to soften. Grabbing her hand, he pressed it to his erection, smearing lubricant on her fingers. "I can't stay away from you, Evie. I don't want you to leave." His throat was hoarse, and he lowered his eyes, looking shamed. "But this is all I can give you. Will you take it?"

God she loved him. Why was he doing this to her?

She turned her face back into the sheets, her cheeks smeared with tears. She didn't want to go, though she knew she should. Unsure, she only lay still instead, and chose by default.

Ford climbed back onto the bed and grabbed her hips, yanking her butt back up into the air. With his knee he spread her legs forcefully. He was not being gentle when he stuffed his slickened cock into her. His erection felt invasive—not right like it normally did. She wasn't wet and soft for him, because he wasn't the Ford she loved.

He fucked her roughly, as if he was angry at her and desperate for her at the same time. Ignoring her tears, he forced his cock into her again and again to the hilt. She knew he would stop if she asked him to—knew it in her bones—but yet she didn't stop him. Her confusion and uncertainty pinned her beneath him. He didn't make a sound, only used her cruelly, taking the only thing he wanted from her. Giving her the only thing he could give.

The lone sound in the room was his skin slapping against hers with the tattoo of his relentless sex. It was a stark sound in the still morning air, and although she didn't want to enjoy what he did to her, her body betrayed her and began to respond to his naturally.

The connection her body had to Ford's would not be denied. Their bodies knew each other and relished the sex between them, and that connection made his denial of love for her all the more painful. She bit down on a moan of pure carnal lust, determined not to reveal any enjoyment in what he was doing to her.

She might have actually orgasmed, with her face shoved into the mattress and her eyes wet with tears, had he fucked her longer, but he thrust hard a few last times and came with a guttural moan, collapsing over her back and flattening her to the bed.

There was a quick knock at the door and Charley entered, carrying two bags of food. His giant smile crumbled as he looked at Ford pinning Evie to the bed and Evie's face, miserable and streaked.

"What the fuck is going on here?" he breathed. Charley looked back and forth between them. He dropped the bags on the floor and stepped to the bed. Gently, he touched Evie's tear-stained cheek. "Ford!" Charley's voice rose, anger and panic evident in his rebuke. "Ford, what the fuck did you do?"

Ford hoisted himself off her, pulling his softening cock out and getting to his feet next to Charley. He busied himself with cleaning up. Evie sat up, grabbing Charley's hand from her cheek and kissing it. "It's okay Charley," she said. "We had a little argument. Everything's fine." She would salvage this and then figure out how to handle it later. She would never let Ford make her feel like that again.

Ford wouldn't look at her, shame rolling off him in waves. Charley took note. "Ford, what's going on? I thought we were good." Charley looked at Evie and she saw the question in his eyes before he asked it. She tried to stop him.

"Charley, don't."

"Ford, do you regret yesterday? Letting me make love to you? Saying you loved us?" His question held such fragile honesty that Evie felt like her heart cracked in half. Charley reached out to Ford.

Ford looked away and lowered his eyes, turning his body

away from Charley's reach. Charley's eyes registered the rejection, and his face fell into the saddest expression Evie had ever seen. Now Evie's anger flashed. She could handle Ford's mistreatment of her, knowing how confused he was, but she couldn't watch him hurt Charley.

"Don't you dare turn away from him!" She got to her feet between them and wrapped her robe around her naked body. "No shame, right Ford? You taught me that." This time she spoke as if she and Ford were the only two people in the room. "Break my heart. Destroy me. I don't care, but look at this." She gestured to Charley. "He is so full of light. Don't ruin Charley. Don't turn him into us." She dropped her arms to her sides, defeated. "At least let him go."

"No," Charley said, his tone serious. "I won't go."

"I know you won't." Evie sighed, looking at Ford. "Charley is a dream come true for anyone, and fuck you for not seeing that." She shook her head. "You've shown me your worst, Ford, and I can take it all. But you've finally found the one thing I can't handle. The one thing that will actually make me go away. I can't watch you break Charley."

She opened Ford's bedroom door and Charley moved quickly. "Evie, what are you doing?" There was alarm in his voice.

"I'm doing exactly what we all need. Someone has to do it before we all go down together."

Charley had her face cupped in his large hands before she could move, locking his eyes to hers. "Don't do this," he begged her. "Don't do this," he whispered, shaking his head, as if they were alone together in the room. Wrapping his arms around her, he enveloped her against him, kissing the top of her head. "Don't do this," he whispered hoarsely.

Her shoulders heaved as she sobbed one time, catching herself with a massive effort lest she let the sobs overtake her. The misery of her decision washed over her. Pushing against Charley's chest, she extracted herself from his embrace and glanced to Ford, who watched them with interest, but immediately looked away. He couldn't meet her eyes, and it strengthened her resolve.

She looked up at the big man, his face handsome even in

misery. "Charley, I love you, but this is bigger than us, and we can't do it without him. He wants to be unhappy."

"That's not true. Everyone wants to be happy," Charley looked back at Ford as if to hope Ford would agree with him, but Ford stayed stoic.

Evie shook her head. "Not Ford. Only if he's miserable and alone will he punish himself enough for who he is. He will make this fail, and when it does there will be spectacularly terrible consequences. I love you, Charley, and I can't watch him do that to you." She suddenly had a crazy thought. "Come with me. You don't have to stay with me. Just don't stay with him."

"Hey!" Ford's angry voice cut through her, but she and Charley ignored him.

"Evie, I love you." Charley kissed her softly on the lips. "I know this stuff with him bothers you, but I can give you all the love you need. We can keep doing what we're doing, and I'll give you enough love for the both of us."

She smiled up at him, tears in her eyes. "Charley, you're breaking my heart. If you're taking care of everyone, who's taking care of you?"

"You will be."

"But you'll never really be happy unless Ford loves you."

Charley screwed his mouth up, not willing to admit she was right. "I'll be happy with what he can give me. I'll be happy with that as long as I have you too."

But Evie shook her head. "I can't watch him do that to you, and I can't love him from afar like you do. I can't." Now the tears fell and she didn't care. She was too miserable to care if she looked weak in front of Ford.

Charley turned to Ford. "Do something," he begged. "Help me get her to stay."

Ford looked over at them, his arms crossed, mashing his lips together in resignation. "Come on, Charley." He gave the man a crooked smile and stretched his hand out to him. "Let's go get in the shower, and then we'll figure this out over breakfast."

Upon hearing words that Charley had never heard from Ford,

he took a step toward the billionaire, but he didn't let go of Evie's hand. "But...Evie..." His voice cut off.

Ford smiled indulgently, as if he'd just agreed to buy Charley a puppy. "Okay, Evie, can join us." Ford turned that hundred-watt smile to her, his face transforming into the one she loved, all dimples and magnetism. The smile that had convinced her to go down this rabbit hole to begin with. He curled his mouth into a semblance of wicked bad-boy.

Those dimples. The shower. She *wanted* everything to be okay. She wanted to believe this morning had never happened. She was blinded for a moment with thoughts of what the three of them could do together in the shower.

Tempted, she stepped forward, but Ford's next words bound her to the spot. "But only if Evie can remember to be the professional I hired her to be. I don't want any more complications like we had this morning."

She stopped. "'The professional you hired me to be'? You mean a whore."

Ford's eyes softened, pain flashing through them, mirroring her own. "Evie, you were never a whore."

"You're right I never was." She took a deep breath. "And I never felt like one until this morning."

Wrenching herself from Charley's grip, Evie ran out of Ford's room to her own, slamming her door and locking it behind her.

CHAPTER THIRTY

EVIE STAGGERED TO her closet to pack her things. She'd let herself do it again—fall for a man like John, a man who didn't need her, a man who'd throw her away when he was done using her. She knew better and she'd let it happen anyway.

But even in her miserable state she knew it wasn't a fair thought. Ford hadn't used her the way John had. Ford had been honest from the start about what he wanted and she'd gone along with the plan willingly. She'd let business become personal. She'd ignored the carefully defined boundaries of their relationship. She only had herself to blame, but that didn't make it hurt any less.

The thought of leaving was devastating, and that was precisely the problem. She wasn't even a month into her commitment and she was already tearing herself apart, looking for more from Ford than he would give her. If she stayed the full year she'd be in a pitiable state by the end, even more desperately in love with a man who didn't want her. A man who would make her leave so he could find a new woman to take her place in his bed, on his rug, over his desk, with Charley.

Her beautiful closet wavered in her vision as tears threatened to spill again.

Pulling out the duffel bag she'd shown up to the estate with, she realized she had little to pack. She'd gotten rid of most everything except the new wardrobe Ford had lavished on her, but she wasn't going to take those items. She couldn't stand to look at the clothes he'd picked out for her, so she took only what she needed to get by for a few days.

She spread out her throwing knives on top of the stack of clothes and carefully zipped her bag around them, cursing herself for not ordering the knife sheath she'd meant to, now that she was going back out into the world beyond Ford's stone walls. Taking one last look around the most gorgeous bedroom she'd ever have, she left, closing the door firmly behind her.

"Evie."

The voice came from behind her, making her jump, and she turned to find Charley sitting on the chair in the hallway, halfway between her room and Ford's.

She whirled away from him and headed for the stairs. "Don't make this harder, Charley." Taking the stairs quickly, she made her way out the side door, heading toward the backyard and the oversized garage that sat behind, and to the side of, the house. Charley followed directly behind her, not speaking.

Stomping down the row of cars she realized hers wasn't there. "Goddammit! Where's my car?" she cried, frustration pitching her voice high. She stopped, not knowing where to go next, and Charley halted behind her, putting his arms directly around her and taking her bag. She struggled against him.

"Evie, stop. Let me carry your bag. Let's figure this out."

"Where's my car? Do you know where that bastard put my car?"

"He's not a bastard."

She scoffed, yanking at her bag but having no luck against Charley's unyielding grip.

"Evangeline, why are you doing this to me?"

She stopped. She'd never heard him use her full name. "Charley, if I have to walk out of here, I'm leaving."

Charley shook his head. "You know what the most ironic thing is? I always thought Ford was going to break my heart. I had no idea it'd be you." She met his eyes, startled. He looked down at her, sadness rolling off him in waves. "I never even saw you coming, Evie. At least Ford loves me enough to give me what he can. You're just leaving me."

She stepped backwards as if he'd hit her, her breath catching in her lungs. "Oh Charley." It was killing her to watch the big man's heart break. "I'm not leaving you. I'm leaving him."

He crumpled onto the bumper of one of Ford's SUVs, no longer meeting her eyes. "He sent me to get you. I would've tried anyway, but when you left, he lost it." Charley looked up at her, and she could see the hurt for all of them churning in his deep, brown eyes. "I've never seen him in that much pain, Evie. He said you wouldn't want to even look at him, so I had to come and find you and make you come back to us."

She felt her resolve start to crumble. "Charley, I need to show you something." She took his hand and he allowed her to tug him to standing. She pulled him along to the front of the garage where she pointed to Ford's shattered back window.

Immediately his posture changed to that of a warrior. "That is a bullet-hole." He stabbed his finger toward the window and looked at her with accusation in his eyes.

"I know! I think it was John. Do you get it now? I have to leave anyway. You both are in danger as long as I'm here. There's no reason for John to bother either of you if I'm gone."

"Evie, why didn't you tell me about this?"

"I was going to, but then yesterday became so...magical. We were happy. I didn't want to ruin it. I was going to tell you today."

He gripped her by the shoulders almost painfully. "I can't let you leave. John could be out there waiting for you!"

She let her anger spark again, feeling even more desperate to get out of Ford's estate and take the danger with her. "I'll be fine if I can just find my damn car. Charley, I can take care of myself! I'll just disappear until John self-destructs. He's more than halfway there already."

She'd barely gotten the last words out when they heard a loud crack from outside. They turned their heads to the sound in unison, and then back toward each other, eyes wide.

"Ford," they both said in unison before turning and running

toward the door.

*****

The only thing she remembered seeing when she emerged from the garage on Charley's heels was the huge wall of windows at the back of the house, splintered now like the one on Ford's car. She gasped, hand flying to her mouth, her mind blanking of anything except fear for Ford. She nearly ran into Charley who was stopped outside the side house door, his fingers to his lips.

With a gesture, he told her to be quiet and stay. She shook her head violently and he closed his eyes, flexing his jaw in frustration. He slunk into the house silently and she followed, both of them creeping until they had a view of the living room.

Evie clapped a hand over her mouth to stifle her gasp when she caught sight of Ford, tied to a chair, his mouth gagged. A trickle of blood ran down his face. *Oh god.* Was he alive?

She nearly sank to her knees, her muscles weakened with fear. Like a swarm of bees, panic overran her brain and she couldn't think. She forced her thoughts to slow. Touching Charley on the shoulder, she asked him with a gesture if he had a cell phone. He shook his head and frustration smacked through her. Her phone had belonged to the firm and she hadn't gotten a new one since she'd come to Ford's.

She spotted a house phone on the kitchen counter. Hope and relief washed over her. Silently, she moved to pick it up and clicked open the line. Nothing.

Dammit! John had somehow disabled the line. An icy terror gripped her belly, and she turned slowly, dreading to look out the window that faced down the driveway. She saw what she feared — the open gate, the one that was never open.

Evie said a quick prayer for Boone, but she knew John wouldn't be in the house unless he'd taken out the loyal guard. Boone wouldn't have stopped fighting, not if he was still able. She looked back, shaking her head at Charley who crushed his lips together in anger. They listened for a minute, straining their ears but hearing no sounds.

Charley pulled her close to him, whispering in the barest voice, "I can't hear him. Maybe he's upstairs. When I give you the signal, we're going in there. I'll untie Ford's hands. You get his feet. As soon as you have his feet free, you go back through this door to my truck. I'll carry him there."

She nodded. "It's John."

Charley looked grim. "I know. That's what I'm worried about. He's not right in the head, I don't think."

Evie blinked rapidly, trying not to panic. She didn't do well handling fear, but she had to keep her head about her. Ford needed her—needed them both—to get out of this alive. She was not going to lose it.

Charley signaled for her to follow him and they both crept out into the living room. Charley was at the chair checking Ford's pulse before Evie was halfway there. She saw Charley's body nearly collapse in relief and her heart soared. Ford was still alive! They might all make it out of there. Stepping softly, she moved low and quick. Charley glanced up at her from his work on Ford's bindings and his eyes popped wide, a look of terror in them.

"Behind you!" Charley yelled.

She had only a moment to register his words when something huge and solid hit her from behind hard enough to make her skull snap forward.

Blackness sucked her down into the deep.

CHAPTER THIRTY-ONE

"Evie...EVIE PLEASE." Someone was kissing her face, and she felt a cold chill on her exposed skin. She tried to will her eyes open, but her lids felt as if they were made of lead. "Love, open your eyes. Please." She felt soft lips murmuring against her skin as the kisses moved over her eyelids, her cheeks, her mouth. She tried to speak to tell the kisser she was okay, but all that came out was a groan that sounded as if it came from inside a tunnel.

"Thank god!" she heard a different voice say.

"Thank god," the first voice murmured too. Then louder, "Evie, wake up!" The voice sounded heady with relief.

She opened her eyes, her pupils focusing on Ford's vibrant, green eyes and long lashes. "Ford?" she mumbled. "Where am I?" She tried to sit up.

"Don't move, love. Lie still for a minute until you feel better." Ford was kneeling on the floor next to her, his face hovering over hers, his hand stroking her hair. Charley was on her other side, moving his eyes from her to Ford and back, as if looking for Ford to fix her.

"My head hurts." She reached up to touch her hair, but he caught her hand in his.

"Don't. Lay still, love."

"So cold." She felt chilled to the bone, her arms breaking out in gooseflesh. Ford lay down next to her pressing his warm body to hers, and wrapped an arm around her, using the other to prop his head up. He looked down at her. "Better?"

"Yes." Her head clearing, she suddenly remembered the events that brought her there. She winced as a rush of anxiety created a fresh wave of pain through her head. She squeezed Ford's hand, her eyes startled. "What happened? Where's John? Are you okay?" Her chest was tight.

"We're in the walk-in fridge—he locked us in here." Ford kissed her cheek again, taking a deep breath in her hair. "What were you thinking, both of you?" He looked up at Charley, who touched Ford's face, wiping away blood with his thumb. "Why did you come back for me? You should have left."

She ignored Ford's question. "We've got to get out of here before John comes back." She squeezed her eyes shut, trying think.

"No." Ford's voice was grim. "The refrigerator locks from the outside. Charley already tried it. And it's strong. Charley tried to kick it down." Ford's gave a lopsided grin to Charley, his dimples threatening to make an appearance. "Rest for a moment, Evie. I don't know how badly you're hurt. He hit you and you hit your head on the marble."

Evie recalled the events, working her way backward through the morning. The pain Ford had caused her and Charley sliced through the last of her fog. She pushed him away from her. "I'm okay. Let me up." Her voice was as cold as the temperature in the mansion's industrial fridge. She sat up slowly, looking for her duffel bag. "Where's my bag?"

"John took it," Charley answered. "He had a gun. After he knocked you out, he took your bag and made me carry you in here. Then he went and got Ford."

"Thank god you were with her, Charley. We can't let him get her alone. God knows what he might do to her."

Evie shook her head, and her voice dripped in sarcasm, "Don't like to share your toys, Ford?" She met his eyes, hers defiant.

He looked at her for a moment, his lips pressed together in a thin line. Then he scooted back against the shelf opposite her and leaned against a box of produce, pulling his knees up. "So you were really leaving me?" he asked, his voice tight.

She braced her arm on a cold shelf and pushed unsteadily to her feet. Ford rose with her, reaching out to help her but she batted his hand away.

Charley moved to her side, supporting her, and she let him.

"Yes. I'm leaving." She lifted her chin and tucked her hair behind an ear.

"For how long? You only had one bag."

"Forever. I'm not taking the things you gave me." She tried to keep her voice even like his.

"And your money?" His voice was cold.

"I don't want it either. I'll find another way to pay off John."

He looked down and ran a hand through his hair, taking a deep breath. "I paid him what you owed him already." He met her eyes steadily, and he lifted one shoulder in a shrug.

Her mouth hung open. "What?"

"He left a message on the house phone intended for you, but I got it instead and I paid him. I wanted you out of danger."

"Why didn't you tell me?"

"Because you wouldn't have liked it. You would have felt like you owed *me* money."

Evie thought back on the day that Ford had spanked her over his desk, and how happy he'd been with her afterward. Before he left, he'd retrieved a fat manila envelope from a drawer. The envelope must have been full of money—money he'd given John to protect her.

"Did you know about this?" she asked Charley, sounding outraged. He shook his head, his eyes wide, looking at Ford with the same surprise that she felt.

She remembered Ford's car. "The gunshot! Ford, you came home from that meeting with a bullet-hole in the back window of your car! Did John shoot at you?"

Now it was his turn to be confused. "How do you know that?"

"I saw you come home. You were really mad. What happened?" She forgot to deny her concern for him. "He tried to kill you?" The high-pitch of her voice betrayed her worry for him.

"He wanted more than the money. He wanted you. I wasn't going to let him have you."

"Ford!" She uncrossed her arms and reached for him, touching one muscular, tanned forearm lightly. "Why didn't you call the police?"

"Because he threatened to keep hunting you if I did."

She lowered her head and closed her eyes, ashamed for all the trouble she'd brought with her decision to get involved with a man like John. It fortified her resolve not to repeat her mistakes. She had to get away from this town and these men and start over.

She dropped her hand from Ford and hugged her arms around her body. If they got out of this alive, she'd find a way to get over Ford and Charley...but she was afraid she was ruined. Being submissive to Ford's demands had fed something in her she hadn't known she needed. She didn't think she could be satisfied without it.

She'd have to find a way.

She looked back at Ford. "Why did you do that? Why did you pay that money for me?" Her voice was small.

"Because I want to take care of you." Ford said angrily, running both hands through his hair again. Looking up to the ceiling, he added softly, "Like you take care of me."

Evie felt her heart jump, but mentally shoved it back into submission. Ford didn't love her. She would not listen to this. He was a master manipulator, just like John.

"I just wanted to keep you safe," Ford finished.

"Why?" Anger rose in her as his words threatened to soften her to him. He'd all but called her a whore earlier. "Is it because you have insurance for all of your precious possessions except me?"

"I don't know why!" Ford's voice boomed, making her jump. "I don't know." He finished more quietly. "I pushed you away as much as I could. I used you. I demanded that you please all of my sexual whims as callously as I wanted so that you'd know me at my worst, know what I was capable of. So you wouldn't *love* me, and so that I would remember your place and not..." He trailed off.

Not what?

Evie stared at the floor, refusing to look at Ford.

"I prayed you both left me."

Charley and Evie looked at Ford in unison, Evie sure that hurt and confusion reflected in Charley's eyes, just as in her own. "I mean when John broke in. I was on my way to the garage, following you both. I couldn't let you leave. But then John burst through the door..." Evie glanced at Charley but Charley was frowning at Ford.

"What happened?" he asked his best friend.

"John came in the front door with a key. That's when I knew Boone was in trouble. He shot at me but missed."

"He hit the windows?" Charley asked.

"Yes," Ford said, "but I could see his second shot wouldn't miss, and I was so afraid he'd follow you two that I just put up my hands and surrendered. He tied me up and hit me with his gun to knock me out." Ford crossed his arms and shook his head, then he looked at them both with eyes as honest as Evie had ever seen them. "I prayed you'd both left and you'd never come back. I didn't want John to hurt you, and I couldn't keep hurting you, no matter how much I want to keep you both." Ford took a deep, shaky breath. "I don't deserve either of you."

Charley was silent next to her, and she wasn't sure any of Ford's words even mattered if he wasn't capable of seeing a new future with them.

"Why did you try and save me?" His question was directed at both of them and his voice held true curiosity. "Why didn't you run?"

Charley and Evie looked at each other, knowing what the other felt. Finally Charley answered for both of them. "There was never a question. We weren't leaving without you. We love you." Suddenly Charley stepped close to Ford. "You told us you loved us. Do you? We might not make it out of this. I have to know if we could've tried to make it work. The three of us." Charley's voice held desperation. "Do you love us, Ford?"

Ford looked from Charley to Evie, and his eyes held something new...surrender. He reached for them. Suddenly the refrigerator door banged open, and Ford and Charley stepped in front of Evie protectively.

CHAPTER THIRTY-TWO

JOHN STOOD AT the door, training his gun on them. He smirked, "Isn't this cozy. Look at the heroes. Don't you know you're supposed to protect worthy damsels? Evie's just a slut." He craned his neck upward in an exaggerated effort to see Evie.

"Evangeline," he drawled her name out, relishing in the power he had over her at that moment. "So you've been here all this time, sucking Ford Hawthorne's dick? His too probably. Am I right?" he asked, gesturing at Charley. She couldn't help it when she felt her face grow red. "Holy shit. Him too? Evie, my god. I thought I was a better judge of character than that, but I underestimated you. You're twice the whore I thought you were."

Charley lunged at John, but John jumped back, cocking his gun. "Now, now, gentlemen." When he felt in control again he turned his small eyes back to Evie, smiling at her pleasantly. "I can't say I'm surprised. You always did suck dick like a pro."

"Fuck you, John!" she screamed at him, and Ford put a restraining hand on Charley's arm, the man barely staying under control.

John laughed, and then his voice turned serious. Apparently he was done tormenting Evie. "We're moving to the library. I've been through rich boy's desk, but I can't find what I need, so we're all going in there so you can help me. Move along now." He gestured with his gun for them to exit the freezer.

Evie looked around frantically for something to help them, and her eyes fell on the cheese platter. Five cheeses and one sharp, well-balanced, all-steel knife. Ford complained every time she'd put the platter back into the fridge with the knife still on the tray. Relief for her irresponsibility washed through her.

As the men slowly moved forward in single file out of the fridge, hatred in their stiff postures, Evie grabbed the knife, tucking it quickly into the waistband at the small of her back, hiding it with her shirt.

When Ford and Charley were in the kitchen, John kept his gun on them until he grabbed Evie by the arm, putting the pistol to her head. Charley and Ford both stiffened, looking like panthers coiled to spring on their prey.

"Turn around, boys," John growled. "Move nicely into the library and your hooker won't get hurt."

Evie jerked her arm out of John's grip. "The gun can touch me, but I don't want you to." She marched into the library behind the two men. John made Ford and Charley sit on the two chairs facing the desk and pushed Evie around to the other side.

"Here's the situation," John announced. "You're going to transfer twenty million dollars into my bank account." He gestured at Ford. "And then I'm going to take Evie and leave."

"No!" Ford lunged out of his chair, but John aimed the firearm at Evie's head again. "Do you think I have anything to lose?" he asked. Ford stopped, fists clenched again at his side, a murderous look on his face.

Ford's eyes flicked from John to settle on Evie. Their eyes locked, and Evie saw the crack in his armor, the acquiescence to what he would do. "I can get you more if you leave Evie. Enough to disappear forever."

Evie narrowed her eyes. What was he doing? She was leaving. If they got out alive, she was still leaving. She turned to John. "No, take me with you." Her voice was unwavering.

John raised his eyebrows at her. "Excuse me?"

"Evie, no!" The plea came from Ford.

Evie raised her chin and squared her shoulders. "I know his passwords. He left me alone all the time — long enough to do all the snooping I wanted to. Do you think I was here for the sex? I can get you fifty million."

"No," Ford's voice held all the betrayal she knew it would. Charley gaped at her.

"And," continued Evie, ignoring both the other men, "I can work for you instead, if you want. Now that you'll be rich like him. I can provide all the same services that I do now for Ford and his friend." John raised his eyebrows, his eyes widening. She made her voice low and seductive, without a hint of tremble. "And in return, you'll take care of me in the manner to which I've become accustomed, right?"

John appeared delighted. His cruel laugh boomed around the room. "How unexpected! Ford, it looks like Evie's not as attached to you as you are to her! She's so willing to trade you in for another sugar-daddy."

Evie glanced around, assessing everyone's positions. Ford and Charley were across the desk. Too far to do anything that would be faster than a bullet. She was their only hope.

She looked at John and tried to swallow her disgust. Dropping her shoulders and cocking her hip, she made an effort to sex up her voice. "I can give you a free sample if you want. I've been practicing." She smiled, and this time the smile was genuine because she was picturing her knife stabbing through his gut.

"Evie," Ford whispered, sounding like he was in physical pain.

"Why?" she heard from Charley, the word almost inaudible.

John ignored them, sounding intrigued. "You really are quite the enterprising little slut, aren't you? I might not have cut you loose so quickly, had I known."

Evie made sure her smile didn't falter. *Jackass.* She'd dumped him, of course.

John slid his eyes down her body, making her skin crawl.

"What have you been learning since you left the firm, Eves?"

"You'd be surprised," she drawled, keeping her words slow and seductive, her eyes intently locked to his. "Let's get out of here, and I'll show you."

Tearing his eyes from her, John directed a nasty laugh in Ford's direction.

"Well, Ford, your precious Evie appears to be ready for an upgrade!"

Evie risked a glance at Ford. He had the look of a wounded man. The damage Evie was doing to him was evident. She swallowed and refocused on John, trying to soothe her dry throat.

John unbuckled his belt with one hand, an ugly sneer on his face. "I'm interested in your proposition, Evie, but I want a sample now," he snarled. He stood and kicked the desk chair out of his way, gesturing to her with his gun. "Take off your clothes. I'm going to try out your new skills right here."

"No!" Ford lurched forward, his fists pounding on the smooth mahogany. Charley simply said, "Evie, stop," in a voice that smacked of betrayal.

"No, John," Ford repeated. "I'll give you the fifty million, just leave Evie alone. Please!"

John cocked his head to Ford, eyes narrowed. "But she doesn't want you anymore, pretty boy."

"I know," Ford's voice held all the bitterness of someone badly beaten at his own game. "But I'll do what you ask. Take my money. Just don't take Evie."

If Ford or Charley made a move, they'd get shot. No way they'd get over the desk before John could fire a round. Evie needed to maintain control of the situation if she wanted to save them. "No!" Evie glanced around, noting the number of steps between her and John. "I want to go, John. I'm tired of him. He's no fun at all. I want something different—something more exciting." John's attention was back on her.

Knife throwing was useless in hand-to-hand combat. The odds of Evie standing at just the right distance away, her target not moving, and her aim being dead-on were all exceptionally slim. But she had to try—she had to get Ford and Charley out of the situation.

"Convince me." John gestured to Evie's clothes again.

"I'm going to take my shirt off." Evie showed him her hands and moved them slowly to the hem of her shirt. With trembling fingers she pulled it over her head. She kept her body angled so John couldn't see the knife.

"Evie, please" Ford moaned, but she ignored him. A lecherous smile spread slowly over John's face.

"I'm going to unhook my bra," Evie's voice trembled slightly, and she held her breath, hoping no one had noticed. Her hands were shaking. She was never going to make the throw.

Not taking her eyes from John, she concentrated on settling her core, visualizing her move.

She had to go for John's stomach or neck—if she went for the chest, there was too much of a chance of the knife bouncing off a rib, causing only a superficial cut. That wouldn't do. She chose the abdomen, knowing it wasn't a killing blow, but hoping it would incapacitate him for the moment they'd need to subdue him.

She prayed Ford and Charley would act just as quickly in the confusion. Ford was the closest to John. If he didn't get to John fast enough, before John could recover enough to use his gun, one of them—maybe more—would be dead.

They had to be of the same mind. Was it too much to hope that they were?

Her fingers brushed the cold steel of the knife in her waistband. She glanced at Ford. Even with blood on his face, his hair matted with it, his clothes disheveled, he was the most handsome man she'd ever seen. Even in his defeat. With the betrayal playing out before him, she knew it was her, not John, who'd defeated him.

Ford did love her. She could see it in the pain on his face. She was sure of his love, now that she'd broken his heart in front of these other men. She took a deep breath—she'd fix it, somehow. She needed him, needed his deep voice commanding her, his strong hands forcing her. It was the only thing that made her feel safe. She would get them out of the situation so he could possess her again.

405

Her hand closed over the hilt of the knife, her mind doing mental calculations as to the distance between her and her target. She took a step forward, estimating the pirouette of the blade, trying to ensure it hit John blade-first, not hilt.

She struck.

Her concentration unwavering, time slowed. She crouched and whipped the knife from behind her, throwing it underhanded — not a method she'd practiced much, but quicker than raising it above her head. She only had a millisecond to get it right.

So many things happened at once. The knife struck John in the left side of his stomach, sinking home as accurate as any throw she'd ever made. He crumpled, crying out as blood bloomed on his shirt.

Ford dove across the desk and grabbed John's gun hand, twisting it around to his back. "Drop the gun," he hissed in John's ear, pulling his arm painfully higher. John let go of the gun. It clattered to the floor without discharging, to Evie's relief.

Ford pushed John to the floor, where he writhed in pain, and Evie kicked him in the face. "Don't move, dickhead, and you won't bleed as much."

Charley slammed his body down on John's, holding him in a choke hold. "Go get help! Take my truck." He threw the keys at them. And then in spite of the chaos, a huge grin broke out across Charley's face. "Hot damn, don't we make a great team?" He beamed up at Evie and Ford. Ford took Evie's hand, hesitating only a moment before wrapping her in an embrace that lifted her off her feet. He smothered her face in kisses of relief.

*****

Charley and Ford came to Evie, who sat on the outside sofa near the pool. Ford settled next to her and Charley knelt in front of her, taking her hands in his. Ford put an arm around her and hugged her to him.

She clutched Ford's hand. "I don't really know your passwords, Ford. I never snooped. Even if I knew them, I would never betray you like that."

Ford chuckled and smoothed her hair off her cheek. "I know, love. I figured that out when you knifed John." He laughed and kissed her forehead.

"You okay? Are you hurt?" Charley's face was a mask of concern. His eyes travelled over her, taking inventory of all of her unbroken parts.

She nodded. "I'm okay."

"You're more than okay, baby. You're a bad-ass." Charley grinned, touching her cheek with his paw of a hand. Evie smiled, bathed in his warmth. Charley had never called her "baby" before. She liked it.

Evie suddenly looked up. "Boone?"

Ford's voice held genuine relief. "He's okay! He was tied up and has a nasty lump on his head, but he's going to be fine. He's already demanded a raise," Ford grumbled, his eyes twinkling with good humor.

"Thank god," Evie breathed. "Did the police leave yet?"

"Yes. The ambulance took John to the hospital, under police escort, of course, and they finally got Charley to shut up long enough to wrap things up."

"I had a long statement to make!" Charley pretended to take offence.

Ford grinned down at Charley, his dimples making a reappearance that nearly melted Evie's memory of the horrible day. "Charley tried to talk them into making us all honorary deputies." A deep laugh rumbled in Ford's chest.

"Hey, I was hoping the position might come with handcuffs. We could have fun with handcuffs, couldn't we?" Charley looked at both of them, and Evie reveled in the feeling. Like they were all three *together*. Together in life, in love, in bed.

What was even better was that Ford seemed to embrace it.

Ford kissed Evie's head and then bent to kiss Charley's lips, his green eyes practically glowing with adoration. He squeezed Evie closer.

She relished the safety she felt in Ford's arms again, but there were questions to which she needed answers. She looked up at Ford, not daring to hope that he'd accept the love she felt all around them. "You were going to save me even when you thought I had betrayed you—that I wanted to leave you and go with John."

Ford's jade eyes brimmed with emotion. "It took me until that moment to realize... I can deny it but it doesn't make it any less true. I'm gone, Evie. Gone. I'm yours. Yours and Charley's." He gripped her to him. "I'm so sorry about this morning. What I did to you—" His face was anguished. "Can you ever forgive me?"

Happiness and relief flooded her. "I'll try if you'll try."

Ford grasped Charley's shoulder with his other hand, his gaze intense. He looked back and forth between them. "Is it really true what you and Charley have told me? Could you love me as just as I am? *Will* you love me just as I am—dominate, demanding, selfish?"

"It's the only way we know how to love you," Evie whispered, her eyes filling with tears.

Ford kissed her with such passion that she couldn't breathe, but he demanded the kiss, commanding her body to respond to his. And it did. Her blood coursed through her joyously, relishing in his control. She broke away, lungs heaving.

"I'm not done," he growled and kissed her again, moving to devour the skin along her neck. Her head dropped backwards, her breath coming in gasps. His fingers tweaked one of her hard nipples and she groaned in response. "I love you, Evangeline." He spoke against her skin, into her mouth, "I love you."

Charley knelt up and he treated Charley to the same overwhelming, deep kiss before pulling back to meet their eyes. Evie's were wet with emotion for the second time that day, but this time it was happy emotion—thrilling, blissful, joyous emotion. "I love you both. I never thought I could say that to anyone. Thank you for fighting for me to see it. I don't want to live without either of you."

"I love you too, Ford," she whispered.

"Love you so much," Charley croaked, his voice thick. His smile was dazzling in its pure happiness.

Ford's mouth crooked in a wicked smile. "And you'll keep loving me, because that's what I want, and I always get what I want, don't I?" He gripped Evie's hand and moved it to his crotch, forcing her to touch his growing erection. "Feel what you started already." He ground her palm against him. "Now that the police are gone, I expect you to fix this."

Evie bit her lip, giving him a coy look. "If you insist."

Ford shook his head, and his face grew ominous with mock disappointment. "Threatening to leave us?" He tsked. "I should punish you severely for that."

Evie's core twanged with yearning in response to his threat of corporal punishment. Now that he wasn't trying to push her away, she knew he'd be focused more on her pleasure...and his. But he'd be no less insistent about it, and god, that got her hot.

She pressed her thighs together and her excitement tingled through her as Ford continued. "But for now, you are going to let Charley and I use you until we're both completely satisfied."

Charley groaned and slid his hand down her thigh, spreading her legs.

"Okay," she whispered, and her panties felt instantly wet thinking about what the two insatiable men might do to her.

"That's 'yes, sir', Evangeline," Ford admonished. "And you're going to come too, more than once, screaming my name."

"Yes, sir, Mr. Hawthorne." And she knew it was true. Ford would ensure it. "But, wait." She had to ask now, before she was too distracted by these incredible men and their hands all over her. "The year. What about the year Ford? I don't how I'll deal with the end when it comes."

"Ah yes, the year." Ford's lips twisted into that bad-boy smirk, and Evie sensed Charley holding his breath. "I'd like to renegotiate," he said.

"Oh?" Her heart leapt. "What length of time did you have in mind, Mr. Hawthorne?" she asked, drowning in the love she saw in his eyes, still not quite sure she could let herself believe it.

"Forever," Ford answered, and his face transformed with a smile so genuine and drenched in peace that Evie's heart stuttered in joy, as much for him as for them all. "Forever. Is that too much to ask?"

"Forever's not even enough," Charley said, looking up at them with the eyes of a man who'd found a home. A family.

"Agreed," Evie laughed. "A deal's a deal. I'll stay forever."

And she closed her eyes, wrapped in the arms of the two men she loved, and she knew she was finally safe. She got more than her fairy tale ending. She got *two* Prince Charmings.

The End.

About the Author

Piper Trace tried to write mainstream fiction, but her characters kept getting naked and using naughty words. Really naughty words. But these lusty characters were so much damn fun to hang out with that she gave up trying to control them.

Piper used to be a corporate lawyer, but now she writes romance full-time, in addition to raising her two kids, hanging out with her husband, and occasionally posting on her DIY blog with partner Sidney Bristol: www.dropdeadthrifty.com

She'd love to tell you all about her writing accolades, but she's pretty sure that, like her, you're a reader who flipped through your mom's paperback romances for the words "breasts" or "throbbing" so you could just read the good stuff. Well, you found it.

Let's have some fun!

Reach out to Piper on social media! She's friendly and loves to chat while you're reading her books.

Facebook.com/AuthorPiperTrace

Twitter: @pipertrace

Email: pipertrace@hotmail.com

*****

Dear Reader,

Thank you for reading *Come When Called*!

I hope you enjoyed Ford, Charley and Evie as much as I do. I was in love with Ford originally, as I wrote the first draft of the book, which is why Ford is the sun around which the other characters orbit (and burn themselves by getting too close). But as Charley began to take shape over time, he quite possibly stole the show. How can you not love a heart that pure?

I read a comment about *Come When Called* noting how on-trend it is (here in 2015), which is ironic because it's unintentional, though fortuitous! I had written the first draft of *Come When Called* before Fifty Shades was published. Now, broody billionaires have sure had their time in the spotlight, haven't they? Ford would assure you, however, he's never changed. He's been infuriating, devilish, damaged and domineering right from the start.

And motorcycle clubs are really hot right now, but Charley is a biker because he had to be the total opposite of Ford. He had to make Ford uncomfortable, which he does throughout the book, usually in super-hot ways. I suppose Charley could have been a forest ranger, military hero or…well there were lots of other choices, but I always pictured Charley straddling some powerful, black machine, making Ford nervous about his safety—not that he'd admit it.

Charley just had to be a biker.

And Evie had to be a spark-plug, because she's the spark that incites everything and everyone to change. She had to be strong enough to take on these two men, along with her psycho ex, and come out stronger, happier and healed in the end. She fought for a place to belong—for someone to really *care* for her in every way—and she deserved to find that. I wanted to give that to her. And it's up to you, the reader, to decide if I achieved it, but I hope I gave her that times two, in the arms of Ford and Charley.

I don't think these three would work in any "coupling" between each other, but together, all three, they make the perfect union. And they will live their happily ever after forever.

I'm so glad I got to share their story with you.

I thought I'd share some background on how I wrote the book, since it was my first! It took me quite a while to write. I'd work on it during breaks from my job and on late nights while my family slept and the house was quiet. I wrote mainly in my car. I'd often write on lunch breaks in the parking lot at my job. Due to the…um…nature of the book, I didn't feel comfortable working on it where someone might see it! I had a tiny laptop I hauled around everywhere.

I also wrote in my car because I had a newborn (at the time) and from her birth until she was about three or four years old, she wasn't a good sleeper and was highly active, so sometimes the only time I got a break was to put her in the car and drive her around until she fell asleep. Then I'd very quietly and carefully pull into a parking lot and write until she woke up.

The process took me five years. I joke that for five years I wrote about Ford in a Chevy.

While finishing *Come When Called*, I occasionally took breaks to write something short. I ended up with five other works out there with two different publishers before *Come When Called* was actually released. Luckily my experiences with traditional publishers convinced me in time to "go it alone". I had sold the rights to *Come When Called* to a publisher back in 2010, but in 2015 I was able to secure the rights back before it was ever published, and so suddenly I became a self-publishing author!

Being a total control freak, this suits me fine.

I have since gotten the rights back to all but two of my other works, but—being the control freak that I am—I want to completely redo those books before I put them back out. Thus, *Come When Called* is the only novel I have out right now.

Trust me, I'm working!! I have nearly forty works in progress right now. Yes, really. But I'm focusing! I promise! I'll try to get you something new real soon.

And I will be so thankful if, when I put out something new, you'd be happy to read it. Because in the end, YOU, the readers, are why we write!

I'd like to ask you a favor. Please take a minute to review *Come When Called*. Even just a star rating is a wonderful gesture.

Until next time,
Piper Trace

PS... so you don't miss that next time, please sign up for my newsletter at www.pipertrace.com! And I'm always looking for street team members, so hit me up if you have enthusiasm for that kinda thing! Kisses!

Sign up for my newsletter at www.pipertrace.com!